# The Comfort Station

## Kelly Cresser

GRAYBEARD PUBLISHING

Kelly Cresser

ISBN: 978-0-9912382-5-5

Cover Design and illustrations by Aaron Provost

Edited by Yolanda McLain, Heather Webb, and Jennifer Mench

# DEDICATION

SEVERAL PEOPLE HAVE CONTRIBUTED TO PRODUCTION OF THIS BOOK OVER THE 12 LONG YEARS IT TOOK TO WRITE IT. BIG THANKS TO JENNIFER CRIGGER, DON CRIGGER, KRISTI KIRSCHNER, FRANCES COLONNA, YOLANDA MCLAIN, HEATHER WEBB, JENNIFER MENCH, AND THE ONE AND ONLY MIKE CARLSON.

_Kelly Cregger_

# The Comfort Station

*Kelly Crigger*

# Prologue

**Cruelty has a human heart, and jealousy a human face; Terror, the human form divine, and secrecy the human dress.**

-*William Blake*

It is a wonderful thing to hold onto a good secret. Bad secrets transfer pain onto others, but good ones enrich lives, especially when allowed to ferment properly. Takeo held onto his secret for six long hours, carefully waiting until they were clear of the Imperial Naval Academy and had crossed the bay to Hiroshima's Ujina Port to tell Genjo. Their classmates would walk quickly to get to their favorite watering hole, *Yonaga*, leaving him behind to tell his best friend the news.

"Tsuchiura?" Genjo nearly yelled. "When did you find out?"

"Captain Minowa told me earlier today after grad..."

"This is a great day!" Genjo embraced Takeo, normally a gesture too affectionate for an honorable Naval officer of the Empire but not for two boys from Kagoshima Prefecture. "Such an honor, Takeo-san!" Genjo shouted, dropping his best friend, jumping back and bowing deeply.

"Thank you, my friend." Takeo grinned, smoothing his stiff, white dress uniform. "In fact, I'm a little surprised."

Genjo feigned a Judo attack at his head, making Takeo flinch. "There you go again, good soul. You refuse to believe in the self. The others would be walking around like roosters in breeding season at such news."

Takeo laughed. "Yes. I imagine they would."

6

"Say it then."

Takeo rolled his eyes. "I am proud of myself." And he *was* proud of his accomplishment. Out of nearly fifteen hundred applicants that year, acceptance to the Tsuchiura Naval Flying School was granted to fewer than 70, and of those an even smaller number would go on to become *Umi no Arawashi* - the most honorable Sea Eagles. But no matter how venerable an institution, Takeo couldn't bring himself to boast about being accepted, especially since the Gods' benevolent gaze failed to bestow an equal virtue on the affable man he'd been blessed to walk the earth with. Genjo was rewarded with a mediocrity that belied his ability, but one that most graduating cadets of 1941 would receive: the dull gray life of surface ship duty and a notoriously short life expectancy. By year's end he'd be manning anything from a destroyer to a supply boat full of cow dung while Takeo soared above the heavens in the latest Zero.

Once, men of their ilk were not considered Academy material because of their middle class upbringing. In pre-war Japan they were the chaff the wind did not bother with. But the demands of war dictated that admission standards be lowered to accommodate more recruits, opening the door to riffraff such as they who yearned to prove themselves. They leapt at the opportunity to become something greater and laughing, embraced their good fortune until the trappings of fanatical patriotism led their proud country to the edge of an abyss they would be expected to jump into without question.

Genjo walked quickly to catch their classmates, his voice repeating "Tsuchiura!" as he told them the news. Takeo allowed himself a brief, pleasant memory of ten- and eight-year-old siblings to drift into his mind—a reminiscence of unsure evenings spent by the riverside where once, in the tall grass, they'd captured fireflies together. The children would hold the glowing insects gently in the palms of their hands and then, crouching in silence by the water, observe the insects' magical flashes until the sky darkened and it was time to release their catch and go home. It was likely the last time he would see that boy again.

But this night was not about that. The plum blossoms had begun to wilt along the warm streets of Hiroshima where everything was still covered in a film of yellow dust carried in from the west on spring winds. Their smiles lit the blocks as they walked and they nodded to their fellow graduates and finest Imperial citizens. They were alpha males unbound, faces lifted to the sky, basking in the last rays of the sun before it bid the day farewell. The midshipmen years now history, they were commissioned officers of the Japanese Imperial Navy, a link in the long chain of seafaring explorers cast into the eternal unknown with only courage to guide them. They were admirable men in a material society that would have left them behind were it not for the war effort.

The two women sitting on the park bench where Takeo knew they would be were each attractive in their own right, but somehow mismatched. It was always like this with her. The starboard girl was a pin-up, the object of every man's desire in a red dress, with meticulously applied makeup, and neatly coiffed, wavy black hair. The portside dame was tall with a plain gray dress and a natural beauty that scarcely needed a short tryst with a brush to be perfect.

She was what he sought week in and week out, stuck in the same place like a flower whose roots dug deep into the park. The woman in red commanded attention, but the one in grey was alluring and elegant. She made desire look easy. He always liked that about her. She was never the eye-catching one, but she managed to catch his eye and his tongue, which never seemed to work properly no matter how many times he made the walk from the port to the bar surrounded by a pack of classmates.

Takeo gazed ahead at his comrades, walking quickly toward inebriation and the same tired tales of past academy shenanigans; exactly what he didn't want. They were the past now. She was the future. Or at least she could be. He slowed his pace, looked down at his dress white coat to make sure everything was in order, stopped, and stood at a crossroads. He looked at her again. An Army officer appeared to strike up a conversation with the woman in red. Behind them, a civilian in a cheap suit made his way toward the bench. Takeo stood still, his feet stuck in the street as if the dirt were quicksand. He wiped his upper lip and muttered. "He who hesitates..."

He arrived at the bench mere seconds before the civilian closing in from the opposite direction. "Good evening, miss," Takeo said. "May I join you?"

"By all means, ensign," the officer responded, not allowing the women to speak. "Did you graduate today?"

"Yes sir," Takeo said, taking a seat on the bench. A smile danced across the pale red lips of the girl in gray. "My name is Takeo Hashimoto. *Hajimemashite.* It is my honor to meet you."

"Pleased to meet you, sailor," the woman said. "I'm Mae."

To Takeo's surprise, the civilian man remained, standing behind the bench, smoldering much longer than seemed natural. He moved behind the girl in red, going unnoticed by the women who were engrossed in conversation but in plain sight of Takeo. The man stared at him, his fists clenched. Takeo smiled politely for nearly half a minute listening to the girl in red talk about herself until his discomfort won over. Takeo rose to challenge the stranger when he suddenly turned and left, walking back in the same direction he had arrived.

"Is everything alright?" Mae said.

"It is now," he said as the Army officer started another tale for the woman in red. Takeo sat, wanting to speak, but found his tongue paralyzed.

"Is there something on your mind, ensign?" Mae asked.

He stared at her, willing the oft-rehearsed words to be set free. "Is it possible to make someone happy without being around that person?" he finally asked.

"What do you mean?" she responded.

"Can you enrich someone's life not by being there physically, but by being there in mind and spirit?"

"That is an odd question. Are you referring to all the times you lacked the courage to talk to me?"

*"All those times." She knew.* "My longing for you has only torn at my heart, but the hope of eventually being here with you always gave me something I didn't have before. And that made my life better I think."

She smiled and let him discover her world. On a park bench in Hiroshima, Takeo explored the life of Mae, a modern woman who believed in hard work, individual responsibility, and not wasting a minute of her life on anything unnecessary. She was a rare and captivating creature in a Japan confused by its own civil war between progress and tradition.

"Why are you always alone?" he asked.

"I am not. I came here with..."

"She is not the same. You are clearly lovely. Why has no man taken you as his own?"

"Maybe you do not know me like you think you do."

"I would like to know everything about you."

"Yes? And what if you learn something you did not want to? What if I am broken inside? Are you going to fix me then, ensign?

Like you're going to fix the world once you become a hero of the Emperor?"

Takeo looked at the ground for a moment. He shifted onto his left hip to face her. "I do not think you need fixing because I do not think you are broken. I think you're under-loved and that's what I will fix."

She stared at him, silent for the first time, unable to find words.

"Ensign," the Army officer bellowed. "I must escort this beauty home. Would you honor me and do the same for Mae?"

*Ground pounders are good for something after all,* Takeo thought, accepting the mission with a smile. Ten minutes later he was walking Mae toward the Ota River flowing from its mountain source into Hiroshima Bay, stopping at a *sake* stand for a quick drink and then again a block later.

"Did I mention how uncommon 'Mae' is in Japan today?" he said as they strolled slowly.

"You have remarked on it a few times actually."

"It's a bit western...somewhat risky with us being at war with the Yankees, don't you think?"

She looked off into the night. "Yes, but I'm accustomed to it. If you haven't noticed, I'm a little less traditional and more...Betty Grable than most."

"I have noticed, yes." She was *seiyou kabure*—ultra Westernized, fascinated by Western fashions and idioms. Times being what they were, this was dangerous. "I'll keep the name if you don't turn me in to the *Kempeitai*."

"Most acceptable," Takeo said, bowing. He was perplexed by his own fragmented culture, one torn between following ancestral traditions, wearing robes and arranging marriages and adopting the mannerisms of modern Japanese in western dress that afforded everyone free will, unheard of previously. This was the chasm that divided a country only recently removed from feudalism.

Takeo felt stifled by his own inhibitions, like a shy farmer forced to do his chores with a pretty girl, alone and unsure of himself, self-conscious in the absence of his friends. Mae was a remarkable subject who commanded his complete attention. Her features were simple and her movements graceful. She grew on him with every click of her heels that echoed in the night. Her dark hair fell to her shoulders in sleek curls, gleaming in a way that made ordinary women seem just that. Her eyes were green as emeralds. An emerald eyed empress if the sake were the master of his words. Turning to him, her face was genuine.

"What a shame. You're so talented yet you just now find your courage," she said.

"A shame?"

"Yes. You will report to Tsuchiura tomorrow and I will never see you again."

"In fact, I must report today."

She cocked her head to one side. "I guess it is Wednesday now. And your courage? Now that you have found it, will you keep it?"

He looked at the ground. All the times he never had the strength to speak to her, no matter how alone she was. It was cowardly to do it on this night when he could fail miserably with no consequence.

"I will try," he said.

They continued in silence, excitement flirting with regret, until they reached a modest wood house with solid doors, rare in the days of war rations, nestled among a long row of houses overlooking the bay. What the house lacked in size it made up for in location, accouterments, and commanding views of the harbor. Persimmon trees and flowering brassica grew inside a well-maintained walled garden. On the hill above them, someone opened a window and drew the rain shutters closed. Glancing up, a candlelight was extinguished.

"My grandfather," said Mae, "He waits until I come home."

Takeo turned and contemplated her for a long moment, only a single word able to escape his lips. "Beautiful."

"The house?" She laughed as she stood in the walkway. Takeo barely had time to blush. "So what do you hope to get out of this, ensign?"

"Excuse me?"

"This is your last night with old comrades before a new life. Your last night walking with a woman...for a spell at least. What do you hope to get out of this?"

"How very forward." He smiled, looking at the ground. He turned, raised his head and gazed out over the bay shining in the moonlight and the dark shapes of naval vessels anchored upon it. "I hear a lot of women fawn over pilots down there. So maybe I need advice from someone who knows what it's like to be in demand," he said, turning back to her with a smile.

"Really? Am I merely someone you can practice banter on so you can do better with another woman another time?"

Her sass was provocative. *She'd tell me to go away if she didn't like me,* he thought. "I hoped...it would turn out like this."

"Well...good night then, sailor." She turned to go.

"Can I write you?"

She turned back. "What will you write?"

He shrugged and looked into her eyes as if he were an ambitious first year cadet again. "Maybe something more interesting than I have said this night."

She smiled like the actress in the western movie that Takeo and his classmates had snuck into earlier in the year—a movie called *Strawberry Blonde*. "That sounds very promising. Then yes, please do." But she did not turn to leave. The two shared a long, silent gaze. "Finding your courage again, Takeo?"

"Yes," he said. "There is something else I want from this night. I want to hold you. For one minute just hold you. No funny business. Just hold you, so I leave here knowing what it's like to feel you and carry something with me that I didn't have before...a moment of us. A moment that is ours. So in those times when I'm alone with nothing but my thoughts, I at least have that moment to savor and the hope that it will happen again. And in a selfish way so you to know what it's like to be held by someone who longs to be with you. In those moments when someone untrue is holding you, I want you to know what you're missing."

She smiled but did not move. Was he being shot down? *I knew it*, he thought. *Too much rehearsing.* But then she stepped toward him, stopping mere inches away, allowing him to wrap his arms around her. Her purse fell to the ground as her arms responded to his, their chests tightly bonded. For one very long moment that was not long enough, they stood on a peaceful street in a chaotic world that didn't exist and held each other.

"Take care of yourself, honorable Ensign Hashimoto," she said retrieving her purse and backing away. "And write often." She was a ghost, gone in an instant without letting him see her face. Was she sad?

"I will," he said as she disappeared up the stairs and through the door. *Worth every second*, he thought as he watched her disappear into the house.

Takeo danced on cloud nine down the hill to the harbor, hoping to catch a late-night cab or off-schedule trolley car. He glanced over his shoulder one last time to look at the house, realizing he was doing just what he'd tried to avoid; reflecting on the evening he'd spent and how lucky he was, instead of turning his attention to the journey ahead. He would miss Genjo and his classmates and now, of course, Mae. But most of all, he'd miss being young. The innocent days of cavorting and discovery were over. Soon his sheltered academy life would give way to pain, heartbreak and the ravages of war. His white dress pants and jacket would be exchanged for a blood-and mud-soaked flight suit. The humid streets of Hiroshima would give way to the misery of the Pacific's myriad jungles and diseases. In a daze of self-discovery, Takeo stopped, suddenly realizing he'd lost his way.

"Shut your mouth and move!" The voice came from a narrow space between two buildings, barely wide enough for a person. Takeo turned to see whom the voice belonged to, instinct telling him to back away, but the scent of Mae clouding his mind. A powerful hand grabbed him by the breast of his jacket and dragged him into the opening, a passage meant to provide crude access to the establishments on either side of the lane. A long katana blade shone faintly in the dim corridor. It was a formidable weapon, but one held by an amateur, or someone too scared to know what he was doing. Takeo was a master Judoka, but sake and pheromones betrayed his reactions.

"Remove your uniform now!" said the man, shoving the blade against Takeo's throat and maintaining the hold on his jacket.

"You want my uniform?"

"NOW!"

*I can defeat him*, Takeo thought. *But all he wants is my uniform.*

He raised his hands to unbutton his jacket as the man released his grip. "You think you're so blasted important, don't you?" the man said. "You just flash this pretty white tails and doors open as if the Gods willed it. Take it off!"

Takeo removed his jacket and handed it to him.

"Pants!" he said, earning a dumbfounded look. "PANTS!" he yelled, as the point of his blade moved closer. Takeo removed his shoes and pants and placed them on a lonely wooden crate next to his new jacket. The pair stood in the alley in the wee hours of the morning, Takeo half-naked, a blade pointed at his chest. "Are you escaped from the asylum?" Takeo asked. He wanted desperately to cripple the man, but also knew he wasn't in his right mind. The assailant moved closer. Takeo stared at the katana bearing down on him and then back to the man's face when it hit him. "I know you…"

The man's eyes opened wide. In a panic he thrust the katana straight toward Takeo's chest, piercing his breast and forcing him to his bare knees on the damp concrete. Takeo let out a long breath, refusing to scream. The man backed away, pulling the undersized sword with him. In the moment of attack, he failed to push the katana deep enough to do any major damage. Takeo had a chance. He delivered a forceful right hand to the assailant's groin and grabbed the blade with his left.

The man doubled over but recovering quickly, brought his left foot up to Takeo's face, delivering a strong kick that sent him onto his back. The concrete was damp and cold on his back. Blood spurted upward as he lay flat, weak and nearly immobile. Another rush of warm blood ran off to the side of his body.

Takeo knew to remain calm. *Panic causes increased heart rate,* he thought. *Heart rate causes bleeding.* He raised his head to see the man clutching his genitals as he leaned against the alley wall, breathing heavily. The assailant took the blade in both arms, lifting it over his head to bring it down like an axe on Takeo. He stepped forward for the killing blow, but found Takeo's powerful right foot in his kneecap that brought him down instantly. Takeo struggled to get up, rolling from his side to his stomach and then to his knees. Takeo turned to strike.

But he was not fast enough. The katana struck his midsection and sent him back to the ground with a hard thud and a desperate gasp for air. Takeo laid on the ground quietly breathing, listening to the sound of the man running hastily away, footsteps receding into the distance. He had to concentrate on the things he knew he must do to survive: do not move, get attention, and above all, do not lose consciousness. He yelled, hoping to alert someone, anyone. But his voice grew weaker. His fingers and toes went cold. His vision grew dark.

*I can't die now,* he thought. *There's still so much to do.*

# 1

## Husking rice, a child squints up
## to view the moon.
### -*Matsuo Basho*

Tae-Hyun fell to all fours and ran a hand across the ribs his little sister had just kicked. Her tiny foot packed the power of a hammer on an anvil, but her apology fell on ears too proud to hurt. "Do not apologize, Ki-Hwa," he said rising to his feet. The little sister stepped back and bowed. "You are right to do this."

"Your Tae Kwon Do has suffered from your journey," Ki-Hwa said.

"And yours has grown stronger." He flinched as he stretched his arm overhead and pain shot to his lungs. "We can't always be there to protect you, so..."

"I have to save myself. Yes, brother. I am grateful," she replied. "I am always grateful for you. Will you tell me now?"

He smiled, not wishing to test her any further for the sake of his own health and knowing her desperate longing to hear about the world outside their little Korean farm. "Yes, I will tell you," he said. But his tales were limited. A year of indentured servitude on a Japanese fishing boat had indeed opened his eyes to life away from a rice paddy, but he didn't wish to destroy her dreams. Not yet at least. Hope was dangerous and he wasn't man enough to kill hers.

"I am so jealous, brother. You have seen the world!"

"The world..." he paused. "The world will break your heart, Ki-Hwa. The question is...what will you do when it does?"

Their father's ragged face was uneasy. The Kim patriarch stepped over the threshold of the front door and gazed up to the roof of the simple home. "Still the strongest one here," he said, running a finger along the eaves, remembering the calloused hands and broken backs it took to build it. "When it rains, we are not wet. When the snows come, we are not cold. The house of Kim may be small, but it is formidable." He looked through the doorway at his wife who remained by the table, expressionless. "Like our children, *oma*." She said nothing.

He turned and strode away from the abode toward the upper rice paddy, and barked a command that echoed across their shallow valley.

"Ki-Hwa!" He waited patiently, but received no response. He stepped forward to get a better view of the lower paddy where his children liked to play-fight in the morning calm. "Ki-Hwa!" Her face peeked up over the stalks, a hand brushing back the long black hair falling into her eyes. "You will accompany us!" he said.

"I'm going to the market?" she said. She turned to Tae-Hyun. "I'm going to the market!" She repeated the words as she ran to the house. The youngest son of Kim, Jung-Hwan, tossed a dried bale of stalk onto one of the family's two ox-carts and spun around to see his little sister run past him, smiling in a way he'd never seen before. "Oma cannot be happy about this," he said.

It took Ki-Hwa mere minutes to clean her slender body at the pump, run to the room she shared with her mother, and drape new clothes onto her lithe frame, and pull her long black hair into a flowered clip. Nearly twenty years of being forbidden to travel into town, and especially to the market was ending. "You are not ready," her mother had said year after year, refusing to explain further. Rumors of women disappearing had circulated since the occupation began, but the culture of fear fomented by locals smelled of paranoia to her and only made the foreigners seem more intriguing. Had she not protested so vigorously, oma would prevent her from attending school altogether. Ki-Hwa loved her mother, but had no desire to be like her-- humble and passive, forever dependent on a husband.

"You'll have to walk," Ki-Chul, the eldest brother said as she joined the family by the carts. "Only the crops ride."

"Gladly," she replied with a smile, taking up a position to the rear left of the second cart, led by Tae-Hyun. Jung-Hwan, closest to her age, but not closest to her heart, shadowed her. "Is that the dress oma made?" he asked.

"Yes!" she answered, lifting a fold of fabric. "Isn't it beautiful?" The traditional Korean *hanbok* was cumbersome and formal and not made for a trek to sell crops, but a peasant farming family could ill afford anything more than what they made themselves or what was passed down. Mother had made the blue and green hanbok using very little money and a neighbor's foot-pedal-driven sewing machine; the greatest invention she'd ever seen. Ki-Hwa was delighted with the result: a brightly colored dress with a thousand pleats and an inseam just below her non-existent breasts. It was one of the few cultural items the Japanese still allowed. Her hair was combed long and straight and pinned back on one side with a borrowed barrette.

"It seems as though *Chuseok* was only yesterday," Tae-Hyun lamented, remembering the annual journey up the valley where their ancestors lay. He gently stroked an ox's head.

"Yes, well, it's come and gone and tomorrow is the start of a new season, so get used to it," snapped Ki-Chul.

With two crop-laden carts, the walk down the muddy, forested road to town was long and arduous, but nothing could dampen Ki-

Hwa's excitement, not even a slight drizzle that set in when they were still a mile from town. She ignored the aching in her feet and the agonizing pace of the oxen, which protested every step.

"Do you think they'll undercut us again this year?" Tae-Hyun asked aloud.

"Of course," Ki-Chul responded.

"But they can't drop the price *every* year."

"Why not? They are the mighty Japanese Empire. They own us."

Ki-Hwa didn't have to ask. With one glance, Tae-Hyun would explain. He always did. "We get less every year," he said, looking across the cart. "They give us just enough to keep the crop coming in, but not enough to prosper."

"It is slavery and deprivation," Ki-Chul added, "Our lives are not our own and it will never stop."

"It's why oma has to make you clothes instead of buying new ones," Jung-Hwan said. Ki-Hwa wasn't surprised as much as she was angry at being kept in the dark. "Why haven't you told me this before?" she insisted, her sex proving to be an obstacle yet again. "I'm a part of this family, too."

"Women don't make decisions," Ki-Chul said.

"Why..." she started when Jung-Hwan turned to her from the front of the cart. "Don't look at them," he whispered loudly.

Three Imperial soldiers crested the hill moving quickly toward them, their rifles slung over their shoulders. They were only ten meters away and closing quickly. One was telling a story, while the other two looked ahead, bored. They wore uniforms the color of recently unearthed clay, Ki-Hwa thought, with buttons and pins whose symbols she could not decipher. No matter the alarm in Jung-Hwan's voice, she simply could not look away and struggled to catch a glimpse over his shoulder in front of her. Jung-Hwan's gaze shifted down to the road directly in front of his feet as he walked on quietly. Ki-Hwa did the same, though her fear, abated at the moment, was a fear of the unknown since she'd never seen a Japanese soldier up close.

"Come," Tae-Hyun muttered to the ox as he tugged its bridle. The beast moved, dragging the cart to the left side of the road and forcing the soldiers to walk on the right, farther away from the young girl. Jung-Hwan did the same with the second cart, allowing the troopers a wide berth, but keeping the carts between them and Ki-Hwa. It didn't matter if they were Japanese, Korean, soldiers, or civilians; they were men—and all four of the male Kim's knew exactly what they wanted.

"What a beautiful day to be a part of the glorious Empire!" Father bellowed happily, tipping his wide-brimmed hat as he positioned himself just to the right of the first cart. But a muffled response from the lead soldier was all that his subservient gesture earned.

*You don't see us*, Jung-Hwan thought. *Keep walking.*

But they did not.

"Stop," demanded the one with more pins on his jacket, holding up a hand. The soldiers walked to one side of the first cart to gaze briefly at its mountain of dried rice. It was standard operating procedure for Imperial troops to scrutinize everything, especially a pile of brown rice, to ensure nothing was hidden. Father knew this and did not panic, but as the cart slowed, Ki-Hwa felt her heart pound. When the second cart drew to a halt, the soldiers looked at the dried stalks, even reaching out to feel their texture. They had not noticed her on the other side yet; the pile of stalks hiding her from their view, reaching seven feet above the ground and perhaps five feet wide, like a small hillock.

But the next instant, one circled around behind her cart. She stared at the ground while watching his movements out of the corner of her eye, praying he would not want a closer look. She

22

felt his eyes searching her up and down, his interest palpable. Without looking directly at him, she could tell he was young, barely out of his teenage years, with the higher nose and slightly more angular features that distinguished a Nippon from a Han. Her own face went numb and her hands tingled as she stared down at the cart's wheel. Ki-Chul clenched his hands, as if anticipating a fight.

*Please don't*, Ki-Hwa thought, noticing her brother's protective stance. *Not over me.*

*Mrrrooooooooohhhhhh*. The first ox suddenly let out a yelp and leapt forward, startling everyone. Ki-Hwa's head shot up to look at the animal. Everyone reeled from the surprise and the air was silent until the soldiers finally chuckled.

"Not as good as ours!" One scorned the incorrigible beast. "...because we use machines!" The three soldiers laughed heartily, suddenly losing interest in the Kim family. They turned and walked away, jesting at the family's expense one more time while the lone soldier gave Ki-Hwa's figure a last look before disappearing over the hill.

"Well done," father said, smiling at his middle son. Ki-Hwa looked at Tae-Hyun, the bridle in one hand and a prod in the other.

"You did that?" Jung-Hwan asked.

Tae-Hyun only lifted his eyebrows and turned to his little sister. "I should have told you before. Don't look at them and don't attract any attention. It only invites trouble."

"How long has it been this way?" she asked.

"1910," Father said without turning, his hands clasped behind his back as he started walking down the path. "They came five years after defeating the white Cossacks to the north across the Yalugang. 'For your own good,' they told us. 'Kyeongju will host an honorable garrison. Even the provincial governor will live here,' they told us. 'We will teach you the ways of our culture and make the Han and the Nippon the same...and we will prosper together as it was meant to be,' they said. 'The chrysanthemum will bless the land so your crops will flourish as it has done in so many other lands' they said. We had no choice. They came across the sea when we were too weak to resist."

He paused as if seeing the occupation act out in front of the carts. "Then our great ancestral treasures disappeared. The tombs of our kings were desecrated. Our women were violated. Our crops were stolen. Our children...raised in secrecy." He motioned at her as the family continued on. "We rose in protest...that was 1919." He paused again lifting his gaze skyward and then looking back to the road. "But we did not know our enemy. The Japanese reaction was as swift as the strike of a crane hunting the frog. They murdered us and sent us to prison. Mounted policemen rode through the crowds, beheading young and old alike. They crucified Christians on wooden crosses in public squares so they could die like their savior and warn the rest of us never to try something so foolish again. They burned churches to the ground, some with people locked inside. 'Independent thinking is unwelcome in the Empire,' they told us. 'It is poison that prevents the chrysanthemum from blooming in all its glory. The punishment for such an act will be eternal suffering' they said."

He stopped suddenly in the middle of the road, hunched over slightly from old age and a life spent behind a plow, staring at the ground. Ki-Chul and Tae-Hyun stopped the carts as his father stood motionless; the unwelcome memories of screams and the sound of pounding horses' hooves returning from their banished place to haunt him. He slowly turned to his only daughter, his face looking as old as she'd ever seen it, filled with a pain he didn't want to remember. "Even the name of our land was stripped away. Chosen became Korea. These are things your schoolbooks will not teach you."

His worn expression filled her with grief. The trip to the market suddenly felt like a funeral procession and Ki-Hwa wanted to turn around and be away from it. The outside world she sought seemed as evasive as the cherry blossom in spring. The only thing predictable was the occupation.

* * * * *

"There it is." Jung-Hwan pointed as the carts crested the last hill hiding Kyeongju.

Ki-Hwa struggled to catch a glimpse. "Where?"

"That building with the umbrellas next to it, with all the steam."

"It doesn't look like much."

"It was once."

"It's bigger inside," Tae-Hyun said.

Father took an unexpected fork in the road away from the market. "Where are we going?" Ki-Hwa asked.

"Business first," Jung-Hwan replied. "We sell the crops and then go to the market," Twenty minutes later the cart came to a rest behind a line of others at a loading dock filled with loitering soldiers and...trucks! Lines and lines of trucks. Ki-Hwa had seen the odd truck at school over the years, but never so many in one place.

"Don't stare," Tae-Hyun reminded her.

"But it's amazing!" she replied as father and Ki-Chul moved to a line behind seven other farmers to see a stately looking man dressed entirely in black. The sights and sounds of such an advanced culture too enticing to heed her brother's cautious advice, even if the place they had reached was simply a logistical depot. Cranes, lifts, and pulleys transferred loads from carts to trucks, and from more carts to railcars. Ki-Hwa wondered how much easier life on the farm would be with these clever inventions. The Koreans were in the dark ages compared to their Japanese occupiers.

"They're doing it again," Ki-Chul said, arriving back at the cart minutes later. Jung-Hwan sighed, closed his eyes, and looked down in disgust.

"We can't let them," Tae-Hyun protested.

"And what do you suggest we do?" Ki-Chul snapped back. "Go in there and demand more? Are you so brave, little brother?"

"It's not fair."

"It never is. But they won, remember? We are simple feathers on their river." Ki-Chul ran a hand across the crops. A year of toil for pennies. Moments later, father returned looking as burdened as the oxen.

"Unload over there," he muttered, pointing to a truck.

"How much, father?" Tae-Hyun asked but got no response.

"How much?" Ki-Chul echoed his brother's question.

"Do as I say!" he snapped, surprising Ki-Hwa. He was not one to yell, much less at his children. A large truck with one family's crops already on board sat thirty feet away, half-empty, waiting to add the Kim family harvest. They piled their crop into the flatbed. Their carts empty, Tae-Hyun moved the oxen to a post and gave them each a pat on the head.

"Now?" Ki-Hwa asked quietly, not wanting to offend her disheartened brothers.

"Yes, now," father said.

A life of waiting was mercifully over. A five-minute walk with Tae-Hyun brought the sounds and smells of the mysterious Kyeongju market, a large and confusing maze with tight quarters, myriad alleys, and endless wonderment. He pleaded with her to stay close as the others faded away, but she ignored him. She was an explorer in a labyrinth of the fascinating and odd. The market was divided into sections by the type of product for sale with each section housing multiple rows of individual stands under an open-air arena. In one area dedicated to furniture, Ki-Hwa saw hand-carved wooden chests, desks, chopsticks, tools, and baskets stacked to the rafters. In a corner she found polished stones of shell and slate, and finely crafted *mah-jongg* tiles that made her think of the maternal aunt who'd taught her to play.

In the textile area she delighted in shoes, pants, hats, hanboks, kimono and all sorts of colorful dresses hanging from wooden posts all the way to the ceiling. Fabrics dominated a section where rolls upon rolls sat in piles so high they were twice as tall as her brother. She marveled at the numerous patterns and colors and dreamed of the dresses she would be able to make with the neighbor's sewing machine.

The food area was a sensual overload. Abundant fish, produce, livestock and herbs were proudly displayed in heaping piles, surrounded by old women who haggled for the lowest prices. The aromas were powerful and penetrating. Ki-Hwa wandered down the aisles looking at mountains of bean paste, cow's intestines wrapped into piles like coiled snakes, bowls of silk worms, Chinese pancakes fried in oil, massive woks filled with heavy rice cakes called *dokbokgi* lined in rows next to a cornucopia of fresh chilies, corn, carrots, huge cabbages, and of course, many varieties of rice.

She found tables where fish and sea creatures of all sizes, from thousands of minnows to one lonely giant squid, all cast their death gaze upon passersby. Herring hung in the air to dry as fisherman quickly sliced open anything that still moved. An eerie mist was ever-present; clouds of steam engulfed the market where women, loudly proclaiming the superiority of their product, called out to entice buyers.

"Before the Nippon came," father spoke as he suddenly walked beside her, "the Kyeongju market was the gathering place for all peoples in southeastern Korea. Now only a lucky handful of farmers and craftsmen are allowed to sell at all." He picked up a set of chopsticks to inspect them. "But these people do not have the highest quality. Those go straight to the Imperial military." He dropped the wooden sticks in disgust.

Ki-Hwa was too enthralled to let father's sad words take away from the moment. She couldn't imagine this wonderful place being any better than it was now and didn't want to. If it had been better at one point in history, then let that be someone else's market. This one was hers.

Father walked on without her just as the brothers spotted a giant cabbage and decided to bargain for it to surprise their mother. Oma loved making *kimchi* and was especially proud of one of her own recipes the boys found spicy and filling. The brothers haggled like auctioneers for the prize cabbage, determined to get it as cheaply as they could for their hardworking matriarch. Ki-Hwa walked on until she found a wall blocking her path; a wall that spoke.

"Excuse me miss," a strong male voice said, so close that she felt the heat of human breath upon her forehead. It wasn't the sudden stop that surprised her as much as the clarity of the voice. She looked ahead to see a strapping Japanese soldier looking slightly down on her. He tipped his hat. She bowed, almost too frightened to stand up straight again. When she had recovered, he seemed a giant, filling her entire world. She considered running away, a move Tae-Hyun would have approved of, but she froze.

"*Joseong hamnida,*" she blurted out, feeling flustered. A mistake she quickly recanted. "Ah...I mean *sumimasen,* sir," excusing herself in Japanese and bowing again just to be safe.

"It is quite all right, Miss," the soldier said calmly as he leaned closer. "I do not completely agree with the Emperor's policy of banning your native tongue." He was handsome and had eyes that seemed to conceal a secret. A scar that began just below the left side of his jaw ran down his neck. She looked at it and then away quickly before returning her gaze to the point where it disappeared under the collar of his shirt.

"Is there anything I can help you find?" he asked. He was eloquent with an ease about him that gave her hope. Hope that all Japanese soldiers were this way and not the barbarians on the road.

"Uh, no...no, sir, I am just admiring the marvelous selection we have today."

"Mrs. Choi has some excellent *gimbap* if you care to try some. Let me purchase it for you." He moved to a nearby stand and motioned to the lady behind it while Ki-Hwa took a moment to study his uniform. It was more olive-colored than the reddish-brown of the other soldiers. He wore red rank insignia on each collar, a pistol on one hip and an immense saber on the other that stretched all the way to the ground. Three medals graced his left breast pocket and a wide-brim cap with the same flower as the others-- a chrysanthemum. His boots were truly impressive; black, well shined, and reaching all the way up to his knees. She gazed down at them in admiration.

*Those must have taken a whole cowhide,* she mused. They were not the same khaki boots with the laced-X worn by the soldiers on the road. They were nicer; shining in a way that was out of place in the usually muddy town. He seemed a sleek warrior, yet his mannerisms and command of the language suggested considerable education.

Behind her small table Mrs. Choi rolled fish, vegetables and rice in a seaweed wrap, sliced it into smaller pieces, and handed it to the soldier, all the while staring at Ki-Hwa.

"It is a beautiful day, " he said, handing her one gimbap. He led her through the loud and steamy market.

"Yes, but the snows are not far off," she replied before biting into the roll. The soldier paused to do the same, creating a silence that made Ki-Hwa uncomfortable.

"So how are we doing?" he asked after swallowing.

"Sir?" she replied.

"In your country. How are we managing it? To your satisfaction?"

Ki-Hwa stammered. "Our lives are peaceful and prosperous. I have nothing to complain about, sir."

"Do you think life is better since we arrived or are we to blame for your circumstances?" He was polite, but his questions made her squirm.

"I believe without the Emperor, our lives would be without guidance and our towns would be primitive clans fighting amongst themselves. The empire enables us to move forward with the times."

He laughed and looked genuinely surprised. A faint smile lingered on his ruggedly attractive face. "Well, I see there still is some education being practiced in the local schools."

He turned to walk and so she followed, unsure of what choice she had. "You have magnificent boots," she said.

"Thank you. They're for riding my horse."

"Were they expensive?"

"They are issued to all officers."

"You're…an officer?"

"Do you know what that means?"

"Yes," she replied. She didn't. She only knew that officers and soldiers were different, and officers were more powerful.

"So you know that I command all these soldiers?"

"Of course," she said taking a last bite of gimbap.

"My name is Captain Inoue," he said bowing only enough to be polite and not show subservience. She wanted to return the introduction, but a mouthful of gimbap prevented her from speaking for a long moment.

"Kim, Ki-Hwa," she said, swallowing. "Where are you from?" The question was purely innocent, but in the time of intercultural hierarchies, it crossed a line of familiarity that she was not allowed to broach. She could be chastised.

But he smiled. "I am from Nagoya. Do you know where that is?" She shook her head. "It is on the main island of Honshu, just to the North of Tokyo, our capital. It is breathtaking in the springtime." With a deep sigh and a longing look toward the nearby hills, he continued, "I miss the salty air that blows in from the sea, the views, the cherry petals that litter the ground like snow."

"'Tis ever common that men are merriest when they are far from home," Ki-Hwa blurted. Her tiny school had precious few books, let alone Western books translated into Hangul. When she was sixteen, a teacher had arranged for a few classics to be sent down from Seoul, including Romeo and Juliet, The Taming of the Shrew, and King Henry V. She hadn't cared for The Taming of the Shrew, but the other two were addictive. Ki-Hwa was always a good student and loved to read; books filled her with hope that something more was waiting for her beyond the sloggy paddies and dirt roads. She read as much as she could and yearned for more Shakespeare or any other classics.

The captain's head whipped around. "Shakespeare? You just quoted Shakespeare. Do you know more?"

"Oh, yes sir. I know Shakespeare well." She didn't, but the attention was intoxicating.

"Although the English are our enemy now, I am very fond of their literature," he said, gazing intently at her.

"As am I, sir."

"Ki-Hwa." A panicked voice rang from behind her. She turned to see Tae-Hyun staring, his mouth agape and fear contorting his face. His eyes darted from her to the officer and back. "Forgive me, sir," her brother said, joining them. "But we must be getting the family back to the farm."

Ki-Hwa narrowed her eyes and stared at her brother. She was enjoying her conversation with the officer and desperately wanted it to continue. She'd experienced an infatuation with a boy before, only to be admonished by her mother who disdained such frivolous emotions. The feeling thrilled her; it was an octopus wrapping itself around her heart, a sensation that she welcomed until Tae-Hyun put a spear into it.

"It is quite all right, young man," Captain Inoue said, "I understand you have much work to do now that the harvest is done." He looked at Ki-Hwa with a smile. "You must prepare to plant winter crops. By all means, take your leave. Be sure to tell your father he has a remarkable daughter. Fortune will call."

"Thank you, sir. Have a pleasant day, sir." Tae-Hyun stuttered as he grabbed his sister by the arm and dragged her away.

"Good day, sir," Ki-Hwa blurted out, turning to look at him one last time. He raised a hand to his brim and tipped his cap the same way he had when they'd met.

"Why were you talking to him?" Tae-Hyun demanded out of the captain's earshot. "Don't you know how dangerous that is?"

32

"He is harmless." Ki-Hwa felt cheated. She defended her actions and the polite officer, but Tae-Hyun was adamant and ushered her through the maze of the market and back to their cart. Still mesmerized by the encounter and even a little lightheaded having never met anyone so enchanting, Ki-Hwa thought about Captain Inoue the whole way home. It would not be the last time.

\* \* \* \* \*

Four full moons graced the countryside and with the passage of time, Ki-Hwa's memories of the dashing captain faded. She begged *Oma* in vain to let her go with the men on another trip to the market, but knew it would never happen again. It seemed the entire family condemned her for talking to him, something she couldn't understand since nothing had come of it.

"But something *could* have happened," Tae-Hyun said time and again. "You have no idea what they're capable of." Only Tae-Hyun had an opinion about the man. Neither of her other brothers or father seemed to care, and yet none of them knew him the way she did. They didn't know the kindness in his eyes and the loneliness he felt for his own homeland. Only she truly understood him.

With the winter crop planted and the snows falling, inactivity turned to boredom. She yearned to see him again, began to resent his apparent neglect, and then finally abandoned all thoughts of him. She grew weary of spending so much time re-enacting the encounter in her head until the memory was as stale as old rice.

On a misty, lazy day with a chill hanging in the air near dusk, Ki-Hwa stood staring over the still paddies when Tae-Hyun approached.

"What are you doing?" he asked.

"Admiring it."

"Admiring what?"

"The land. It's so peaceful."

Tae Hyun stared out over the snow-covered cropland and furrowed his brow. "Are you feeling ill?" he asked, "I thought you wanted more than this."

"I do. But I enjoy the quiet of it, too," she replied as she walked away.

"Where are you going?"

"Bulguksa."

"Your private palace," he muttered. He watched her until she disappeared around the corner and headed off toward Toham-san, her footprints the only blemish in the freshly fallen snow.

Reaching the sad ruins of Bulguksa Temple usually took Ki-Hwa thirty minutes, but today, the ankle-deep snow added another ten minutes to the trek. As a little girl, playing here had been a fantastic escape, a chance to run in the footsteps of great ancestors and hide among ghosts. Now that she was a young woman, it was a hidden solace of uninterrupted silence and natural bliss. When she was thirteen, a monk had come from Taegu and taught class on the history of Buddhism in Korea. The precocious Ki-Hwa immediately asked about Bulguksa, and he was only too happy to divulge the story as it had been told to him.

She made the journey weekly, providing her chores were done. She walked over the remains of Lotus Flower Bridge, past the still-standing Dabotap Pagoda, where four magnificent stone lions once stood, and sat where the Hall of Great Enlightenment had burned to the ground. Her mind raced with images of how life must have been at the height of the Temple's influence and she reached her hands out to try to feel the forgotten ones whose lives filled the place before the occupiers destroyed it...or so they said.

The crisp sound of boots crushing the snow underneath them reached her across the ruins. Whoever was wearing them was moving fast—perhaps running. The sound grew louder, coming from the west, from the direction of the Lotus Bridge. Then she saw them: three Japanese soldiers.

*Don't show fear. Sit still. Bow respectfully,* she thought. Still they came, their intentions clear. *"Konnichi wa,"* she said. No response.

The first one bounded effortlessly up the stairs and grabbed her arms. "You have been ordered into the service of the Emperor!" he demanded.

"What have I done?" she asked.

He wrestled to get both arms behind her back where another soldier attempted to tie her hands together. With three older brothers, she'd been in this situation before. Ki-Hwa leaned back against the second soldier and used his body weight to support hers while delivering a formidable kick to the lower jaw of the one to her front. With her right foot on the ground, she pivoted and delivered a knee to the groin of the second. Her hands broke free and she threw a desperate punch at the head of the third. Her speed was formidable, but her strength was not. The small woman did not have the force to incapacitate the young trooper and he grabbed her arm before she could turn to run even one step. In an instant he had Ki-Hwa face first in the snow, straddling her.

"Tie her hands, you idiots!" he ordered. "Just don't rough her up."

"Why?" She struggled, fighting back the tears. "What have I done?" She let out a little yelp as the final binding clamped down on her hands. The soldiers stood her up, forced a rag into her mouth and covered her head with a sack. When the world went black, Ki-Hwa began trembling with fear and at the same time, was engulfed in an all-consuming sadness. Her heart raced as tears streamed from her eyes in the darkness. A soldier threw her over his shoulder as the others jeered at her fighting spirit.

"Oma?" she whimpered quietly.

# 2

**If you prick us, do we not bleed? If you tickle us, do we not laugh? If you poison us, do we not die? And if you wrong us, shall we not revenge?**
*-William Shakespeare*

The Hankyu railway train from Osaka to Kyoto was not built for speed or comfort, especially for a man of fifty-two years with a weak spine born under the irascible sign of the Tiger. But when the cause noble, even the weakest of reeds stand steady against the wind.

Dismounting the train on aged knees, he found his way north through the busy streets to Gion Kobu and then to the *okiya* he sought. He peered at the placards on the outside of the house announcing the names of the *geisha* who resided there. Finding the name he secretly hoped he would not, he groaned. His worn hand knocked on a solid door of oak, rare in these days, which opened before he could think of something to say.

"Ah, young *shikomi*, is the Okasan available please?" he bowed just low enough to appear respectful, though this was not the way he felt. A very young looking girl knelt gingerly at the door, her gaze fixed upon the ground at his feet.

"A moment please," she replied, reaching to close the door. "But I am a *minarai* now sir."

"My deepest apologies," he bowed, this time sincerely, embarrassed at the mistake. Still, he found it irritating to be corrected by a girl who probably lacked the skill to properly pour him tea were he a customer. He waited outside for several minutes, his collar itching before a bony pair of hands slid the door back open.

"Ah, Hashimoto-san, *Konnichi wa*," a proper voice welcomed him as a tall, thin woman stepped through the doorway and bowed. She was just as alluring as he'd remembered, adorned in a brilliant purple kimono with soaring white cranes that disappeared into her *obi* belt.

"May I see her?" he stammered.

"You are always welcome to see her, sir. But..." She paused and lowered her voice. "...are you certain you want her to see *you*?"

He looked down at his expensive modern suit and his eyes moved to the handcrafted *zori* that adorned her slender feet poking out from under her kimono. She wore *tabi* socks with a split between the big and second toes so the thong slipped comfortably between them and remembered the tales of agony women were expected to endure to wear them. "I have traveled far," he said. "I am certain."

She nodded and motioned for him to follow. The interior courtyard was as modest as any Japanese home of the day; nothing like the ornate entrance suggested, a purposeful ruse. It was tidy with many exotic plants filling the space, creating a more claustrophobic feel than was necessary. "I always wondered what was behind the doors here," he said.

"I do hope it meets your expectations."

A pleasant odor of blooming spring flowers and tealeaves hung in the air. "I must have just missed a gathering." His voice cracked. "It looks very comfortable."

A smile graced her dangerously thin lips and for one surreal moment, he wondered if consciousness would leave him were she to smile in earnest. "Would you mind waiting here, please sir?"

He nodded and bowed more deeply than necessary as she disappeared across the courtyard. As the economy deteriorated, so had the reputation of her house. Perhaps the future of her girls was also at risk he wondered. Rumors swirled of women in such okiya lowering standards to earn their keep; *korobi* geisha willing to roll over for any guest and taking less than necessary to play the jade flute. His eyes explored the dimly lit interior, but he took none of it in. He could have been in the belly of a whale for all he cared. *Calm yourself,* he thought. *Or she will see right through you, old man.*

Without a sound, she stepped from behind a corner. Had he not been looking in the direction of that very spot, he never would have noticed her. His breath instantly abandoned him. With small steps she approached as silent as a mist. A blue kimono decorated with orange and white koi swam around her body. He'd seen a number of geisha in his life but she was stunning. The oval shape of her youthful face, the almond color of her eyes, the perfectly brushed hair, and the cupid's bow of a mouth that hid her radiant smile all at once reminded him of her mother. She carried herself with poise and finesse that would break a man made of stone, a sight that all at once filled him with pride. Without a doubt, she was the most beautiful woman he'd ever seen. But he could not enjoy the moment.

"Why are you here, father?" she asked, stopping in front of him.

"Hello, Tamiko. You look very well." Guilt beat back pride with such ferocity that it humbled this man whom, until this moment, had not understood what the word meant.

"As do you." Trained to recognize exquisite fabrics she glanced at his suit. "You can afford a fine tailor now?"

"I have done well since you left."

"I left?" She craned her head forward. He shut his eyes tightly to avoid looking into hers. "In that case, I apologize for leaving, father. But I must say, those you sold me to were rather adamant that I was their property."

He opened his eyes, wondering for the thousandth time if this visit was wise. The agony just to come to this place was enough to last him the rest of his days. But he also expected this and it was time to speak his peace. "Someone has dishonored our family. I request your assistance to make it right."

She stared at him, turning her head. "Are you asking me for help, father?" The composure drilled into her for years by totalitarian geisha was forgotten. Her arms dangled and the fan concealed in her sleeve slipped to the floor.

"It is true I have made misguided decisions, but I have also made reparations for my past-- except for you. Please let me complete my journey."

"As I was allowed to complete mine? As I recall, it never started for me, father. I've lived in an okiya since almost before I can remember. I scrubbed floors, dishes and toilets for years before even being allowed the privilege of carrying a *geiko's* makeup or taking my first lesson. I was not even permitted to experience puberty without Okasan's guidance."

"I never wanted this for you, Tamiko."

"Do not call me that!" Her childhood nickname was unwelcome.

He stood up straight. "Do you usually shout at guests of the okiya?"

"I am a scorned daughter. I have earned the right to shout at you." She tamed her emotions the way a kite tames the wind. "You may not have wanted to do this, but you did it nonetheless. You have profited well from the sale of your daughter. Look around, father. There are no walls and locks, but make no mistake: this is a prison and I am a convict."

He tried to remember the speech he'd rehearsed on the train. "Our family were once Samurai, Tamiko, but with all the changes the Empire has gone through..." He paused, searching for the right words. "We had to find new ways to live among the people, or we would be in the hillsides in rags. Money was always scarce when I was a boy. So when my pockets were heavy, I did not know how to manage it. I lost sight of what was important. I could not bear the shame of returning to poverty when our finances left us. I deeply regret making this arrangement. You were sacrificed so the family could continue."

"So your son could continue, father," she corrected him, "Your passion was always for him. The favored child."

"Your mother begged me not to-- "

"You would have been wise to listen to her. We would not be having this conversation if you had. I loved mother enough to dedicate myself to this life for her good name. I worked hard to become what I am for her. But you..." she withheld her assault. "Now you need my help because someone has dishonored the family I never knew." She shook her head and crossed her hands in front of her. "Why?"

"How I wish this visit was only about your forgiveness," he said. "But it is not for myself. It is for Takeo."

# 3

**With one chained friend, perhaps a jealous foe,
The dreariest and longest journey go**
*-Percy Bysshe Shelley*

Ki-Hwa could not see the men talking on either side of her as they bounced like so many potatoes in a sack on the rickety road from Bulguksa. The cab was certainly better than the man in the back who was undoubtedly jostled, but he at least was not hooded and bound.

"We could stop right here. No one would know," the driver said.

"We could also be run through by the captain's sword," a voice to her right replied. "She is not to be harmed."

"Yes, sergeant."

"If you are so anxious, take care of yourself when we get to the barracks. I will not hear of this again."

The sergeant's warning resulted in total silence for the rest of the ride. She was seized, tied, blinded, and squeezed between two men in the cab of a truck not meant for three people while her captors bartered over her virtue. Instinct told her to cry and beg for life, but rigid discipline kept hell at bay. This was more frightening than the time Tae-Hyun was nearly crushed by a stack of cinder blocks falling near the house. They had been playing when her brother fell against the six-foot high stack, causing it to collapse and bury him. Scrambling to dig him out from underneath the pile she was sure she would find a corpse, but the bricks turned out not to weigh much. That was when she discovered the difference between heavy, expensive bricks, and lighter, cheaper ones made with more straw in them. Father was incensed and immediately returned them to the vendor, not willing to weaken the Kim house. How she wished she were buried beneath cheap bricks instead of in the cab of a truck.

They stopped. The engine's silence and dismounting soldiers brought a swarm of locusts buzzing in her stomach as they eased her out of the truck like a glass bowl. Someone groped her breast and she wriggled to the other side while the man in the truck bed fumbled with her feet.

"Get her up the stairs," the sergeant said.

She counted thirteen steps when they put her down and unbound her feet, but not her hands. Someone pushed her and she stumbled, still blind.

"Faster," the driver insisted with a shove.

"Five lashings with a cane if you do that again," the sergeant said. "Would you prefer to park the truck instead of having the honor of presenting this to him?"

*Present me to whom?* she wondered, trying hard not to let the tears well up. Her heart pounded in her ears, echoing inside the hood like a bell. She retraced her steps a hundred times on the ride and once more as she walked.

*I hiked up to Bulguksa, sat in my favorite spot, alone with my thoughts in a place no one ever goes. Men came from nowhere. Why? Who were they?*

Warm air. The smell of a fire. They must have passed through a door. The men slowed their pace and stopped, grabbing her by the shoulder to do the same.

"Sir! May I present-- " the sergeant started.

"Do you think me a fool, sergeant?"

*It cannot be*, she thought. But it was. The hood flew from her head, revealing the strapping Captain Inoue standing mere inches in front of her.

"*Anyeong haseyo,* Miss Kim," he said, greeting her in Korean.

"Thank God!" she cried out, running to him. "I don't understand what's happening. These men attacked me and brought me here. I don't know why. Please tell them who I am. I'm not who they want!" She placed her bound hands on his chest. The man she had dreamed of for so long would help her. It was all a misunderstanding and he would take her home.

"Oh, but you are, Miss Kim. You are exactly who they set out to rescue." He turned and walked to a massive wooden table in the center of the room and removed his sword. Just past the table was the largest hearth she had ever seen where a pile of embers smoldered, wasting most of the space it was built for. She looked to his sword where it lay on the table, which he noticed. "Oh this is not your fate, little one. You are destined for much more."

"You? You have done this to me, sir?" She held up her tightly bound hands.

"It is the natural evolution of things. The big fish swallow up the little ones." He was stone faced, void of pity. "Because the nail that sticks its head up is the one that gets hit."

"But what have I done?"

"Quite the contrary, miss. You did not do anything. But you did say something." He leaned closer and smiled as if he'd told a joke.

"But you can't..." she started.

"But I can. Your fate is better left in our hands, Miss Kim." He took two slow steps toward her as she inched backward. "You need direction and mentorship, so the gracious Emperor will provide you the opportunity to flourish under the Rising Sun."

She stood alone in a room bigger than her entire world, the target of contempt. A swarm of emotions buzzed in her head and she shooed each one away as an ox swats flies with its tail—all except anger.

"Is that what we are in your eyes? Wayward children in need of enlightenment?" Her voice cracked. "Are the Korean people being saved by the gracious Empire for our own good?"

"A tiger's heart wrapped in a woman's hide." He said, smiling. "We will assimilate your culture into ours and make the herd stronger. It is the natural way."

"Assimilate us? Do you not mean exterminate? Like the Chinese?"

"What do you know of China save for your schoolbooks?" he raised his voice. "We brought prosperity and hope to a godforsaken band of inbred tribesmen in loincloths. We brought the hand of God to rid the land of its infernal pestilence! You know nothing of the world; nothing of life and death. Your very existence is at my bidding and yet, you lecture me on virtue as I offer you providence and a meaningful destiny." He paused to study her form. "You weep for Korea and condemn me as the enemy of your country. Tell me, Miss Kim, what solution do you propose for your people's plight? Do you have one? You can stand there and cry about the need to find the way to a better life, but you have no path to get yourself there. That is why you need our help."

He stood inches away, leaning in with a scowl until she saw every flaw of a well-maintained set of teeth. Her right foot began to slide backward until she commanded it to stop. "We are not your underlings."

He smiled. "Darkness reigns at the foot of the lighthouse, Miss Kim. You would be wise to look up to us."

Words failed her. She stared at his back as he slowly walked to the table to retrieve his sword. An impeccable hat sat next to the blade, adorned with that lovely flower she had seen before. The beautiful chrysanthemum in bloom perched atop the headgear of a murdering liar. In front of him the fire popped as an ember shot from the hearth. Her breath quickened. Her blood pulsed and the anger turned to rage.

"You have barely been off your farm, Miss Kim, but you will travel now," he said.

But she was not listening. She lunged forward with all her might and kicked him squarely in the back, sending him falling toward the fireplace. It was instinct without reason; a malicious kick with bad intentions with no thought of the consequences.

Captain Inoue fell, placing his hands briefly on the glowing embers that lay strewn on the hearth. He leapt to his feet and let loose a muffled groan of pain, looking down at his singed palms. He turned to her, the sadistic smile engulfing her with fear. With remarkable speed Inoue was on her. Before she could even turn he had clamped one burned hand down on a long strand of hair and shoved the other, swollen and blistering, into her face.

"This? This is not pain!" he shouted as spit flew from his mouth. "You will learn about pain. I know who will teach you!" He exhaled moist, warm air into her eyes and nose. But recoiling as suddenly as he'd attacked, he gave her a sidelong glance and laughed.

"Sergeant!" he yelled, letting her go and folding his arms behind his back.

"Hai!" the young man said, running into the room.

"You know your orders. Do not come back if you fail," he sneered at the sergeant before turning to Ki-Hwa. "Farewell, for thou art too dear for my possessing."

Defeated, bound, and wrapped in the arms of a strange soldier, Ki-Hwa sobbed as the two turned and walked into the unknown.

\* \* \* \* \*

*I still have my virtue at least,* Ki-Hwa thought, bouncing down a rutted dirt road in a new truck with a new sergeant who said nothing. The lights of Kyeongju faded. Within minutes her tiny life was a great distance away but her strength did not fade with it. If she could talk to a captain she could talk to a sergeant.

"Where are we going?" she asked without response. "I asked where we are going." Silence. It didn't matter. He could have answered with anything other than Kyeongju and it would be the same; some other place that was not home. She peered out of the window, struggling to make out shapes in the dark. They passed a farmhouse and she imagined her mother looking for her, calling out over the Kim's little valley, her voice echoing in the snow and answered only by the same silence that the sergeant afforded her. She wanted to lay her head against the window and sleep, but the pain of her bound wrists on the seat behind her and the bumpy ride ruled that out.

*Control yourself,* she thought over and over. *Bide your time like Tae-Hyun on that boat.* They drove slowly through night even as the snows began to fall, east until the sun rose gracefully in their faces, resting only once at a river for a hastily heated breakfast of Army rations which she had none of. The mute sergeant was watchful while he ate and even when he relieved himself. But when he unwrapped her bindings so she could do the same, Ki-Hwa struck. She kicked him in the groin and turned to run, but he was fast. He threw a hand out and grabbed her shirt and held on tight. She didn't get one step from him.

"Miserable little..." he barked, but stopped short. Her punishment was tighter bindings and having to hold her pee because she wasn't going to do it with him watching. She could relieve herself in the truck just to annoy him but then she would have to sit in it. Maybe the half-hearted escape attempt wasn't such a good idea after all. *Where would I have run to anyway?* She thought.

Back on the road he was more than quiet. His silence conveyed resent. He hated her for some reason far deeper than her kick to his scrotum. Something bothered him about her, but it did not matter. He could be Satan and the journey would be no different. Her eyelids fell and closed without a fight. She woke to find the truck stopped and the sergeant placing her head against an extra Army jacket that had been sitting in between them in the cab. Her head comfortable enough for sleep he sighed and cut the bindings around her wrists, but left the ones on her feet. Finally he spoke.

"One wrong move, " he said holding up his knife. She slumped against the jacket, waking some time later to find the truck still plodding on. She rubbed her eyes and took a moment to study the landscape and then her captor. He looked fit, more so than the other soldiers she had seen. He was cleaner too. His hands were not rough, his face shaven, his uniform neat despite the wet and mud. Without looking at her, he pointed to the front of the truck and Ki-Hwa turned to see smoke rising in the east. Another city. Even from a distance it looked larger than Kyeongju as it lay nestled between two massive mountains. Alone on the road since the previous night, they found cars passing them now, travelling in the opposite direction, kicking up dust each time. Her head whipped around to see the first few, studying their features.

"Pusan, Harbor City," she read a sign aloud. "Pusan? Why are we in Pusan?"

The sergeant said nothing. Pusan was the main port in the southern half of the country. A teacher once told her of the various people who passed through this city—sailors and traders from all over Asia; Russian, Chinese, Filipino, Malay, Indo, Thai, Australian and even French from Indochina. Half of the news of the world that reached Korea came through Pusan. Everything was bigger, wider, longer, and faster. She tried to see as much as possible as they drove from one end to the other without stopping until the sight of the ocean filled their windshield and knocked the breath right out of her. Her first thought was of Tae-Hyun and how he lived on it for nearly a year. She missed her brother, she worried about the family she had been taken from, and she was awed by the magnificence of God's great ocean that stretched to the end of the earth before her.

With a heave on the brakes and a violent shudder from the engine, the truck stopped at a dull building made of rotting wood that sat precariously on a wharf. With layers of paint chipping away in the breeze it was several hues of gray and looked like the grandfather of all the warehouses there. The sergeant reached down to her ankles and sliced away her bindings with immaculate precision. "Get out," he said as the engine, nearly an old friend by this time, finally got a rest.

She dismounted and stood in a dirt lot. Her eyes darted around for something, anything that she could run to and hide behind to escape him. Maybe she could vanish into an alley and find her way home in a few months. A wind kicked up and an overpowering stench of rotting fish invaded her nostrils that made it hard to think. Chips of paint flew from the building's exterior like leaves from a tree in a gale. Ten soldiers squawked like crows at another man sitting guard by a door, who only shook his head in return. She felt more alone than ever.

He took her by the arm and they walked past the guards and soldiers and into the stinking building. The men stared openly, as though Ki-Hwa were a cow at auction. Two soldiers continued to peer into the window and gawk at whatever was inside. Over the door, two large Japanese banners ruffled in the wind.

"With service of mind and body," she read.

Once through the door, she immediately wanted out. Though thankfully warm inside, the sergeant sat her down on a bench just under the main window through which the soldiers continued to peer and now directed their attention at her.

"Wait here," he muttered, stepping through a doorway to an adjoining room. The warehouse was large and even duller inside than it was on the outside, if that was possible, and the stagnant air stubbornly held onto the odor of death. Crates were piled in neat rows with various markings— wheat, sugar, coffee, salt, and rice with drums of oil and gasoline and racks of timber mustered alongside. The interior was stifling and resembled the Kyeongju weigh station where crops were stockpiled until they could be shipped. About ten women, mostly poor and dressed in farm clothes like hers, or in old hanboks, sat on benches on the opposite side of the building, looking at the ground as if they were waiting for it to move. None took notice of Ki-Hwa except one; the woman closest to her who could not stop staring.

"Woo, Seo-Sung," the woman said. Finally, here was someone paying attention. "Where are they taking us?"

"Someplace else," she said. "It's our turn to give more to the Empire." She looked at the others. "Well, most of us at least."

Ki-Hwa had a thousand questions, none of which made it to her lips. She searched for the sergeant, but he was gone. "We should run now," she said.

"You're a fighter. Good. You'll need it." Seo-Sung eyed her up and down. "But maybe not. You're pretty. Maybe nothing will happen to you. At least nothing too bad."

"Nothing too bad? We've been taken from our homes. What could be worse?"

The sergeant returned chewing like a cow and handed Ki-Hwa a plate of *bulgogi* and rice, sitting next to her to inspect her bruised wrists. "Left them on too long, damn," he said as he slid the plate of food to her. She was famished and decided not to conceal her hunger, much as she wanted to. Within seconds it was half empty.

"Hey Sarge, have any more?" Seo-Sung asked.

"I don't feed the mutts," he replied.

"Will I have new clothes as well? Or shall I wear this forever?" Ki-Hwa asked.

With a quick breath that almost sounded like a laugh, he got up. "I guess you'll need something," he said with his back to her. He removed his hat and dropped it on the bench. "But before you get any ideas, look around. Ask yourself why none of these women have made a run for it. There aren't any guards in here. Should be easy to get away, right? Just push that door open and go?" Ki-Hwa said nothing. "Ask her why she hasn't yet," he motioned to Seo-Sung before walking away.

Disappearing quickly around a corner, Ki-Hwa slid her plate over to Seo-Sung and offered the remnants of her bulgogi. Seo-Sung was attractive, but her face was strangely older than her years would imply. She was taller than the average Korean, but lean with a raspy voice and swagger she'd never seen. Her hair was shoulder-length and fell in easy curls. Korean hair followed a predictable pattern of curling after age thirty. It was as consistent as tree rings. Ki-Hwa guessed she had a big-city background, maybe born and raised here in Pusan. "What's happening to us?" Ki-Hwa asked.

"Us?" Seo-Sung leaned back, swallowed and slowly rolled her eyes skyward. "Well, we're in high demand, you know." She cleaned her teeth as she spoke. "The Japs don't have enough of their own women to go around see, so they contracted us to help out the war effort."

Ki-Hwa only stared at her. "You know, show your glorious cooperative attitude and support the Empire." She cocked her fist and swung it upward, grabbing her bicep like the American woman on all the war posters.

Ki-Hwa hated sounding so naïve, but she wasn't making any sense. "I don't understand."

"I mean we'll get the opportunity to bend over for the Emperor, literally. It's an easy job. We'll spend most of our time just lying on our backs with our legs spread, waiting for flies to enter the trap."

"Please be clear. He will return soon."

Seo-Sung stared at her.

"Please."

"You really don't know?"

Ki-Hwa shook her head.

"No one told you why you're here?"

"No."

Seo-Sung leaned in closer. "We're bound to be comfort women, at comfort stations for the Imperial military. Do you know what that means?" Ki-Hwa was silent. "You don't, do you?"

Five minutes later Ki-Hwa was sitting like a chicken held down on the chopping block watching the axe fall. Her eyes darted around the room as her chest surged from rapid, short breaths. Her heart raced as though the bag was over her head again. Tears fell from her eyes uncontrollably. "Sex slaves?" she nearly yelled out as Seo-Sung tried to calm her. She was nothing more than property; no longer a girl, a schoolgirl, a farm girl, or even a person. Merely a nameless and subservient thing that would be expected to dispel her virtue for someone she did not know. Many times over.

\* \* \* \* \*

Time is an enemy when fear rules the roost. The sun traversed the sky while Seo-Sung, Ki-Hwa and her escort sat quietly on hard wooden benches most of the day. Near suppertime the sergeant put his coat under his head and lay down to nap. Across the small room, Ki-Hwa stared for the millionth time at the other women destined to give their bodies to the Empire like she.

"Can't put you finger on it can you?" Seo-Sung said.

"What?" Ki-Hwa answered.

"There's something different about them and you're wondering what it is, aren't you?"

She looked at them again. "Yes. We're in the same room but they seem a world apart from you and I."

"Why do you think those girls have bags?" Seo-Sung asked, pointing to a few satchels at their poorly shooed feet. "Do you have a bag? You don't. Why? Because you didn't know you were going to be dragged from your home this day. You weren't allowed to prepare."

"They are here of their own will?"

"Some are professionals. Some were sold. Selling a daughter is a quick way to not be poor in this land. Did your father..."

"No!" Ki-Hwa turned away from Seo-Sung at the floor and then back at the group. Some were pretty. Some were not. Some cried. Some slept. All were rice on the back of the cart heading to market.

"Don't go anywhere," the sergeant said suddenly rising, putting on his jacket, and rounding a corner. Twenty minutes later he returned with two new dresses for Ki-Hwa and an order. "Time to go."

"I'll find you," Seo-Sung said with enough confidence that Ki-Hwa believed her. "It's a boat. Where can you go?"

The sergeant and Ki-Hwa boarded and settled into a cabin the same dull gray as the warehouse, but with a different odor. The warehouse smelled of fish, the cabin of man sweat.

"Where is Seo-Sung?" she asked.

"Don't know, don't care," the sergeant responded, tossing his duffel bag into a corner. He placed his rifle gingerly next to the duffel, removed the ammunition clip, stuck it in his pocket and left the cabin.

"I will find her if you do not," Ki-Hwa shouted down the hall after him.

"Don't fall overboard."

She glanced around the cabin. A bunk was attached to the far wall that bore a small bare mattress. A small steel chest of drawers with a mirror was built into another wall. She walked down the hall and peered into each open door expecting to see life, but they were all empty. At the end of the corridor, a placard hung on the wall.

| Kinai Maru |
|:---:|
| Commissioned to the service of the Emperor 1938 |
| 8000 tons max. capacity |
| Lifeboats→ |
| Fire Extinguisher→ |
| ←Galley (downstairs) |
| Officer's Mess→ |
| ←Bridge |

The sound of footsteps forced a retreat to the cabin where the sergeant was sprawled out on a new sleeping mat on the floor, his possessions lined up neatly against the wall, a worn book in his hands. "Satisfied?" he asked without looking up.

"How did you...You are not staying in here."

"Where do you propose I go little one? It's a boat and the quarters are limited."

"There are empty cabins. Sleep with the pigs, but not in here."

He didn't move. Three new clean white sheets and a decorative blanket were folded neatly on the bunk next to two sets of small men's pants and four plain white shirts. "Where did you get these?" she asked.

"I'm good at getting things." He flipped the pages of his book. "And I am not going anywhere until we are both at our destination. Now be quiet."

"And where is that?"

"I said be quiet or I will stuff my sock in your mouth. My job is to deliver you unharmed. Not talk to you."

She sat on the bed and ran a finger over the clean sheets. She'd been awake a very long time and was about to journey across the ocean into the unknown. She didn't want to sleep, but knew it was time to rest. There would be plenty of days to fight.

She made the bed, removed her shoes for the first time since the previous morning, and lay down. She pulled a sheet up to her chin and rolled away from him.

"Tokyo," he said. "We're going there first."

She rolled over to look at him. "The capitol?"

He let out a sigh, keeping the book in front of his face.

"And then where? What about this person who is supposed to teach me about pain?"

"You would be wise to not think about him."

"And what am I to call you during this trip? Sergeant? Master? Glorious representative of the Empire?"

"If I tell you my name, will you let me read my book?"

"Yes."

"Isogai. Sergeant Denbe Isogai. Now be quiet."

True to her word, she stopped asking questions, rolled over, and gave in to sleep. *Tokyo,* she thought. *I have that for now.*

* * * * *

On the first day at sea Seo-Sung found Ki-Hwa and took her to the galley to eat. The women were silent and bore the same sullen expression as Ki-Hwa's family when part of the rice crop would become too heavy with water during the night and lay on its side, rendering it worthless. The girls spoke in hushed tones and devoted a great deal of attention to another Korean girl named Cha-Young. She was bruised around the eyes and had trouble eating.

"What happened?" Ki-Hwa asked.

"One of the crew got forceful with her last night," Seo-Sung said shaking her head, staring at the battered girl. "She's nineteen. She thinks it's her own fault." She turned to look at Ki-Hwa, but found only an empty place.

Halfway down the ship, Ki-Hwa stopped running and leaned against a railing. She stared at the water slipping by the hull, trying not to throw up. "Raped!" Ki-Hwa screamed at the ocean. She ran to her empty cabin, sat on the bunk and sobbed. She cried for her plight; she cried for her parents, she cried for her home, and she cried for Cha-Young and the crewman who couldn't control himself. And then she cried for herself, knowing it would soon be her. *How can men do this?* She thought. *Why are we nothing more than property to them?*

Denbe returned to the cabin some time later. "Did you know a girl was raped last night?" Ki-Hwa asked before he could even sit.

"I did not."

"Does it not bother you?"

He sat on his mat and stared blankly at one corner of the cabin. "Well it's not something I would do, but I really don't care much if someone else did."

"What if it were me?"

"Are you planning on being raped?"

"What if it were me?" she raised her voice.

"It will not be you."

"Because you have a duty to safeguard me. Because you would fail if I were hurt."

"You could say that."

"Well, then I have a demand. Protect Seo-Sung as you protect me."

"Your friend with the arrogant tongue?"

"If anything happens to her, I'll be no good to anyone. I'll be the flower that never blooms and may even throw myself overboard. Your goods will be damaged or lost upon arrival and you will fail your mission."

He stared at her. "You are in no position to make…"

Ki-Hwa stood and ran into the opposite wall face first, cutting her lip.

"What are you doing?" Denbe yelled. Ki-Hwa backed up two steps and did it again. She turned to him, blood streaming from her nose. "I want her protected!"

"You are crazy! Why anyone wants you so much…"

She turned to face the wall and threw her head back.

"Stop! I will do so, but she'll have to move in here. That is the only way I can watch over her." The cabin was cramped with two people and would be even more uncomfortable with three. "Are you at ease with that?" Denbe asked.

Ki-Hwa wiped her nose on her white shirtsleeve. "I am."

\* \* \* \* \*

Being subjected to the whims of a farm girl was dishonorable for an Imperial Army Sergeant, but Denbe had learned his first important lesson about Ki-Hwa: if she wasn't happy then no one would be. He was talented at procurement and keeping his mouth shut, so he said little but got the things she and even Seo-Sung needed in Tokyo. Ki-Hwa's swollen lip and nose were well worth the pain for having Seo-Sung and a new set of *mahjong* tiles in the cramped cabin. A life of Tae Kwon Do with three brothers made her nearly immune to facial pain, a secret Denbe would never know. On the third day trucks, crates, and timber were loaded into the main holds and the Kinai Maru was under way.

"You know kid," Seo-Sung pressed Denbe that evening. "You don't strike me as the soldier type. I think you were a student, probably a bright one. Then the Emperor called you to his glorious service, and you followed. I think you could have been so much more, but now you'll die on a beach or in a jungle like the rest of the pack."

"And you?" he replied, dropping his book. "Where were you studying when the war started? A western movie theater?"

She smiled. "I was learning how to get things from people. Like you. Like this."

"*Soju?*" Ki-Hwa gaped at the green bottle Seo-Sung pulled from her blanket. It was a potent Korean libation made from rice that her father always kept hidden away from his children, unsuccessful with three sons.

"Where did you get that?" he asked.

"Same place I got these." Two bottles of Japanese sake then appeared from her bottomless blanket. "I haven't been sitting here doing nothing, sergeant. Why don't you try the soju and we'll drink the sake? We'll call it a cultural exchange."

He grabbed the soju bottle from her hand and inspected it. "Is it any good?"

"Would I steer my captor wrong?" With a smile, Seo-Sung handed Ki-Hwa a bottle of sake. She stared at its fine Japanese kanji inscription. She could speak Japanese but her ability to read it was lacking. She had seen father under the drink, but had never done it herself. Two glasses later she sat on her bed with her back against the wall, a turtle hiding in its shell. Sergeant Denbe Isogai was not so placid.

"My family was good," he said. "But I was not meant to be an officer like father." When the Emperor asked for volunteers...I left his precious academy and enlisted in the cavalry. I thought it was my destiny. But it wasn't to be." He took a pull of soju. "Instead of glory on the battlefield I was sent to your country to sit on my hands and then got a babysitting mission." He motioned to Ki-Hwa, who sat motionless and silent on the bed.

"I'm sorry we can't be more glorious for you," Seo-Sung replied.

He stared at her. "And you?"

"I am a menu on a wall, sergeant," Seo-Sung said. "I can be whatever you want me to be. If you want to think of me as an honorable child allowed to do almost anything she desired as long as it didn't burden her parents then I can be that. If you want to think of me as a street urchin with no morals who wasted her life with other wayward youths, working odd jobs to get by, not all of them legal, I can be that too."

He stared at her and then turned the bottle over to look at the ingredients. "I do not think women are so challenging as many men make them out to be," he said. "They just don't know what they're made of." He lied back on his sleeping mat. "But I do."

Seo-Sung turned to Ki-Hwa and whispered. "This is how you win a man."

"So which one is true?" Ki-Hwa asked.

"Which one?"

"About you. Which one are you?"

"Have you not paid attention, little one?"

"Do not talk to me like I am a burden." Ki-Hwa looked at the sake and felt the need to lie down like the sergeant, but refused. "I am no one's burden. Father only wanted boys to tend to the fields. He never saw the need for a girl. A girl is nothing but a burden on a farm. I was tough like them. Tried to win his affection. 'Boys make money,' he told me, 'Girls cost money.' Mother was different. She understood."

"Don't ever tell anyone that again," Seo-Sung said, taking the bottle from Ki-Hwa. "Never let them see your true self."

\* \* \* \* \*

Two weeks on the open ocean is a journey to the ends of the earth for anyone discovering what it means to have "sea legs." Even worse is being relegated to a cabin with nothing but a worn set of mahjong tiles as the boat pitched like a see saw in the South Pacific. One a desperately clear morning the Kinai Maru finally steamed past an island the First Mate called Corregidor and into the busiest bay a destroyed, smoldering city could hope for.

"Manila," Denbe said as the three leaned against the railing and stared in wonderment at the charred remnants of what must have been a lovely place not many moons ago. The Imperial Navy in the bay and dominating Army in the city were ants deconstructing the carcass of something recently perished. The city's skyline was a mishmash of pointed buildings as big as full-grown trees with Christian crosses on top in between blackened, destroyed piles of stones and timber that Ki-Hwa thought once were someone's proud homes. The searing heat was nauseating, but below decks was too familiar so the three stayed out of doors and felt war smack them in the face.

"Your friend's work?" Seo-Sung asked, looking over the city.

Denbe was silent, almost embarrassed at the wanton destruction left behind by the Fourteenth Imperial Army. The Navy was busy hastily rebuilding docks and warehouses to transform Manila into another hub of the extensive Japanese supply network. Even from the safe distance of the Kinai Maru's main deck, the city was positively frenetic with activity, but unlike Tokyo the people lining its streets all wore uniforms.

"You don't get off the boat," Denbe insisted.

"Afraid of them?" Seo-Sung asked.

"Yes," he replied, turning to her. "Because they're just like me. Only worse."

For the first time since Pusan Seo-Sung kept her mouth shut.

Just before its departure, crates of bananas and tropical fruit were uploaded to the Kinai Maru along with a new cargo of fantastic beauty. Ten more comfort women, this time Filipinas, boarded hours before departure and bunked with the Korean girls in the general quarters. They were unlike anyone Ki-Hwa had ever seen and the first day out of Manila, her curiosity got the better of her. She stood outside the door of their quarters, barely more than a cattle pen, and stared openly at two Filipinas as they spoke in a flowery language she wanted to know. Their skin was like coffee and their eyes were rounder than any she'd ever seen. Their mouths were wider and showed more teeth than the Nippon or Han mouth and their curves made Ki-Hwa feel pale, flat, and uninteresting. They were exotic and breathtaking. And like her, their beauty would soon be destroyed on the anvil of the Imperial hammer. The first smile she'd felt in weeks turned into a familiar scowl as she walked back to the cabin to find Denbe.

"How many countries have you conquered?" she demanded more than asked.

He looked at her and paused for a long moment, knowing this was coming. When he spoke, he spoke as a schoolboy recalling a rehearsed message. "We do not conquer. We liberate. We exercise our divine right to make the people of this hemisphere better than they were born into." His voice cracked.

"By invading, killing, occupying, destroying cultures? You do not think this is true." Denbe remained silent as he lay on his mat. "I want to know more," she said. "You take all these places, my home, and no one has stopped you or said that it was not right? The world just...lets you?"

"Who would oppose the rising sun? There is no country in Asia that could stop us and the rest of the world doesn't care."

"That does not make it right."

He sighed and looked at her, too indifferent to care, but too beholden to the imp not to. "This is the belief of *hakko ichiu*: to unite eight corners of the world under one roof...a Japanese roof. A pan-Asian alliance would liberate everyone and stabilize economies." It was a textbook response written by the Emperor's own men and they both knew it. He rolled away from her to face the wall. "I do not wish to speak of it anymore."

"I do."

"Speak to your friend then."

"I do not know where she is." Denbe didn't respond. Ki-Hwa stood and crossed to the porthole to stare into the darkness. There were no lights, just dark water illuminated by a half moon on the wave crests. "I do not know where I am. We are lost. All of us. Rafts on the ocean. No chance to live. We bide our time until the great darkness takes us. This is not even living."

Denbe let out a long sigh, allowing Ki-Hwa to stare out the portal and vent. "Rabaul," he finally said.

She turned to look down at him, little more than a defeated man beaten by a simple girl with a purpose. A small victory. For a moment her heart, so empty for so long, was suddenly awash with something. Not hope. But something. She wondered if all men would be so easy to tame, but knew that was folly.

"We are going to Rabaul," he said. "Deep-water harbor, airstrips, volcanoes, and about a hundred thousand troops. I hear the war has barely touched it."

"Tell me more," Ki-Hwa said, lowering her voice the way Seo-Sung would when she wanted to coax a man.

"This isn't the time or place."

"Why not?"

"Because it isn't." He pulled a sheet up to his chin. "And because...I don't want to go there as much as you do."

Ki-Hwa looked out the window again and saw the same all-powerful ocean she'd seen for weeks. Still there. Still looking back at her as if it didn't care. She crossed to her bed and lay down, eyes open, staring at the ceiling, saying the name of the place again and again until Denbe covered his ears.

"Rabaul. Rabaul. Rabaul."

# 4

## Misery acquaints a man with strange bedfellows
*-William Shakespeare*

Denbe leaned against the salt-blasted forward railing of the Kinai Maru and stared at the island fortress of Rabaul. "Unpredictable reefs," he said. "It will take more time to travel less distance." A deckhand had told him this and many more secrets of the Pacific in exchange for security in case the new mechanics wanted a fight. Sergeant Denbe Isogai wasn't above trading his fists for information to look smart in front of women. He had a penis after all. The ship was five days out of Wewak and two days since a Filipina girl had gone missing, leaving everyone on edge.

"How does a person go missing on a boat anyway?" Ki-Hwa kept asking. She scanned the horizon at every hour of the day along with several others who shared her apprehension. They were like children waiting for the doors to open on the first day of school. One day a pod of dolphins rode the bow wave of the Kinai Maru and she named the three that jumped the highest after her three brothers. She was a constant on the forward railing until the afternoon something loomed in the distance; a cancerous lesion on the face of the pristine blue ocean.

"Tovanumbatir," Denbe said as she dragged him to the rail. "It's a volcano, the highest peak in New Britain." Her heart pounded the way it did at harvest time when father paced endlessly up and down the dikes between the paddies smelling, feeling, and studying the crop. Every hour was critical to its success and the children stood by waiting, tools in hand to cut, chop, and stack at a moment's notice.

The journey was ending, but it had consequences. The personal protection agreement she'd enjoyed with Sergeant Denbe Isogai would be over, and without him, Seo-Sung's future was in doubt. The women could be sent to different parts of the island, or worse, Seo-Sung wouldn't get off the boat at all. Ki-Hwa's breath raced as if she'd run up all the stairs in the ship and then slowed to the drumbeat of a funeral march before racing again. She perspired and her long, dark hair became damp and matted in the humid South Pacific air. "Don't let fear control you," Tae-Hyun had often told her. But it was so hard not to.

* * * * *

Ki-Hwa was up before the sun, not really sleeping her last night on the Kinai Maru, and standing at the railing, holding Kazushi the over-anxious deckhand by the sleeve. The enormity of Rabaul was in front of her as if she stood on the Bulguksa pagoda preaching the word of Buddha to an audience of monks.

"You have been here, yes? What's so special about this place?" she asked him.

"It can hold all sorts of boats."

"There are different sorts of boats?"

"Some have shallow drafts, some deep-water keels, some are submarines." His voice cracked the way Denbe's did when she pressed him. What was it with these boys? Why did they waver in front of her so?

"Submarines?"

Kazushi nodded. "I met a guy at the compound who drove submarines. I can't imagine being underwater in those things. When I joined the..."

"At the what?"

"What?"

"You met a man at the what?"

The youngster looked at the water below. Calm for the first time in weeks. "You shouldn't…never mind. Look, this has been interesting, but the Chief will be looking for me." He turned to go and then ran.

"Wait. Tell me about those." But her words bounced off the boat's gray hull and back at her as he disappeared. Ki-Hwa remained on the deck, watching and waiting. When the sun hit her back Seo-Sung joined her, but didn't even have a chance to say good morning.

"What do you think that is?" Ki-Hwa pointed.

"Slept like a log. Thanks for asking, doll."

"I'm sorry. What do you think…"

"Well, you certainly are a curious one. Are you pointing at that bird in the water? It looks like a float plane."

"A what?"

"A float plane. See those big…things underneath it. Those are floats. This kind of plane takes off and lands on the water. I saw some in Pusan. Great for smuggling I hear."

Nestled in between a family of volcanoes, Rabaul wasn't as grand as Manila but a thousand times busier and made Pusan port look forgotten. Trucks of all sizes littered the harbor while planes buzzed overhead in formations of four to twenty, rising from airfields far off in the jungles beyond the main city. The sounds alone were more than all the sounds she'd ever heard in all her life on the farm.

"We're in line to unload," Denbe said joining them. "Should be today."

From the upper deck Ki-Hwa studied the wharves and rows of Rabaul's warehouses. At the mouth of the harbor, two craggy coral formations jutted out of the sea like guardians inspecting all who passed. One was large and skinny with varying foliage growing on top of it while the other was short and fat without much of anything, reminding her of a bald uncle.

Wherever man had not touched, a giant palm tree shot high into the sky, providing cover for the thick undergrowth at its base and a refuge for workers lounging underneath them on a break. An inviting fragrance permeated the air, carried from the island to the boat on the warm breeze. Dust rose from the streets as cars and trucks hurriedly raced about. The sounds of construction echoed off the ship's hull, reverberating long distances across the calm waters. It was the busiest place she'd ever seen. But something was out of place too. She struggled to put her finger on it and finally mumbled.

"The houses have legs."

Every structure was elevated seven to ten feet from the ground by huge tree trunks, like women wading into the water and lifting their skirts to keep them dry. "Why would they build houses that way?" she asked.

"Floods," Denbe answered. "I guess."

By the time the Kinai Maru had docked, painstakingly pushed and prodded by tugboats, dark was closing in and the captain announced that unloading would wait until morning. For one last night the Kinai Maru was a sanctuary that Rabaul could not infiltrate. The three were unable to tear themselves away from the main deck, staring at the lights of the city well into then night, unique fears eating at each.

"It hasn't even slowed down," Ki-Hwa said near midnight.

"No," Seo-Sung said. "It seems to be as busy as ever. Especially that place." She pointed at a large, white building near the center of the city. Cars continually arrived and departed, dropping off and picking up nicely dressed men and women.

"Probably an officers' club," Denbe said. "I saw one long ago."

Ki-Hwa stared at the place as cars came and went. She wondered if the person she was meant for was in there right now, having a drink. He must be close. If not in there, then somewhere in this city a man was preparing to take delivery of his new belonging. A new thing to put on a shelf and adore like a doll or strap to a bed and violate like a peasant. She leaned over the railing and fought the urge to throw up.

"No weakness," Seo-Sung said quietly looking at her. "Be strong. Whoever he is, do you want his first impression of you to be like this?"

Denbe looked up at the night sky. "Maybe you should ask Buddha for…"

"It does no good to tell my problems to the stars," Ki-Hwa said. She looked up from the water to Denbe. "Only action will free me. And free you. And hope is not action."

The morning broke pessimistic over Rabaul. Denbe's uniform was immaculate as he waited at the gangway, a rifle slung over his shoulder and a duffel bag at his feet. He said nothing, reverting back to the pre-oceanic Sergeant Isogai with a chip on his shoulder and a mission to accomplish as Ki-Hwa wondered where he found an iron to make his seams as crisp as a dried leaf. He walked in front of her like a warden leading a prisoner through another putrid warehouse to a dirt opening where a woman with a badly scarred face waited. She was flanked by a dark-skinned man with frizzy hair who Ki-Hwa stared at while they corralled all the comfort women onto a waiting truck.

"That boat was the pits," Seo-Sung elbowed Ki-Hwa. "Never thought I'd be happy to be on my way to a comfort station." But she got no response. As the last to board the pickup truck, Ki-Hwa sat in the unenviable position of tailgate rider, enveloping her in dust, but affording the best view of the city. The fine mist rising from the streets behind the back wheels stung her eyes. The buildings were covered in a light brown layer of dust making them look hazy and out of focus. The heat was stifling and the humidity oppressive. Perspiration trickled down Ki-Hwa's skin under her shirt. And still she stared out the back at one new thing after another.

The truck turned quickly from Mango Avenue onto another road before stopping at a series of barracks-style buildings that not only looked uninviting, but downright dangerous. A large cloth banner hung over the main door.

"Long live the Imperial Japanese Army." Seo-Sung read it aloud in Japanese before changing to Hangul. "Long live us if we play our cards right, gal."

The walls were incomplete and left about a foot open under the overhanging roof. Several women glared from tiny windows at the truck and its fresh inhabitants as its noisy engine shut down. The building they had stopped in front of had a well-made roof of thickly woven *kunai* grass, but that was its only redeeming characteristic. A series of similarly dull buildings sat behind it in neat rows. The scarred girl opened the tailgate, motioning with her hands as if she did not know how to speak.

"Guess that means this is our stop," Seo-Sung said.

Ki-Hwa dismounted first, followed by Denbe and his irritating silence. Seo-Sung jumped down and stood beside her as the two gave the building the once-over. Beyond the hood of the truck a small crowd of men gathered to see the new recruits. This was it.

The comfort station. The den of perversion, deviancy, and surrender.

"Get in line!" A bossy blonde Caucasian woman in a very nice dress demanded in Japanese. Come along now, line up ladies."

The scarred woman, who still hadn't said anything, handed her a clipboard. She walked down the line calling out names, checking them off and giving the girls a good sizing-up. She stopped directly in front of Ki-Hwa without looking up from the clipboard.

"Where is this girl?" she asked in flawless Japanese, pointing to a name on the manifest.

"Never got off da boat," replied the native truck driver. "Captain say she vanish."

"Nonsense! He's hiding her for himself. After you drop dem all off, you get back there. You set dem straight, big fella you see?" She resumed her inspection, looking at Ki-Hwa. "And you are?"

Denbe thrust a piece of paper into the woman's hands, earning a scoff at his impertinence.

*How long has he been carrying that?* Ki-Hwa thought.

The blonde woman read it and paused, looking Ki-Hwa up and down. "Well...," she said dropping her voice. "It's clear where you're going." She stared at Ki-Hwa for an eternity while the young farm girl maintained a respectful gaze at the amulet just above the white woman's breasts. She was clean, combed, and curled in the most modern style, her hair ending just at the shoulders and held back with an expensive jeweled brooch. Her perfume overpowered the salty, fragrant air, a chore in these humid, windy parts.

"And this one," Denbe blurted suddenly, "This one stays with her." He pointed at Seo-Sung.

"Don't tell me my business, sergeant! I determine where they go. You've come a long way and have accomplished your mission.

Choose which you would like as your reward." She motioned toward the women staring over the station's walls, but Denbe didn't so much as turn his head.

"I have not completed my mission until I've met with him, madam." He bowed slightly.

"Fine, see to it that you do so today. She'll show you where." She flicked her hand dismissively at the scarred girl. Sergeant Denbe Isogai gave one parting look at Seo-Sung, an apology in his eyes as he walked to the truck.

"My name is Victoria Foster." The white witch spoke in perfect Japanese, her voice commanding. "Rule number one here is that I am in charge. Rule number two is I am always right. Rule number three is if you think I am wrong, refer back to rules one and two. Rule number four is you will learn your place and live accordingly. We have a hierarchy here. Some girls are on top, some girls are on bottom. Right now, you all are on bottom." She turned and glared at Ki-Hwa. "Except you of course."

Victoria tucked her hands behind her back the way an Imperial officer inspecting troops would and walked slowly down the line. Her off-white camisole and predatory stride reminded Ki-Hwa of the tall storks back home that hunted small fish in the paddies, spearing and swallowing them in one quick movement.

"You will all have to work your way up to earn rewards. But no matter what your place is on the ladder, make no mistake as to your purpose here. You are comfort women. Your job is to make the Imperial servicemen who have committed their life's blood to cleansing the world of its evils comfortable. They are God's chosen warriors and deserve to relish in the fruits of your flesh in those rare moments when evil is not encroaching on our doorsteps and demanding their Bushido rise to the occasion. Whatever they want, they get." She spoke about her policies, their living conditions, working hours, supplies, medical checks, roaming privileges, and the troops in general. They would not be paid, but Victoria would certainly collect money in their best interests to provide the things they required without question.

"You," Victoria said pointing at Ki-Hwa, "and you and you, get back on the truck. The rest of you go inside. Quickly now!" Seo-Sung was not among the three selected, despite Denbe's disapproval. Ki-Hwa watched her disappear with the rest of the lineup through the single wooden door of the comfort station without so much as glancing back over her shoulder, the gate of hell swallowing her whole.

* * * * *

Denbe struck out on his own, driven by duty and impatience. The quartering of comfort women were not his problem, but the streets of Rabaul were. Navigating an island city shouldn't be such a riddle but it took him an hour to find the headquarters of the 6th Field Kempeitai and another hour waiting for an audience with the end of his mission.

"He'll see you now," announced an elegant female receptionist. *You have nothing to fear. You are a Bushido warrior,* he thought, searching for courage sapped by the sea.

"Your jacket," the receptionist said. Denbe looked down to see a fine coat of dust on the uniform he'd kept meticulously clean throughout the journey. He dusted off and held his head as high as he could before striding through the door to stand in front of a giant mahogany desk in the grandest office he had ever seen. He bowed deeply and waited to be spoken to before the esteemed Colonel Nibori Kanegawa.

"Sergeant?" Kanegawa said, not looking up from a document in his hands.

"Sir! I bring a greeting from the honorable Captain Kenji Inoue, sir!" He extended his left arm to offer a letter, still sealed in wax. The colonel remained silent, staring at the document. Denbe's eyes focused straight ahead, fixed on portraits of the Emperor and Empress that hung on the far wall, not daring to look at the man. Slowly the colonel looked up, studying the young sergeant for several uncomfortable moments.

"Is your weapon loaded?" he asked.

"Sir, yes sir!"

"You enter my office with a loaded weapon?"

"Sir, yes sir!"

"Is there an enemy in here, Sergeant?"

"Sir?" Denbe froze, his extended arm beginning to shake.

"Do not answer my question with your own question. Am I threatened by something that you see, which I cannot?"

*It is war,* Denbe thought. *There are enemies everywhere. Of course I'm going to keep my weapon loaded.* "Sir, I do not want any harm to come to the colonel while I am present, sir!"

To Denbe's left an open window allowed a tiny ocean breeze to enter the room. Papers on the desk moved. One threatened to blow away until Kanegawa grabbed an ornate letter opener and held it down with the tip. He was quick, certainly the result of a life spent wielding a sword. Denbe was impressed, but his fortitude was being tested. His arm shook and his shoulder burned. *I carried this piece of paper across half the Empire for you...*

"While your concern for my well-being is flattering," said the colonel, running the tips of his fingers down the opener, caressing the tip. "Do not...come into my office with a loaded weapon again. Is that clear?" His tone rose just enough to provoke a rush of anxiety. A bead of sweat landed audibly on the floor.

"Sir, yes sir!"

The colonel finally reached out and took the envelope and Denbe dropped his arm feeling the sweet rush of blood refill his hand. With the accuracy of a seasoned butcher, Kanegawa cut the parchment open with a single, efficient slice.

"Patience, Sergeant," he said. "You must exercise patience."

"Sir, yes sir!"

"You are a cavalryman, yes?"

"Sir, yes sir!"

"A good cavalryman with such dedication to duty is difficult to come by. I could use a man like you for my personal detail. Unless, of course, you desire to return to occupation duty in Chosen."

"Sir, it would be an honor to serve the Emperor here, sir!" He bowed again.

Kanegawa read the letter, smirking. "Yes, of course it is. It seems you have diligently escorted a woman halfway across the Empire, so it stands to reason you could escort me around this island. It is March now. If you're lucky you will get a chance to defend the Empire by the summer. Report to Sergeant Takahashi immediately. Miss Arai will instruct you where."

"Sir, yes sir!" He bowed and pivoted quickly to leave.

"Sergeant," Kanegawa said, making him spin back around to his previous position of attention. "A reputation of a thousand years may be earned in the time of one hour."

"Sir, yes sir!" He bowed and spun again, but this time left the colonel's office as rapidly as possible.

In his office Kanegawa dropped the letter onto his desk and swiveled his chair to the great window facing Simpson Harbor. His fingers skimmed along his katana as he stared blankly at the azure waters lapping calmly against the shore.

"Captain Inoue has sent me a gift."

"Comfort Station Forty-One." Seo-Sung read a proclamation in the dingy hallway, "This must be the infamous compound."

An older woman led the group to one end of the building, assigning rooms as they went. Her blouse was clean and relatively new while the other girls wore threadbare dresses. "Three here, two in this one, two here. Speak Japanese only." The compound was a buffet of Pacific women. She estimated two hundred women from all corners of the Empire lived in the six barracks-style buildings: Japanese, Korean, Filipina, Thai, Chinese, and Polynesian. They stood in doorways and stared like prisoners at new meat as she stared back.

*Why would any man want to leave?* she thought. *Why would any woman want to stay?* She craned her neck upward. The ceiling grew to a great point that the walls could not reach and without doors the rooms afforded no real privacy. But at least they had walls. Most buildings on the island were constructed in the traditional way; platforms on stilts with a giant thatched roof resembling a large triangle that ran straight into the ground. There was no running water, only scarce electricity, and the windowless walls made the compound hotter than the Kinai Maru's boiler engine room. Like the warehouses in Pusan and Rabaul, an unpleasant odor of fish, mildew, spicy foods, disease and defeat hung lazily in the air along with the sweat of tightly quartered women.

"There are three women in this room, Koreans only," said the guide, standing in front of a door near the end of the building. But the remaining women froze, each unwilling to enter first. Seo-Sung made her way past and inspected the room that was little more than a bare box with a large mattress in the center. Two clean sheets were draped nicely over it and five small hooks hung on the wall, presumably for clothes.

"I bet the finest gentlemen holiday in this very spot," she said.

"You get what you deserve," a voice said down the hall. Seo-Sung stretched her neck to see past the guide. A tall, drunk Japanese girl in her mid-twenties stared back. "If you want something better, you must work for it. We did."

"Your parents must be so proud. Have you a sash that says 'Mrs. Rabaul whore'?"

"*Senjin* bitch!" retorted the girl, charging Seo-Sung.

But she had no chance. With the precision and speed of a sparrow, Seo-Sung's size seven shoe planted itself squarely in her chest. The blow threw the Japanese girl against the opposite wall with a resounding thud.

"No one calls me Senjin." Seo-Sung yelled at the girl who scrambled to get up and flee down the hall clutching her chest. Though well placed, her kick had not been meant to cause major damage. She wanted to make a point, not kill her. Not yet anyway.

"Miss Foster will hear about this!" the guide shrieked, running to check on the kicked girl.

"Bullies are everywhere," she said to the gawking women. "No matter where you go there's always someone who wants to belittle you." But her encouragement was lost on them. She could see these women were too beaten down by life to hope for a better one. It was the same face of the oxen just before death when he'd given up and knew nothing could hurt him anymore. People who had already quit surrounded her. The fear she'd always managed to beat back into a rabbit hole peeked its head out once again and threatened to run wild through the woods of her soul. She went to her room and within minutes, a pair of seasoned Korean girls joined her with green tea and the compound's commandments.

"There are about five hundred comfort women on the island," one said.

"Koreans?" Seo-Sung asked.

"In total. Most are Japanese and *Hanguk-In* like us. We're divided into four groups—the specials, the premiums, the regulars and the unfits."

In this hierarchy, the specials had it the best. They were the apex of the comfort paragon; the best looking, top-shelf girls who were fit only for the highest-ranking admirals, generals and visiting VIPs. Many of the specials were Japanese geisha, rigorously schooled in the varied arts of personal entertainment and usually assigned to one man only. There was a rare Korean, Chinese, Malay, Filipina, Thai, Dutch, and even an Australian girl for those gentlemen who preferred them, but among the different ethnicities and groups of comfort women, the hometown Kyoto-trained geisha was the gold standard. They lived on an old copra plantation just outside the city with bigger rooms, clean linens, better food, and even windows that overlooked the harbor, and all the best amenities the island had to offer.

"I bet that's where they took Ki-Hwa," Seo-Sung said. "Lucky gal."

On the next level down were the premiums, but they still led a relatively comfortable life. They were attractive, but not beautiful. Sultry, but not seductive. Proper, but not educated. They lived in a big house overlooking the city that was nicer than the compound, with each girl having her own room, a futon and some scattered furniture. The premiums were mostly for officers and senior soldiers who had more time in the service.

"And I wasn't included in that group?" Seo-Sung said. "This just keeps getting worse."

The woman continued, "We're regulars. We're at the bottom of the working class barrel. Strictly for the common soldier. We have no rights and we earn everything we have through work. We service all troops, whether we want to or not. Some get rough. Even the unfits have it better than us. They're unworthy of sex. They have the disease. They only perform labor."

The girl who had cried in front of Victoria started to cry again.

"Don't do that here!" Seo-Sung snapped. "There will be no weakness among us."

"Not all of the women here are forced," the woman continued. "Some are *karayuki*--traveling prostitutes, many from poor farms and fishing villages-- like the woman you kicked.

"Who was the mute? With the scar?" Seo-Sung asked.

"Chitose. She was lucky enough to get a position as Victoria's assistant and be put in charge of premium house after her accident." Seo-Sung didn't have to ask. These women liked to talk. "She was once a premium until she was beaten and burned by a soldier a few months ago. He even cut her tongue out."

"Oh my God!" the crying girl exclaimed, placing a hand over her mouth.

"It is true," the older woman said, nodding, "Victoria insisted the Kempeitai conduct an investigation, but no one was ever charged. The unfits don't have to lie on their backs, but they also get nothing in return."

"She has a room in this other premium house, though, yes?" Seo-Sung asked. "And she's close to the boss lady, right?" The woman nodded. "I'd say that's leverage. And leverage is power. You should all develop an appetite for it."

\* \* \* \* \*

*Be strong,* Ki-Hwa told herself a thousand times. She rode in the cab of the truck with a local, dark-skinned driver. They'd dropped the other two girls at premium house and driven back into the city before taking a right turn onto North Coast drive. The truck struggled to get up the steep ridge before turning right again onto a new dusty road. Skirting the ridgeline overlooking Rabaul and the bay Ki-Hwa could see nearly everything from the commanding heights. The city, its encompassing volcanoes, and the harbor with its full complement of boats at anchor would probably be stunning if she cared to enjoy it. Her hand gripped the door handle tightly. Out her window, the land fell away steeply before curving down to the water and disappearing into the surf. It was a dichotomy of land dominated by thick, canopied jungles on the hills and barren moonscapes of dust near the volcanoes.

The lush ridgeline gave way to row upon row of palm trees ripe with the coconuts she saw on the Kinai Maru and now knew where the hard, round fruit came from. Beyond the palms were expansive groves of another type of a new tree with spiral strips cut from the trunks that ended just under the lowest branches and were purposely planted in neat, straight rows. They reminded her of the rice on her parent's farm and the tears threatened to loose again.

A strong breeze blew in from the ocean, cooling the cab and filling it with a salty scent. It was a comforting fragrance and she struggled with her desire to admire the beauty of the place and not think about the impending outcome of the journey. The lush jungle, the wet air, the tropical smells and the warm sun caressing her skin begged her to relax and soak it in, but she wouldn't. The green paradise was really a prison.

The truck finally passed the last tree to reveal the front façade of the plantation. It faced the city and the three volcanoes that silhouetted it. Palm trees surrounded the main building, swaying in the breeze, singing the song of the tropics as the wind whipped their dried leaves into a frenzied dance. A huge porch wrapped around the entirety of the main house, made of a fine wood with a sturdy rail two women leaned on. Colorful paper lanterns hung over the porch like butterflies wrapped in cocoons, waiting to hatch their incandescent light upon anyone choosing to sit under them. The roof appeared strong, made of wood and metal with a grass thatch on top probably to ward off the heavy rains that now brewed over the harbor.

Ki-Hwa exited the vehicle, looked toward the city, and wondered how long it would take to run there from this ridge. Two hours? Three? The driver grabbed her few belongings, and led Ki-Hwa up seven wooden stairs to the great porch. Through a window and past an antique lamp, she saw Victoria berating another Asian woman who wore little more than a silk robe. She glanced hastily down at her feet and sped past. The driver, his muscular frame and sun-bleached hair leading the way, showed Ki-Hwa to a sliding rice paper door that was open, and dropped her lonely satchel in front of it. Her jaw dropped at the sight of the suite. It was a large and elegant room that she inspected from top to bottom.

"Electricity?" she said aloud. She stared at the four-post bed in the center of the room as the driver's footsteps faded down the verandah. The large, wooden shutters opened to a view of the coconut groves that stretched forever, but the window itself was what caught her attention. There was actual glass in the windows of her living quarters, an item she'd only seen in portholes on the Kinai Maru. To the left of the bed were two chairs, one made of fine leather and the other bamboo with a hardwood table between them. An antique oil lamp rested on its top, decorated in stained glass like the windows in a church she'd once seen in a photograph.

On the opposite side of the room was a dresser full of clothes and there were even fine silk robes. She sifted through them, the fabrics feeling soft in her hands, but then noticed tubes of gel concealed under the blouses. She struggled to read the Japanese labels and cringed when she deciphered the word 'lubricant.' She backed away as if finding a snake as a wave of goose bumps rippled over her skin.

In front of the dresser was a finely decorated screen made of wood and rice paper painted with a glowing sunset, scattered cherry blossoms, and a long, sinuous dragon that wound its way through trees. It was the finest thing she'd ever seen. *It must be priceless,* she thought.

By the door where her raggedy sandals lay was a new pair of very finely made zori. *Geisha wear these,* she thought, slipping them on. They caressed her feet with a soothing roughness, but she kicked them off quickly. *I am not one of them.*

On one end of the room was another doorway. She walked over to peer inside and gazed upon a grand porcelain tub. Her eyebrows leapt in amazement and her knees felt weak. It was large enough for two people, which prompted another shudder of disgust at the thoughts of what might take place there. She allowed herself a moment to run fingers along its smooth rim and caressed an object her family always dreamed of owning. Affixed to the wall by the bathroom door was a large mirror that hung independent of the captivating wrought iron boudoir that she found stocked with makeup; compacts with pale, fragrant powders, soft brushes, and shiny cylinders of lipstick.

In the corner near the window were several well-worn books. She reached for a slender green volume with a gilded spine and was surprised when a sheet of disintegrating notepaper fell out

from between the pages. Reaching down to retrieve it, she found
a poem, handwritten in pencil.

*Who is this person staring at me so sternly?*
*The martial bones I bring from a former existence regret the*
*flesh that covers them.*
*Once life is over, the body itself will be seen to have been a*
*deception,*
*And the world that has not yet emerged will be real.*

*You and I should have gotten together long ago*
*And shared our feelings.*
*Looking out across these difficult times our spirits garner*
*strength.*
*When you see my friends from the old days,*
*Tell them I've scrubbed off all that old mud.*
                                    *— Qiu Jin*

She stood alone in the largest living quarters she'd ever seen
and thought only of the tiny farm her parents and brothers
crammed into and then the horrid building Seo-Sung disappeared
into.

"Is this a blessing or a curse?"

"That depends on where you came from." A slender woman in
an intricate flowing silk kimono entered through the washroom
door that only now did she notice was a shared washroom.

"Oh! You startled me," Ki-Hwa said, bowing politely.

"My apologies. Hello, I am Asako. *Hajimemashite.*"

"*Hajimemashite.* My name is Ki-Hwa."

Asako smiled. "I was wondering when someone was going to
move into this room." If the Filipina women were pretty and
exotic, Asako's beauty was indecipherable. She had a serene voice
and perfect skin and teeth, rare in the war years. Her eyes were

lighter and rounder than the average Japanese woman and she moved confidently, almost floating above the ground. She was plucked and primped, and smelled nicer than any blooming flowers Ki-Hwa had ever known. Asako took Ki-Hwa's arm and sat her on the bed to get acquainted. She was coy and candid and seemed to know things about Ki-Hwa before she could even reveal them. Soon, other specials came to watch through the open door. Like a pack of wolves circling their prey, Japanese girls began slinking by to steal a glance at the Korean in their midst.

"They are simply curious," Asako assured her. "You're allowed to roam freely around the plantation because Victoria-san believes you have nowhere to run and no reason to leave anyway."

*Like the ship*, Ki-Hwa thought. *Why is everyone so confident I am so obedient?*

"It is a thousand acres of trees. There are cliffs toward the water so do not venture too close, and there is jungle down the coast that gets very thick. The local people who work the crops are also our guards, but do not be alone in the groves with them."

"They are dangerous?"

"I would not want the opportunity to find out. Their stares alone are frightening."

"Is there something we need to be guarded against?"

Asako paused. "Soldiers get anxious. Occasionally those who are not allowed here display poor judgment."

"They try to sneak in."

Asako nodded, rose, and crossed to the door, motioning for her to follow. The two toured the grounds as Asako dismissed the unapproving women. "Repeat after me. This plantation was built by Europeans who stole the island from the indigenous people to exploit its copra, rubber, palm oil, and coconuts before the Great World War, but then we liberated it."

"Why should I repeat a lie?"

"Because you may be asked by a visiting dignitary someday and if you answer truthfully you will be dismissed."

"So I will be sent home?"

Asako only looked at her. "The military has a very strict regimen," she continued. "The more rank one has or the more important one's position is, the better the rewards one is entitled to in the payment of food, spirits, cigars, and women. I'm told Victoria acquired the plantation after the general moved closer to the city and was allowed to direct comfort operations, though I do not know how. She must be a very good negotiator to be an Anglo women of power in a Nippon bastion."

Two row houses resembling theirs stood end to end, forming a near-perfect square around a well- maintained central garden. Across the garden Ki-Hwa saw a soldier, probably an officer, walk down the verandah of the opposite building. He entered a room, removing his hat as a woman closed the door behind him. Asako continued to walk, but Ki-Hwa stopped and stood silently on the verandah. The sun was fading behind the western ridge, but several fingers of light found their way through the palms to touch her face. She looked to the sky and then the ground.

"It will be painful, won't it?" Ki-Hwa said.

Asako stopped and turned. She walked over and took her hand.

"You are the only Korean girl I know of here at the plantation." Asako continued. "You will stand out. You will be wanted."

Ki-Hwa looked away. "Until they know me."

"And what will they learn?"

"That I don't know what I'm doing. That I am not experienced in the bedroom. That I would rather cut them than touch them."

"Come. Let us get some tea," Asako said. She did not press the subject and allowed Ki-Hwa to keep her secret to herself. She was the newest member of a country club of vice and privilege, but she would never fit in if she could help it. She would not become Asako.

# 5

**It is night and one is expecting a visitor.
Suddenly one is startled by the sound of raindrops,
which the wind blows against the shutters.**
-*Sei Shonagon*

The chambermaid would not let Ki-Hwa so much as pick up a rag when she dropped one. An unfit girl, she cleaned the spaces of her room that didn't need cleaning, forcing Ki-Hwa out of the way at every turn. Obstinate, Ki-Hwa made her own bed before the girl could. She'd lost control of her life, but in this small space she could at least control her bed, for now.

The rain was steady. And not just rain, but buckets the way it did during monsoon season on the farm. Only she was not home and it was not monsoon season. It was a maddening third day on New Britain and it was raining because God hated her.

The warm water danced off the strong roof, filling her room with a cacophony of noise that reminded her of children clapping at school. She didn't mind the sound. The roof was solid and there was a dresser full of clothes tugging at her curiosity to explore. She avoided it the day before, knowing that giving in to admire the finer things would chip away at who she was; the girl who wore field clothes, tied her hair up in twine, punched boys, and liked the feeling of wet mud between her toes. But now she had no choice. The fragrant soaps and relative abundance of fresh foods had not sapped her identity, and neither would draping herself in exotic textiles make any difference to the person she was. She stood behind her dressing screen in a thin cotton robe, a kimono in one hand and a blouse in the other, unsure of which one was right.

The sound of footsteps striking the wooden boards of the verandah echoed, as though made by horses' hooves. Distant at first, the sound grew louder until it overtook the drumming rain. The maid grabbed the used breakfast plates and disappeared out the door, bowing to the unseen man who approached as she scurried away.

The steps were irregular as they approached. *Is he limping?* She hoped he would pass by her open door and go to Asako's room.

"Miss?" a voice said.

The blouse and kimono fell from her hands, her body paralyzed.

"Miss?" he said again.

"A moment please?" she squeaked. Footsteps backed away from the door. She threw the blouse on and then draped the kimono over her body as well, adjusting it several times but still ending up crooked. She stepped from behind the screen, her heart begging her not to, but courage beating it back.

Filling the doorway stood a man who appeared even more regal than Captain Inoue, if that were possible. He wore the same officer's uniform as the captain, but there were striking differences. It was tailored to his body and void of even the slightest wrinkle. He wore six ribbons on his left breast, twice as many as Inoue, and though Ki-Hwa could not distinguish rank yet, his epaulets suggested he held more than a captain. His face had age lines and she guessed he was somewhere around forty years old, nearly twice her age. She stared. The blood drained from her face and her ears pounded with her own pulse. The room grew hot and the sound of rain, once deafening, disappeared.

He removed his cap, dropping his hands to his sides and bowing ever so slightly, his eyes staying on her as a sign of superiority. He was bald, a thin goatee tracing the shape of his jaw. His eyebrows curved upward, giving him an appearance of contemplation. His forehead either perspired or was damp from the rain and his gaze burned through her like the scorching South Pacific sun. He was worn as the old oak, but just as sturdy.

"Beauty doth persuade the eyes of men without an orator," he said with a raspy voice. Ki-Hwa managed a fake smile and bowed, introducing herself formally.

"*Hajimemashite,* sir. Kim, Ki-Hwa. *Yoroshiku onegaishimasu.*"

He entered the room slowly, surveying it with purpose, his limp now unnoticeable. "I am very pleased to meet you, Miss Kim." His voice fell an octave, going from rasp to gravel. "Captain Inoue sends you his highest regards."

*Inoue.* She prickled at the name. "Would you like to sit, sir?" she motioned to the large leather chair facing the window. He moved to the chair and sat, but did not remove his boots, a sign of either contempt or control.

"How do you like our island?" he asked, his voice resonant in the empty room even over the raindrops. Before she could answer, the sound of approaching heels echoed off the walls and stopped at her door.

"Colonel Kanegawa," Victoria exclaimed with a bow. "I did not know you were coming this early."

"It's quite all right, Miss Foster. I have a busy day today and wanted to put Miss Kim's mind at ease before I got started. She's had a long journey and needs to be welcomed properly."

"Yes, well, we like our people to be as presentable as possible..." Victoria looked at Ki-Hwa, mortified by a cockeyed kimono over a blouse.

"You may dress up your dolls as much as you wish, Madame, but it is a woman's kindness and not her looks that wins my respect, as you well know."

"Ever the gentleman," Victoria replied.

"Yes, now if you will do us the pleasure of allowing us to be acquainted."

"Very well. Good day, colonel," she glared at Ki-Hwa on her way out.

"Now, where were we?" the colonel asked.

Ki-Hwa said nothing. She moved to the bed and sat directly opposite him. She would not make the same mistake she'd made with Captain Inoue; misplaced trust born of naïveté and boredom. She was a cow being introduced to the butcher and for twenty minutes they made polite, informal conversation about her home, the voyage and her views about the Empire. She kept her guard up and offered nothing personal and said only what Asako had taught her to say.

*He is like a spider,* she thought, *patiently waiting for his prey to cease struggling.*

He told her about himself, speaking slowly and deliberately, forming each word before pronouncing it correctly, and uttering nothing without purpose. His influence on Captain Inoue was clear. Colonel Nibori Kanegawa had been raised by a cavalryman and desired only to be a part of the same esteemed tradition. Born into a respected family on the island of Kyushu, he adored his father and followed in his footsteps, attending the prestigious Toyama Military Academy. A graduate of the class of 1918, he was fond of spirited horses, admired courage, and had an affinity for classical literature.

"I've had a...remarkable career you could say." He looked out the window as if remembering his best and worst experiences at once. He tried to woo her with tales of his travels in China, Manchuria, and the Philippines, in a calculated effort to impress.

*He is not easy to dislike,* she thought. Were the circumstances different he would be an attractive man, albeit older, or at least a very respectable one. She respected her own father and found maturity an attractive quality in men. But she fought the empathy that he tried to plant in her. *Service of mind and body,* she remembered. She was so distracted addressing her own internal conflict that it barely registered when he mentioned that he had once served in Chosen.

"I would like to ask you a question, Miss Kim." He sat forward in the chair and looked directly into her eyes. "What is the greatest virtue? Reason, valor, compassion, or fidelity?"

*A riddle. I can play this game,* she thought. She crossed her legs and furrowed her brow. "Well, sir, are we referring to me or someone else?"

Her response earned a smile. It was small, but the ends of his mouth moved and his eyes narrowed. "To you and to me," he said.

"Then for myself, fidelity. For you, valor."

He smiled fully as she waited to hear an explanation that never came. He merely stared at her, studying the way a painter would his subject. She was sure her response was exactly what he wanted to hear, but his long, silent pause created doubt.

"You seem wise beyond your years," he said. "Why do you think you are here?"

*To be your wench,* she thought. "To serve you and the Emperor." The answer Asako gave her.

He nodded. "Bid me discourse and I will enchant thine ear." He leaned back in the chair, his smile fading. "You are here to take care of my needs alone and I will return the favor both now and when this war is over," he said. His gaze remained fixed on her, unblinking.

"If I may, sir...will that entail returning me to my home in Chosen or to yours in Japan?"

"Whichever you prefer, Miss."

She did not believe him. "Very well, sir. I am yours alone."

Saying this phrase, actually committing herself to serving him, whether it was a lie or not, scared her to the core. She pledged her adolescent purity to a stranger who would— at his whim— bring an end to the privileges of youth she'd always known. In doing so, she was making a deal with an adversary, if not necessarily the devil, to become his butterfly and to be pinned into an album he could exhibit.

With a wide smile and a deafening silence, Colonel Nibori Kanegawa rose to his feet, kissed Ki-Hwa's hand and turned to depart. "I will take my leave then. But I will see you soon, Miss Kim." The rain, noisy and disruptive when he arrived, had ceased.

She walked him to the door when the tip of something protruding from inside his uniform caught her eye.

"Does this interest you?" he said reaching inside his jacket and withdrawing the item.

"My apologies, sir. It caught my eye."

"It's quite all right." Colonel Kanegawa produced a magnificent katana-like object as long as her forearm with what appeared to be a hand-carved Buddha on its handle and a serpent gracefully winding its way down the length of the blade. He handed it to her gently with both hands, the blade pointing toward him. She was afraid to handle it, yet excited to inspect such a magnificent object.

"It's a letter opener. Have you seen one before?" he asked.

"No," she replied staring at it, turning it over. She wanted to stab him in the face with it, but thought better. Maybe she could steal it while he slept and use it on him or Victoria.

"This is Bishamonten," he said placing a finger on the head of the small carving on the hilt. "He is the God of Warriors, the

Guardian of the North, and one of the Seven Lucky Gods of Buddhism. It is hand carved from pure ivory."

Ki-Hwa ran her fingers down the length of the carving, mentally cataloging its shape and texture. Bishamonten was short and fat with a long spear in his right hand, a pagoda in his left, and an expressionless face. She remembered Bulguksa and thought of all the wonderful treasures such as this that must have perished along with everything else in the Temple the Japanese destroyed.

His index finger ran down the blade. "This is a Chinese dragon flying through the clouds."

"He's chasing a...pearl?"

"Yes, that's exactly what he's doing," the colonel replied. "Dragons are believed to be the source of rivers and springs and they decide where and when the rain falls. The pearl of wisdom he pursues is the source of his power. He will protect it with his life." He gently grasped it from her fingers, but not without a protest. She wanted to keep it not to open letters, but throats.

"I had several of them made in China. I give them as gifts from time to time," he said returning it to his coat. He gave her a long glance before bowing slightly. "Good day," he said, the clacking of his cavalry boots on the verandah the only sound but for random splashes of rainwater falling on palm leaves.

Ten paces later he stopped, placed his hat back on his bald head and executed a precise turn. "By the way, the sergeant who escorted you here-- what is his name?"

"Sergeant...Esokai?" she replied.

"Isogai I believe it was. He will stay here on the island. I have enlisted him in my service. I thought you might want to know after such a long journey together."

"I didn't spend much time with him. He kept us locked away for most of the trip. For our own safety."

"Locked safely away? But you shared a cabin, yes?"

"Yes, sir. But his manners were impeccable and he insisted on sleeping in the hallway outside our door."

"Did he now? He is well disciplined then." Colonel Kanegawa tipped his hat, turned and left, his limp once again noticeable. Reaching his waiting car the colonel addressed the new driver, Sergeant Denbe Isogai. "Time?"

"Nine o'clock, sir."

"And already so hot," he said, looking to the clearing skies and waving a hand to shoo mosquitos. He turned to see Victoria standing in the parlor window and waved to her.

*I knew you would be there, predictable woman.*

A strong ocean breeze blew in, muffling the sounds of another staff car as it pulled up. Colonel Kanegawa turned and breathed a shallow sigh of discomfort, knowing he could not avoid the man inside it.

"A little early for the lash, is it not Chief?" the colonel said, getting his barb in first.

"And a little early to recite poetry to your new *bijin*, isn't it colonel" the Chief of Police replied.

Kanegawa chuckled as he tried to duck into his car, but came up short. "Don't you want to know how the rebuilding is going?" the Chief asked.

Kanegawa straightened up and sighed. "Oh yes, of course."

"The camp's population is growing again. It's up for the second month in a row. Those Imperial engineers are doing wonders down there."

"It is the least I could do." The colonel smiled.

"Yes it *is* the least you could do."

*And now we parry*, Kanegawa thought.

The Police Chief moved in closer. "The investigation is complete, but there's still a mystery, colonel." Kanegawa heard the same speech since Chief Sato arrived on the island a year before. "How in the name of the Emperor did those troops think their actions were acceptable?"

The colonel remained silent, but did not blink as the two powerful men stood nearly toe-to-toe in the heat. Denbe took a step closer in case his new boss needed protecting. "Were they just misguided, caught up in the heat of the moment? Or was it more? Poor leadership perhaps? Or its complete absence?" the Chief was insistent. Colonel Kanegawa stood, not backing off an inch and stared into Sato's eyes as he had so many times before.

"I pray you learn the answer to that question. You are the island's Chief of Police after all. Justice is your job."

"And justice will be mine, colonel."

* * * * *

Ki-Hwa sat on her bed. All was out in the open now. There would be no more suspense or waiting. Her suitor had been revealed and he was far from horrible, but he was still an unwilling arrangement. Her shoulders slumped and she heaved until a lone tear dripped between her fingers and fell to the floor.

"I can see why you're crying. This place is a dump." Seo-Sung appeared in the open doorway, startling Ki-Hwa. "You have a boudoir! I saw one once but never knew anyone who..." Before she could finish, Ki-Hwa was across the room, hugging her tightly. "Okay...it can't be that bad," she said, patting her lightly on the back.

"Get inside before Victoria sees you." Ki-Hwa pulled her into the room and slid the door shut. "How did you get here?"

"Walked."

"To see me?"

"What else do I have to do? Get accustomed to the glamorous life of a regular?"

"Very considerate of you."

"You can repay me by not crying. Remember?"

Ki-Hwa wiped her face as Seo-Sung sat in the leather chair, still warm from the Kanegawa. "So who is he?"

"A perfect gentleman. One who will do bad things to me I fear."

"I doubt it could be any worse than what happens every night at the compound."

"She told Ki-Hwa the story of the girl she had kicked and the welcoming committee of Korean women and then the story of Chitose. "Remember the scarred girl who picked us up at the port?"

"Yes."

"I cornered her last night and struck a deal. I liberated some antibiotics from the hospital for her."

"You stole them?"

Seo-Sung nodded. "I said I had stomach cramps and when they weren't looking-- "

"But why?"

"Because she needs them. Her tongue is infected. So is one of her scars."

"But why risk yourself for her?"

"Why did you risk yourself for me?"

Ki-Hwa was silent. Seo-Sung picked up the conversation. "She's one step removed from the most powerful woman on the island. Earning her trust could mean something for us later on. Besides, maybe some Jap bastard will need those antibiotics when he gets venereal disease and there's none left, so he can live an eternal life of pain. Think of it as my small way of fighting back."

Ki-Hwa smiled, but the rest of the story saddened her. The men who called on the regulars after dark were not the charming clientele the colonel seemed to be. They were barbarous cretins who treated women like filth, unworthy to be in the same room with them. One man, complaining to his friends, said he "couldn't believe he was fucking a Senjin bitch!" but what choice did he have?

For Seo-Sung, sex had once been a pleasurable act, but now it was mechanical pain. If it weren't for the deal she'd made with Chitose, who provided extra tubes of lubricant, she'd be even worse off. Discomfort, degradation, and trauma were her new bedfellows and her life at the compound made Ki-Hwa guilty. She was receiving special treatment because of her appearance, while her friend was living through hell for being less attractive. Who they were as individuals meant nothing. For all the Japanese knew, Ki-Hwa worshipped the devil and Seo-Sung was a Saint. But her superficial appearance entitled Ki-Hwa to greater care and status, as though she were a child's favorite doll carefully placed on a pedestal and idolized while the other toys were kicked around the floor and never put away.

"Insanity," Ki-Hwa declared.

"Don't be silly. It's completely fair," Seo-Sung replied. "You have no reason to feel guilty about something you have no control over. Beauty is the design of God, not a choice of man. Does the *mugunghwa* choose when to bloom? Does the snake choose when to shed its skin? This is the natural way of things. We have no vote, no voice, no say in how we are born or what we're born into. You can control how pretty you are as much as you can control the tides. You have nothing to regret, nothing to apologize for. You're beautiful. Accept the way you look and wield it as a power, not a curse."

Ki-Hwa nearly cried for the love she felt for Seo-Sung. "You should be up here. You're a beautiful woman."

"Oh, sweetie." Seo-Sung cocked her head to one side and smiled as the light brushed her face. "My best days of catching flies with honey are past. I'm not so foolish to think I'm as attractive as you are—or as she is." She motioned toward the bathroom. "You can come out now."

Asako emerged from around the corner. "I wanted to help but did not want to intrude."

"You see," Seo-Sung said, "she's beautiful *and* polite. You're a cut above, the two of you. You have talents that men want. Why fight it? I hear the regulars talk about equality and how they're just as good as you are, but they're not. There is nothing wrong with earning privilege."

Asako sat next to Ki-Hwa on the bed. Ki-Hwa introduced the two and before long, Asako knew all about their journey on the Kinai Maru up to Ki-Hwa's encounter with the colonel. Asako sighed at the mention of his name.

"Kanegawa..."

# 6

**Grief teaches the steadiest minds to waiver**
*-Sophocles*

Date: April 9, 1943.
Flight report: Lieutenant Takeo Hashimoto
Aircraft: Mitsubishi A6M5 type 52 Zero
Unit: 251st Fighter Squadron, Tainan Kokutai
Departure Airfield: Lakunai, New Britain

Takeo wiped the sweat from his face, rotated his head, looking at all four corners of the operations tent, and stretched his neck. The g-forces of a dogfight strain the soul more than the body. He took three deep breaths, remembering every deadly detail and put pen to paper.

General Comments: At 1300 hours we scrambled to meet enemy bombers with fighter escort moving toward Wewak garrison. I mounted Samurai Zeke and taxied, bumping a mechanic with the left wing in my haste to kill Yankees (my plane was unharmed). Climbing to 12,000 feet, our flight of seven made course. At 1600, we made contact with 20-30 American Corsairs, 12-15 Hellcats and another 20-30 twin-tail devils the English call Lightning.

*What can I tell you, faithful reader?* Takeo wondered. *The cool air at altitude was such a welcome change from this island inferno that I wanted to stay up there all day.*

As usual, the Lightning's stayed at higher altitudes and made only random diving runs into the fight. We plunged into the enemy and I was able to get behind a Hellcat quickly. One gun jammed but the other remained operational and I splashed him two minutes after contact. The mechanics need to inspect that gun (though perhaps not the man I bumped). A Corsair with skull and crossbones on the tail tried to get behind me, but I shook him with the reliable barrel roll / split-S combo.

*I'll bet that Yankee pilot is still wondering where the 'yellow monkey' went.*

I spotted two Corsairs chasing Petty Officer Iwakura's plane at 5,000 feet to my 10 o'clock low and dived to assist. I got behind the trail Corsair and blasted several rounds into him when my cockpit fogged up during the dive. By the time I regained visuals, they were gone, but one was smoking and plummeting fast below me. I will claim it as my kill. Unfortunately, Petty Officer Iwakura was also shot down by the lead Corsair and did not bail out. Bullets raked the nose of my aircraft from a Hellcat at 3 o'clock high. The plane passed directly over my aircraft at about two feet separation, but without causing major damage. The pilot had blonde hair and a dimpled chin, and the numbers 48 on his nose and 15 on the fuselage.

*...and he needs remedial training at the firing range. There was no excuse for him to miss me.*

I pursued a bomber and splashed it with two unopposed runs. While there was great honor in this, the nose art of this bomber had a topless lady and I was sad to see her lost. I'm sure the crew spent many hours painting her.

*...probably as much time as I spend on these reports.*

She managed to get a few miles southeast and out to sea before going hard-over. I saw three parachutes and a flying boat instantly land to pick them up. Another Corsair got behind me and fell victim to my barrel roll / split S-combo. I pulled out of the maneuver and found myself behind a Hellcat with no wingman. I made quick work of this slow dog and narrowly avoided a friendly parachute as I pulled away. I did not see who it was. A Corsair got behind me. This pilot was very good. I only managed to shake him by flying directly into the path of the Allied bombs and between the flak coming up from our anti-aircraft guns. Again I was not hit.

*...or I wouldn't be writing this.*

Turning South, I saw the main formation egress and gave chase despite low fuel. The Corsairs were still heavily engaged with planes from the 201st and 204th Squadrons. I got behind someone from the 204th and took up a wingman position as he tried to get a shot on a Corsair but failed. I was unable to reach him by radio and eventually maneuvered my way in front and he broke off.

*Like cutting in line at the mess tent.*

I was only able to damage the Corsair with a few rounds; this pilot was a master of the air. However, he was smoking when I broke off. I saw only a few Lightning's come down from their altitude to engage in glorious combat and they flew out at the same altitude. Their cowardice is a disgrace.

Total count-2 Hellcats, 1 Mitchells, 1 Corsair possible.

<u>Signed:</u> Takeo Hashimoto, LT, IJN, Ace-14 kills

Takeo handed the report to the flight officer who quickly scanned it.

"Are you the court jester now?"

"As long as I keep splashing Yanks, I can say what I want, sir. " He smirked and walked straight through the gauntlet of pilots filling out reports and exited the tent. Seeking refuge in the shade of his favorite palm tree, he lit a cigarette.

"You *must* be the tallest damn tree on this island," he said, patting the immense trunk. The palm was mighty, reaching high into the air as if to pull the sun closer. He leaned back against it to gaze across the runway and admire his plane. The lines were clean and simple; its engine powerful and responsive. Life and death were separated by millimeters and few enjoyed the symbiotic relationship of Takeo and Samurai Zeke. "I may not be much down here, but up there...father would be proud." He was one of the privileged few picked to fly the new Zero when the first four were delivered a month earlier.

"You see," he told the tree, "the A6M5 type 52 is heavier, but the weight is offset by the additional thrust provided by new exhaust stacks. The wings are smaller with a heavier gauge skin and the folding tips are removed, making it turn tighter and dive faster." He stared at his plane. "You should have seen her today. She did well. It's an honor to own such a thing of beauty."

The Tainan Kokutai, the Chitose Naval Air Group, the Army Fighter Regiments, and the mighty Kanoya Naval Air Group littered the airfields of New Britain. They were split into five airfields and a floatplane base in the harbor. They flew, trained, took target practice, flew, reconnoitered, did maintenance, flew, had classes, and flew some more. The days were not as plentiful as 1942 when there was unlimited gas, ammunition, spare parts, and time to sharpen their skills, but they were still in good supply. The one dwindling resource was men.

Takeo couldn't imagine another force capable of defeating this great collection of warriors. Yet there they were-- the Allied Air Force, in increasing numbers. They never gave an inch, never wavered in their commitment to crush the Empire. They were as tough and determined as he'd heard they were. They regularly bombed northern New Guinea, Irian Jaya, and the Caroline Islands from their growing list of bases. They took the refueling base at French Frigate Shoals on the fringe of the Empire and at Guadalcanal shot down almost every Imperial torpedo bomber in the air that day. They destroyed four aircraft carriers in one battle outside Midway Island, crippling the fleet. It was only a matter of time before they invaded Kavieng, Bougainville, and eventually Rabaul. He ran two fingers across his undershirt, feeling the scars on his chest beneath it. "Victory to the strongest."

The cigarette done, Takeo walked across the dusty tarmac to the officer's tent and fell into his cot. He reached for a canteen of fermented coconut juice that he brewed in a homemade still. It was a volatile concoction that he was mostly impervious to now, but did its job. Sake was once the standard drink for officers on the island, but it had grown scarce as the war progressed. The drunkard in Takeo was forced to brew his own booze from the most abundant plant on the island. Alcohol was more than a release for a man who had a comfortable relationship with death. It was proof that Buddha loved his people. It nullified the belief that a higher power desired his subjects to live in fear.

*A vengeful God would never allow us to discover fermentation, after all,* he thought.

He took a long tug as four pilots boasted of their victories like adolescent boys after their first experience of a girl's breast. "Brave fight up there, lieutenant," someone said, walking past his cot.

*Brave fight up there, lieutenant!* Takeo mocked him. *Your skill is next to that of a samurai. ...not that we have or need those anymore, but if we did, you would be honored to be one of them! Can you ride a horse? Shoot a bow and arrow?*

Takeo said a quick prayer for Iwakura, hoping he'd bailed out and was on a serene, uncharted sandbar surrounded by beautiful mermaids, but knowing he was probably in the depths of the deep blue Coral Sea. Had he survived, the other pilots would have to return the personal belongings they had already pilfered from his chest. Nothing was worse than an officer with no scruples.

"To Iwakura-san," he said to no one in particular. He raised his canteen high into the air. Two pilots looked at him and nodded in agreement, but the rest couldn't be bothered. The ritual was too familiar. He rolled over to one side, placing the canteen gently on the ground as his eyelids grew heavy when the sound of a duffel bag hitting Iwakura's empty cot startled him.

"Sir. May I use this cot, sir?" a voice asked in rigid adherence to rank structure. Takeo looked up to see a young ensign, fresh off the boat and still in a clean uniform, standing at attention awaiting his response.

"The last man who slept there died today," Takeo said, "But be my guest. It's probably not cursed."

A day later, Takeo sat in the shade in the second-to-last rattan chair on the corner of the premium house. It creaked like a squeaky truck brake and warned anyone brave enough to sit next to him not to do so. The warm mid-afternoon was peaceful but for the intermittent shrilling of cicadas. Ki-Hwa stepped from the house. "When are they expected to arrive?" she asked.

"Any time now," Asako replied.

"What does she want us to do?"

"Be her support," Asako answered. Chitose is with the regulars this morning and Victoria doesn't like to be around new girls alone. She uses me often to welcome new specials and premiums. You are here because I think your life energy is wasting away in that boring room that you never leave."

"I like my room."

"Only because you know nothing else of this place."

Ki-Hwa had not ventured away from the plantation since arriving and didn't want to start today, but Asako insisted. "Your Ki will thank you," she said. "Ironic, is it not?" Asako said.

"What?"

"Your name. Ki in Japanese means life force, like Qi does in Chinese."

"It is a common name where I'm from."

"Oh." Asako turned to see Takeo sitting quietly on the porch, staring at the city below. Without a word, she walked straight over to him and sat in the adjacent chair leaving Ki-Hwa alone in front of the main doorway.

"Asako?"

An Army major appeared from inside the house and stood next to her. "The sake is inside, youngling," he said, reaching out to lead her into the house.

"I am for Kanegawa-san."

"*Sumimasen deshita.* Excuse me," he said tipping his hat, bowing and backing quickly away. A truck roared up the hill, followed by Victoria's personal car. "Asako-san!" She nearly shouted. Victoria was getting out of her car and inspecting the new girls who stood before her in the circular driveway. In an instant, she would turn and walk up the twenty stairs to the verandah and find Ki-Hwa alone and unable to speak, paralyzed while Asako fraternized with an unknown officer. She stared at the white witch when...

"I am here," Asako said, standing next to Ki-Hwa.

"What were you doing? I thought we were not supposed to talk with anyone outside the plantation."

Asako ignored her, looking at the new girls instead. "Is she Korean?" Three pretty women stood in the driveway as Victoria inspected them, her clipboard in hand. Two were calm, but the third was frightened and was indeed from Ki-Hwa's homeland. A sense of relief filled her at the sight of another Han and then the moment dissipated like a fog lifting in the late morning sun. The pride she felt turned to pity; these were merely the latest to enter a life of misery. For each Korean girl in premium house, there were three more at the compound trying to procure a meal while staving off the hungry advances of an Imperial attack.

Ki-Hwa looked over at the officer still seated in the chair. "Who is he? What did you talk about?"

"It was refreshing to talk to a man my age for a moment, that is all."

"A man of your age?"

Victoria motioned at Asako to show the new girls to their rooms and shot a disparaging glance toward Takeo before mounting her car to leave.

"I don't think she approves," Ki-Hwa muttered as the new girls, the Korean one near tears, climbed the stairs to their new life.

"She has no reason to be suspicious," Asako said, turning to leave. Ki-Hwa turned to look again at Takeo as she entered the house, but saw only an empty rocking chair.

*Should I?*

# 7

**What dire offense from amorous causes springs,
What mighty contests rise from trivial things.**
*-Alexander Pope*


"This place is not beautiful?" Kanegawa asked.

"It is certainly different from Chosen." Ki-Hwa responded. "Much warmer."

"You are distracted."

"It is hard to find beauty in a place where I don't want to be."

They walked along the ridge near the plantation overlooking the ocean. In the distance dust rose from Rabaul's streets and the sounds of hammers repairing a ship pierced the air. He was dressed in a khaki brown garrison uniform; she, in a white dress adorned with red orchids. Her lips were red, the waxy lipstick cumbersome like an allergic reaction. Her long hair was curled under in the modern Japanese style, a departure from her usual straight, but Asako insisted she wear it this way. She ran her fingers through the uncomfortable coif as the wind tousled it.

"I think your hairstyle doesn't suit you," the colonel said. "I think the other way was unique. It expressed who you are." He squinted in the sunlight.

"And who is that? An obedient farm girl?"

"It was different. There is nothing wrong with being different."

"Different...like a poor Korean girl in a house of well-to-do Japanese?"

"Does that bother you?"

She looked from him to the ocean. "I feel like the gray pelican in a flock of white seagulls."

"Beauty is like art. The interaction between the viewer and the art is all that matters. If the viewer thinks a stain on a wall is art, then it is. Others may call it a stain, but to that one person it will always be art."

"Is Kanegawa-san saying beauty is in the eye of the beholder?"

He smiled. "It would be rather uncreative to use a phrase more worn than my boots."

She smiled, but then stopped and covered her mouth. "Do you resent me for being so cold?" she asked.

"Will you warm to me?"

"I'm in a situation I didn't ask to be in, sir. I hope you understand."

He stopped and placed his hands behind his back. He stared at the ground and took in a deep breath. "You have a long life ahead of you. And that life will have choices. Do you see that tree over there?" She gazed where he pointed and saw a rubber tree in the distance. "Life is like that tree. It's a series of choices that lead you down one branch or the other, each one being its own distinct journey. You could take the branch that leads to happiness or the one that leads to sorrow, though you won't know which is which until you take it. That requires a decision. Your life is defined by these decisions because in your dying days you will find yourself at the end of a tiny branch, looking back at the great tree of possibilities and do one of two things; fall back to earth like a wilted leaf, filled with regret and the thoughts of what might have been...," his voice trailed off.

"Or?" she asked.

"Or you can bask in the sun and the radiance of destiny at the top." He turned and walked away, satisfied with his teaching while she stared at the tree.

She thought of her father and of his inability to ever share this kind of wisdom and how Tae-Hyun did it in his place. *Soon he will teach me a new lesson...one about pain.* She reminded herself. She walked briskly to keep up with him. "You have taken an extraordinary amount of time to talk with me," she said. "Do you always try so hard?"

"With some people, yes. I like to know as much as I can. With women I like to feel a connection before..."

"It's hot today," she interrupted.

A strong wind blew, nearly taking his cap with it. "Not so hot actually," he said, adjusting his hat. "But unfortunately, I must excuse myself. I have business to attend to in town. I may call on you this evening if the general does not require my presence."

She bowed as he touched the brim of his hat and left. She thought of something Tae-Hyun had told her when he had a quarrel with a rival over a girl.

*He's the worst kind of enemy...patient.*

\* \* \* \* \*

Living on New Britain caught a man between the sun's hammer and the ground's anvil. Dusk brought some relief, but it was still one of the most inhospitable places for humans to exist. On the back steps of the compound a pair of comfort women smoked cigarettes with two soldiers whose attention they desperately tried to maintain to procure more when Seo-Sung burst through the door and nearly tripped over them.

"When are you dames gonna learn they pay you NOT to talk!" The troops spun around to look at her as the girls fell silent. One laughed. "Well, we sure didn't come for the conversation," he said getting to his feet and leaving. His friend followed.

108

"They would have given us more," one girl said.

"You care about cigarettes when we're all hungry? Tell them to bring some food down here so we don't have to get by on the throwaways from the mess halls," she bellowed as the girls ran inside. Seo-Sung, a native sarong around her waist, stepped onto the dirt and noticed a tiny black and gold bird of paradise picking apart a fallen guava, the vivid pink flesh of the fruit surrounded by the fresh green of young leaves. Normally so elusive, the magnificent little creature seemed unaware of her presence.

"I know what it's like to be hungry too little one," she said. A moment later it flew away into the palms. "And on the run."

With a sigh, she looked in every direction to ensure no prying eyes were on her and strolled to the road on the west side of the compound. Two minutes passed before a staff car stopped in front of her. Without saying a word, a boyish corporal walked over and dropped three packs of smokes in her hands, holding her hand a moment longer. She caressed his face and smiled, the way a praying mantis might regard her mate before consuming him. With a flushed face, he returned to the car and drove away.

*Your real crime, ladies, is bargaining for so little,* she thought. She looked at the boxes of Lucky Strikes flipping them back and forth and puzzling over the English words.

"I don't need a translator. You say, 'Good damn smokes. Better than any Jap brand. Very popular on island.'" She looked back over her shoulder toward the compound. "Disgusting habit, but I know someone who really wants you and will pay for it."

Seo-Sung had quickly become a top earner for Victoria because of her unwillingness to let any soldier leave without paying up, but she also bullied the non-Korean regulars, causing the madam a few unwanted trips to the compound to correct her tightly run ship. Seo-Sung brought in money, but disrupted the system at the same time, so removing her was tricky. She wasn't educated enough to be a premium and her reputation scared the higher girls who knew of her. Moving her up could cause trouble in premium house, but keeping her in place when she had rightfully earned a change in scenery could be detrimental too. *I'm a problem,* Seo-Sung thought. *It's so gratifying.*

Two days later Seo-Sung sat in her new room at the premium house with Ki-Hwa. No matter her disdain, Victoria was first and foremost a businesswoman and knew how to exploit success.

"I'm not one to wallow in self-pity," Seo-sung told her. "I'm going to shut that book and leave it on the shelf forever."

"Good for you," Ki-Hwa replied. The sight of her friend away from the stench and filth of the compound was a small victory that earned a genuine smile. "So how did you accomplish this?"

"Well, you know the girl with all the scars, Chitose?"

"Yes."

"Have you noticed how much better she looks?" Ki-Hwa had indeed noticed her skin looked smoother and the scars were less noticeable. The abnormal shine on her face from burned and stretched skin had dulled and the girl with no tongue was able to form a few crude syllables.

"You had something to do with this?" Ki-Hwa knew her friend well.

Seo-Sung closed the door. "I managed to meet someone in the hospital. He lost some antibiotics at the same time I lost my undergarments."

"And why did you risk such a thing?"

"Because she's Victoria's pet and has leverage. Look where it got me." She threw her arms out wide at the room.

Ki-Hwa shook her head and sat on Seo-Sung's futon. "You are more compassionate than that. You may have done it for yourself, but you did it for her too."

Seo-Sung smiled, proud that her gift of reading people might be rubbing off on the young girl. She crossed the room and gazed out her window at the compound in the middle of the city below. "Survival is the victory of the poor, so I win. This round at least."

Ki-Hwa walked into the hallway and looked around. premium house had individual rooms with real futons, dressers, and linens. Half the rooms had a bathtub and the girls ate regular food that wasn't gourmet, but was consistent at least. Local workers helped with laundry, cleaning, and cooking.

"There's no violence here at least," Seo-Sung said. At premium house there was order and a list of rules with sharp punishments for breaking them. The men who visited were mostly officers with manners and bearing; men who actually took the time to undress and the occasional Godsend who even liked foreplay to warm up the engine before starting it. Girls didn't get smacked around or called dirty names unless they submitted to playing those games.

Being a premium meant no more caring for someone else's children. Twenty-one feral whelps of various ages lived in the compound, all of them very malnourished and possessing nothing other than what they could find or steal. When the younger children's mothers had to service a customer, someone else had to watch them and when it was a Korean girl who needed help, Seo-Sung obliged. There were two whom she thought sweet and lovable but for the most part the kids were scrappy miscreants who justified her choice not to breed. They had nowhere to go, nothing to do and always wanted more to eat, more to play with, more to wear, more to see, more entertainment, more answers to questions, more everything. They were insatiable little sponges of energy and inconsolable nuisances at the same time.

So it was a good day when Chitose grabbed Seo-Sung and drove her up to premium house in close proximity to where generals and admirals commanded their own kingdoms from on high. If they had any clue how disruptive she was in the compound, they would never have let her within a mile of their headquarters.

# 8

**And maps can really point to places**
**Where life is evil now:**
**Nanking. Dachau.**

*-W.H. Auden*

*Gossip*, Ki-Hwa thought in that undefined space between dreaming and waking. *They love to gossip here.* She lay in bed listening, wishing her rice paper walls weren't so thin and the other women would find a more suitable place for their ranting, like inside a volcano. She rolled over, but there was something else. Amid the voices, she made out the unmistakable sounds of tools...no, farming tools?

She dressed and walked onto the verandah to find three girls staring over the railing at construction workers. Or were they? Their clothes were tattered and they were not Japanese. In fact, they were not even Asian. Pick axes and shovels tore apart the central garden that just last night had filled the air with a pleasant scent and vibrant colors, its magnificent flowers blossoming among the plantation's row houses. Only the small bloom of sacred chrysanthemums survived. Until this minute she had not known of a man on New Britain of non-Japanese descent, save for the native New Guineans. But in front of her labored twenty men with dark skin, but not as dark as the locals alongside white men who must have been...

"English?" she whispered.

The hole grew larger by the minute. She stared at the white men, having never seen one, examining their physique and the way they talked and worked. *Not the purple ones*, she thought as

113

the last of the beautiful flowers disappeared. Her impulse was to sprint out and save the discarded flowering bush, but reason intervened. She had no intention of being brave, nor was she yet fully awake.

Victoria appeared at the end of the porch from the main house with Colonel Kanegawa closely behind. They stared intently at the workers. Unnoticed, Ki-Hwa stepped behind the other watchful women and then sidestepped to get closer, straining to eavesdrop.

"How long do I have them? Victoria asked.

"Until it's done," the colonel replied.

"I appreciate the colonel's assistance. I don't want my assets harmed."

"Nor does the Imperial Command, Miss Foster."

"How long..." Victoria started in near-perfect Japanese. "Before they come?"

The colonel took a long moment to think about his response, both pained by the inquisition and sensitive to the security of such information. "Two months, maybe three I suspect."

"Then it's eventual?" Victoria pondered, staring at the construction unfolding in front of her. "There's no turning them back?"

Ki-Hwa snuck another step closer, keeping her back against the wall and looking away from them.

"It seems they have the momentum now," Kanegawa said. "There are almost one hundred thousand soldiers of the Empire on this island. It is unavoidable. They will either conduct a lengthy bombing campaign or invade. But either way..." The colonel paused in his dramatic way, "They will come."

Panic welled inside Ki-Hwa. She had been so focused on her own war that she forgot there was a bigger war being waged around the globe. The rumor among the women was only reconnaissance aircraft dared patrol the skies over Rabaul, but they were quickly shot down by the skilled Imperial air defense. She knew now this was wishful thinking.

"Will this take them away from the other projects?" Victoria questioned.

"Digging has not been a popular endeavor yet. The generals are concerned that preparing fortifications for the defense is contrary to the Bushido Code. We are required to always take the offensive, so waiting for the enemy to attack would send the wrong message to the soldiers." Kanegawa fiddled with his hat.

"Well, as I told the high command, none of the enlisted men ever see this place thanks to you and the Kempeitai. Your secret is safe with me."

*She must have threatened someone to get this done,* Ki-Hwa thought. *But what is this monstrosity filling our courtyard?* She stumbled sideways on the creaky wooden porch.

"What are you doing there?" Victoria sounded like the squawk of a hungry crow. "Get inside!"

Ki-Hwa retreated immediately, but in such disarray that she fell headlong into Asako's room.

"I'm sorry Asako-san!"

"It is perfectly fine, Ki-Hwa. What is the matter?"

"I heard Victoria and Kanegawa-san talking about the Allies. They're coming."

Asako smiled. "They are already here, Ki-Hwa."

She looked out the door at the laboring men, staring at a white man who looked as thin as a sapling, but who worked harder than her strong-backed brothers did at harvest. Half of the men were tanned a deep brown and the other half were milky white; some had green eyes and some blue. They all wore scraggly beards and only enough clothing to cover them sparsely, garments that clung to their bodies by final, obstinate threads. They took the excess dirt away in baskets to a waiting truck that drove away full and returned empty a while later only to be filled again. The guards were harsh and frequently kicked, shoved, or even spat on them.

"Is that English? Their language?" Ki-Hwa asked.

"Yes."

"Why do they all speak the same language?"

"Do they?"

"They look like they come from all over the world...but they all speak the same language. Is it English?" Asako had no answer.

Koreans spoke Japanese but not by choice. Had the English done the same to the rest of the world? Was everyone now subjects under the iron fist of England?

\* \* \* \* \*

"What is your greatest sin?" Kanegawa asked. Ki-Hwa hung his jacket on a hook near her dressing screen. She ran her fingers over the silver buttons, staring at the inlaid chrysanthemums in each one. "Sir?"

"Sin, bad deed. Something you feel guilty of. What is it?" He looked at her through barely open eyes, his voice deepening and his words slurred. "And I don't mean an apple stolen from the local market on a dare. A real sin."

"You've been at the New Guinea club this day, yes?"

"Yes, but your sins are the topic of discussion now, young one." His voice held an intimation of something unsaid. Like the black water snake hiding in the paddy, something lurked beneath the question. She removed his sword and placed it in the corner next to the door, took his coat and hung it over the screen before assisting him into his chair.

116

"I would think my appearance is my sin."

Kanegawa smiled. "That is not a sin. Guilt maybe, but not a sin." He attempted to lean closer, but the sheer weight of his own body betrayed him. Like an aged oak, he crashed back into the chair, breathing heavily.

"In thy face I see the map of honor, truth, and loyalty." He smiled and raised a hand to his forehead, rubbing it with a long sigh. "Henry the Sixth."

She straddled his legs, her back to him, and one at a time slipped his boots off, propping his feet up on a small foot stool. She unbuttoned his shirt, undid his suspenders, brought him sake and then retrieved a cold towel to rub the back of his neck. He said nothing. She finished and moved to the corner of the footstool next to his feet to massage them. The work disgusted her, but it was better than the alternative. If she could delay long enough for him to fall asleep...

Every other night for a month they danced this dance. He would arrive, sit in his chair, and take off his boots and drink. Tonight he wore an expression of lust, but it was not the first time, so she did not expect him to behave any differently from the way he had other evenings. He told her of his job as the head of the Kempeitai military police and compared it to a "peculiar prison sentence lacking a fair trial."

She wore only a silk kimono and undergarments because that's what he liked: class with subtle sexuality. He had yet to consummate the relationship, but no good fortune lasts. "Remove them," he said in his gravelly sake voice.

Her hands stopped. "Sir?"

"Remove them," he repeated.

She stood slowly and faced him. Her kimono slipped from her shoulders onto the floor to expose a girl in her underthings. She was a doll on display, completely alone like the scarecrow in the winter field. Asako had prepared her for this, but Ki-Hwa remembered none of it. Without a word he rose from the chair. He took her in his arms and laid her down on the bed, standing over her for a few long moments, his eyes going from top to bottom and back again while hers stayed fixed on ceiling. He ran a finger over her ankle and sighed.

"Magnificent," he said.

She lied perfectly still, unmoving to her own surprise.

He shook his head and walked to the window while she lay on the bed. *His plaything*, she thought. *Not even a person.*

"Why did you not choose reason when we first met?" he asked looking out the window.

She sat up on her elbows. "Reason is not for a woman who serves a man, nor a man who serves his Emperor," she replied.

He smiled. "Why do you think I asked you about those things?"

"To determine where my values are, I believe."

"Ah, but it also told me so mush more." His words slurred. "I learned that you treasure loyalty to your suitor. That indiscretion is not in your character, that you understand the warrior ways and want to feel pride in yourself and your mate. You are woven of the fiber needed to accompany a great man in Japan."

She stood and crossed to the chest of drawers with the sake, pouring a small cup for herself. He turned to her, but his eyes were empty. He was somewhere in the past again. "Reason is hemlock to a warrior, anathema to the practitioner of the art of war. I try not to reason, but it invades my mind again and again. The memories haunt. The screams of the dead and dying never fade." His eyes darted around the room as if it were another place, surrounded by the enemy. "There is no place for reason when the trumpet sounds the charge." He stared past her toward the door. "It is only after the battle has been won that we question. We reconsider. We regret." A spasm of pain crossed his face as she drank. "We-- you and I-- are not in the business of reason!" His voice grew louder. "We do not ponder the meaning of an order or trifle over the particulars of planning. We act, yes?"

She nodded.

"When valor preys on reason, it eats the sword it fights with, as my own charred soul is consumed by shame." He stared at her, wanting conversation while she wanted him to pass out so she could get dressed. She stood as still as a sculpture from a bygone era with one arm across her midsection and the other holding the cup.

"The Bushido warrior is deeply rooted in philosophy but learns to separate reason from action. There is a time to think and a time to act. And after the act, a time to reflect and learn." He held up his right hand, pinching the tips of his fingers together as if grasping at some subtle, evasive thought before it escaped.

"Then should I reason more about my situation and take action...or accept it as it is?" Ki-Hwa pushed him. He toyed with her, so maybe she needed to return the favor.

"Well, you are not subject to the Bushido code, so you may do as you like," he said.

"Are those men who dug the hole allowed to do as they like as well?"

"No," he laughed. "They are the enemy, they deserve nothing more than what we give them."

"And how much do you give them? Do they work for you?"

"In a manner of speaking, yes. I have jurisdiction over their lives and their camps. They live comfortably, though not so well as yourself." His eyes narrowed into a warning glare, which she heeded. She wanted to crack him like a coconut and see how rotten it was, but now wasn't the time.

He leaned back and chuckled again. "Ah, the good captain has repaid his debt with a divine gift." He finished his drink and looked into the cup, knowing his meticulously careful tongue had just betrayed him.

"A gift? Am I...a gift to repay a debt?" She trembled at her own suggestion. A man of his stature could slice off her head and dump it among the groves for no one but God to find if he felt insulted.

For all her apprehension, the colonel struggled as well. "It was not a material debt," he said looking away. "Simply one of honor." His words were suddenly void of any hint of drunkenness. "I saved the young man's life in Nanking...and earned myself a limp in doing so"

"Nanking...you and Captain Inoue were in Nanking?" As a girl, Ki-Hwa had overheard two teachers mention Nanking in a hushed, secretive sort of way that puzzled her. It was something the Japanese hierarchy wished to forget. Through much prodding on the Kinai Maru, she had convinced Denbe to tell her what he knew of the infamous story and then wished she hadn't. It was an orgy of death and murder.

"I've been told it was a grand battle with the Imperial Army winning much glory." She lied.

He paused and stared blankly at the ceiling. "Yes, " he said, "Much glory."

"And you saved his life there?"

He sighed again. "I was atop my horse addressing my staff. Four Chinese soldiers appeared from behind a building shooting at us. I positioned my horse between the men and the enemy and received a few bullets in the thigh." He made slight hand motions as if he were still there atop his mount; younger, fitter and commanding troopers in the thick of battle. "The horse was much worse for wear, however." He paused. "I adored that gelding."

"The staff eventually pulled me to safety. I guess Inoue has felt he owed me a debt of gratitude since then."

"And I am the repayment?" she said barely hiding her disdain.

"My dear, some men take a moment like that to their very soul." He closed his eyes and stumbled as she grabbed his wrist and led him three steps to the bed, crashing onto it spread eagle. She removed his trousers and glared at the sight of legs covered in local Tolai traditional tattoos.

"What are these?" she said running her finger down his thigh.

"Local tribesmen decorated me." He rolled to one side away from her. Ki-Hwa stood looking at the tattoos; there, visible down his right thigh and extending up into his groin. Five scars appeared where the skin was bumpy and uneven.

"That's the leg you limp on," she muttered. The scars were perfectly circular underneath the veil of dark ink and she stared at them for a long moment. And all at once it dawned on her: perhaps this was why he hadn't tried to consummate their relationship. Maybe he couldn't.

The colonel cared for, Ki-Hwa sat in his chair, unable to sleep, and began piecing his life together. He had graduated from Toyama Military Academy in 1918 and become a cavalry lieutenant immediately afterward. If he was assigned to Korea, it was possible he had been part of the mounted police or Japanese cavalry that rode down and slaughtered demonstrators that fateful day in 1919. It was certainly within his ability and demeanor. He'd already dug himself into a hole by revealing his relationship with Captain Inoue and then dug deeper by admitting he'd been a willing participant in the rape of Nanking. It would be unforgivable if he also had something to do with the massacre in her homeland that still traumatized her father as well.

*Does he seek forgiveness? From a farm girl?*

She looked at him, helpless on the bed. For all his might, pomp and circumstance, he was completely vulnerable at this moment. *The sword in the corner.* She could kill him now. This beast that probably deserved to be put out of his misery. She could retrieve his saber from where it sat just feet away and run him through in an instant. He wouldn't even wake in his drunken stupor. She could drag him outside and into the jungle until someone could help bury him.

But she didn't hate him enough nor did she possess the courage to do such a thing. It was not his idea to have her kidnapped and sent here, or so at least he claimed, she reasoned. Hating him was difficult. She hated the situation, but not Kanegawa...yet.

*But,* the devil inside her bellowed, *he may still take the greatest gift of your young life.*

This man she not only felt nothing for, but whose motives were unclear and most likely insincere. But kill him...she couldn't do that. *And they behead criminals here.* She walked to his coat where it hung on the screen, and ran her finger along his medals. He had the same ones as Captain Inoue but higher. He'd told her what they were one night but she only remembered the Order of the Rising Sun 2$^{nd}$ Class. Now she knew what the personal valor badge was for...and the limp. And the tattoos.

*I know your secrets now, colonel. But what good will they do me?*

# 9

## Tempt not a desperate man...or woman
*-William Shakespeare*

"So do you have one of those American nicknames like all the rest of the Joes, mate?" the big Aussie said.

"Like what?" replied the shabby American lieutenant.

"Lucky, Buddy, Cookie, Swabbie?"

"Swabbie is what we call those dirty Navy boys, and if I had any of those other nicknames, I'd have to beat myself up."

The Australian Coastwatcher wasn't satisfied and stared silently at the American pilot in their hide spot in the jungle. "Crash...I was called Crash, okay pal? I wrecked a couple of planes back home in California."

"That's easy to believe. The only plane I saw you pilot got shot out from underneath you."

Lieutenant Frank Collins was a good pilot who'd caught a bad break. His redesigned P-38 Lightning was modified with photographic equipment and sent out on lonely reconnaissance patrols, perfect for a loner like him, until he ventured too low for a shot and got jumped by a flight of four Zeroes. He didn't have a chance. In minutes, his plane was ablaze and he was in waist-deep water off Kokopo point with shrapnel in his thigh and a parachute above his head.

"Over here mate. Be quick about it," Dave Ladd yelled at Frank from the beach before the Japanese could get to him.

Dave stabilized his wounds and helped Frank to the safety of one of his many covert jungle observation posts, all named for pinup gals, like OP Jayne and OP Rita. Walking was painful. For nearly a month afterward, he resigned himself to sitting in this hole keeping notes on enemy movements until he could be rescued. He was determined not to jeopardize the Aussie's mission and to get himself out alive whenever the opportunity presented itself. But Rabaul was too crowded to risk a rescue operation, even by submarine. The Japs were everywhere. His wound healed nicely after a few weeks but then deteriorated after a bad slip on a wet root. He was also ailing from an encounter with a toxic red cedar tree that caused severe headaches, stomach cramps, and burning skin.

"It's ironic, you know," Frank said. "I was born and raised in the Mojave desert, which shoulda made the Army Air Corps see how perfect I am for the North Africa campaign. But instead I'm in the bush listening to a kangaroo crackin' wise on me."

"Well, it's not a holiday for me either," the Australian said. "Waiting is the devil."

"Really? Then you're in the wrong business, pal. You Coastwatchers do a lot of it if you hadn't noticed."

"Well as many planes as you've lost, maybe I'm not the only one in the wrong business, eh lieutenant?"

In the jungle the harshest agony was boredom, so Frank started a game of who-can-laugh-last. The rules were simple: no matter how funny something was, you couldn't laugh. Whoever laughed, lost, and Frank was getting used to losing.

"A horse walks into a bar and the bartender says, 'Why the long face?'" Dave said nothing. "You're just as thick as a coconut, ain't you? Well, those things have husks, buddy. Ones that peel away, too. I'll get you in the tank soon enough."

"Use your mouth for what it was meant. Have a feed," Dave replied tossing fruit at him like a lemur in a cage. His days of finding anything amusing were long gone. He was a repatriated islander to the bone, having moved to New Britain with his brother and father at age eight. After losing his wife to tuberculosis, Dave's father felt Cairns was no longer suitable for the Ladd boys, so they pulled up stakes. His father had few skills but a strong back, so when the opportunity arose to take the family to New Britain and work the fields, he took it. Dave embraced his new life. His brother, Jacob, didn't.

By the age of fourteen, Dave knew everything there was about extracting copra and palm oil from the local trees. He went on walkabouts to keep himself occupied and to satisfy his sense of adventure. He learned everything about the bush; what to eat, touch, smell and avoid. He learned to forage for food, to cook over embers using hollowed-out bamboo, to snare cassowary and bow hunt wild pig and rusa deer. By twenty, he knew the island like few others, including the natives, whom he knew as well. It was one thing to teach a man to shoot or communicate, but it was something completely different to teach him how to survive in the jungle. No white man did it on New Britain like Dave.

Even his father, reluctant to let him join the ranks of the Australian Coastwatchers, saw the boy's natural aptitude for jungle survival and relented. The Coastwatchers were just what he needed; a covert civilian group supporting the Royal Navy that gathered intelligence on any suspicious activity threatening Australia and the territories surrounding it. As Japan's expansion loomed, five hundred Watchers guarded Australia, New Guinea, and the Solomons; their nations' first line of defense. It was a pair of Watchers who warned Rabaul when a Japanese invasion was imminent, though there was little the paltry Lark Force stationed there could do.

When the Japs came, Dave evacuated hundreds of civilians, including his ailing father and brother, over the Bainings Mountains to Palmalmal Plantation, before going into hiding with his trusty radio and machete. He developed a network of spies that would be the envy of any intelligence officer. The Japs hired his native friends to do various tasks they couldn't, but that only gave him an ace in the hole. The locals trusted Dave and provided him with up-to-date information on almost every facet of the Imperial hierarchy. The Japs didn't have a chance against him. Too many ridges, too many forests, too much area for him to move around in no matter how many tens of thousands of troops they brought in, and too many locals who trusted him over the Nippon strangers. He was a formidable thorn in the Japanese side and proud of it.

"We really need a deck of cards," Frank said following it up with a burp. "And some bicarbonate soda. Whew."

"I prefer Chess," Dave replied, grinding his machete on a whetstone.

"Really? Didn't figure you for the chess type, but now that I think of it, you are quiet and conniving, like those kooky chess players."

"Two Kates rising up from Keravat," Dave said, pointing to the southwest without lifting his head from the blade.

Frank turned to see two torpedo planes taking off from the dirt airfield and pulled out his journal. "Training mission I suspect."

"To be honest, Yank, I prefer rugby, but I think the Japs might have a spat about us playing on their airfield."

"Ah, rugby. Another sport the English exported to its colonies along with oppression, taxes and prisoners."

"At least they didn't export the guillotine like the French." A long pause followed as they looked down the mountain toward the city.

"When is she supposed to be here?" Dave asked.

Frank looked at his well-worn watch as a bead of sweat dripped onto the dark leather band. "30 minutes." He was gazing back down the trail that ran dangerously close to their Observation Post when something moved on it.

"Oh, for Christ sake!" Frank's journal flew as he dived onto his stomach. Dave instinctively did the same and brought his Arisaka rifle to bear next to Frank's. "Helen Keller is early and she's not alone!" he whispered.

"Bloody hell!" They both looked nervously in the direction of Chitose, who was striding quickly to get up the steep slope with Seo-Sung in tow. Chitose knew the general vicinity of their OP, but could never remember its exact location. Dave silently moved twenty meters down slope to signal her, but then hesitated.

"Whatcha waiting for big fella?" Frank muttered.

Finally Dave rose to a knee and waved a hand. Chitose stopped in her tracks, as did Seo-Sung, who nearly wet herself.

"Great God Almighty!" she exclaimed. "A white man! This is why you brought me up here?" The pair ran up the slope and off the trail into dense jungle with Dave leading them. They arrived at the OP to find Frank's sidearm pointed at them, the mistrust painfully obvious in his face.

"Who the bloody hell is *she*?" Dave turned and demanded in Japanese.

"Nuth." Chitose said pointing to Seo-Sung and then to Frank's wound.

"What?" Frank said.

"She's trying to tell you I'm a nurse," Seo-Sung said slowly in Japanese, unsure how good their language skills were.

"A nurse? And you brought this dame here to take care of me?"

"She fix leg," Chitose signed back.

"Great gravy, you brought her up here for me?" Frank repeated.

"Guess she's still trying to repay you," Dave said. "Look, you *cannot* do this."

"Well, it's a little late now," Seo-Sung said. "Let me look at your leg."

"Fine I am," Frank retorted as he brought his weapon back up and aimed it at the Korean.

"Look, I'm not Japanese. I'm Korean and I'm a prisoner down there. Let me help you, tough guy. What are you going to do, pout and send me home?"

Frank stared at her, looking for some reason to be convinced. She was right. There was no sense in sending her back now, but letting her tend to his wound? "It's just scratch."

"No, it's not," Seo-Sung said. "Or she wouldn't have risked this."

He conceded, lowering his pistol. But Dave was not as nice and took it out on Chitose in both Japanese and sign. She'd compromised his secrecy without consulting him, a decision she was unauthorized to make. Her job was to provide information, not determine who was trustworthy enough to bring in.

Seo-Sung inspected the wound with a slight smile. An early morning hike had just turned into good fortune. Two white men, one wounded and needing her help, were hiding in the enemy-infested jungle. She wasn't exactly a nurse, but two months as a hospital volunteer was coming in handy on New Britain.

"You're going to get us killed, mate," he scolded Frank before holding a finger up to Chitose. "This is not a game!" He turned back to Frank. "We're going to have to abandon this spot now, you realize."

"Why?"

"We don't know who saw them come up here. The Japs could be following right now."

"But Rita has the best line of sight to everything. All five airfields, the harbor, the channel."

"Jane is just as good," Dave said. "Less food, but good vantage points. It's time to move anyway. I saw a couple of boot prints on the trail a few days ago."

"They're too scared to get off the trail. They never venture into the bush. You know that."

"Just as well. We need to move."

"For crying out loud!" Frank protested. "I like Rita."

"You're the one who had to save her, Yank," Dave said, motioning to Chitose.

Frank went silent, glad that Chitose didn't speak English. "You would have too, champ. Besides, it paid off. She's brought in good info." Frank had to defend his decision, even if it might have been a bad one.

Just three weeks after Frank was rescued, Dave left him in OP Carol to go off and collect sugar cane, papaya and fruit from an ambarella tree he'd spotted. It was the first time Frank had been left alone. Near dusk he took shelter under the massive leaf of a pandanus tree as it started to drizzle and sat there fighting off the overwhelming boredom.

"I can think of a hundred places I'd rather be...let's try to name them all...Tahiti, Hawaii, Australia with the REMFs, Comiskey Park eating a jumbo dog..." Suddenly the sound of movement alerted him. He hunkered down and aimed his pistol downhill. Moments later a Japanese officer walked into view with a large bag over his shoulder.

"What are you up to Japo?" he muttered.

The officer stopped in a tiny clearing just below him, dropping the package to the ground. He wobbled slightly, sweat glistening on his face and head. He removed his jacket clumsily and doubled over trying to breathe.

"Not an easy climb is it, pal? I don't suppose you brought your laundry all the way up here to dry, did you?" But Frank's flippant attitude changed when he saw what, or who, was in the bundle. It was a girl. She had dried blood around her nose and red patches around her swollen eyes. Her blouse and dress were both torn open, exposing her breasts and legs up to the thigh.

"How did no one see you bring her all the way up here? Guess this really is a good hiding spot." Frank's indifference betrayed him. This man had obviously beaten her, something he loathed. But the life of one Japanese woman was secondary to his own, so he looked away when the officer did the unthinkable--woke the girl and raped her.

"You sick son of a bitch." His moral code told him to stop the lewd crime, but his head told him to stay put. He was an American Army officer on a mission that was much larger than one Japanese girl who'd run into the wrong guy. He chose not to watch as she struggled but didn't scream because he commanded her not to. When the soldier finished he punched her twice in the face until she passed out. Frank cringed, gritted his teeth and pointed the gun at him.

*It's too loud, even in this wet jungle. God dammit!*

The officer then pulled a small packet of liquid out of his trouser pocket and poured it on her. *Gasoline!* Frank smelled it immediately. That's one of the funny things about the jungle. An unnatural smell resonates immediately. It happened every time Dave opened the peanut butter packets his natives brought him.

Frank faced a real decision. If the drunken soldier lit her on fire, it wouldn't be long before someone noticed, especially since it was almost nighttime. But killing an Imperial Japanese officer would also not go unnoticed. Someone would miss him. Frank was stuck until the Japanese officer made the decision for him. He pulled out his bayonet with his right hand, grabbed the girls' tongue with his left, pulled hard and sliced it off cleanly, discarding it into the jungle. Blood spurted out of her mouth like a geyser and it was clear she was in danger of drowning in the pool that was building up in her mouth.

That was it. Lieutenant Frank Collins would stand no more. He reached down and pulled the tanto knife from his boot and slithered on his belly down the hill toward the officer. Twenty meters, ten meters, five meters. The Japanese officer muttered as he lit a match. Frank jumped to his feet and rushed forward despite his painful leg injury. The officer turned his head at the sound of crushing foliage.

Panicking, he dropped the lit match, catching the girl's arm ablaze, and reached for his own blade. But he had no more time to think when Frank's tanto found its mark. He buried it with surgical precision, aiming through the man's jacket and chest cavity to his heart with a hand clamped over his mouth. The two fell to the ground with Frank on top, holding the position for several seconds to ensure the deed was done. All the while the girl's arm burned.

He jumped off the officer and smothered the fire with a large, wet leaf. Picking up several more, he covered her burns with them. He checked the officer—twitching but definitely dead—and then looked at the girl. Amazingly, she was still unconscious.

"Lucky for you. But you'll be in hell when you wake up." Frank looked at the corpse.

That night he explained his decision to Dave, who reluctantly agreed that he'd done the right thing. They had to move, though. There was no sense staying in OP Carol since they couldn't know if anyone had seen the officer come up the mountain.

They carried the body high up the mountain to bury it under a dense thicket of brush and palm fronds. They then took the girl, confused and in searing pain to OP Rita where they cared for her. In turn she became their informant. She made up a story and went back to premium house after a week of rudimentary healing and rivers of tears. That girl was Chitose, the head of premium house.

"You should have seen me take him down," Frank smiled. "Just like the college days when I was a linebacker." He punched Dave's arm.

"American football." Dave mocked.

"I'll get you info," Seo-Sung suddenly offered.

Frank's ears perked up. "Like what?"

"Anything. You give me the mission and I'll come through."

Frank stole a glance at Dave, who heaved a deep sigh. "Bugger me, she knows everything as it is."

"And what's your price? Don't tell me you'll do it for God and country," Frank said.

"Get me off this island. Before things get too bad here. I want out."

"Ha!" Frank bellowed.

"Define 'too bad.'" Dave replied.

"It's only a matter of time before your countries invade this place or bomb it into dust. Even the officers are worried. Before that happens, you two will get gone and take her I assume," she motioned toward Chitose. "Take me too."

Frank was impressed with her swagger. "How about this," he said. "You get us some details on the POWs here, where they're held, how many, guards, shifts, everything you can, and when we grab them, we'll grab you too."

Seo-Sung didn't even need to think about it, but paused for effect anyway. "Deal." She held out a hand for Frank to shake, who in turn began to bow.

"I thought you Yanks shake hands to seal a deal."

"He's going through an identity crisis," Dave said.

Frank shook, looking slightly embarrassed. "We shake. But know this...you cross me and you'll be swimming with the fishes in the harbor. Understand?"

"I do."

\* \* \* \* \*

Dave and Frank watched the women disappear down the trail. "Are you bonkers mate?" Dave said. "You gone loopy in the bush? You can't hold up that bargain."

"Well don't worry, we won't have to make good on it."

"You don't think she'll come through?"

"It ain't that," he said, running a hand through his sandy blonde hair that was longer than he cared for. "My government can't even put together a rescue mission for me, let alone those two."

"So why give her the POW mission? We know most of that stuff anyway."

Frank shrugged his shoulders and cocked his head to one side as he sat on a stack of leaves that doubled as his bed. "Give her something to do, make sure she's on our side, you know. You object?"

"I object to sending an untrained girl who knows about us into the belly of the beast. If she gets nipped and questioned, we could be facing the firing squad."

"They wouldn't waste the ammo. They'll behead us instead," Frank joked.

"This isn't a thing to make light about, lieutenant. You don't know these bastards like I do."

"Relax. I have a good feeling about her. I think she may surprise us. But the chances of the Allied Forces rescuing a civilian nurse are pretty slim."

"Why so? I sent a few hundred out during the invasion."

"Well, the US of A isn't in the business of taking care of civilians unless they're...militarily significant let's say." Frank lay back on his bed of leaves.

Dave continued to stand and watch the trail well after the two disappeared. "Ah, the high and mighty Yanks, only take action when it's convenient to you, eh?"

"Home of the Brave, pal."

Dave stood silent, watching the trail until an engine roaring overhead snapped him back to the present. "A single Mavis. Recon flight."

"Isn't it ironic?" Frank said as he sat up and retrieved his journal. Dave ignored him and grabbed his kit bag, slinging it over his shoulder. "I'm going to take some food to the priests at Ramale tonight. The guards haven't been feeding them."

Frank scribbled a note and wiped his forehead as Dave prepared to leave. "It's ironic," he repeated. Dave finally looked back at him. "We just had that entire conversation in the language of our enemy. Don't you find that out of the ordinary?"

"No...*we* just had that conversation in Japanese...*you* tried."

\* \* \* \* \*


Seo-Sung practically skipped down the mountain in delight, her mind filled with all the things she wanted to do for her new friends. But as the sun broke through the morning mist signaling a new day, she first she had to come clean with the woman who dropped this gift into her lap. A few hundred yards shy of premium house, she grabbed Chitose by the arm and wheeled her around.

"Look, you trusted me with your great secret so I should return the favor. I'm not really a nurse, not fully at least." Seo-Sung confessed about her brief stint in the hospital in Pusan, embellishing it only slightly. "Those guys up there don't know I'm a comfort girl," Seo-Sung said. "I'd like to keep it that way." She was awash with the high of responsibility. For one of the few times in her life, someone depended on her, or so she wanted to believe at least. She was suddenly a respectable nurse and covert agent, not someone's lustful plaything for the night. If they wanted a spy, she would be their Mata Hari. Chitose was surprisingly content. She had plenty at risk as well and simply nodded in agreement.

"I was walking through the house this morning and noticed a couple of empty beds," Victoria said as the pair stepped onto the verandah. She sat motionless in a wide rattan chair wearing a thick veil of disdain. "When did you two start taking morning walkabouts?"

"Ee...uh..." Chitose stumbled.

"We wanted to enjoy the sunrise over the city," Seo-Sung intervened. "We've been meaning to do it for a long time now, but could never get up early enough. It's magnificent. Have you ever seen it from the mountain, Ma'am?"

"No! Nor do I care to. And nor do I care for you to! There are many hidden dangers in the jungle and I don't want my girls exposed to them! Do you understand me?" Her voice was near a shout, but she remained seated.

"Yes ma'am, but a little mountain air does a person good. In Kor...uh, Chosen, we often hike the mountains in the morning. Perhaps you would enjoy an occasional walk on the trails?"

"The only mountain air around here is the stinking methane belching out of that great hole in the ground," she said throwing a thumb over her shoulder toward Mount Tovanumbatir.

"You mean sulfur?"

"You are not to go near that mountain again or you'll both wind up regulars. Do I make myself clear?" Chitose nodded in fear, inching her way toward the front door. "Speaking of sulfur, where did you get those sulfa tablets on your dresser?" Victoria asked.

Seo-Sung froze. The truth was she'd stolen them from the hospital, but admitting this would surely mean a move back to the regulars and maybe even judicial punishment. She couldn't hesitate to answer, though, or Victoria would be suspicious. Time for a change in tactics.

"Did you go through my stuff?" she countered accusingly.

"It is *my* room, dear. I loan it to you at my pleasure."

"Pleasure? Are you sure you know what that means?"

"No profit grows where no pleasure is taken. You have the burden of providing the pleasure while I become the most profitable person on this island."

"I'm unhappy about the intrusion, ma'am," she said. "But you're right. It's your house and these are your rules. And I will follow them." She turned to go inside.

"You still haven't told me where you got the sulfa."

She spun around. "A customer from the hospital left it in the room. I guess it's not that important to him."

"Really? And what customer would that be? No one from the hospital comes up here."

"I didn't say he worked at the hospital, I said he came from there. It was Captain Aoki."

"And why would Captain Aoki have sulfa. It's fairly rare, after all. " Victoria rose from the chair and crossed the verandah to stand in front of her, grinning like a fisherman returning to port with a prized tuna.

"I don't know why, but he is Kempeitai and I know he's been spending a lot of time with the regulars, despite his rank. He fancies Mari, even if she is not the cleanest so I suspect he's seen the inside of the hospital more than once. You really ought to do something to keep men like him from bringing diseases up here. Your exams and quarantine policies for girls with the spots aren't working too well."

She hurried up the stairs so Victoria would have no opportunity to take the conversation further. Was she not running she might have noticed her old friend, Sergeant Denbe Isogai sitting in the front parlor.

"What is her problem anyway?" Seo-Sung said as she entered her room, not expecting a response, but receiving one anyway.

"She's afraid of losing what she has," said a familiar voice. Seo-Sung whipped around to see Asako and Ki-Hwa walking through her open door.

"You scared me half to death!"

"I am truly sorry. We were waiting for you to return."

"Seems like everyone is this morning." Chitose joined them, making her gesture for a car driving away. She began making tea, the aroma filling the room.

"So what do you mean, she's scared of losing what she has?" Seo-Sung inquired.

"Well, it is not much of a story..." Asako started, "but I know she worked at the plantation making copra when the invasion came." She stared out the window, trying to remember exactly how the story went, not wanting to miss anything. "She came here from Australia a few years before the war to find work. There was nothing for her in town so she convinced the plantation owner that she could do the same work as a man out there. They hired her, which was unheard of for a woman and did not go over too well with the male workers, as you can imagine." She paused to sip her tea and made a face when it scalded her lip.

"I can," Seo-Sung said. "Had to work twice as hard as the others to earn her room and board. I've experienced it. "

"Yes and I suspect that is why she has such a hard attitude." She blew on her tea. "After the invasion, she was rounded up with most of the other women and put into that camp where the Indian men are now. Before they could decide what to do with her, she persuaded them to let her be a comfort girl, along with the other Australian girl, Emma."

"Was Kanegawa here at the time?" Ki-Hwa asked.

"Maybe. He was on the island then, I believe. The plantation became the first comfort station and was only for the upper-level officers. From what I am told she only required a few weeks to take control of all comfort operations."

"How?" Seo-Sung asked.

"I do not know but it must have had something to do with the plantation's ownership. She did not own it before the war, but she does now."

"Really?" Seo-Sung said in amazement.

"She owns it?" Ki-Hwa nearly fell out of her seat.

"I think once the comfort women started arriving in force, she was asked to oversee the whole lot of them because the Imperial Navy and Army didn't want to. I think they were too preoccupied trying to prepare the island for operations and build the airfields and that sort of thing. So they gave her jurisdiction over the plantation, the compound and premium house and she has been in charge ever since." Her words trailed off into silence as a breeze rattled the window.

Every topic wears out its welcome, even a juicy one like complaining about a boss. Within moments they turned to inspect Chitose's wounds, impressed at how well they were healing. Still, Seo-Sung felt something was missing from Asako's story.

*Victoria must be an opportunist like me. Something doesn't add up though,* she thought. The other girls talked, but Seo-Sung wasn't listening, lost in her own daydreams. She walked to the window and stared at the beautiful panorama, but without really seeing it, unable to block out the enormity of the morning's main event. She wanted the others to leave so she could get to work. The roar of engines turned her gaze turned toward the sky.

"The 251$^{st}$ is leaving," Asako said.

"Who?"

"The 251$^{st}$ Squadron. They're relocating to the island of Truk to regroup. I expect they'll return in a few months." Seo-Sung and Asako watched intently as wave after wave of the 251$^{st}$ flew low over the island's headquarters as a show of respect to their dear leaders.

"Why does the coming and going of soldiers interest you?" Ki-Hwa asked.

"Information is power, my friend," Asako said.

"We are their captives. Have you forgotten?" Seo-Sung added.

"Of course not," Ki-Hwa replied.

"Good." Seo-Sung turned back to the window. "Because I do not enjoy being a captive and will not be one forever."

The last flight of Zeroes roared overhead before arcing slowly around to the north for the long haul over the open ocean as Seo-Sung and Asako could not be torn from the window to watch. Seo-Sung finally went to use the washroom, but Asako, alone in an airy white silk dress, watched until every last plane of the 251$^{st}$ had disappeared into the pale blue sky.

"Are you angry?" Ki-Hwa asked her.

"No. Why?"

"Your fists are clenched."

Asako looked down to see Ki-Hwa was correct. She opened her hands. "It is merely chilly in here. We must go." Asako and Ki-Hwa left for the plantation, leaving Seo-Sung to pace her room and wring her hands, anxiety building to an almost feverish pitch. She didn't want to be just another informant, but rather an extraordinary spy. Good information the Allies could use wasn't enough; she wanted to impress them by providing more intelligence than they had imagined her capable of. She resolved to provide perfection when only mediocrity was expected. She wanted to shake the mighty house of Hirohito itself. Before Chitose abruptly woke her this morning, she was a simple comfort woman. Now, she was a collaborator, a traitor, and a seditionist. She was guilty of collusion with the enemy. One careless move and the Kempeitai would break down the door and arrest her. After painful torture and eventual beheading, they would do the same to the Allies hiding in the bush.

*It's worth it. What else have I got to do?* she thought. She looked toward the door as a girl with a hollow face and drooping jowls shuffled past in a worn nightgown, hung over and hurting.

*This isn't living.* She couldn't approach this like an amateur. She had to be cunning, professional. She had to scrutinize her game plan all the way to the end state, not just the first few moves.

*What to do first?* She stopped pacing in the middle of the room, her teeth clamped down on the end of a thumbnail, mumbling. "My mission is to collect information on the prisoners. How should I do that? Get close to the ones who know. Identify them and come up with a way to suck the information I need out of them." She spat out the nail and resumed pacing across the creaky wooden floor. "How is it that this whole island smells so beautifully sweet, yet this room reeks of mildew and sweat?" She opened her window and lit an incense candle. There were only three people she could think of who worked at the prison camps: Colonel Kanegawa, Captain Aoki and the young translator. She'd seen the translator at the compound one night as he taught a girl there a few English words, like "Hello," "Goodbye," and "Wednesday." He was a charming kid, but couldn't be more than eighteen.

"Young and unpredictable. Good candidate."

Kanegawa was risky unless Ki-Hwa was willing to help and Aoki was a lecherous man who couldn't be gotten rid of once you'd given him any attention. She then made a mental list of definite and potential allies. Her team would almost certainly have to be women since she worked among so many and knew precious few men on a personal basis. Mostly Korean too. Ki-Hwa was definitely in, but Asako was questionable. Maybe too fragile for something like this. A couple of reliable premiums rounded out the list.

She paced the room a while longer, scheming, mumbling, perfecting the plan and its players. The critical first steps were complete. "Ki-Hwa will help. She has to."

# 10

## He wears the rose of youth upon him
*-William Shakespeare*

Ki-Hwa stood on the verandah and stared at the massive hole, ever increasing in size where a serene garden once flourished. The construction continued nearly every day and each time the workers came Ki-Hwa could be found standing outside her room watching men do menial labor, just as for years she'd watched her father and brothers working on the farm until she was old enough to join them.

*Olive skin, white skin, blue eyes, English...fascinating.*

The hole grew deeper and bigger, encompassing the entirety of the courtyard. Partitions for several rooms, storage spaces, stairs and even sleeping quarters took shape. Concrete was mixed, brought in wheelbarrows, and poured over massive posts that arched high in the center for strength, or so Asako said. She would know since her services were being offered to the chief engineer until the project was complete. He seemed to enjoy talking her ear off about the project's technicalities, explanations she would patiently listen to before removing his clothes and silencing him. She wasn't a special for nothing.

"Asako-San?" A mousy voice came from down the verandah. Ki-Hwa turned from the construction to gaze upon a magnificent sight. Saeko, a fully trained geisha in magnificent splendor stood radiantly in Asako's doorway, decorated elaborately in the most beautiful kimono Ki-Hwa had ever seen. It was deep blue with a gold and white embroidered cherry blossom tree arcing its way across her midsection and a series of cranes flying majestically across her shoulder. It must've taken ten thousand silkworms a lifetime to produce the amount of fabric that hung perfectly from her lithe form and ended just short of the floor so her zori were barely noticeable.

Her face was a ghostly white with red pouty lips painted like the colorful dots of a koi fish. Her face was so pale, it made her teeth look a dingy yellow when she spoke. Her eyes sat strikingly forward on her face, nuanced from the skillful use of makeup and charcoal with an almost undetectable hint of red at the edges. Her cheeks were tinted a light shade as if she'd caught a cold. Her hair was combed and tamed into perfect order. Ornamental pearls dangled weightlessly from her lobes and accentuated her lavish makeup. Her beauty was staggering and Ki-Hwa was astonished that someone could change her appearance so completely.

"Would you tie my obi please?" She held out her right hand and gave Asako a piece of deep blue cloth.

"Certainly." Asako appeared in the doorway and quickly tied the cloth behind her back. She stared at the costume that had obviously taken an immense amount of time to perfect. She felt plain. "How long before he arrives?" Asako asked.

"Any minute now." For someone who was short on time, Saeko was well composed.

When Asako was finished, she adjusted the *eri sugata* collar that lined the kimono around the neck. "Do not forget your fan," Asako said as Saeko turned and floated like a goose on a steady tailwind down the verandah to her room.

"How do you know how to do that?" Ki-Hwa asked.

But Asako merely smiled.

"Ki-Hwa," Victoria summoned from across the courtyard. "A word please." She went to the main house. "Sit," Victoria demanded once inside the parlor. "I want to ask you about Seo-

Sung. What line of work did she have back in Chosen?" Victoria wasted no time in getting to the point. She was a mongoose attacking before her prey could defend itself.

"I'm not sure. She's rather vague about those days."

"Did she ever nick anything from you?"

"Nick?"

"Steal."

"No!"

"Well, I'm not convinced she hasn't stolen from others and I know she's been up here to see you."

"We are friends from the same country. We spent a long time together on the boat from Chosen. We just like to visit with each other."

"Her room is very tidy. It's odd for a Korean."

"She believes messy people are lazy. And laziness leads to complacency." Ki-Hwa guarded her answers like mahjong tiles.

"Is she afraid of being indifferent to this profession?" Victoria asked.

"I don't know. Should she be? Should I?" For a moment, Ki-Hwa thought that perhaps she'd been wrong about Victoria. Maybe she was a caring ear to confide in. Maybe she cared about her women on an emotional level.

"Is she a lesbian?"

"What? No. And she does what she pleases. I can't stop her from coming out here."

"Well, I could stop her from coming out here...if I wanted to." Victoria was reaching, but for what? Her rule about premiums not coming out to the plantation was never enforced, so what was she after? Specials walked to premium house and premiums walked to the plantation or into town. Everyone knew it and no one cared.

"If it displeases you, I will tell her to stop and when I want to talk to her, I will go there." Ki-Hwa took a lesson from Seo-Sung and let Victoria think she had the upper hand.

"I'm concerned that she doesn't know her place and she needs to." Victoria's eyebrows turned upward.

"Yes, ma'am."

"Right then," Victoria said with a sigh. "You will help me get that across to her. Now do me a favor and fetch my teacup in the next room." She pointed toward the hallway.

"Yes, ma'am." Ki-Hwa rose and walked down the dimly lit hallway past two antique pieces of local furniture and turned left at the end to enter the dragon's lair. To her surprise, the room was bland with dark, simple dressers around the walls and a large four-poster bed in front of the window. A set of handmade China dolls sat on a chest in the far corner. Several expensive silk robes hung on a standing valet next to the immense bathroom that reeked of perfume. Ki-Hwa felt as if a man had recently been there. *Maybe she still takes a patron occasionally.* A shudder ran up her spine at the thought of Victoria with a man. She saw the teacup on the boudoir and picked it up when something on a dresser caught her eye. It looked familiar. On the dark wood dresser next to the bathroom door laid a shiny object she'd noticed before. It reflected the light streaming in through the window as it sat between two ceramic Foo dogs and next to a pistol: a silver and ivory letter opener; one of Nibori's letter openers. "I give them as gifts from time to time," she remembered him say. Reaching out to examine it, a thousand questions swirled through her mind.

*Why does Victoria have one? Do they have a history? Is he involved with her? Is this why he provides labor for her?* She seized the letter opener and examined it closely. There on its hilt was Bishamonten looking grand and stately, and there was the dragon chasing his pearl. There was the exquisite detail to the whole thing gazing back at her, laughing at her, mocking her as though Bishamonten himself was saying, "She is worthy of me, but you...?"

"My cup please!" Victoria shouted from the parlor.

*Clunk* went Bishamonten onto the dresser, his arm snapping off as he fell, the pagoda still in his hand. *Oh, no! Oh, NO!* In a dizzying flurry she picked up the letter opener and Bishamonten's broken arm, holding a piece in each hand and turning quickly to the door and then back again to the dresser, panicking. She stared at the miniature deity, eyes wide with fear.

*What to do?* She looked to Bishamonten for help. Victoria would be sure to notice it was broken or worse...missing. *But you have to fix me or she'll have a fit when she finds you've broken my arm off. And if you don't leave now, she'll be suspicious.*

Ki-Hwa shoved the letter opener into the waist of her loose dress and walked quickly out of the room with the teacup in one hand and Bishamonten's arm clenched tightly in the other. She covered the length of the long hallway in seconds, practically tossing the teacup down in front of Victoria, who was engrossed in her accounting books. Ki-Hwa continued out the door without missing a stride, even as she jumped into her shoes.

Once in the safety of her room, she plopped heavily onto the bed, her mind swimming. *I should have just left it there and then it would just be broken. Now it's missing and I've stolen it.* She was near tears. *And I'm a thief...I've never stolen so much as a kiss!* She drew the letter opener out of her blouse, raising the hilt to eye level and pressing the arm gently against the place where it had broken free.

*You foolish girl.*

146

# 11

## Dreams...are the children of an idle brain, begot of nothing but vain fantasy

*-William Shakespeare*

Ki-Hwa's days were routine. She ate a mango, drank a cup of green tea and fetched a basin of fresh water from the tank at the end of the verandah to wash her face and brush her teeth. After, she threw the water out, used the toilet, flushed it using the gravity tank, and stood outside her door, leaning on the railing as the bunker took shape, only to return to her room and be bored.

Spending her life rotting in a kiln was maddening. The sheer misery of living as a woman abducted from home seeped into her soul. Though she was lucky enough to entertain only one chivalric patron who had yet to consummate the relationship, she lived in a state of disbelief, surrounded by women whose lives were suspended, few of them able to accept their fate. This pattern of idleness had to be broken, even if only temporarily.

She picked a plain dress and blouse, applied some basic makeup, brushed her hair, chose a pair of comfortable shoes, and convinced Abongo, the truck driver, to take her into town after his daily supply pickup. She peered at the main house briefly, still wanting to return the broken letter opener. With every passing day she expected Victoria to search her room like the Kempeitai searching for a traitor and find Bishamonten and his broken arm sleeping between her mattresses. She had to figure out a way to fix and return him.

She stared out the truck's window at the ocean, grateful in spite of everything, for having the opportunity to see it every day. She studied the ever-busy Simpson harbor, the gently sloping volcanoes, New Ireland Island in the distance and the unmistakable Rabaul. She turned her attention west, toward the opposite side of the island where no one was allowed to travel. She stared at the Bainings Mountains in the distance, wondering at the secrets hidden there.

Abongo dropped her at Rabaul's main open-air market where she took in the sounds and smells. She bought a can of juice purchased with the few Yen she'd managed to hide from Victoria and meandered through the rows of tables, comparing them to Kyeongju. Leaving the market, guilt fluttered around her heart when she passed two regulars surrounded by soldiers on a street corner. One of the men looked her way and she looked at the ground as she walked, quickening her pace. She found her way to a part of the beach closest to the wharf and sat in the shade of a palm, gazing at the sheer size of the docked ships. Giant frigate birds performed an aerial ballet, swooping and diving in a frenzied fight over a few scraps of fish tossed from a trawler. She sat alone, a breeze against her skin, watching the waves rippling up the beach, folding over themselves and receding back again into the vast ocean. She shouldn't allow herself to relax, but this day was hers; a brief, blissful interlude in an otherwise sordid drama. She only wished her family were here to feel it too.

But for all the beauty of New Britain, she was destined to return to life as a comfort woman, a sex slave, the belonging of a tortured man who would surely torture her soon enough. She returned to the confines of the plantation as the daylight slowly surrendered to darkening skies and a storm brewing in the west. Rounding the corner into her room, she found someone waiting for her.

"Let's take a walk," Seo-Sung said as she slid her door open.

"I just finished a long walk. Can't we stay here?"

Seo-Sung was adamant. "We have to go where no one can hear us," she whispered. They walked down the driveway and veered quickly into the coconut groves as the last rays of the sun disappeared behind dark clouds. Seo-Sung confessed her covert operations, telling Ki-Hwa everything about the Anglos in the jungle and their opportunity for escape.

"It's much to take in," Ki-Hwa said. "Everyone's preparing for the Anglos invasion, and now you say they may be taking us away from here?" She turned away from Seo-Sung and picked at a lonely piece of sawgrass that jutted up from the ground.

"It's wonderful," Seo-Sung said to reassure her young friend. "This is our opportunity."

Ki-Hwa shrugged her shoulders. "If what you are saying happens, it means another long trip into the unknown. And even farther from home. It's like being kidnapped again."

Seo-Sung sighed and ignored Ki-Hwa's concern, choosing to remain focused on her mission. "Tell me about the kid, the one who speaks English." Ki-Hwa described everything she knew about the tall interpreter whose flawless complexion made even the specials feel envious. Ki-Hwa guessed he was about twenty years old, but he'd spent his first fourteen years on a livestock farm in Hawaii until his parents moved back to Japan just before the war. He was forced to accompany them and renounce his American citizenship; not doing so would have disgraced his family. He'd even had to renounce the English name his parents had given him and resort to using his middle name, Chikaki. Having mastered English in Hawaii, Chikaki volunteered to be an interpreter and was assigned to the Imperial Army, eventually landing in the POW interrogation program. Colonel Kanegawa and the 6th Field Kempeitai got their hooks into him first.

"What about the prison system?" Seo-Sung asked.

"Can we do this another time?" Ki-Hwa's voice was nearly a whine in the tropical breeze.

"Just a little more."

Ki-Hwa confessed what little she knew about the prison system from Kanegawa's bedroom banter and a visit she'd once made to his office after drinks at the New Guinea club. "The Kempeitai are a combination of military and political police," she said. "They keep everyone in line, not just the military but foreigners and perceived threats as well." Ki-Hwa droned as though she were giving a class to basic recruits. "But rank doesn't matter to them. In fact, the average soldier isn't whom they're concerned with, except when it comes to law enforcement. They keep a very close eye on high-ranking military officers and civilian officials for any indication of... what's that word...? 'Sedition.'"

"Breaks in the ranks?"

"Yes. They're ruthless when it comes to getting information from POWs or anyone else they think is a threat. Their power comes directly from the Kempeitai headquarters in Japan that answers only to the Emperor. They have absolute authority over local commanders, whenever they see fit to use it. And once they get what they want..." She made a motion of a blade cutting across her throat.

"So everyone has to stay valuable...string them along? How many camps are there?"

"On the island? I think four or maybe more. They number them. Three are on the outskirts of the city and One-Fifty-One is in town. I know Camp One is mostly Australians, Camp Seven is mostly British from Singapore and One-Fifty-Two is all men from an Indian Regiment...and a mishmash of other foreigners and locals. Can we please do this another time? I'm tired and it's going to rain." Ki-Hwa looked up as the unmistakable smell of an approaching storm filled the air. She turned to walk back to the plantation.

"How bad off are they? The prisoners. Like the ones we saw working on the bunker?"

"I don't know, but I suspect very bad.

Seo-Sung walked with her as a flock of birds flew away from the blackening clouds. The wind was kicking up, providing some relief from the enervating heat.

"Here's how we do this. I'll go meet with the Hawaiian kid and invite him up to premium house for some service, which he won't refuse, and establish a little relationship with him."

"Victoria won't like that," Ki-Hwa interrupted.

"She won't know. And that will add to the excitement for him. Sneaking around her, right? I'll get him to see me a couple of times before I start asking him about the camps. Or I'll introduce him to a younger girl if he doesn't want me."

"He won't talk."

"He's twenty! He'll say anything to get sex, especially with a premium. I just have to seduce him the right way." She talked with conviction, as if her powers of persuasion were undeniable. "Now with the colonel, what we need to know is when and where they move the POWs, or if they even do at all. Are they staying put in one camp or are they moved periodically to throw any rescuers off?"

Ki-Hwa began to speak, but waited until the roar of three Betty bombers landing at nearby Rapopo faded. "I'm not sure I can do it," she finally said.

"What?"

"I'm not sure I'm strong enough. He's very smart." She smoothed strands of hair that the wind whipped into her face, tucking them into her collar.

"Of course you are! You've been strong enough to handle abduction and servitude. You can do this!"

"You can get what you need without me."

Seo-Sung's jaw dropped. "This is the same man who had you stolen from home and shipped thousands of miles away like a piece of luggage. The same man who forces himself on you, who uses you like a plaything, and who wants to return you to Japan to be his back-door mistress!" She nearly shouted.

"We don't know that." She looked away, unable to look at the friend she was disappointing. "And he hasn't forced himself on me."

"Yet. He will. Do you think when the war is over he'll just say, 'Hey that was fun, see ya around doll' and let you go home?"

"He can't. At least I don't think he can." She looked at the ground.

Seo-Sung stared at her young friend in disbelief. "So what then? You're his trophy?"

"He's taught me poetry and history and other things I want to know. I was never given the chance to have an education, remember? He teaches me things. No one else has done that."

"Are you telling me you care for him now?" Seo-Sung spun around with her arms outstretched. "What happened to you?"

"I do not care for him in that way, but I don't hate him either. I've had plenty of chances to do him harm, but what's the point?" High in the trees dry palm fronds hissed, sudden gusts whipping them against each other.

"I don't believe this. We have an opportunity here to help cripple the bastards who invaded our homeland, right? Or at least get some of those poor prisoners off the island. Do you remember the way they looked when they came out here? They're thin from not being fed. They're scarred from being tortured. They're sick and given no medicine. They're afraid for their lives because of what the Kempeitai does to them..." She lowered her voice and moved closer. "And they have families too. They're someone else's sons, husbands, fathers, uncles, nephews, whatever. And you're choosing him over them?"

"I don't choose him. I just don't have any desire to hurt him."

"He's a butcher!"

"Maybe I don't choose him then. Maybe I choose here. This place. A farm, a ship, an island...a father, a sergeant, a colonel. I thought they were all different, but they're not. They're all the same and we can't win unless we make something of it. Unless we do something with what we're given. That is the only way to defeat them. To make them see they were wrong in thinking they could break us." Ki-Hwa was near tears. Seo-Sung only looked at her, gaping in disbelief. "So you want to make something...of this?" she motioned toward the plantation.

"I've told you everything I know. You can get whatever else you need from Chikaki."

"He's a worker bee. The king of the hive is sleeping in your bed. All I need you to do is ask some more questions. Get inside his head."

"I...," she stopped. How could she let her friend down? But to betray Kanegawa made her stomach turn. Seo-Sung took a deep sigh and looked at the storm surrounding Mount To. The temperature dropped mercifully as the wind grew even stronger. Seo-Sung raised her voice, shouting over the sound it made in the palm fronds. It was no mere wind. A typhoon was coming. They needed shelter.

"You do what you have to, Ki-Hwa. And so will I."

They walked back to the road gripped in uncomfortable silence as the first few drops of rain pattered on their heads. Ki-Hwa turned to walk toward the plantation, but Seo-Sung stopped her.

153

"His position does not give him the right to dictate values," she said. Ki-Hwa stared quietly, only wanting to go home. "And yours shouldn't either." Seo-Sung stepped closer. "And just because we're near the lowest rung on the Empire's ladder doesn't mean we have to act like martyrs. I told you this once before, remember?" She put a finger in Ki-Hwa's chest, poking it with her fingernail. "Now keep this to yourself and act normal."

Ki-Hwa nodded without thinking as Seo-Sung walked off. The rain came in torrents, plastering her hair in long, heavy strands against her head and neck but she didn't care. She ran to the plantation, eager to feel its shelter like the impervious roof her father had built. In the middle of this dark storm, its glowing lights were a welcome sight. It was home now. Mother, father, and her brothers were all gone, and Victoria, comfort women and the colonel had taken their place. Her poor, simple farm home had been replaced by a finely decorated house of prostitution with a bathtub and a four-post bed. Her arms fell to her sides and she stood motionless, wondering what had become of the hopeful and defiant girl in the blue and green hanbok.

# 12

## Straight trees have crooked roots
-Japanese Proverb

"Admiral Yamamoto is lost," the general said, felling a room full of the most boisterous people in the Japanese Empire into deadly silence. "His flight was ambushed by enemy aircraft after leaving here this very morning. Our Imperial leader is one with the Buddha now." Only mumbled prayers and the muffled sounds of dashed hopes floated through the headquarters of the Rabaul outpost. Even Colonel Nibori Kanegawa sat quietly in the back row, contemplating the effects of such news. *A rare man of honor and trust,* he thought. One of the most powerful men in the Imperial military and the architect of the Pearl Harbor attack who sat in this very room only twelve hours earlier was gone. An Empire reeled.

"This cannot be coincidence," Rear Admiral Iseki scoffed. "Someone on this island is aiding the enemy."

"That much is certain," the calm Major General Fukuda said. "But who and how is the question we need to answer."

Rear Admiral Iseki refused to yield. "Yesterday they hit five supply ships off New Ireland as if they *knew* we would be there. They are targeting logistics areas and resupply shipping instead of tactical assets. They know where and when to attack us."

"Are you implying we have a spy, Admiral?" responded the general.

*The battle line is being drawn,* thought Kanegawa as he sat quietly. *Army versus Navy. Delightful.* Fifteen of the island's highest-ranking officers sat around the former governor's meeting

155

table, searching for someone to blame and taking none of it themselves. Equivocating was not the usual Japanese way, but this would surely mean the dishonor of someone.

"We all know the Australian Coastwatchers are situated throughout the Solomon's and are probably even right here on New Britain, but these attacks were far beyond even their capabilities." The Admiral said.

"Improbable," replied the general. "My soldiers scour the jungle daily and we monitor every known radio frequency."

"But we do not know theirs," replied the Admiral. "They change it more often than the hours. And whether we want to admit it or not, they have the ability to monitor our coded message traffic. We have something more than a spy, gentlemen. We have a high-ranking traitor with access to sensitive information."

"You are paranoid."

"We all should be. Their fighters ambushed ours at our weakest point, when they were too far away to send reinforcements."

"Perhaps your pilots are just not as capable as you would like to think, Admiral."

Admiral Iseki's face reddened, contrasting against his white service uniform. He sat forward, sweat staining his collar, preparing for a fight when a well-timed cough dispelled his rage.

*And just as it was getting interesting,* Kanegawa thought.

Clearing his throat was the commander of all forces on New Britain and New Ireland, Lieutenant General Imamura. He sat in a leather chair, raised a few inches off the ground to compensate for his short stature. Looking your subordinates in the eye was for captains. Looking down on them was the business of Imperial flag officers.

"There is a disparity between the number of planes we destroy and the number we lose." He paused and took a puff of his cigar, blowing the smoke over his shoulder and out the large wooden window propped open behind him.

"I agree with Rear Admiral Iseki on the unusual tactics we saw this week. Instead of attacking our fighters in the sky, they sought specific ships and targeted our supply chain which they know is stretched so far from home." He reached across his body to flick ashes into the tray nearest the naval contingent. "But this could be attributed to anything...undetected recon flights over the island, poor radio discipline, a spy, as the Admiral suggested. The rumors we've all heard about the Allies breaking our coded message traffic." He motioned toward the Navy side of the room, shrugged his shoulders, and pressed his lips together with a dubious expression. "Nothing is certain."

Sweat glistened on his mostly bald head and smoke wrapped around him like a contrail. "We cannot live in the past, dear gentlemen. If we are to learn anything from this it is to ask ourselves what this means to their overall strategy? Do they intend to continue attacks on our supply chain until we have nothing left to fight them with? That would take a very long time. Or are they merely testing us? Perhaps they want to know how we will react to such attacks so they can predict what our response would be to a frontal assault?"

He leaned back in his chair and looked to the ceiling. "Our mission is unchanged, but we must be more wary. It is very possible that information is being leaked to the enemy. It is also possible that they will invade New Britain, though I believe that day to be further away than our illustrious Kempeitai cavalryman would like us to think." He glanced at Kanegawa, who bowed his head ever so slightly in return. "If we have a traitor among us, he will find him. But we must also remember not to let him affect who we are. We are the greatest warriors on earth. A spy is but an insect that is whipped away with the flick of a horse's tail. We cannot allow these events to come between us. It is not our way to lay blame upon each other's doorstep." With his pearls of wisdom distributed, he stood and bowed, signaling the end of discussion.

"*Hai!*" The men all rose and sounded off, bowing to the general and preparing to leave. *Purposely vague so everyone hears what he wants to.* Kanegawa thought. *Only I know who the real insect is.*

\* \* \* \* \*

The next evening near dusk Seo-Sung strolled down to the compound and talked with the girl Chikaki taught English to. "He hasn't been around lately, but he should be soon. He owes me a lesson. Why?" the girl pried.

"Oh, I'd just like to learn some English myself." Seo-Sung looked over her shoulder and leaned in closer. "You know, in case these guys lose." She winked and pointed toward a departing soldier.

The girl chuckled. "That's why I want to learn it too." They both giggled. But Seo-Sung was no closer to learning English than she had been before, though she did learn his full name-- Chikaki Kahalehoe. She repeated it several times to herself after leaving. She had to find him, seduce him, and make it look genuine. *Cake.*

But it would have to be a chance encounter; probably on the street so he would think it was a situation of his own making. She walked toward the Kempeitai Headquarters, stopped a block short and waited. Four times a staff car drove down the road and four times she walked innocently toward the building. But none stopped. Doubt seeped in until the fifth car, kicking up a gritty cloud of dust, held what she wanted. It stopped in front of the headquarters and spat out the colonel. She counted to three, fixed her hair and started toward the car whose driver remained obediently in his seat with the door open for air. Only it wasn't the person she'd hoped to see.

"Denbe?"

# 13

## By the pricking of my thumbs.
## Something wicked this way comes
*-William Shakespeare*

Seo-Sung's window at premium house couldn't have been more perfectly designed for an informant whose mission was to watch and record the comings and goings of everything in Rabaul's Simpson Harbor. Only that wasn't her mission. Her mission was to gather intelligence on the Allied POWs, but if she could use her room to produce bonus material for Frank and Dave then that made her more valuable.

She surveyed the harbor and went over her notes, mumbling to herself. "Seven transports, four cargo lighters, nine guard boats, five submarines, five submarine chasers, two oilers, three special service ships, four troop ships that look to be loading in a hurry, two stores ships, two minesweepers, three light cruisers; though it looks as if the Naka is heading out to sea, five heavy cruisers, the same five wretched fishing dumps moving out and...," Seo-Sung stopped, noticing something out of place. "Three destroyers." She stared at them. "Well, you're new. What's your name big boy? Looks like you'll be in the company of the sailors from the Minazuki. They're a fine lot." She toyed with her hair, curling it around her fingers and holding it to her nose to inhale the fruity aroma of the islands embedded in her long strands. But it was time to go. Ten minutes later she was at the bottom of the stairs, striding into town while her guardian angels watched from the jungle.

"She heading off to fetch the goods, boyo?" Dave asked.

"Right on time," Frank replied watching her through shaky binoculars. His malaria tremors were worsening, so the sight of Seo-Sung walking toward the hospital filled him with a little hope. Even without the binoculars her white dress was a beacon in the afternoon sun that was easy to spot from OP Betty. They'd moved from Rita during the night to get a better angle on the city for the show that was about to begin.

"How long?"

"Seven minutes," Frank said looking at his shaking wristwatch.

"I don't hear anything."

"You will, wise guy."

"Not going to come up lemons today, are we?"

"Do we ever?"

Dave looked toward the sky and scoffed. "You Americans."


As Seo-Sung walked through the streets, a low rumble filled the air and grew steadily until it shook the very earth.

"Oh my God!" a girl walking near Seo-Sung exclaimed. "Eruption!" The panicked girl stared intently at Mount To and, finding nothing to support her fears, scanned the rest of the surrounding caldera. But there was no ash, no smoke, nothing. Still, the rumbling was there, steady and strong; shaking coconuts from trees and permeating the air with waves of a droning roar that grew ever louder.

"What the hell is that?" a soldier said, joined suddenly in the street by two other panic-stricken troops. A Zero raced overhead from Lakunai, followed by two more along with three Raiden "Jack" interceptors. Their fierce Mitsubishi engines rattled and growled as they streaked over the town, straining at the edges of their performance envelopes to get to altitude. Seo-Sung continued to walk calmly, but watched the harbor as boats raced in all directions.

*Just as he said they would*, she thought. Seo-Sung, now within striking distance of the hospital, saw a girl silently pointing to the sky and looked up. Silhouetted against the white, billowing clouds, ominous dark spots moved from southeast to northwest, slowly cruising directly at them. There were hundreds of them, swarming like a plague of locusts, the big slow ones in the center while smaller, faster ones raced about the edges. The lead bombers had already unleashed their cargo and were peeling away while neat lines of death fell from their still open bellies.

Seo-Sung picked up her pace and broke into a run. When the first wave struck, she was on the lower verandah of the main hospital. The concussion waves made her ribs feel like tiny twigs snapping under a swinging gorilla. The impact threw her against the wall and deafened her momentarily. She raised her arms to protect her head from falling debris. The bombs were close, probably just down the hill near the edge of town.

*Perfect.*

Watching from OP Betty as the first bombs found their marks, Frank began to hum. Waves of steel struck the center of town and the wharf, then shifted east, slamming into Lakunai airfield and the harbor. The air resonated with a chilling *WHUMP* every time one exploded. Some were spot on target, but many fell in the jungles and the water, shattering palm groves or killing schools of fish, their bodies quickly floating to the surface. Dave took mental notes of the impact damage while Frank's humming grew louder until he broke into song.

"Mine eyes have seen the glory of the coming of the Lord..."

Dave raised an eyebrow and turned his gaze upon Frank, who was singing at the top of his lungs through the fierce cacophony of chaos and pressure waves blasting the island.

"He is trampling out the vintage where the grapes of wrath are stored," he sang.

Dave's Tolai spy, a large, shirtless man with a brooding bone through his nose, peered at the silly white man who was behaving as though a demon had taken hold of him.

Frank's voice grew louder until he raised himself slowly from a prone position to a kneeling one. "He hath loosed the fateful lightning of his terrible swift sword." His heart leapt with pride; he was fully engrossed in watching the full power of his nation bearing down on this speck of jungle halfway around the world. He stood with outstretched arms as if he personally orchestrated the pandemonium and continued to trumpet the melody. "His truth is march-ing ooooooonnnnnn!!"

"Mate!" Dave finally shouted. "What the fuck, man? We're in enemy territory."

It would have been impossible for anyone to hear them over the thousands of bombs raining down in short order, but since the usual fate of Allied POWs was execution by beheading, he heeded the warning.

"Sorry," Frank said as he slowly lay back down. "Just caught up in the moment. Hell of a sight, eh? Home of the fucking brave. Glory, Glory Hallelujah." He continued humming.

"Him bad medicine fella," the tribesman said.

Dave nodded. "He'll crack a fruity on us before this is over. Mark my words."

At the plantation, the bunker was going through its first test by fire, and not a day too soon. Nearly fifty terrified women and ten plantation workers huddled in the steel, concrete and timber box, built specifically for this occasion. *WHUMP WHUMP WHUMP* went the bombs. Some of the women wept openly while others showed steadfast courage. They sat with their backs against the wall, feeling every impact as it shuddered through the earth. Asako sat calmly with Ki-Hwa at her side, a leather bound journal taken from Kanegawa's office on her lap. She'd decided that if the bunker were ever put to use, she wasn't going to sit in its cold walls and cry. She needed something to keep her mind occupied.

"We should stay here more often," Asako joked. "The air is more comfortable." A few electric lights flickered, but failed to provide enough illumination to allow everyone to see clearly. They hung from the ceiling, swaying and trembling with every bone-shattering explosion. Ki-Hwa took a nervous look around, opened her journal and through shaking hands tried to tame her fear.

*When we were children, we longed to read*
*Tales of journeys, conquests and greed;*
*Now we are grown, true greed lies*
*Too many places in thin disguise.*

*The day will come when bombs run out,*
*When men return to cities that burn*
*To find the fires of home gone out,*
*And we who are lost sail swiftly home,*
*To farm and village and ...*

*And what?* wondered Ki-Hwa. Her fingers clutching the pencil, she tried to bury her back into the wall, fear grappling with sorrow. From this distance, in darkness surrounded by terrified strangers, home seemed no more substantial than a dream.

But across the island, Seo-Sung waited, as far from a dream as a woman could be. Behind a thin curtain in examination room number four, by far her favorite of all the rooms in the 8th Naval Hospital, she sat quietly, listening as the staff panicked, their first time under fire. Just what she wanted. Her routine was rehearsed and executed with near flawless precision:  open the window, grab the bag, sneak across the hall, pick the medicine closet, hide behind the laundry cart that never moved, stuff her bag, make sure to get chloroform, return to bed, throw the bag out the window-all in two and a half minutes.

But the uncontrollable variable-- fear-- disrupted her carefully laid plan. The bag landed with a crash on the jungle floor just as the big orderly rounded the corner to take a blood sample. Scared by the assault, he strode through the halls with a greater sense of urgency. Japanese honor dictated showing no fear in the face of combat, so the hospital staff acted as if it were just another sunny day, but they moved with a quickness of foot she could not have predicted.

"Why were you up?" he asked looking at the window.

"Just getting some air," she said, sitting back on the bed and trying to control her breathing.

"Don't move," he commanded as he approached. He took out a syringe and drew blood with shaky hands, glancing toward the window once. "A moment," he said leaving the room as a series of *WHUMPS* shook the building. She went to the window. The underbrush was too thick to spot the bag below, but she knew it was there. *I should leave now,* she thought. *No. Be calm. Might as well get a shot.* She lied back, allowing herself to become comfortable.

"So, Miss Woo," a doctor said, startling her as he entered and peered at her steel chart. "Is this your name? Still feeling stomach cramps?"

"Yes, they really hurt this time, like it's my appendix." She knew enough to know the symptoms of appendicitis and how hard it was to accurately diagnose and lead him toward her conclusion.

"Well, I don't think it is appendicitis. I think its kleptomania."

"What is that?" she said, flashing a puzzled look.

"Kleptomania. A need to steal." The big orderly stepped in and produced her handbag, taken from the jungle floor only moments earlier, as two more orderlies entered with wrist and leg restraints. "Don't struggle, Miss," he started.

"Like Hell!" The agile Korean delivered a precision kick to the lower jaw of the orderly on her right, contorting his face, but not knocking him down. Rolling off the bed she dived for the window. But the biggest orderly was too fast and grabbed her around the waist, shoving her to the floor with his full weight on top of her.

*Carelessness is the fatal flaw to a thief,* she thought. *Damn careless!*

At the plantation all was silent; the bombing had ceased. Ki-Hwa took Asako's watch in her still-shaking hand. An hour and a half since they'd fled the upper world. Girls milled about, some leaving out of need and others out of curiosity, but most too afraid to move. Suddenly the journal was torn from her grasp, causing a line of pencil to gouge the length of a page like a stab wound.

"And what exactly is this you've been writing?" Victoria asked.

Rage overtook fear and the Korean farm girl quickly found her footing, standing eye-to-eye with the madam. "Personal notes," Ki-Hwa exclaimed, taking the book, closing it and turning her back to Victoria. "It's none of your business." She was cross, not normal, but after what they'd just survived, forgivable.

"Everything here is my business." Victoria paused and looked to the stairwell as the mass of girls found the courage to exit. "But you can have your little diary...for now." She moved away, trying to round up her assets.

The air outside was surprisingly clear. Had their part of the island really been spared after all that commotion? Ki-Hwa and Asako walked to the front of the main house in a world that was different from the one they'd left before entering the bunker. They moved to the ridge's edge where the ground fell away to the town, not realizing that all the other girls followed. One screamed. Below them Rabaul was ablaze. Five ships and a submarine had been sunk or were sinking, their bows standing on end in the harbor with men clinging to them like rats. Another ten or so were on fire. Sailors swam about looking for something to grab onto, panicking. More floated lifeless in crimson pools. Patrol boats scooped up the ones worth saving and left those who wouldn't see the end of the day. The devastation was horrid, even from this distance through clouds of smoke and dust. Several craters pocked the city where buildings had stood before the women retreated into the earth. A wharf was reduced to a pile of splintered logs. Lakunai airfield smoldered. Buildings burned. People died.

Ki-Hwa stared the long, piercing stare of someone who'd witnessed too much. She looked into the face of war and would never again see the world the way she had only seen it hours before. She scanned a land she once thought untamable and saw a toy that could be made or broken at the will of man. Her eyes landed on where premium house should be but they weren't visible through the thick smoke that was rising ever higher into the mid-morning air. "Seo-Sung!" she gasped, waking her legs and running to the road against common sense.

"Where are you going?" Asako yelled, raising her voice for the first time since Ki-Hwa had known her. But she was gone. In full flight down the little road toward North Coast Road with three girls following she jogged toward the inferno now making its way from building to building.

"Get back here!" Victoria yelled, but no one listened. She was a mere step from rage as she lost control of her harem, half of which wandered aimlessly about, all of which were in shock.

Asako had managed to conceal her fear well in the bunker but this was overwhelming. The incessant pounding of the bombs echoed in her head and she trembled. All she wanted to do was go back to her room and sleep for days. She turned to go as the other girls continued to watch with morbid curiosity. She stumbled into her room and collapsed on the bed, happy to be in the comfort of her familiar and undamaged surroundings, alone with her own breathing.

But an uneasy feeling came over her, as if some evil were present. She sensed movement and turned over and lay on her back, listening. There was a faint rustling and then, something dropped onto the wooden floor. *A piece of clothing? Are those boots?*

"Where's your friend from Chosen?" a man's voice said.


"Bring her," the big orderly demanded. A trio of staffers walked Seo-Sung, her wrists bound behind her back, down the hall and out the back door of the hospital that faced uphill toward the high ridge of the caldera. They forced her to her knees in front of Colonel Nibori Kanegawa and two of his Kempeitai, including one Seo-Sung immediately recognized as Sergeant Denbe Isogai.

"Leave us," the colonel demanded. The orderlies disappeared back into the hospital as smoke from the bombing raid wafted over the building and new casualties were brought into the front entrance. Kanegawa unsheathed his Katana and held it outstretched. Denbe took out his canteen and poured water across the immaculate blade in the Samurai tradition, his hands shaking and sweat dripping from underneath his hat.

"Our flag officers will be delighted to learn of the capture of the spy who brought down our beloved Admiral Yamamoto," Kanegawa said moving closer to Seo-Sung.

"I would take credit for that were it me, colonel," she said. "But you've got the wrong girl."

He moved close to her face, smiling as he stared into her eyes. "Steal drugs? Trade sex for cigarettes? I might believe that if you didn't establish a pattern. You targeted all the same people. Sergeant Isogai, Corporal Endo, my interpreter. You're gathering intelligence for someone." He backed away and held the blade to her throat. "And now you will tell me who."

From his vantage point in OP Betty a white dress outside the hospital caught Frank's eye through his binoculars. "Oh shit," he mumbled.

Asako sat up, alarmed by the sinister, shirtless man in her room. The bombing had shaken her. She wasn't sure whether to play the part of a good hostess or yell for Victoria.

"I really want to give it to your Chosen friend. Ever since I saw her on that ship."

"This is not her room and you should not be here, Mister...?"

"Sergeant!" he insisted. "I'm a fucking sergeant, you officer's whore!" He lunged, clenching her arms with an iron grip. He threw her back onto the bed and straddled her midsection with his whole body. She had no time to react and no strength to fight, mentally or physically. He slapped her across the face, following it up with a powerful blow to the cheek. She was dazed, unable to fight back.

"You think you know your place, eh? You think you belong to the high-and-mighty's, do you?" He hit her again. "I'll teach you your true place! You're a whore, no matter who you fuck!" He jammed a hand down into her crotch and ripped her underwear off so quickly the band cut into her waist. "You and that Senjin bitch both need to learn your place!"

Asako lost focus, too stunned to fight back. She yelped and tried to regain her senses, her arms instinctively covering her head. But the Sergeant gave her a hard right backhand across the face, almost knocking her out. She felt nauseated and when he penetrated her, it seared pain throughout her body that awakened her, but only for a second before he delivered a final, crushing blow.

Seo-Sung looked past the colonel's gleaming sword at Denbe. The man she once trusted stood motionless, looking at the ground, sweating.

"I want to know who is helping you," Kanegawa said. Who are you passing information to? And why do you care about our enemy prisoners?"

"I have no idea what you're talking about, sir. I stole drugs and got on my knees for smokes. You got me there. But spying? I am innocent, sir."

Kanegawa sighed. "Lies. I know you are not that simple. I am the head of the Kempeitai. I see everything."

"Too bad you don't feel everything as well," she said, staring at his crotch.

A lifelong Cavalry officer with a long history of swordsmanship, Kanegawa made a simple wrist movement to lift his blade before putting his shoulders into the strike and bringing it down on Seo-

Sung's neck. In less than a second he'd separated her head from her shoulders.

"Sir!" Denbe yelled as her body slumped to the ground and blood covered the white dress. His canteen hit the ground with a metallic thud. "You said you were only going to scare her! Why did you do that?" His breath came in fits.

Kanegawa turned slowly to gaze at him, the bloody blade held in both hands below his waist. "Did you grow attached to this girl on your voyage, Sergeant? Maybe you two were better friends than you led me to believe." Denbe stood quietly, regaining his wind, the look of terror still etched on his face. Kanegawa stood up straight and turned his entire body toward his driver, the blade now pointed at him. "Are you certain you are in command of your loyalties?"

Denbe stared a long moment at Kanegawa's splattered chest. A drop of Seo-Sung's blood clung to one of his silver chrysanthemum buttons before falling to the ground as her body had. He snapped into a rigid position of attention, relaxed his countenance and spoke clearly. "I am your loyal servant, sir," he said bowing before moving around the colonel to retrieve Seo-Sung's head.

Kanegawa, the bloody katana still in his hands, stared at the surrounding hills as Frank stared back at him from the jungle. "Yes...I see everything."

# 14

**Home is where one starts from.
As we grow older the world becomes stranger,
the pattern more complicated;
of dead and living**
*-T.S. Eliot*

Friends in wartime are black and white. They're either passersby who won't be alive long enough to get to know or they're blood brothers for life. There is no time for anything in between, especially for fighter pilots who have a life expectancy shorter than a sunset.

"You'll like Rabaul," Takeo said to his new wingman, Hideki. "It's bigger. More to do there." Two months of refitting the 251st on Truk Atoll was an eternity for someone who so desperately sought action. Finally they were heading back to Rabaul with a rebuilt Squadron and new pilots, even if one was becoming a friend against his better judgment. The pair walked to their planes, sweating in the Pacific sun. Hideki's jacket was clean and his scarf was still the bright white of a novice while Takeo's had long since grown discolored with the blood, honor, and pain of combat; the stains that never wash out. A man who cannot stop seeing the faces of the dead is not welcoming of the living and so Takeo had no desire to become acquainted with anybody new, especially since they were all doomed to spiral down over some pristine blue lagoon, coral outcropping or malaria-infested jungle. They were comets given just enough direction to meet a fiery end in the bowels of the sun. But it was hard to dislike Hideki.

"So I am told," Hideki replied. Hideki Tanaka was a consummate professional, the antithesis of Takeo's seat-of-your-pants recklessness. He studiously memorized altitude, formation, emergency procedures, radio signals, and everything else about the flight while Takeo let the wind guide him.

"Lakunai has the shortest runway, but it's not as dusty as the other four since it's mostly concrete. You won't have the same visibility problems there as at Tobera or Vanukanau. Just don't slide off the western edge or you'll be sushi for a crocodile."

"I hope you are not serious, sir," Hideki said as the pair mounted their steeds. Takeo hated leaving Rabaul. It might not have been the best assignment in the Empire, but at least he was flying against worthy opponents on the front lines of freedom. Sitting on the sidelines at Truk was miserable. His plane was already top of the line and didn't need refitting, so he was forced to train the new recruits, fresh from a hurried flight school on the mainland. He led hours upon hours of classroom tactics and boring, level flights until the new batch of younglings, all too eager to die for the cause.

The only upside of Truk was sake, several cases of which were stowed away under the seat of his Zero for the long but easy flight to New Britain. It was good flying in a full formation of brand new Type 52 Zeroes with the 251st. Even if his pessimism was morbid, he felt a part of something bigger than himself, looking out over his wingtips at more planes than he'd seen in months. Maybe they could win this war after all.

The Imperial garrison of New Britain welcomed the Squadron back with open arms and legs. The temporary absence of the 251st and the relocation of other units to Lae and Wewak had an unintended side effect. With a smaller officer pool to choose from, previously banned men gained access to the specials, but with the return of the 251st, there was a hope that some normalcy would return as well. That night Takeo made the walk from Lakunai to premium house with Hideki in tow, questioning the need for the trip the whole way.

"I don't think you serve the Emperor well when you drink, sir," Hideki said as Takeo took a long pull from his flask.

"You may be right. But I serve myself well enough. Are you afraid you're doomed to become like me?"

Hideki chuckled. "You are a likable person, a good pilot and a well-respected officer in the Squadron, sir."

"But?"

Hideki paused the uncomfortable pause that usually precedes an insult. "But you're also a drunk with a bad attitude and a lust for comfort women sir."

"Fair enough," Takeo stopped walking and hiccupped. "So let's examine this. Is it my fault? Is my weak mental state to blame or has the war been too difficult for me to cope with without spirits?"

"I haven't known you long enough to make that judgment, sir."

Takeo collected himself and took a deep breath. "Ah, but what is the cause of my moral demise? Perhaps I no longer care for the glory of the Empire. Am I no longer imbued with the spirit that spawned the Bushido code and crushed our society between fanaticism and nationalism?"

Hideki was taken aback. Either Takeo wasn't a drunk as he'd thought or he was a great orator under the influence. "You clear your head nicely when you want to."

"Answer." Hideki tried to resume walking, but Takeo took a few steps in front of him and turned the youngster, capturing a glimpse of moonlight off Hideki's brass insignia.

"Bushido demands national acceptance of military rule, especially in wartime," Hideki said. "This is the spirit of the

Samurai. It craves battle and condemns weakness. Its foundation-
- "

"Was forged in bravery, loyalty, allegiance to orders and a forbiddance of surrender. I know, young lad, I know. The question is, do I still embody this spirit or has the war beaten it out of me?"

Hideki reached into his jacket and pulled out a pack of cigarettes and matches. He stared at Takeo for a moment while lighting one, coughing slightly. "The Yamato race is noble, superior to all others. If we don't believe in our glory then how will the rank and file? I think you know that."

Takeo nodded. "Death in combat is more honorable than any other form. And you will get many chances to find out." He held up a finger, preventing Hideki from responding. "Gentlemen must drink before tackling such topics," he said, reaching for his flask and turning to continue the evening's march.

This was dangerous talk and Hideki scanned the road as they continued. They were halfway between the airfield and the outskirts of town. A dark road, but one that could easily hide a Kempeitai who would throw them into the brig for a lack of faith. Takeo didn't want to make a new friend, but Hideki had a passion for flying and Judo, driving the two together. During all their training flights in the skies over Truk, Hideki was the only student worth training. In the air, Takeo would seek out his tail number and go straight for him, winning the engagement most times, but having an increasingly difficult time as the months went on. He was getting better, smarter, and even inventive. He might survive this butchery so humiliating his friend in the sky was Takeo's way of saying he cared.

"Smart men learn from their mistakes," Takeo would tell him when they were alone. "But wise men learn from the mistakes of others." In truth, there was little the talented Hideki needed to be taught. Flying was a natural gift he was blessed with. Takeo saw great potential in him, except for one thing. "Why do you feel such dedication to the Emperor, Tanaka-san?" Takeo asked.

"Your life is as light as a feather, but your loyalty is as heavy as a mountain. I believe that to my core," he responded.

"And you don't think that is too reverent?"

Hideki sighed. "How can the man descended from God be too reverent?"

"And how do we know we are descended from God? Who's to say he is not actually perched atop a fiery throne of lies ruling over the damned? That would be us, in case it wasn't clear."

"The Emperor is the divine spirit of God!," Hideki said. "You just have to believe. Faith, sir." Hideki began walking again, the sound of shells crunching under his boot heels. "If we are not the chosen people, why do we continue to conquer the world? We wage a divine crusade to bring civilization and harmony to unsaved people. We are the righteous ones in the world of shame and misery. We must prevail."

Takeo had to be careful. His appetite for war and the glory of the Empire had waned, but saying so would likely earn him a one-way ticket to a back-room interrogation that some never return from. He didn't want to believe this youth was so anxious to die for the Emperor. He wanted to believe Hideki could still be reached. Somewhere down in that chastened soul was a rational human who knew the difference between wrong and right. But this was a question that would have to wait. "Yes," he said walking onward toward the lights and sounds of Namulan Hill. "We must."

Walking was something Lieutenant Takeo Hashimoto comfortable with. He'd been raised without the ability to afford transportation and had learned to rely on his God-given legs to get him anywhere, so the next day he walked out to the plantation alone after failing to find what he was looking for at premium house the night prior. He was in a fog, straining to think; struggling under a tortuous sun that forbade him from opening his eyes, and a crushing headache that made every movement a lesson in regret.

He pulled out his flask. "A hair of the dog that bites you," he'd once heard an American say over his radio before they pounced on the unsuspecting flight. They monitored the Allies' radios during dogfights and even had an English-speaking Imperial soldier yell propaganda at them on their own frequencies.

He approached the plantation stealthily from the backside. He was not supposed to be here, but logic is seldom found in the human heart and his judgment had long been shot down. He kept a wary eye on the main house, but kept his feet moving slowly forward, knowing he had to reach the sanctuary of her room before anyone noticed.

"Lieutenant," Colonel Kanegawa said, stepping onto the verandah from Ki-Hwa's room and adjusting his jacket. Takeo had nowhere to hide. "What is your business here?"

"Sir, I was just curious to see how the construction was going."

"The construction?" Kanegawa and Takeo both turned toward the bunker where the garden once was. It was mostly complete, but one side was still exposed.

"Yes sir. My uncle directed mines and I've always been fascinated by the digging, of course, but this looks to be something else."

"Yes, it is quite different." Kanegawa stepped closer and gazed at him, his garrison uniform pristine and his boots shined to a glaze. "As you can see this is not a mine, but a project for protection." He took a long pause, but made a slight hand gesture so Takeo would not speak. "Tell me, what mine did your uncle operate?"

"Sado," he blurted out. His answer wasn't too far from the truth. His uncle worked in mining. That much was true, but he was a common miner, not a mine director. His cousins were poor, possessing none of the opulence and stature of the refined colonel standing before him. Takeo was a drunk and acted foolishly, but he wasn't ignorant. He knew what this man could do to him and stood at attention in deference. "He directed the mine at Sado, sir."

"Sado is an island, is it not? A place of exile for unwanteds until gold was discovered during the Tokugawa Shogunate. So he lives in Ryotsu?"

Behind Kanegawa, Ki-Hwa stepped from her doorway, saw the exchange and retreated back into her room.

"No, sir, he lives in Aikawa with his family."

"I have heard it is a beautiful place to behold. And how do you intend to improve the effort out here? " he said, waving a hand toward the bunker behind him.

"Sir, I was told the buttresses were made of tree trunks and placed fifteen feet apart."

"Yes, but they are temporary. You should know we use tree trunks only until the concrete can cure."

"Yes sir, but as I said, my uncle's work was in mining."

"And?"

"You have built this on volcanic rock that's mainly composed of pumice and limestone. It's soft and porous and therefore expands greatly because of its ability to trap air. It also dissolves quickly under pressure from anything acidic, such as vinegar. It will expand more than you think and break those supports now that the structure is sealed and the temperature is rising inside. If the new buttresses aren't put into place immediately, the trunks will collapse before the concrete cures and the roof will sag, maybe even crack."

Kanegawa looked at him and furrowed his brow. "Good observation," he said, beginning another long pause and gesturing with his hand to keep Takeo from talking. "I will take this up with our Chief Engineer, Captain Mashita." Kanegawa placed both arms on the railing and leaned over it, looking intently at the roof of the bunker. The two said nothing for a very long moment until Kanegawa stood straight and looked away into the coconut groves where men stripped the trees of their fruits.

"You have done well here, lieutenant," he said slowly, maintaining his back to Takeo. "But venturing out here unannounced was foolish and I do not suffer fools well." He spun around. "Now leave, and do not let me catch you here again. Is that understood?" He stared directly into Takeo's eyes so there would be no misunderstanding.

*"Hai! Wakarimashita!"* he said with a bow and turned to go, feeling Kanegawa watching as he walked away. Passing down the verandah, all the bedroom doors were closed, so he couldn't even peer into hers.

*So close,* he thought.

## 15

### A woman always has her revenge ready
*-Moliere*

Rape. Nothing could be more wrong or unforgiving to Ki-Hwa than a man attacking and beating a woman. Seo-Sung's story of how Chitose had lost her tongue was the most awful thing she'd ever heard, but Asako's rape was horrifying to the very core. Asako, her friend and the only person who welcomed her at the plantation, had been suddenly and savagely attacked and after nursing her back to near-normal health, she determined it was her duty to do something about it. There was only one person who could help. "So will there be an investigation for Asako?" she asked.

Kanegawa didn't even look up at her as she dug her thumbs into his shoulders, rubbing until they started to cramp. He slumped forward in the leather chair as she worked his leathery skin through a cotton shirt damp with the day's sweat. "Et tu Brute?" he sighed. "Everyone wants something."

"I am merely curious."

"Then you should take it up with the police instead of me. I told Miss Foster that already." He gulped down his sake and slammed the cup down with a thud. "But she insists on using me as leverage."

"Do you know anything about the man who did it?"

"No. It's not my jurisdiction. My mission is the military, not a civilian crime. You know that." He turned almost all the way around to look her in the eye. She'd never seen him lose his temper and didn't want to tonight. But what had happened to Asako was like a hundred bee stings. She rubbed his shoulders again, forcing him to turn his back to her.

"Yes, I know what you do. Are the men in your camps military criminals then? Will they be executed?"

"Eventually, yes. Are you going to tell me that execution of prisoners is morally offensive too?"

"I just want to know more about you," she whispered.

He turned to the side to gaze at her from the corner of his eye. His voice softened. "My job and those men have nothing to do with who I am. If I am a better man it's because God has left their fate to me, just as he's left the fate of the world to the Emperor. Their lives depend on me and on my judgment of their worthiness, but how I treat them is no reflection on who I am as a person. Nor is your occupation a reflection on who you are."

"Isn't it? I am just as much a prisoner. Another body to manage until my usefulness is gone."

He leapt up from the chair and turned to face her. "I treat you like an Empress. I give you what you crave. Companionship."

"I crave more than an older brother." She moved out from behind the chair to challenge him, standing face to face with him in the middle of the room.

He lowered his voice and spoke sternly, leaning forward so his face was mere inches away. "You desire more? Romance perhaps? Sex with younger men? Love? These things are not necessary. Only friendship and understanding are." He paused, holding up a finger. "But forgiveness is essential."

"Should I forgive you then? Tell me what it is you seek forgiveness from? What sins do you expect me to grant you salvation for?"

"You give me the satisfaction of knowing men can start anew. You give me the privilege of a 'tabula rasa' and I give you the

181

attention you need. It's a symbiotic relationship, one that benefits us both. 'When the lion fawns upon the lamb, the lamb will never cease to follow him.'"

"Is this your way of fawning? Withholding gifts from me that your former mistress proudly flaunts?"

He glowered at her, but she stood firm.

"How did you know about Victoria?" he demanded.

"I only suspected, until now."

He smiled. "So much more cunning than I gave you credit for." Then the smile vanished. "My relationship with Victoria is in the past. And like everything else that's in the past, it is meant to be forgotten!" He walked to the washroom. "You are a presumptuous little girl who should not meddle where you don't belong!"

Pride filled Ki-Hwa. She had confronted the most fearsome man she'd ever known, either bravely or foolishly, and forced him to retreat and regroup. For that's what his trip to the washroom was: a chance to collect his thoughts. But she had also misjudged him. He was in this relationship solely for himself, just as Seo-Sung had warned her. She was a mere tool he was using to wipe his conscience clean, though she still hadn't a clue how. *That's what priests are for,* she thought.

She glanced at the mattresses, between which Bishamonten lay hidden next to his broken arm. She stood alone in the center of the room, arms crossed, unsure of what would happen next. He emerged, water dripping from his head and reached for his jacket. Ki-Hwa stood quietly waiting for him to say or do something. She wanted him to make the next move. In one sense, she was desperate for him to prove her wrong; to show her something inside that would make her believe he was still a good man and

she'd made the right choice to stay. In another, life would be easier if he were the devil himself.

"I expect you will be here when I return later," he said.

"Of course," she replied. Before she could say anything else, Kanegawa rolled the door open. "Sergeant!" he yelled. "What are you doing here?" She listened to him berate a soldier, caught where he shouldn't be for only a moment before closing the door on him. Inside her heart the death knell sounded for what little feeling she may have been forming; a naïve belief that maybe in this island of evil, she'd been handed over to the one good person who was simply misunderstood. That maybe his reputation was unearned, that maybe he was truly virtuous deep down inside. She wanted to find purity in him, not greed and blind malevolence like the rest of them. But this was wishful folly. She saw it now. Seo-Sung was smiling somewhere, the masterful judge of character that she was.

Ki-Hwa went to Asako's room, saw her sleeping peacefully on her bed, and thought of her brothers, sleeping on the floor in the same room of her small home. She thought of the farm, nestled between two unspoiled green, forested hills that the Japanese had not yet raped for their precious timber. It was the middle of October, so Chuseok would be over and they were probably preparing for *shinmai*, the first rice harvest of the season. Ki-Chul would be prodding his brothers incessantly, ridiculing their lack of strength as he harvested the lower paddy in less time than it took them to complete the smaller, upper ones. Tae-Hyun would stoically ignore him while Jung-Hwan raced to beat him, but fall short again. Father would be supervising quietly from the house with an occasional command as he prepared the oxen and carts for the trip. Oma would prepare food for them all as she pondered her only daughter's fate nearly a year after her disappearance.

After the harvest, white cranes would descend from their lofty perches to stalk the naked paddies in search of a frog, exposed with nowhere to hide once the rice was gone. Slowly and patiently the crane would dig into the mud, and then lifting one leg, spike its beak into the water with sniper-like accuracy to bring the hapless victim to the surface and swallow it with one gulp. Captain Inoue was probably also doing some hunting of his own; preying on other girls like her to harvest for the good of the Empire. She said a prayer for a poor crop for the captain, a prayer for a bountiful crop at home, and a final prayer that she would see it again soon.

* * * * *

The next morning Ki-Hwa was halfway up the stairs to the main door of premium house when the sight of Takeo caught her eye, sitting in the same chair as before and staring out over the city, an outdated newspaper on the table in front of him. He tipped his hat. She bowed in return and continued to the doorway until she realized something.

*He's here for Asako. Oh dear...he doesn't know.*

"*Konnichi wa,* Ki-Hwa-san," Takeo said politely, inclining his head and rising from the chair.

Ki-Hwa froze in the doorway and turned to him. "*Konnichi wa.* I wasn't aware you knew my name."

"Come to see someone?" he asked. She walked down the verandah and took a chair next to him. A breeze blew in and she shuddered.

"I don't care to sit idle this day."

"As I don't."

She looked back toward the door and then to him, noticing the aviator wings on his chest. "Have we lost many planes out there?"

"We? I am surprised to hear you say 'we' considering your situation."

*Asako must be telling him about me.* She looked at the ground, both embarrassed and insulted, and yet her breathing slowed. His affect was strangely calming. She found herself wanting to open up to him; to tell him everything that was happening and then hope he had a miracle in his pocket to loan her. Maybe a way out in his plane. She could see him as her knight in shining armor, or at least a sturdy shelter in the hurricane of deceit she lived in.

"It must be great to fly," she blurted out.

"It is a deadly business."

"Why do you do it then?"

"I don't like marching, I detest horses, and those tanks are always targets, so flying was the logical choice." He smiled, prompting Ki-Hwa to do the same. She sat back in the chair for a moment, looking out, away from the house and wondering what to say. "What about you?" he said. "Why do you do it?"

She sat up straight. "I am not in a position to do otherwise. I am a gift from one bastard to another."

"Kanegawa," Takeo said, pulling his pewter flask out of his jacket and offering it to her.

She stared at it and back at him, considering the offer, but shook her head. Ki-Hwa took a deep breath. "He is the cause of my dismay, but not an entirely bad man." She shifted sideways in the chair to face him and placed her arms between her knees.

He smirked and took a drink. "Then how did he get you here?"

"Isn't it a little early for that?" she motioned at the flask. He said nothing but nodded in agreement and put it away. "So tell me about flying."

"Not much to tell. You just go up, kill, and land."

She looked straight into his eyes, which didn't seem like the eyes of a killer, but she knew how poor she was at judging character. "And just how do you do what you do?"

He took a long breath, pursed his lips and looked away. A Mavis seaplane landed as gracefully as a seabird on the calm morning harbor. "It's not simple, or easy for that matter," he looked back at her. "I call it merciful anonymity."

"Merciful anonymity?"

"It means I don't think of the plane I'm shooting down as a person; just a hunk of flying metal. So I don't ever know who I'm sending to their death. I never have to look at them close up unless we nearly crash into each other. They stay anonymous, mercifully."

"You separate yourself from the responsibility."

"Not from responsibility, from death. I am responsible for killing them, and my soul will pay for that. But death itself I keep it at a distance. I choose not to look it in the eyes like the others."

The two sat in silence until a strong breeze separated the pages of the newspaper and scattered them around the verandah. Reaching to gather the ones that had blown her way she paused, reading a Fuku-chan cartoon. In it, a little boy was looking into a mirror and painting a moustache on his reflection with black ink.

"Is that how you look at us? Comfort women aren't real people either?" The words leapt from her mouth before she could stop them.

"You mean do I think of you the same way I think of an enemy plane? Just something to shoot down with no soul inside?"

Ki-Hwa nodded.

"No."

"You would be the first."

"Hmmmph," Takeo snorted. He brought one leg up to cross the other and picked at his boot. "You don't have a monopoly on bitterness," he said. She looked at him, his face an expression of sincerity that made her feel small. "Everyone has suffered in this war. Every person here has a sad story to tell and if you ask them they will speak of it until your ears bleed."

The clackity-clack of shoes at the front door echoed in the morning air. They both turned to the front door to see Chitose, dressed to leave.

"I have to go. It was a true pleasure to see you again, lieutenant. I apologize if I seemed..."

"The pleasure was all mine." He rose and the two bowed in farewell.

She began to walk away, but three steps later stopped and turned to him as he settled back into the rattan chair. She hesitated, bit her lip, and walked back. "I am so sorry to be the one to inform you of this, but..." *Be blunt. Just say it.* "Asako was attacked while you were on Truk. She was raped. And she's taken some time to recover. She's not the same. I know you two..."

"Raped?" Takeo stood, fists clenched. "By who?" He raised his voice.

"No one knows. I am truly sorry."

"Where is she?"

"In her room."

"You should have said so from the beginning, little girl!" He walked past her, brushing shoulder to shoulder. Takeo walked away from premium house without another word, and as much as her heart said to go after him, her head had a more pressing issue. Chitose was also walking rapidly away from the mansion in a different direction, uphill, until Ki-Hwa sprinted like the day she caught Jung-Hwan along the main dyke before he could get to dinner before her. She grabbed her by the shoulder and spun her around. "Where is Seo-Sung?"

Chitose kept climbing, not wanting any part of the conversation, but Ki-Hwa placed her body squarely in her path. "You introduced her to those men and now she's gone. What happened?"

Chitose held a finger up to her mouth and her eyes grew wide with fear. She turned a complete circle, gazing at the surrounding jungle.

"What are you...?" Again she held up a finger to silence Ki-Hwa. It was as if she was assessing the earth itself. She walked uphill, motioning her to follow. They walked slowly around behind the hill as if out for a stroll before doubling back, picking up the pace, climbing two ridges and disappearing into the dense foliage above the city. They stopped several times as Dave had always instructed to make sure they weren't being followed. Ki-Hwa protested and perspired, but Chitose lost hardly a breath and said nothing. It was maddening. Thirty minutes later they stood in front of the big Aussie on the trail.

"Oh my!" The Anglo stopped Ki-Hwa in her tracks. He wasn't like the white men who toiled over the bunker. He was healthy, larger than any man she'd ever been in the presence of with relatively clean clothes. Where his sleeves were rolled she could see the veins and muscles of his arms and just below the hem of his shorts were legs muscled from years of climbing mountains. He wore a belt with two canteens and his rifle was slung over his shoulder so as to not scare the new girl. But the rifle did the opposite, driving her fear home and forcing her to confront the truth. Seo-Sung had taken a side and gotten herself mixed up in the war. That something terrible had probably befallen her best friend. And that she had no idea what she was doing.

"What news from down below?" Dave asked, but only got a shrug for an answer. "I figured as much." He turned his attention to Ki-Hwa. "Is this her?" Chitose nodded. "Well, come along then."

A few hundred yards later they strolled into OP Rita where Frank waited, seated on a thick bed of palm fronds and clearly suffering from one of the many tropical diseases that so easily afflicted white men in this part of the world. "Hey toots," he said to Ki-Hwa in English. She said nothing as Chitose moved to Frank and sat next to him.

A few items of gear were strewn about, but in an orderly fashion that reminded Ki-Hwa of her own tidy room. Canteens, a machete, a pistol, ammunition, and a radio like the one she saw in Kanegawa's car once.

"Water?" Dave said grabbing a canteen from what Ki-Hw? suspected was his bunk area and holding it out. She wanted refuse, but the hike was exhausting and the scent of sulfur f one of the nearby volcanoes was strong. She took the can and waved her hand in front of her face. "Stench keeps the away," Frank said.

"Look, I'll get to it straight away," Dave said in Japanese. friend was very good. She gave us information that we r and now that she's disappeared. "

"Do you know where she is?" Ki-Hwa asked, dropp? canteen to her side and fighting back tears.

Dave paused, but Frank did not. "I wish we did. Do y^ow what could have happened to her?"

"No."

"Did she tell anyone else about us?"

"I don't know."

"What did she tell you?"

Ki-Hwa paused to go over the conversation in the grove again. That awful talk that she knew would end badly. And now had. "She wanted to get off the island. She wanted to know about the prisoners. The white ones. She wanted to know everything about them so you could take them away. With her. What has happened to her?" Ki-Hwa's chin quivered and her eyes filled with tears, but she refused to let them loose.

Dave looked at the ground, but Frank didn't flinch. "Why do you think she told you all that, doll face? About us. Our plans. Because of your friendship?"

"Because she knew I have a relationship with Colonel Kanegawa."

"And he is?"

"Please don't act as if you don't know." She paused to look at each of them and wipe her eyes. They were asking questions they knew the answers to but wanted to hear her say them. Why? "He's the head of the Kempeitai. Surely you know that."

"What did you tell her?"

"Everything I knew. She was my friend. Why? Where is she? And hat do you want from me? Why did you bring me up here?" She ⟩ked at Chitose as. What was the point of all this? There was thing they could do for Seo-Sung or Asako and they were the rities.

ve stepped toward her. "Look. She was good. I don't know but she was. She got us information we could not have ourselves and we think a lot of it came from you. So it w ⟩e dinkum if...it would be very generous if..."

vant you to help us now that she's gone," Frank took cont ⟩nce again.

"So ⟩ is gone? You know what happened and you're not telling n ⟩ and now you want me to help you?"

190

"Well, yes."

"And risk meeting the same fate as she did, whatever that is?"

"For all we know she's..." Dave started. But Frank cut him off.

"She's dead. You're right. You have a right to know. They caught her outside the hospital and killed her."

Ki-Hwa couldn't control the tears and let them flow. She sat on a felled tree near Frank and sobbed. But in less than a minute she regained control and looked at Frank. "Thank you for being honest with me." She sniffed and wiped her eyes. "Seo-Sung...you crazy girl." Ki-Hwa wanted to reminisce about her friend, but not here. Not now. "So why not her?" She motioned to Chitose.

"She has a job," Frank responded. "We have things for her to do already. Besides, no one has a relationship with the colonel the way you do. He knows where they are and when they move."

"Why escape? Won't they be treated well in Japan?"

"We don't leave people behind." Frank was adamant. "Before our Armies and Navies bomb this place back to the Stone Age we need to get them out. They can't become casualties."

Ki-Hwa looked at the ground, wanting to end the conversation. Her stomach felt like a butterfly in a jar but only one thing was certain: she would not make a decision this day. She turned to look at the city below through the trees. It was a magnificent view and in the distance she could make out the plantation and probably even pick out her own window with the binoculars if she wanted to. She imagined her comfortable room and wondered if she were dedicated enough to trade it in for a bed of palm fronds and insects like these men had. She stood to leave. "This is a difficult thing you ask. I need time."

Dave started to protest, but Frank held up a hand to stop him, shaking his head to let her go. "I understand," Frank conceded. "But listen up. This offer isn't on the table long. We have plans and if you want to be part of them then we need to know."

Ki-Hwa nodded. "I see." She bowed and motioned to Chitose that she was ready to leave. A thousand questions buzzed like gnats in her head, but she already knew the important points: they wanted her to squeeze Kanegawa for information, Seo-Sung was dead, and the Anglos were coming.

# 16

**Knowing others is intelligence; knowing yourself is true wisdom.
Mastering others is strength; mastering yourself is true power.**
*-Lao-Tzu*

*October.* Ki-Hwa gazed into the coconut groves one morning, watching the trees bend by strong gusts of wind. "There should be brown leaves on the ground." At home, her parents and brothers would be thanking the Gods for the year's harvest and praying for peace. It was this time last year when she was taken. The low roar of engines filling the air destroyed her reminiscence.

"Already?" The siren's call came earlier than usual, sending everyone scurrying like insects before the noon meal and planes frantically aching for one more horsepower to take the fight to the invaders. Ki-Hwa hurried through a sweltering day and pushed in past the others to take up her spot in the bunker. She waited for the impacts and the ferocious torrent of sound and pressure that always followed. Every shock, every painful pounding in the ears, every impact meant someone not afforded the sanctuary of shelter was dead or maimed.

"Merciful anonymity." She repeated Takeo's catchphrase and thought of those not as fortunate as herself. She prayed for the safety of everyone she knew. Ki-Hwa gazed at the crowd in the dark cavern, made up almost entirely of Japanese women now and Abongo, his frizzy hair and white smile unmistakable even in the low light.

*The bombs discriminate less than they do. How ironic.*

The earth heaved suddenly beneath her and the walls of the bunker collapsed inward. A close one followed by two more. Ki-Hwa felt a rising panic. But as quickly as the bombing run had started, it stopped, and the sound of explosions retreated back toward the city.

"One bomber, either off course or dropping early," Asako said. "It was just one."

Ki-Hwa closed her eyes and tried to relax, her journal falling to the floor. She retrieved it and resumed writing. Seeking inspiration, she looked at Asako and thought of the young lieutenant who pined for her. Their relationship was strange. It couldn't be described as a classic affair by any stretch. In fact, it couldn't be described at all since Ki-Hwa had never so much as heard the two talk. He was up there now among his comrades, fighting to keep her and everyone on the island safe from the enemy sky raiders. His life but a fleeting afterthought to an enemy pilot. They were so young. Just as in every war. She turned to a fresh page.

*Underground, brave hearts*
*Await news of lovers and friends*
*Who soar among eagles,*
*Rising beyond the clouds*
*To beg the favor of the gods.*

*Descending to earth,*
*Seventeen-year locusts*
*Come to rest awhile*
*And take flight once more.*

Slipping her pencil between the pages, she closed the journal. The bombing stopped and like fragile creatures crawling out of a

burrow, the women surfaced. Once again, Rabaul was devastated. It seemed nothing could stop the onslaught of the Anglos. Ki-Hwa surveyed the town from the cliffs. What she'd thought impossible had become terrifyingly real; a waking nightmare. Earlier bombings rendered the town immobile for a few days, but this was much greater devastation. Half the city looked reduced to rubble and half a dozen ships were ablaze in the harbor. The air was acrid with black smoke that covered the town like a brooding storm, and a wind blowing in off the bay fueled the fires still burning. Flotsam was scattered over the surface of the sea, and bodies floated quietly alongside broken, burning shards of wood that was once a wharf.

"So much fire this time," she gasped as Asako stood quietly beside her. "Why is there so much fire?" And then she saw them. Several white parachutes hung in trees on the slopes surrounding the town, silhouetted against the thick, green jungle.

"Parafrags," Asako said. They were bombs that slowly drifted, suspended under parachutes, onto their intended targets, detonating upon impact. Occasionally the parachutes got caught in trees or wouldn't detonate because the force of the impact wasn't enough to set them off. Parafrags had claimed the lives of many unsuspecting natives walking through the jungle and children who were too curious for their own good. She moved to the porch to get a higher view when she noticed that nearly every special had their backs turned to her.

*They're distracted.* She looked around quickly, confirming her suspicion. The verandah was empty. Her heart beat faster. The need to return the stolen object filled her mind. *But if I'm caught in the main house and the arm still isn't fixed...*

She must act. She took one last look at the crowd whose attention was squarely on the burning city. Ki-Hwa slipped her shoes off and sprinted to her room. She plunged a hand between the mattresses and pulled Bishamonten out, along with his severed arm.

Exiting her room and turning toward the main house, she caught a glimpse of something moving off the verandah in between the buildings. *A man?* She paused to look into the groves, but saw nothing. She stuffed Bishamonten into the belt of the cotton *yukata* that she still wore. Her legs carried her quickly down the length of the wooden porch to the front of the house. She surveyed the crowd, but saw nothing that would change her mind. As she backed toward the door, her heart pounded.

"Is that the postal depot?" One girl screamed as the flames jumped to a new building. Ki-Hwa stood in front of the door, reached behind her, grabbed the knob and turned. But the door opened on its own.

"Chiyo!" Ki-Hwa said, turning to see the young girl. "I'm sorry. You startled me. I was just leaning against the door." But Chiyo didn't care. She exited the house and walked past her to watch with the others as the city burned.

*She's too close. She'll see me,* Ki-Hwa thought as she stared at Chiyo's back just fifteen feet away. But Bishamonten disagreed. "You want rid of me too badly! Don't pass up the chance!" he screamed from inside her robe. She dashed through the door and ran back to Victoria's room at the rear of the house. But grabbing the doorknob to turn it, Ki-Hwa was stopped in her tracks by the one thing she had not considered.

"Locked!" she said aloud. She turned the handle repeatedly, but the door wouldn't budge. *Why is it locked?* Her eyes darted, looking for anything that might help. A vanity stood in the hall with a hairbrush, an ornament, a spoon with a tea stain, nothing. Running back down the hallway to the front door, she stopped. Footsteps clearly echoed up the stairs to the verandah.

*Hide!* she thought. She'd only been in the main house once, but knew exactly where to go. Victoria's favorite chair was a high-back wicker model with a wide headrest that fanned out like the tail feathers of a massive peacock. She darted behind it and made herself as small as possible, looking through the wicker to the front door.

*Whoever you are, just go away!* She prayed as her stomach turned with anxiety. A shadowed figure graced the glass in the front door, too blurry to make out, and a hand started to turn the brass doorknob.

"Masami, come here," Chiyo yelled.

Masami stood at the front door with her hand on the knob. "I do not wish to see any more. I am going inside," she said, not caring to look at whatever the naïve Chiyo from Hokkaido thought was interesting. Ki-Hwa stared at her outline through the frilly, white valance as she turned the knob.

*Just drop the letter opener right here so at least you're not caught with it.*

"Do not be rude, Masami. Go see what she wants to show you," a soft voice suddenly commanded.

*Asako!* Ki-Hwa craned her neck to see more of the front door. A female silhouette stood alone in the entrance as the light pitter-patter of Masami's footsteps faded. Ki-Hwa scampered to the door. Asako moved to the end of the verandah toward Chiyo and Masami, pointing toward the city and making them look away.

Ki-Hwa cracked the door open and made herself as thin as a reed to slip out and softly close the door behind her, keeping an eye on the sea of women staring at the city, their backs still to the house. *Luck of the Gods,* she thought as a bruised Asako, out of bed for the first time today, turned to look at her and smile.

# 17

**The sin they do by two and two,**
**they must pay for one by one**
*-Rudyard Kipling*

Colonel Kubota stood on the verandah of the Governor's mansion, lit a cigar and looked up. Warm rain began to fall, resonating off the corrugated tin roof. "It seems there's always something falling from the sky here," the Army Chief of Staff said with a laugh. Another meeting of the Imperial brass had just ended with more questions than answers. On the verandah the conversation broke into numerous parts, with two to three of the power clique taking positions in small circles for their own strategizing. Colonel Kanegawa leaned over the railing to admire the view of the town below. Next to him, General Fukuda spoke to the Island's Chief Engineer, Colonel Takemura.

"I believe it's time to dig fortifications into the hillsides," he said quietly. "The Allies are having too much impact on daily operations. We must protect ourselves from this incessant bombing until we can regain the offensive. Are you ready to execute the plan we discussed?"

"Yes, sir," the engineer said.

"How long will it take to build the first command and control bunker?"

Kanegawa interrupted. "I can provide some of the workforce. Captain Mashita and my men built two bunkers in forty days that have not buckled a bit despite several close calls." He beamed with confidence.

"Yes, I remember," the Chief Engineer said. "We have machines for this, colonel. Using sick men is unadvisable."

"What else shall they do? Many of them are fit to work."

"But not as efficiently as our engineers."

"Yes, of course." Kanegawa replied curtly. "And how many of those remarkable machines are there now?"

The Chief Engineer paused. "We lost a few backhoes and some excavating equipment in the last two attacks, but we're able to continue with the mission."

General Fukuda interrupted, " We may want to consider the Kempeitai's offer. Too much manpower is better than not enough." He turned to Kanegawa. "I assume, colonel, you will also provide the guards for these men as they work? That way Colonel Takemura's men won't have to worry about caring for them."

"But of course, sir."

"Very well, then. I want the command and control tunnels dug first, followed by the hospital and the ammunition stores. We need to get those underground immediately. Let me know when you're ready to begin and provide me with daily updates." He turned to Kanegawa. "Keep me informed."

Both men bowed. *"Hai! Wakarimashita."* responded Kanegawa. Takemura was silent and shot Kanegawa a look that would make a falcon fall from the sky. "I will be in touch." He walked down the stairs and disappeared into one of the many waiting staff cars.

Kanegawa started to do the same when a voice stopped him. "So what do you think, colonel?"

*The one person I was hoping to avoid.*

The unmistakable voice of the Police Chief Sato came from behind him. Kanegawa rolled his eyes skyward and turned slowly. "About what, chief?"

"About all this talk of spies," Sato said. "You know, I think the general is onto something. Maybe we have someone working on the inside, helping the enemy target all the right places that hurt us the most."

"You subscribe to his theory. Good. He is a wise man. Now we only have to find this traitor." Kanegawa smiled.

"Yes, but who could he be? Or is our spy even a man? Maybe a woman?"

Kanegawa pursed his lips and held a finger to them. "That is very possible. Perhaps you should pursue that theory." He tried to leave only to find his way blocked by the larger policeman.

"Well, where should I start? How many women on the island have access to vital information and the means to broadcast it?" Sato crossed his arms and brought a hand to his mouth, mocking Kanegawa's own pose of deep thought. "Victoria Foster is really the only woman who fits that description. Where do you think her loyalties lie, colonel?"

Kanegawa's smile faded. "Yes, well, if it is a female you're after, there is the harbor master's wife and the manager of the New Guinea club. They both have access to higher-ranking individuals. There are also at least a hundred women of non-Japanese descent who would jump at an opportunity to sabotage the Empire. You just have to find out who among these fine gentlemen is talking in his sleep." He motioned toward the officers on the porch.

"Maybe that's far-fetched." Sato looked down and held a finger to his mouth. "But you know what else the general said that made me think?"

"I dare to imagine," Kanegawa said, inspecting his boots.

"He said if there is a mole, he'd be someone patient. You're a patient man, are you not?"

The colonel put his boot back on the ground, raised his head slowly, making direct eye contact with the chief and took a step closer. "Your suspicions of me are unwarranted, as is your disapproval. You coddle the poor Chinese refugees of this island and seek to discover why some distasteful things happened to them while judging me with no cause or basis. I have done nothing you suspect, and have neither the time nor the inclination to justify my actions to you or the Inspector General, with whom I know you've had parlay. You search in vain to find a path for me to the executioner's table, chief. We'd all be better served if you spent half as much energy on more worthy causes."

Chief Sato did not back down an inch. "You were the cause of that barbarity. It was you and we both know it whether a tribunal finds you guilty or not, you sick bastard!" Sato roared mere inches from his face, but then calmed himself and lowered his voice. It was the Japanese way. "Bigotry wrapped in apathy is no excuse, colonel. Maintaining discipline among your troops was part of your job. Complacency or dereliction of duty; whatever you want to call it, your men slaughtered them and you're guilty."

Kanegawa smiled. He was never sure why the Chief, a man he had not met until New Britain, had taken the destruction and rape of Rabaul's Chinatown district so personally--until this very moment. In his rage he'd misstepped. Sato was part Chinese. He could hear it. His accent came through when his emotions ran high, a dead giveaway. Ever so faint, but certainly there. Sato had become very keen at hiding his Chinese connection, but in a split second he betrayed himself-- and to the one man who would make him pay for it.

"You know nothing," Kanegawa said quietly. "You have never experienced the heat of battle or the temperament of the Chinese people. You sit on the side and criticize while the real men fight."

The two stared at each other for several long moments until Sato finally nodded, smiled, pulled back and walked away as Kanegawa watched. But the confrontation had not gone unnoticed.

"Why don't we send the comfort women home?" suggested Colonel Imamura, the island's commissariat and younger brother of the Commanding General. "Fewer mouths to feed that way. We can send them to Japan with some of our personal effects."

*Dear God, the little idiot is right.* Kanegawa thought. They were non-combatants; civilians on the battlefield with no reason to be there except to earn a profit, though only Victoria made any money. Sooner or later, a series of bombs would get lucky and hit the food stores, the fishery warehouse, or the gardens where everything was grown. Simpson Harbor had already ceased to yield its precious bounty and there were fewer boats to catch them anyway. And rice, the main staple of the Japanese diet, was also in short supply. The island's logistics were getting tougher as supplies dwindled in the face of mounting attacks.

Moving hundreds of comfort women off the island could help their situation, but it could also lead to violence toward the local population and rapes of local women. The comfort station system was designed to control the urges and emotions of the soldiers and limit the spread of venereal disease, with only mediocre results in both departments. Removing it could result in the very thing it was designed to prevent.

*But strategically, it makes perfectly good sense,* Kanegawa thought.

"Very well," General Fukuda said. This doesn't require General Imamura's decision. I'll make it now." Junior officers scribbled in their notepads. "We'll offer the women of Japanese descent a choice—they can return home or stay at their own risk. We will not be responsible for their safety if they choose to stay. Anyone owned by a Japanese gentleman who wants to move back to the homeland will go if both parties agree."

"And the others, sir?" Kanegawa asked.

"It is not our responsibility to protect non-Japanese citizens and they are not the priority when supplies get low. They will stay but will have to fend for themselves." He smiled. "After all, we can't go without all of our...comforts." The officers laughed, but only because they were required to feign enthusiasm at the whims of the general. "Of course we need Miss Foster's input on this. See what she thinks." He motioned to one of his aides.

"Why not rid ourselves of the POWs as well?" Kanegawa interjected. "We sent so many Australian POWs to the homeland back in June last year to put them on display and scare the Allies. We can load them onto the Subuk Maru or Tamahoko Maru, both anchored in harbor, and send away more."

The general looked surprised. "As I seem to remember, the Montevideo Maru never made it to Japan, colonel. A submarine sank it."

"Fewer mouths to feed still."

"It also means one less cargo ship and crew that we can ill afford to lose."

"Sir, I've just pledged a workforce to Colonel Takemura, but that will only employ the ones who are physically able to work, which may number around sixty percent. The other forty percent can be sent to Japan as trophies of war. We have several high-ranking officers here who know much about Allied operations, not to mention the enormous honor the general would receive for such a generous gift to the Emperor."

The general quickly glanced at the faces of the group and saw no disagreement.

Kanegawa continued. "This fortress has not been engaged fully in battle yet, so what better way to show our worthiness to the Emperor? Have we any other trophies of war to show him? Inflated and exaggerated reports of enemy aircraft shot down?"

"This move would not have personal reasons, would it colonel?" inquired General Fukuda.

"I could never do anything that wasn't for the good of the Empire, sir."

General Fukuda nodded in agreement as the air raid sirens came to life and sang their tired song. "Make it so then."

# 18

## Come not between the dragon and her wrath
### -William Shakespeare

"What a wondrous thing it must be to fly when no one is trying to kill you," Ki-Hwa said taking up her spot in the bunker next to Asako.

"This will mean foraging in the morning," Asako said, placing her weary head against the Korean girl's shoulder. Ki-Hwa winced not because she didn't like Asako sleeping on her; she did; but because Asako didn't know the meaning of foraging. She would walk into town and poke around a fallen house or look under a timber in the road just to do her part for the Empire, but she was dainty. She was not one to get dirt under her fingernails or eat a half destroyed mango so it did not spoil on the ground and go to waste. "Do they know even it is nighttime?" she whispered.

"I was just wondering that. Maybe I will make a note of it in my..." Ki-Hwa felt the ground around her. "Where is it?"

"Are you asking me?" Asako replied.

Even if the light in the bunker was so poor at night, her journal was a comfort item and not something she dared let the unknown forces of chance or a stray bomb take away. The first series fell in rapid succession, loosening some dirt from the walls, but they were not close. Not enough to dissuade her. "I'll be back."

"No," Asako protested. But she rushed out the main hatchway, passing Victoria who only gazed at her, speechless, and pushed her way past several other dumbfounded women. She ran as quickly as on the day she sprinted to retrieve Bishamonten. She opened her door and looked around the room that was lit only by the reflections of anti-aircraft searchlights. There—on the nightstand. Feeling its familiar, worn leather cover brought Ki-Hwa relief. She turned to leave when her door suddenly slid closed with a thud. Blocking it was a brooding figure wearing nothing but a scowl and mechanic's overalls, the red cotton rank of a sergeant visible on the collar.

"Hello," he said as he moved slowly toward her. Outside, three powerful explosions rocked the ground.

"I don't take customers," she said standing perfectly still, the journal covering her chest.

"You will now."

"Who are you?" Ki-Hwa stopped. The Sergeant was vaguely familiar, but she couldn't place him in the dim light.

"Don't you know?" he hissed. "I came here for you, senjin. Just as I came here before but had to make do with your neighbor."

*Oh, dear God. He raped Asako!*

He smiled, his excitement feeding on the terror he saw in her eyes. She sidestepped his first lunge, but he came again, grasping her arms, pinning her to the bed with almost no effort. "I came back here looking for you but your bastard colonel caught me!" He slapped her across the face and shouted. She yelped as he threw his entire weight on her, pinning her arms against his body as she clutched the journal tightly.

A hand ripped her panties off in one quick, painful jerk. Almost instantly, she felt his manhood flopping around between her legs trying to find its way in. She twisted, drawing up her knees and clenching them together as tightly as possible. Frustrated, he raised himself up to deliver another slap. As he lifted his arm to strike, she thrust her arms up and jammed a corner of the journal directly into his eye.

"Ahhh, bitch!" he yelled, releasing his grip on her crotch to cover the unexpected wound. He was momentarily off balance. She pushed him to one side and rolled quickly away to the other. But the sergeant grabbed wildly and snatched a handful of her shirt as they both fell off the bed.

An explosion followed by another flooded the room with light and an overwhelming pressure in her ears. They were on the floor, scrambling like fish trying to get off a hook. Ki-Hwa found her feet underneath her, but he seized the loose blouse, yanking her to her knees. He maintained a firm grip on her shirt and fought to bring her down to his level, struggling to see out of one eye. They grappled for what seemed like hours, all the while cursing and moaning, neither one able to get an edge. She slapped at him and pounded with her fists, determined not to be a victim. But staying on the defense was no way to prevent that. It was time to strike.

With her back to him, Ki-Hwa quickly turned over and drove the heel of her hand directly into his mouth with all the force she could muster. His lip split open and gritting her teeth, she recoiled for another strike. Another massive explosion, followed by a third left Ki-Hwa deaf to the sound of her own voice as she hit him again, once in the nose and once again in the mouth. His teeth turned red. Screaming soundlessly, she drove her hands into his face one after the other. The thought of coming all this way to be torn open by a rapist terrified her, and the sight of blood enraged her. The combination made her strong.

She struck him again and again, driving her aching hands into his face. Six solid blows to the same side of his jaw gave her inner strength. But the seventh tempted fate. He anticipated the blow, caught it before it made contact, secured her wrist in his grip and turned her onto her back with catlike nimbleness.

*WHUMP WHUMP WHUMP WHUMP* went a close series.

One powerful hand suddenly clenched her throat as the other reached back into her crotch again. She saw his mouth making words and the sound came to her as though she were under water.

"I will kill you when this is over!"

Between her thighs, Ki-Hwa felt him trying to penetrate her again and began to panic as blood from his mouth dripped onto her face and mixed with her sweat. He rose up and crashed his fist hard into her temple. Her arms went weak and her head swam.

A massive explosion lifted the ground under her body and collapsed it again, and as the building shuddered, fragments of plaster fell from above. She was dazed, unable to focus and beginning to feel defeated. He laughed like a demon thrilled at the sight of a dying human and threw himself back on top of her, ramming against her with all his weight, trying to get inside.

Ki-Hwa slapped at his head and wriggled her way backward, but it did no good. She pulled his hair and tried to bite his face, but couldn't sink her teeth in. The bombs were close and loud. No one would hear her scream. She would be like Asako. Found after the fact, whimpering in her own blood. He pushed her legs apart.

*WHUMP WHUMP WHUMP.*

She was tiring, flailing her arms in every direction trying to find something—anything—that could be used as a weapon when suddenly, there was something...her hand brushed against a hard, slender object—metallic—jutting slightly out from between the mattresses. Something pointy. Gripping the hilt with all her strength, she brought Bishamonten's steel blade arcing through the air and rammed it into the Sergeant's back just below the neck.

He screamed as bombs struck the earth nearby. Rising up off her he reached for the weapon still stuck in his body with both hands, but she wasn't about to let him have it. She sat up, grabbed the hilt and snatched before he could, the blade tearing muscle as it exited. His screams of pain fueled her determination. She stabbed at him again, but he arched and raised his torso, making it impossible to drive the blade in with any force. She brought the weapon around to his front, stabbing him directly in the chest with both hands wrapped around Bishamonten. He tried to block the blow with his arms, but Ki-Hwa's strike was surgical, passing directly between them.

He fell back, scrambling to get away like a wounded animal. He pushed an arm forward to keep her away. Blood began oozing through his overalls, but she had no intention of showing any mercy. She was on him as quick as a mongoose on a snake.

"Back!" he yelled with one arm outstretched.

"NO!" she screamed, lunging at him. Her rage set free, she would not be stayed. She straddled him and stabbed and stabbed and stabbed, panting hard and driving the blade home time after time. She screamed until she was hoarse, plunging the knife in and out of his chest. He was going to hell this night if she had any say in the matter.

*WHUMP, CRACK* went a close pair that shook the earth and the house around her as brilliant, flickering light illuminated the chaotic scene like massive fireflies whose bellies light up and disappeared before you can get a hand on them. Missing its target, the blade momentarily stuck into a floorboard. The stained glass lamps swayed and flickered. Hair flew in her face, wet with the blood now spurting out of him.

But still she did not stop. She screamed and stabbed the rapist Sergeant long after he had stopped defending himself, not wanting it to end. Everyone who had hurt her; Captain Inoue, Colonel Kanegawa, Victoria, the racist comfort girls who called her senjin, and even Seo-Sung for making her trust a friend and then leaving her life without a trace: she paid them all back with his sacrifice.

Only exhaustion stopped her. She paused with both hands clenching the weapon high in the air, poised for another strike, breathing heavily. She looked at him, certain he was not getting up, and let her arms dangle to her sides. Her head and body slumped forward. She tried to clear the hair from her face but it was tangled, matted, and soaked in blood. The Sergeant's eyes were slightly open and fixed on nothing while his jaw hung as if startled. She convulsed, trying not to heave and slowly looking around at the blood covering her hands, arms, and shirt. It was everywhere, as if the walls and floor themselves bled from the fight. The small rug in the center of the room turned scarlet as it soaked up his life. Still straddling him, she slowly brought her hand forward and inspected her weapon. She stared for a long interval, reflecting on how it got there. She gripped the exquisitely carved ivory handle so tightly that it left an impression on her palm and was painful to release.

A pair of explosions sounded some distance away, faintly rattling the windows. The bombs were getting more distant and less frequent. In an hour everyone would leave the bunker and come back upstairs.

*Oh no. I have to hide him!* She jumped off the body and looked for something that would tell her what to do. She searched frantically around this room that she lived in every day and found nothing. It wouldn't matter that he was in an area that was off-limits to him; that the colonel had directly ordered him not to come out to the plantation, or that he had raped another girl. It wouldn't matter that he had tried to rape her. None of that meant anything. All that would matter was their positions; he, an Imperial Japanese Army sergeant, and she a Korean comfort woman. The playing field was not level and justice would not favor her. She was sure as dead if anyone found this mess. She mustered all her strength and rolled the small rug around the limp body.

*WHUMP WHUMP*

She stood at the edge of her small window trying to find a way to get the heavy body and rug over the sill. She had a strong back, but not that strong. She dragged the roll back to her bed that stood a good six inches off the ground with a bed skirt covering the bottom. Ki-Hwa stuffed the rug underneath, pushing against it with her feet. Now she just had to worry about the blood that was everywhere. Her room looked as if a child had run around wildly throwing red paint. There were splatter streaks all the way up her screen and dresser that seemed impossible to clean.

*WHUMP*

*Still time. I have to try.* A full hour later Ki-Hwa had managed to restore the appearance of the floor, dresser, walls, bed and chair; she had even managed to reclaims her own appearance. It took another half hour and buckets of vinegar and water to clean it all again as the sound of exploding bombs faded. She got on her hands and knees and scrubbed for her life at the stains that littered the room like stars with brushes and towels until she was satisfied they were no longer visible. But her scrubbing left an odor and removed the top layer of varnish on the dresser, leaving uneven streaks that someone surely would notice. She broke a bottle of vinegar on the dresser and let it spill all over the floor on purpose. "A bomb must have knocked it off," she rehearsed. Now she needed something more; an alibi. Victoria would ask why she had not come back.

"Where have you been?" Asako entered the room, looking frightened.

"I came up here for my journal and heard a close one and decided to hide in the groves."

"Great goodness, whatever for?"

"Yes, tell us what you think you're doing?" Victoria charged into the room, her voice raised in anger.

"I just thought the trees would be safer with some of the bombs hitting so close." She tried to appear shell shocked so they would go away.

"That bunker was constructed for a reason. To keep us well protected! You never leave the bunker! Do you understand?" Victoria shouted just inches from her face.

"Yes, ma'am. I was confused and didn't know where to go." *Please don't notice the rug is gone,* she thought.

"Don't ever do it again. You don't think. Just do as I say!" Victoria yelled at her, spitting in the process.

Ki-Hwa flinched, feeling the Sergeant's blood as it squirted on her face again. "Yes, ma'am," she replied politely and bowed.

"You look very tidy. What have you been doing washing up and doing your hair—in the middle of a raid?"

"I felt dirty after hiding in the brush. I wanted to clean up."

"You're sweating."

"It's the heat...and you're frightening me."

Behind Victoria, on the other side of the bed, Asako peered curiously down at her feet. Victoria looked back at her. She crossed to the shared washroom and into her own room.

"Well if you'd listen to me I wouldn't have to shout." She lowered her voice.

"Yes, ma'am." Ki-Hwa bowed, trying to end the conversation.

Finally Victoria turned and walked to the door, but stopped short for a parting shot. "And clean that broken bottle up. You're not a regular."

Whether it's on a truck rambling through the night, a ship on an ocean, or a small room with a dead sergeant under the bed while ruthless military and civilian police searched for a murderer, waiting is agony. Standing on the precipice of the unknown and staring into its blackened abyss can destroy the most determined soul. All it takes is a whiff of the odor of death and a prying nose to push Ki-Hwa into the pit, so she kept the window open and sprayed perfume every hour. She even clipped a bundle of Victoria's flowers and placed them in a vase on her dresser in an effort to make the place more natural. She couldn't bring herself to leave but had to keep up appearances and did so to forage with the others briefly the next day. She had no appetite, nauseated by the thought of what lay under the bed. She kept the door shut to discourage any would-be visitors and refused the chambermaid, which had the unwanted side effect of raising the temperature in the room without any airflow. For the first time, she looked forward to seeing Kanegawa.

"It feels like a hot spring in here," he said entering the room without a knock that evening. She leapt from the chair, rolled the door closed behind him, whisked him to his chair, removed his boots, and placed slippers on his feet with the precision of a ground crew. She'd rehearsed her speech a thousand times and then a thousand more, but now he was here and she could not find any breath.

"I have done something terrible," she blurted out.

"What's the prob--"

"I've done something that would get me executed if anyone were to find out. I need help but I won't tell you about it if it puts you in jeopardy. If this is something I must face on my own then so be it. I am ready to take responsibility for what I've done, but if you have a way to keep me safe I will forever be indebted to you. I will make it my life's work to bring honor to it." She spoke rapidly, staring him in the eye, unable to hide her fear. She knelt next to the chair and waited for his response, but it was a long time coming.

"If you need help, I will consider it. But not telling me what you have done will be worse."

Ki-Hwa sighed. She knew he wouldn't make it easy, but what choice did she have? She led him by the hand around the bed, lifting the bed skirt to reveal the rolled rug underneath. The dead sergeant's head protruded slightly from inside the heavy rolls. He shot her a stunned look, unsure of her intentions.

"It's a sergeant. I killed him."

He looked back at the rug. "It would appear so. Who is he?"

"I don't know. Someone who tried to rape me. The same man who raped Asako. He admitted it."

"And you know this for sure?"

"Yes. He admitted it."

"Unfortunately an admission does not hold any weight when the suspect is dead. How did you kill him?"

"I stabbed him. I don't know how many times. Perhaps a hundred."

"Well, that will do it." The colonel was cordial and understanding at first, but without warning he changed, standing upright and raising his voice. "You killed an Imperial soldier. This is a death sentence."

"Would you please be quiet?"

"Hmmph." He crossed back to his chair and sat. "Sake."

She fetched a cup. "It was in self-defense. He meant to kill me."

"That makes no matter. He was an Imperial Soldier and you are *ianfu*. Your word means nothing to a court *if* you are afforded that luxury, which you probably will not be. This will go straight to the general and he will condemn you with very little debate." She was thankful that he kept his voice down and accepted a drink. "You will owe me forever for this."

"Yes. So you will help me?"

He only stared into the cup. He was trying to scare her, the way her brothers had done when she dropped oma's favorite vase and they threatened to tattle as she cleaned up the pieces in tears. She knew it, but had to play along.

He nodded and held his cup out for more drink. "We have work to do." The colonel's body had seen better days. He struggled to lift the sergeant and his death roll over his shoulder. Ki-Hwa started toward the door, but he motioned at the window instead. "Less eyes this way." He shifted his burden and let it fall out the window, watching as it fell through wet foliage, hitting the ground heavily. "Now," he paused to catch his breath, "I'm going to give my driver a speech about how his unwavering loyalty has earned him an evening with one of your friends while you find someone to keep him company. Then I'm going to get in my car and take this package and get rid of it." He crossed the room to retrieve his hat.

"Yes." Ki-Hwa nodded and bowed. "I know one who will do so without complaint."

Kanegawa left Ki-Hwa alone in her room for several quiet minutes until boot heels echoed off the verandah approaching her room. Moments later her jaw dropped as she saw him for the first time since the compound.

"Denbe?"

*   *   *   *   *

An hour before sunrise, Kanegawa returned, his uniform a deep shade of brown, damp with the sweat and rainwater that had soaked it through.

"Where did you take him?" Ki-Hwa asked.

"A drink first," he demanded with a scowl. In one fluid motion his jacket hit the floor, his boots fell from his feet, and his back slumped into his chair. She rushed a cup of sake and another of water to him, spilling a little. Both disappeared immediately and he waved the empty cups in the air demanding more.

"Where is my driver?"

"In the next building with Juri."

"The wailing wench who wouldn't shut up when the 253$^{rd}$ left?"

"Yes."

"Do you have any idea what you have done? What *we* have done?"

"I defended myself. And if I had not I would have been the one buried tonight."

He chuckled as he took the two full cups from her. "I have to admit I am impressed with your skill. You killed an Imperial Soldier. That is worth a toast." He held up the cup of sake and emptied it, slamming it down on the table.

"Now, let us discuss your debt of gratitude for saving your life tonight." Ki-Hwa's shoulders slumped as she reached for the empty cup. "You are vulnerable until the disappearance of that soldier goes unnoticed, which will take a while. Therefore, the only place safe is where I can protect you." Ki-Hwa felt the air around her turn cold.

"And where is that?"

"You will return to Japan and wait for me as my consort." Her heart stopped and her voice was lost. Her legs felt weak. She stumbled and sat on the end of the bed, staring out the window.

Hope, that damnable feeling, fooled her into thinking this would turn out differently, but Kanegawa was not the type to ever let a debt go unpaid, especially when a soul was to be claimed.

"Did you think I would take care of your problem and say 'Good day, madam. Please do call again when trouble comes your way'?" He mocked her. "This will be just the beginning of your servitude. Up until now your services have been voluntary, but henceforth will be mandatory."

"Voluntary? I am not here of my own free will. You know this."

"But you could have left. At any time you could have walked out of here. There are no shackles on your feet. You are not a prisoner." He raised his voice.

"Would you please keep your voice down, sir?"

"Did you keep your voice down when you butchered that sergeant?"

"I didn't have to. The bombs...there was only chaos."

He held out his cup and stared at her until she rose to fill it. He drank quickly, the sweat on his head finally slowing. "Little one...why do you think you are here?"

"Sir?"

"Do you think Captain Inoue saw you that day at the market and just decided then and there that you were a prize to be given to his mentor? Do you think it was a spontaneous decision with no forethought?"

"Yes."

He grinned and held out the cup once more. "Naïve young woman. He never travels to the market. He avoids it at all costs. He curls up at the sight of those vile things you people eat." He took the refilled cup, drank, and smiled. "He was there solely to find you. He knew you'd be there. And how do you think he knew this?"

"I assume he was there looking for people...girls in general. He is the Governor of the province and the market is the largest gathering of the year." She fetched a bottle of sake and poured him more, her tone hushed.

He sat up in the chair and leaned toward her, still smiling. "He was there waiting for you, and only you, because your father sold you to him." He lifted the sake to his mouth, keeping his gaze fixed on her. "He sold you."

"No, that's not possible." She looked away as the blood ran from her face. "My father is a good man. He couldn't."

"Ah, but he could," Kanegawa said, staring at her. "Especially having spent years watching his little farm grow poorer and poorer each season. A commodity like a young virgin in a land of wealthy gentlemen is hard to dismiss. Good man or not, he was hungry."

Ki-Hwa sat back on the bed, frozen, trying to control her tears. "Don't be a victim!" Seo-Sung's voice echoed in her head.

"Why do you think he let you go to the market after so many years of denying you the pleasure? Do you think he had a sudden change of heart? Did he wake up and suddenly feel it was your recompense?"

She lowered her head. Her face disappeared behind her long black hair. Kanegawa let the barbs sink in as she quietly sobbed. But she didn't cry for her father. She cried for the rest of the family who would never know; the brothers who wondered where she was; the cousins who prayed she was alive and safe. She cried for oma, sitting in the doorway holding out hope that her only daughter would someday return, never knowing the man to whom she'd pledged her life had secretly sold her little girl. Those who never question the truth are the first it betrays.

"How much?" she asked through sobs.

"What?"

"How much did he get for me?"

"It does not matter."

"It does. Was it at least enough to take care of the family? Will they still struggle season to season?" She looked into his eyes.

Kanegawa hesitated. "That is up to you." He finished his sake and held out the cup, but she didn't move. "More."

She dragged herself off the bed and crossed the room to fetch another bottle of sake. A tear rolled off her nose and fell into the cup, but she refused to change it for a clean one. *If you want my soul then you can drink of its pain.* She gave him his drink and stood before him.

"Sit."

She returned to the bed.

"No. Here." He motioned to his lap. Ki-Hwa stared at him and finally sat gently on his good leg but looked to the front door, unwilling to gaze upon the beast. He caressed her back, stroking it gently through her silk robe and spoke slowly. "You have nothing in Chosen so you will return with me to Japan after the war and repay your debt in kind. You will be my mistress and you will be proud of it." Her gaze shifted to the spot on the floor where the sergeant took his last breath. "You will enjoy Japan. Consider it your home now." The colonel drank in silence, the sound of his swallows filling the void. "Do you wish he had killed you now?"

"No." She noticed his katana in the corner and remembered that night long ago when he was drunk and passed out; the steel blade and the vulnerable man at her whim. "But I wish I had killed you."

219

# 19

## Better to be an unbroken tile on the housetop than a broken jewel in the house
*-Japanese Proverb*

"I don't envy them," Asako said, watching from Seo-Sung's old room in premium house as the Subuk Maru departed with two hundred and fifty comfort women on board. "That's a long journey." The compound was mostly empty and the ones who were not sent home moved up to premium house. About a third of the premiums left, along with five specials, but not Ki-Hwa. Colonel Kanegawa, despite his threat of getting her out "soonest" did not place her name on the ship's manifest, but continued to insinuate that was her fate. "As soon as I can get you out," he would say as she rubbed his shoulders and poured his sake. Days later, many POWs were gone on the Tamahoko Maru, leaving the rest to suffer under light guard.

"What will they do with the compound?" Ki-Hwa asked.

"That is up to the locals," Asako replied. "It is theirs again. If they have any compassion they will open it to those whose homes have been destroyed."

"Like everything else, compassion is in short supply here."

Asako crossed the hallway to another empty room where she could gaze upon the heights behind premium house through an open window. Ki-Hwa and Chitose followed.

"They are up there now?" Asako whispered.

"Yes. They move around a lot, but they are there."

"Seo-Sung is dead after getting involved with these people. That doesn't bother you? It could be you next. Or you."

"What other course of action is there? Inaction?" Ki-Hwa replied.

"I've heard very nasty things about the Americans," Asako said, gazing at the hillside. "It is said they rape and murder everyone. They have an insatiable blood and sex lust that stems from their capitalist ways. Too much competition in them."

"And how is the Empire any different?" she replied.

"Why do you want to do this?"

"You were raped, Seo-Sung is dead, Kanegawa intends to make me his geisha. Why not?"

"You will not be geisha," Asako retorted. "You could be caught and beheaded. Does that not worry you?"

Ki-Hwa looked out the window at the bustling harbor. A boat exactly like the Kinai Maru was pushed by tugs into the same dock she once walked down. She took a deep breath. "I've been dominated my whole life. Since before I could climb onto a stack of dried stalks I was told this is the way it is. That we are women. That we are not in control. That we do not question why. That we simply say 'yes sir' and move away, looking at the ground because that it is our place to do so. Because we are too weak not to."

She turned to Asako and raised her voice. "Well I will follow the leader no more. If it's my fate to die an obstinate woman than I will and I will do it for those who cannot like Seo-Sung. For what is living otherwise? If I did what they expected of me then what kind of disappointment would I be? As much as these men want me to be their plaything I will not. And I think they will respect me more for that even as they bring their blade to bear on my naked neck and snuff out the one who would not shut up."

Asako looked at the ambitious Korean girl and sighed, unable to find any words. *So passionate to fight but too blind to know better,* she thought. Asako was no stranger to risk, but this was madness. Still...her hope was inspiring. But if it was going to work they needed more of everything. More people, more planning, more preparation, and more guarantees from the Anglos.

"Are you insane?" exclaimed Sergeant Denbe Isogai the next evening in the very same room. Chitose sought him out during the day and asked him to come to the house where Asako brought him upstairs in case any prying eyes noticed. It all had to look legitimate. Just a Kempeitai Sergeant visiting a comfort station. Ki-Hwa and Chitose scampered across the hall to join from Seo-Sung's room when the coast was clear. They were careful, but Denbe was unmoved.

"There are nearly one hundred thousand Imperial Soldiers on this island preparing for an invasion on every corner," he said.

"Not every corner. We know of a few beaches they have not prepared," Ki-Hwa said.

"They think the coral is too high for any ship, but at high tide a shallow draft boat can get over it," Asako added.

"And how are you going to get a hundred prisoners into such a vessel? And once you do won't it be too heavy to get over the coral? Before all that how are you going to get them away from the camps and to your embarkation point? Steal a truck? Break them out? Have you ever shot anyone?"

Asako, Ki-Hwa, and Chitose did exactly what they did not want to. Stayed silent. If they were going to convince him they had to be confident. Finally Ki-Hwa spoke. "If you helped us..."

"Stop! I do not want to hear of it or I will have to turn you in. You know who I work for."

"We are not powerless."

"You are three women against an Army and a Navy, preparing to fight another Army and Navy, drunk on hope. But you don't see that it is completely misplaced." His words cut. They expected resistance, but not violent opposition. "Do you know what will happen to our families when they find out?" This, above all, stopped the conversation. Each one of them thought about their loved ones back home and what might happen to them when the word came back that their daughters had turned on the ever-caring heart of the Empire.

"Why don't you go back to Japan with the next ship?"

"Will there be another one?" Asako asked, but Denbe would not answer, knowing it was confidential information.

"No," Ki-Hwa interjected. "He sent back the healthy ones and kept the sick ones here to die from labor. They barely need guarding. It was on purpose." Denbe stayed silent, knowing what she meant, but she continued. "With so few people to watch and most of them infirmed anyway, he could strip all the camps of their guards to make them soldiers. He'll lead them into glorious battle himself. Even you have been training more, Denbe. He's always despised this assignment. No horse to ride, no naïve children to stand in front of and yell at." She stared at Denbe, a direct challenge to his hubris.

"I am no more fond of this place or the horrors our leaders justify as necessary for the greater glory of the Empire than you are. But to plan an escape with a bunch of sick and lame men is preposterous. Look around you. This is the mightiest outpost in the Pacific."

"But it gets weaker every day," Ki-Hwa said. "The Anglos are more powerful. They defeated the Imperial Navy before and are coming straight for this island."

Denbe held up his hand. "I do not wish to speak of this." He turned to leave. "I commend you, but no. I will not speak of it to anyone. You have my word." He left with Chitose close behind to make it look like he was being escorted from the house.

"He may be right," Asako said.

"He's not. We can do this without him." They both stared out the window watching the hills for a sign that never came. Chitose returned, closing the door quietly.

"How can you be sure the Anglos will hold up their end?" Asako asked not expecting a response but putting the question on the wind for her own benefit. "How do you know they will take us out of here? How do we know they are not the ones responsible for Seo-Sung dying?"

Chitose made a muffled sound, stomped her foot, and shook her head.

"We don't," Ki-Hwa responded. "I don't think we can trust any man. They only do right by themselves. At best they can be manipulated into doing something predictable."

Asako sighed and looked out the window again. "Then we need to offer them something else."

Ki-Hwa turned to her. "Like what?"

"Something they cannot refuse."

# 20

## I know a trick worth two of that
*-William Shakespeare*

"If there is one great irony to the Allied bombing campaign waged over this fair island," Colonel Imamura slurred as he raised a toast. "It is the complete failure to have inflicted even a scratch on this immortal gathering place! To the New Guinea club!"

"Here, here," the crowd roared.

"It is fair to say the establishment had some help, though," he continued. "Thanks to our much overworked Chief Engineer, the sturdy walls are reinforced with pillars of steel forged from destroyed Allied aircraft." He patted the closest wall to him as someone provided him with another cup of sake. "To the Allies. May they never know what we've done with their airplanes. And they to our morale!" All were merry.

The New Guinea club had earned its reputation as a palace of exclusivity with the island's power elite. As such, it lured individuals well trained in etiquette and food preparation, resulting in a first-class staff and an extraordinary menu, despite the war. When the decision was made to dig tunnels for protection, the club was selected to receive a storage cave to protect its food stores and give workers a safe refuge. But it quickly turned into a social establishment for one particular reason.

"Seventy-five degrees. Thanks to the iron ore at the base of the caldera," the engineer stated. "If this were the usual limestone, we'd be baking to death right now."

"It's as soothing as a mountain waterfall," Kanegawa responded. "And under a volcano even."

"One day they'll get lucky and hit this place...and then we'll really start a war!" A new officer boasted.

"It would not matter if they did. None of my structures will ever buckle," the engineer responded.

"Engineers," Kanegawa snorted. "Even a hog knows how to dig a hole." He bowed to a polite but raucous laugh from his table of Kempeitai and climbed the almost vertical stairway back to the main floor, stopping when he spied a figure and detoured. "Lieutenant Hashimoto and two esteemed colleagues." Kanegawa chuckled. Standing before him were Takeo, Hideki and another lieutenant from their wing who waited by the front door for a table. He walked closer, grinning, his breath reaching the young officers long before he did. They all snapped to a rigid position of attention.

"Good evening, sir. We are winning!" Hideki said.

The colonel took a deep sigh. "Of course we are. Is there anything that would make you think otherwise?" His gaze was direct and briefly lucid.

"The Imperial forces of Japan will surely triumph with the blessing of the Emperor," Takeo said, unable to hide his sarcasm.

"I'm not convinced of your conviction." Kanegawa slurred, losing his balance and putting a hand on the wall. A momentary loss of control was the one thing he hated and three junior officers stood before him witnessed it. The embarrassment jolted him back into superficial sobriety. He grabbed Takeo by the arm, motioning for the others to stay as he led him out the door." Tell me something, lieutenant," he huffed as his car pulled up. "Where is it you're from again?

"Etajima, sir."

"But you said your father worked in the mines at Sado. The two are very far apart."

"That is my uncle, sir."

"Yes. Of course." The colonel looked at him, still wearing a smirk of satisfaction.

"Is there something you need from me, sir?"

"Ah, the privilege of youth. The audacious mind that thinks it can get away with anything simply because it is young." He paused as Denbe opened the passenger door. "Let's be perfectly clear. I am the law here, not that imposter Sato. You know something about imposters, don't you?"

Takeo stopped breathing. "Imposter?" he said looking away. He waited a long time to look back at the colonel, weighing his options, trying to determine exactly what he knew. "I do not know what you mean, sir. If there is an imposter here then he must be found. Unless, of course, he is making the Emperor proud and helping win the war."

"An imposter is an imposter by any name. The ends do not justify the means, lieutenant."

"Well, sir. Let's hope this imposter makes a mistake and you find him."

"But I already have, lieutenant. It's just a matter of when I want to expose him." Kanegawa's eyes narrowed as he stared into Takeo's. "I see everything." His words growled across his lips mere inches from Takeo's face. He wanted a fight, and was praying Takeo would take the bait, but for punching their commander, the Kempeitai would surely emancipate his head from his shoulders and nothing good could come of that. Takeo bowed and backed away, staring down the ulcer of New Britain.

"I thought not," Kanegawa said smugly. He stared until he collapsed into the car. Hideki and the other lieutenant stood at an uncomfortable position of semi-rigid attention, but Takeo did not take his eyes off Kanegawa. Just as the car door closed he saw something in the back seat-- a pair of legs, white legs, half-covered by a skirt that Takeo noticed.

*I am not the only one with secrets, colonel.*

\* \* \* \* \*

"Warrant Officer Tanaka?"

"Fourth bunk down on the left sir," a petrified new ensign said as he leapt from his bunk and stood at attention in front of Takeo. His reputation was getting around. He liked it.

Takeo entered the Junior Officer tent without so much as a knock or an announcement of his presence, making everyone uncomfortable. The younger officers were required to stand and call the tent to attention when a superior officer arrived. Failure to render this courtesy could result in severe punishment, but Takeo couldn't have cared less. He thought nothing of pomp and circumstance, even if it was in keeping with the highest traditions of the Imperial Navy.

"To what do I owe the pleasure, sir?" Hideki asked as he stood erect and placed his book on his bunk.

"Get your gear," he commanded as if the younger officer had no choice; and he didn't. "Let's spar."

"Yes sir."

They drove a Toyota truck, one of the well-maintained ones that still had all of its own parts, away from the airfield, through town to the North Coast Road, up over the main ridgeline, and then took a right onto an obscure dirt road through dense jungle barely touched by human hands.

"Where are we going, sir?"

"Found a beach that looks pretty deserted," Takeo yelled above the whining engine and the wind screaming in through the windows. Moments later the brush cleared and they had a small beach on the north shore all to themselves. It was littered with fresh deposits of kelp, driftwood, dead fish, and wreckage from shipping destroyed in the channels but it was also a small oasis of calm in the busy circus of war.

"Winter swells. When the waves get bigger they deposit all kinds of shit on the beaches," Takeo said as he stopped the truck in the deep sand where the road ended. "Sometimes a pilot will wash up. And after days at sea, it's not a pretty sight."

Hideki winced. A strong ocean wind smacked Takeo in the face as he exited the truck. He breathed the unmistakable scent of the tropics deep into his lungs. "You can smell the sea as far inland as the Warangoi River."

"You've been that far in?"

"Once."

Hideki shook his head. They wasted no time removing their boots and jackets and getting down to business. They were each exceptional at their craft, honed from years of training. Before long they were covered in sand and sweat as action countered reaction and each threw the other or used leverage to defeat a throw. Judo is all about balance and both had plenty. They pulled punches mere centimeters away from their intended targets, but as the workout progressed their kicks slowed and punches found their way through defenses with considerably less force. Missing with a roundhouse, Hideki scored a combination of kicks on Takeo's midsection, throwing him heavily to the sand.

"Impressive," Takeo said, holding his ribs. He raised a hand to stop Hideki's advance and request a break in the action. "Was that for your glory or the Emperor's?"

Hideki backed away and let out a sigh. "Please do not do this again."

Takeo had trouble breathing. "I just want to understand you better, Hideki-san, that's all."

"Understand what?"

"The blind leading the blind...or is it the blind leading the stupid...or is it just blind ambition. I can never remember. Don't the Yanks have a name for your type? Lemmings?" He laughed to ease the tension, but it fell short.

"Why do we have to go through this every day, sir? Must our friendship suffer for a disagreement on belief?"

Takeo got up and moved to the front of the truck, placing a hand on the hood to support himself, but removed it quickly. The dark green Toyota was scorching hot in the noontime sun and despite a layer of sweat on his palms, his hand was still singed.

"Why do you believe in him? Has he spoken to you personally? Did you have a divine vision of him on his white horse with a golden aura?"

Hideki wiped his face with a rag. "No."

"Did he speak to you and tell you that following him would result in your eternal salvation?" He was treading in dangerous waters. Openly mocking the Emperor was a game for the drunk and the dead.

"I don't have to tell you that as an officer of the Imperial Navy, I'm bound to report subversive activity or persons deemed not to be in support of Imperial policies."

Takeo rolled his eyes. "You know I'm not subversive."

"But you're insubordinate, and in direct violation of standing orders."

"And how is that different from any other day?" He sat on the truck's bumper, pulling a canteen from a knapsack.

"Have you been drinking already? Or is it that you have not been drinking today?" Hideki said finding his breath again. "When did you lose faith? You must have felt something to join the cause and spend so much of your time becoming the ace that you are. That did not happen by sheer luck. It was your destiny. You trained and trained, just as you do now. You must have heard a calling at some point, as I did, to do something for a greater good."

Takeo looked away and studied the beach, slowing his breaths. He gazed at the palm trees just a few feet away, wrinkling his brow and making a face as if straining to remember. He took a deep breath and felt the scars on his chest.

"Once...maybe. So?"

"So you must have felt the Bushido spirit at some point to devote yourself so fully to the Emperor and the Navy. When did you lose that drive and why?" Hideki put it to him forcefully.

"It's not important."

"Yes it is. You want to understand me. I want to do the same."

"No...it isn't." Takeo said quietly, dropping his head to the ground. Sweat soaked through his sand-covered khaki pants and undershirt, deepening their color from olive green to nearly black. He placed the canteen on the bumper, walked around the truck and grabbed his flask from the driver's seat. Instead of comforting him, the burn of a long tug only fueled his angst.

"You're a pompous boy," he said as Hideki leaned against the front fender.

"And why is that?"

"Because you think you know everything. You think you've got it all figured out. The Emperor has a plan for us all, divinely sent down by God and regaled to us for none to question."

"Well..."

"You are completely devoid of your own independent thought, are you not? You have no original ideas floating through that head of yours, except to trust unfailingly in the Empire and know wholeheartedly that everything we do is just and true according to his will."

"His will is God's will."

"God's will? To be a pawn? Why do you accept that? Why do you believe that your fate is whatever they wish it to be? You sound like the old Samurai. As long as it was good for the Emperor, they did it. And you know what happened to them!"

Takeo stopped. He didn't want it to come to this, but inside knew it would. He walked into the sand and kicked at it.

"It is the Bushido way," Hideki said.

Takeo spun around. "It is not the Bushido way that I crave. I yearn to be free, not dependent!"

"It's not ambition that guides me, but loyalty."

"Loyalty?"

"Yes."

"Well, your loyalty will lead you to perpetual enslavement. I don't care to have my life dictated to me by another man. And yes, he is a man. Like you and me, born from a womb to a mother's bosom and a father's lash, prone to his own failings, not absolved of imperfection, and not the mouthpiece of God!" he shouted.

"You should stop, sir," Hideki muttered, reaching for a canteen.

Takeo calmed himself. "He's a man, Hideki. Flesh and blood. And our fate, our destiny, our reason for living is not preconceived by him." He wiped sweat from his brow and breathed deeply, looking out over the ocean. "When does it all end?" Takeo asked.

"When we make it end," Hideki answered.

Ki-Hwa stared at the body, not wanting to remember the night she killed him. For some the human brain is remarkably adept at blocking out its most traumatic events. The rapist deserved a shallow grave halfway up a mountain where no one would ever find him, but she still reeled at the sight of him again. Dave reached down and moved part of the rug that enshrouded him. "And you say Kanegawa brought him out here?"

She nodded.

"Usually sergeants have to carry colonels to bury them. And being buried on a mountain is a very honorable thing. But I don't think that is the case here." He studied the rotting corpse. "Damn lucky my fellas saw him leaving this little spot or we wouldn't have found it."

Ki-Hwa forced herself to look again, to remember why she was doing such an insane thing with people she didn't know or entirely trust. "This will give us leverage, yes?"

Dave nodded. "Mind you, we need to figure out the best way to use it. Don't suppose the Kempeitai would deal with him had they found it?"

Ki-Hwa shook her head. "He is their leader. It only takes a flick of his hand to send them away."

"Right. Anyone else have it in for him?"

"Everyone."

They stood quietly in the small clearing for several moments, waiting for an obvious answer that never came. Kanegawa's work was sloppy. He'd chosen a spot barely off one of the main trails on the backside of the main ridge above Rabaul, only a few miles from the plantation as the swallow flies. The grave was so shallow that it only took a few scrapes with bare hands to uncover the cache. It was more of a lazy case of dropping an unwanted object under low palms and tossing dried leaves and dirt on it than an actual burial. She was disappointed in him.

"Look, I don't want anyone else to know I did this. I don't want them looking at me like a murderer. Not Denbe, not Chitose, not the Yank, not anyone."

"But it was in self-defense, right?

"Yes!" She was adamant. "I would appreciate your discretion."

Dave nodded and looked at the body again. "What is that?" Nestled in between the body and the rug, just barely noticeable, was a rigid object made of steel and ivory. He reached down and plucked it out, brushed the dirt away and brought it up to his face to examine.

"That is Bishamonten."

\*   \*   \*   \*   \*

Denbe dropped a cigarette next to the front tire of Kanegawa's car while his boss was in the plantation with Ki-Hwa again. The sun had set and all ambient light was running west. Kanegawa could be gone an hour or the night. Either way it was his duty to wait within shouting distance of the car. So he walked the same walk he always did until a voice stopped him.

"Before you yell, let's just say Seo-Sung sent me," Frank said.

Denbe froze and then looked toward Ki-Hwa's room. "Don't call him. Just listen. Have I got your attention?"

He nodded.

"Ki-Hwa has presented you with an opportunity. You should take it."

"Why?"

"Because you need them and they need you."

"I don't need them."

"Sure you do. You respect them for at least thinking they have a chance. Plus you don't want them to know you got Seo-Sung killed, right?"

His jaw dropped. "How did you know?"

"I saw it all. They know she's dead, but they don't know you could have stopped it."

Denbe looked at the ground and then at Frank. The American's rifle was slung across his back and he did not appear to wish him any harm. "I didn't think Kanegawa would kill her."

"But he did. And it was because you turned her in. She told you about us and her plan, so you gave her up."

"I was afraid after Admiral Yamamoto was killed. They were searching for anyone whose dedication was in question. My loyalty was to the Empire, not a woman.

"Listen, we'll keep what happened between us, but you're in whether you like it or not. My country is coming and you can bet your last plug nickel that we will overwhelm this place."

"How do I know you won't cross us?" Denbe asked.

"I won't. But you need to do this for them, not yourself. You need to do it because you're not like...him." Frank motioned over his shoulder toward Ki-Hwa's room.

"How do you know?"

"Because you have a soul."

\* \* \* \* \*

Christmas came and went with the anticipation reaching peaks and valleys. The few girls who celebrated Christmas crafted homemade gifts to trade with one another for the holiday. Ki-Hwa made a bra of coconuts for Asako, who gave her a grass skirt in return. It was modeled in the local tradition and Ki-Hwa adored it.

"And I'm not even a Christian," Ki-Hwa declared proudly.

A few girls exchanged trinkets made from whatever they could muster. One girl took an ammunition can, made a pillow for its top from an old futon and gave it to Victoria as a footstool. But any holiday spirit Victoria felt was short-lived; the business of making money didn't stop. As a Christmas gift to the higher-ranking men of the island, she provided free sex vouchers good for an hour with the girl of their choice, provided their patron did not object.

After months of resisting, Police Chief Sato finally gave in to temptation and used a Christmas voucher as well. A Chinese girl called Chang, whose befitting name meant 'slim and graceful', enchanted him. He soon became her sole patron. One clear, cool evening after the New Year his car appeared in front of premium house and she practically leaped in before it could stop.

"Hello dear," she whispered in his ear, purposely using her hot breath to provoke him. "Did you bring what we need?" The chief threw a thumb back over his shoulder and pointed at two blankets. For weeks she'd begged him for sex outdoors to appease her wild side, the side that intrigued him the most. He always refused, but this week she nearly insisted in order to keep his preeminent place at the head of her line. It had to be tonight.

"It was a good day." The police force, not the Kempeitai or anyone else for that matter, had caught an American west of the city searching for food. It was an immense personal victory for the police over the rival military police, even if he was required to turn the man over for interrogation. Chang was ecstatic.

She pulled a bottle of sake from a canvas bag.

"Banzai," he said to himself, not wanting to find a reason to back out.

"We're going to be naked in the jungle!"

"Not so loud, please," he implored. But Sato soon found himself feeding off her excitement though still harboring the apprehension of a man his age as he pulled away from the house. "This will be either the greatest or stupidest thing I've ever done," he mumbled.

"Here," Chang said ten minutes later. "Stop here. I see the clearing." Sato stopped the car as far off the road as he could and the pair quickly ran into the jungle hand in hand.

Down a moonlit trail they went, running at first, then walking, the chief stopping several times.

"How about here?" He breathed very hard.

"No, this is right in the middle of the trail...up a little farther."

"How far?" Sato was exhausted.

"Come on!" The vivacious young woman exhorted him onward.

Chang grabbed his hand once again and ran up one trail and down another like a child in a hedgerow maze. "Right over there. That's it," she exclaimed, running a hand strategically along the length of his crotch. She turned and ran the final fifteen yards to a clearing just off the trail and threw down a blanket. The chief arrived and lazily flopped his tired body on top of it. Sweat dripped from him as Chang excitedly began a strip tease that took Sato from hesitant to overly willing. If he was going to risk an embarrassing discovery then he might as well fulfill all his fantasies first.

Sato was fully aroused when she placed his hat on her head and straddled his lap. He embraced her tiny frame and laid it down on the blanket. In moments the two were fully engaged and spent the better part of an hour in many positions. When he finished for the second time and silence fell over the jungle again, they moved in opposite directions to relieve themselves. The chief groaned as he forced it out.

"What is that?" Chang asked.

"What?" Sato said, turning. He crossed the clearing to investigate.

"I stepped on something. It felt hard." She stepped away as Sato drew back several thick banana leaves to investigate.

"I don't see anything," Sato said.

"There." Chang pointed.

Sato saw it and moved brush out of the way and kicked the dirt until he knew what it was. "I was right about one thing. This was either the dumbest or greatest idea I'd ever had."

# 21

## He who is prudent and lies in wait for an enemy who is not, will be victorious
*-Sun Tzu*

"Where did you get this hideous foot stool?" Kanegawa asked.

"My girls made it as a Christmas gift," Victoria responded.

He leaned forward in his chair to inspect it. "It smells like ammunition."

"But it has a certain charm to it." Victoria crossed the front parlor of her house at the plantation and retrieved a bottle of sake.

"You like it because it reminds you how far your consorts will go to please you. You like the power of having them shower you with gifts. Your tongue is three inches long but it can kill a girl six feet tall."

"Well, it is comforting to know the Kempeitai is willing to take the rubbish out if anyone who crosses me." She handed him a cup and poured a drink.

He couldn't help but think of the irony of that statement, having recently hidden the body of someone who'd crossed one of her girls. "Yes...a powerful tongue indeed." He looked around the parlor, his eyes settling on an intricately carved buffet. He'd seen this piece a hundred times, but now it looked different. Victoria was usually too preoccupied with managing her assets to re-arrange her things or change anything even slightly, but something was not the same. Something was...missing. And then he knew. He crossed to the buffet, his eyes widening. *It's not here*, he thought, looking over the piece one more time to be sure.

His brow furrowed. "Where is your letter opener?"

She paused to think about the question. "I took it to my bedroom a long time ago."

"Is it there now?"

"You know...it's been absent for months. I suspect one of the girls flogged it, but I haven't a clue who would be so dodgy."

"Go look," he demanded.

"Nibori..."

"Look now."

She rolled her eyes and walked to the back room to her dresser where she saw it last, speaking as she went, Kanegawa following. "It should be here somewhere. I don't really think anyone stole it." She searched her room briskly as he watched.

"It's a lovely piece, but it's just a trinket. I'll find it. Why are you so..."

"Just a trinket?" He turned, leaving his sake on an armoire. "You have no idea how valuable those 'trinkets' are. Remember that I gave it to you as a personal gift. Obviously it meant nothing if you lost it months ago and did not care enough to find it or tell me about its disappearance!" He erupted.

"There are a few more urgent events going on here than fretting over a letter opener that you had an enslaved Chinese craftsman make," she said. "I'm not exactly getting bags of mail everyday that call for a tool to open letters more efficiently."

Kanegawa was not pleased as the pair walked to the front room. "You truly care for no one but yourself! I give you the life you desire and an item that is precious to me, but it's not enough for you. You always want more! You are selfish and have abused my good nature once too many." His disdain was sincere as he walked through the front door, slamming it behind him.

He walked toward his car, but moments later he doubled back down the main verandah to Ki-Hwa's room, making sure to step quietly and avoid Victoria's windows. He entered the room even more stealthily than he intended to find her sleeping quietly. Kanegawa sat on the bed next to her and grabbed her arms above the elbows, shaking lightly. She awoke with a fright.

"What did you kill him with?" he whispered to avoid rousing Asako in the next room.

"What?" Ki-Hwa jumped backwards and brought her hands up as she tried to focus on the intruder.

"What did you kill him with?" He repeated the question slowly and deliberately.

"Uh, a knife of some sort. No...it was a..." She struggled to think, squinting and answering in a sleepy voice.

"*What?*" He demanded forcefully, grasping her arms and squeezing hard. She winced.

"A letter opener. Like the one you had when we met."

He released his grip, looking out the window as bats launched themselves off coconut trees to hunt in the dark. He sat still for a tense moment, evaluating this information as Ki-Hwa slowly entered the present from her slumber.

"And I assume it's wrapped up in the carpet with his body?"

"I think so."

"You careless wench!" he snarled. "Why did you leave the instrument of murder with the body? That's a sure way to get us both executed if anyone finds it!"

"But they won't. You took him into the jungle."

He stood and put one hand to his forehead and the other on his hip. "They are mine and mine alone!"

"But you've given several to people on the island."

"And they can all be traced back to me. Everyone knows they're mine," he thumped his chest.

"I thought you said..."

"I know what I said!" He stopped and lowered his voice again. "Why didn't you tell me you used it to kill him? Where did you even get it?"

"I don't know. It was just there when he was attacking me on the nightstand." She wasn't about to admit that she'd taken it from Victoria.

"And how did it get there? I wonder."

"I may be your consort, but I'm not a thief!" She placed her feet on the floor, but continued to sit on the bed. She was not a skilled liar, but had already rehearsed her alibi and knew enough to stick to it.

"Then where did you get it?"

"I think it fell out of your jacket."

He had to go, but couldn't leave her upset. It would only make his predicament worse to have a loose cannon who knew too much. Besides, he'd already angered Victoria this night; another agitated and jittery woman could be the end for him. "Go back to sleep then. I will take care of this," he said like a father calming his daughter after a nightmare.

"Will you? I'm the one who killed him. You could be offering me up to the executioner."

"You are correct, I could be if that was what I truly desired. But we have plans, you and I, remember? Now guard your words against the wind." Like a ghost he slipped out of her room, closing the door gently.

Colonel Nibori Kanegawa was an infinitely patient man capable of meticulous planning, never leaving anything to chance and rarely letting a minute go by that was not accounted for. He was fond of the letter openers; they held a priceless, nostalgic value. Their acquisition came at too high a price to leave one rotting away with the body of a worthless rapist. And more urgently, what if it were found by one of the hundred thousand prying eyes on this armpit? He had to retrieve it.

He stood in the driveway and gazed at his timepiece. "Nearly midnight. I should return before sunrise." But he didn't have transportation. For once he dismissed Denbe for the evening, sure he would not need him until morning and making the long walk on a bad leg with limited time wasn't wise, but there seemed to be no choice. If that opener were to be retrieved this evening he had to move out...and now! He quickly walked to the rear of the plantation and retrieved a compact shovel left behind after the bunker was completed.

"My kingdom for a horse!" he muttered as he walked into the night. He hiked up the road and around the mountain with no pause, despite a throbbing leg and a sweat-soaked shirt. Mount To was steep in places, but climbing was certainly easier without a body over his shoulders. The moonlight shone brightly through the trees, but even without it he knew exactly where to go.

Arriving at the small clearing, he finally allowed himself a moment to rest before digging. Moments later he fell upon the mound and shoveled the dirt away.

*Dig quickly, old man!* he told himself. But something was off. *This is too easy. The dirt shouldn't be this loose.* There was a faint rustle in the trees. Probably a bandicoot.

But it wasn't a bandicoot. Or any animal for that matter. Kanegawa felt the cold steel of a gun barrel behind his head accompanied by a voice. "Don't move."

# 22

The drunkard wallows: Maru sits upright.
The girls are giggling: Maru only smiles,
And crossing to the window, sees the moon
And quotes a verse about an octopus
Caught...in a trap
*-William Plomer*

Dawn on Rabaul brought a new beginning for an old man. Kanegawa sat alone on a steel chair in a stone prison cell; a lonely box built to suck the morale out of its inhabitant through isolation, sensory deprivation, and blasted furnace heat. He chuckled at the ridiculous notion that it would affect him. He was ready. When they came for him, he had no doubt who would win. Around noon the door swung open. Sato entered with a chair.

"So how is this going to go, colonel?" he asked sitting across from him.

"Well, which part?" Kanegawa replied.

"You and I are no strangers to this process." The Chief's words echoed off the smooth walls. "You know what I have to do. You also know the means I possess to do it. So I'll repeat my question. How is this going to go?"

"It is your interrogation, Chief."

Sato stared at him. "This doesn't have to be difficult. You could make it easy."

"On whom?"

"Well certainly not on me. I'm not the one in question here."

"And why am I, exactly?"

They sat mere feet from each other. A deputy stood in a corner, taking notes as all three perspired heavily in the humid airtight chamber.

"You're here because you've been caught red- handed. How is this going to look when I inform the generals?"

"How will it look indeed, Chief?"

"So you're opting for the hard way?"

"Actually, you are. When you state that you've apprehended me, and falsely I might add, who will believe you? Who would take you seriously after your display of uncontrollable anger at the general's mansion where you attacked me? Everyone on this island knows you harbor a grudge born of misinformation. It is not I who will have to do the explaining. Whatever you are accusing me of, you will need undeniable proof to discount personal vengeance as the motive of a corrupt police force."

Sato sighed. "Very good speech, colonel. You did not fail to cover anything I did not expect you to." Kanegawa shifted in his seat. Sato continued. "How long have you been covering this up?" he asked.

"I still do not know what you mean."

"It's a simple question, how long?"

"I have not covered anything up."

"Colonel, please. You're insulting me now."

"Pity." Kanegawa looked away.

"What other reason would you have for being on the mountain in the middle of the night with a shovel? We found it, colonel. We caught you digging it up. Just admit who you are."

"Are you still implying that I am a murderer? Have you not let that one rest? The tribunal-- "

"This is not the tribunal. This is my court, and I know you're a murderer."

Kanegawa leaned back, crossed a leg over the other. Though a man of considerable wit and resource, he found himself backed into a corner. "I am prepared to make a deal."

"And what is that?"

"I will give you the real culprit. At best I am only an accessory."

"There are others?"

"Just one. I did not do the actual killing. I only buried him."

Sato paused and looked at his deputy. "Tell me more."

Kanegawa stopped, sensing insecurity. He could see it in the deputy's slack-jawed expression. *He doesn't know. He's trying to get me to confess because he's clueless.* "I do not remember much more."

"You don't?"

"No."

"You were about to say you killed someone."

"I was not."

"You said you buried him."

"I do not recall saying that."

"You said you were an accessory at best."

"Did I?"

Sato stopped. He looked back at the deputy who still stood with his mouth open and knew he'd been betrayed. He shook his head and motioned to the deputy. "Bring it in." The deputy disappeared. "We'll get back to that later. Why you were on the mountain digging in the middle of the night?"

"I felt like gardening. The volcanic soil is wonderful for azaleas."

Sato could not suppress a smile. Kanegawa was as adept as everyone gave him credit for. The deputy re-entered the room and handed him a brown canvas bag. "I'll give you one last chance to talk to me, colonel."

Kanegawa leaned forward. "I am usually the one using that demand on prisoners, Chief." He stared Sato down. "Is that a battery? You will have to put my feet in water to make it really hurt."

Again Sato smiled. He opened the bag and pulled out an object Kanegawa had seen before. A radio-- an American radio—the type the Anglo pilots use for survival when they bail out. "What is that?" Kanegawa asked.

"Now colonel...I know you've seen one of these before. Your men have brought them in with pilots they catch in the jungle, which also makes it an easy thing for you to procure." Sato held it in his hands, turning it over and inspecting it repeatedly.

"And how does that concern me?"

"Because it's yours."

"Mine?"

"Yes."

"How on earth did you come to that conclusion?"

"Well, this is what we found in the hole you were digging into. I found it a few nights ago.

"Then the question is what were *you* doing on the mountain?" Kanegawa took the offensive.

"Hiking if you must know. I'm trying to be more fit," Sato replied, patting his belly.

"Really?" Kanegawa laughed an angry laugh. "Do you mean to say you think I am using that radio to transmit to the Allies? Why would I do that?"

"I'm not sure, colonel. You tell me."

"I would not."

"Then why were you digging it up?"

Kanegawa uncrossed his legs and adjusted his shirt. He gazed at the dim-witted deputy behind Sato. "I was not. You put it there yourself. This is an attempt to frame me."

"That may be believable if we hadn't caught you up there, in the middle of the night-- "

"Digging a hole, yes, I heard you before. This is ludicrous. I am innocent and this is a monkey court." Kanegawa turned away and crossed his arms.

"Don't try to turn this on me, Nibori." Kanegawa hated being called by his first name, especially by someone he didn't respect. "You've been passing the Allies information. You've been guiding in their planes and telling them when their POWs were being shipped out." Sato threw out his whole card.

"That is absurd!" Kanegawa raised his voice and shifted in the metal chair to stare at Sato.

"Is it? Why have none of the POW camps been hit by a single Allied bomb? Why is it that those places you hold dear to you have also gone untouched? Your quarters, the New Guinea Club, premium house, the plantation. All unscathed. Coincidence?"

"Yes."

"I don't believe so, and this discovery doesn't lend itself well to your cause, colonel. You're the spy the brass warned us about."

Kanegawa clamped down hard on his tongue and shifted in his seat in an attempt to control his fury. "You are mad, Chief, and will hang from the tallest tree on this island. But I am impressed by your theory. Did you think it up by yourself?"

Sato smiled. "I did."

"And what would my motivation be for doing these things?"

Sato shrugged. "That's easy. A combat-forged cavalryman accused of war crimes and unhappy with the Imperial Command's decision to place him in a position beneath his abilities cuts a deal with the Allies for his freedom. I will have no difficulty proving that piece."

"But how did I help them? You haven't shown how they benefit from this relationship?"

"That's simple.  Two boatloads of POWs intercepted and liberated. It makes the Americans happy."

"Two boatloads?"

"Yes, two boats full of prisoners; the Montevideo Maru and the Tamahoko Maru. Both left here full of Allied POWs and were never heard from again. Probably intercepted by the Americans. You knew where and when they were going. In fact it was you who suggested getting rid of them, wasn't it?"

Kanegawa's blood ran cold. He knew the accusation to be baseless but the perception was damning. "They did not arrive? And you believe I am clever enough to control that from here?"

"Imamura informed me a few days ago. He was about to tell everyone, including you. It's just a happy coincidence you got to find out this way. But you know what's not a coincidence?"

Kanegawa looked down at the ground and let out a brief laugh. "You ask many leading questions, Chief."

"Two boats disappear, the Allies never hit your favorite spots, and you're caught digging up a radio. And you volunteered the remaining POWs to be a digging workforce so you could concentrate more time on spying. Doesn't look good, old buddy." Sato was satisfied.

Kanegawa tried not to fidget in his chair. "I regret to inform you that your theory, though amusing, is false, whatever the perception may be, Chief. I have done nothing wrong and what's more you have no proof except a dirty radio that probably doesn't even work."

Sato turned the radio on, filling the room with static.

"Pointless," Kanegawa smirked.

"I suspected you would say so." He turned to his deputy who exited the room.

"Him? Do you think anyone will believe a deputy over me?"

Sato turned back around to face Kanegawa. "No, but they'll believe him." A gaunt, handcuffed American pilot fell through the doorway. The skinny, malnourished officer had clearly been beaten for show, a tactic Kanegawa had used many times himself. Everything about his body language confessed. He stared at the floor for a long, guilty moment before lifting his eyes to meet Kanegawa's. He shrugged his shoulders, almost apologizing to the colonel, something that did not go unnoticed. "Can you believe we caught him foraging for food in the open?" Sato said. I thought you would've trained him better than that, Nibori." Kanegawa stared silently at Sato. "He says you've been the source of his Army's success here."

"Really?"

"NAME!" Sato barked at the American in Japanese. Chikaki translated.

"Collins, Francis G., 312-12-9579, US Army Air Corps," he said looking at the ground. A chair was placed under him and he swayed in it, his blond hair tousled and his face unshaven and bruised. The effects of the beating had left their mark.

"And how would I know this man, Chief?"

"I can only presume, but he knows you. He was near the mountains to the west, close to where the last Anglos were seen."

"Then why was he not turned over to me? I have jurisdiction over prisoners of war!" Kanegawa tried to change the subject, but Sato wouldn't have it.

"Well, I would if he hadn't implicated you as his accomplice during preliminary questioning. As soon as he did that, it became a police affair."

"You are fabricating this."

"Tell us about this man here, Yank?"

Chikaki translated. "He is Colonel Nibori Kanegawa, Commander of the Kempeitai."

Kanegawa rolled his eyes. "That's adorable. Does he do any other tricks? Roll over, play dead, that sort of thing?"

"Well yes. Yes, in fact he does." Sato was suddenly dead serious. "Tell us more, Yank."

Through Chikaki, Frank told them everything he knew about Kanegawa and detailed how he had developed target data for the island's infrastructure. He described how Kanegawa passed the information to him and that he used the information to guide Allied aircraft to their the most crucial targets with lethal accuracy. His performance was flawless. When he finished, Frank looked at the ground as if he were bound to die on the gallows at daybreak. A tear even forced its way when he spoke of wanting to see his wife and children again, though he had none. Frank confirmed everything about Sato's theory, telling how he struck a deal to defect in exchange for vital information, including the times and dates of the Montevideo Maru and the Tamahoko Maru.

But none of it was true and Kanegawa knew it. The accusations combined with even the slightest bit of evidence would have been enough to condemn anyone else for treason. But this, of course, was no ordinary man. "Great acting, Yank," he said. "An admirable performance deserving of plaudits and praise. Chief, you should promote this man."

"Still in denial?"

"This is all a meaningless ruse." He sat forward. "Let me tell you my theory. You captured this man somewhere on the island trying to infiltrate. He was probably part of a team, but your incompetent men failed to capture the rest. You trained him to say what you wanted him to, buried his supplies up on the mountain and decided to frame me as revenge for your slaughtered fellow Chinamen." Sato tilted his head. "Yes I know about your true heritage. It is by pure coincidence that I suggested the Tamahoko Maru take those prisoners away, for a reason different from the one you suspect. I am innocent. You are the one who has questions to answer and this is over." He rose to leave.

Sato stood in his way and the two stared at each other. "Do you think anyone here cares that I'm half Chinese? Do you think that's an issue?"

"It is forbidden in the Imperial military."

"Yes, it is forbidden in the Imperial military, but I'm the police. I have no ties to the military. I belong to a civilian organization, and I've been cleared to do this job."

"These allegations are still false. You have no evidence."

Sato allowed a lengthy pause before looking down at Frank still seated and quiet. "You know, I can see why your men followed you so loyally. You just don't give up." Sato motioned at his deputy who handed him the final trump card. "So explain why Yankee lieutenant here had this on him." Kanegawa's body went numb as the blood drained from his extremities. He sat back in the chair as the nauseating rush of mortal fear gripped him for the first time in years. In Sato's hands, staring back at him was Bishamonten.

\* \* \* \* \*

It was a day like any other on New Britain. Except it wasn't. It was D-Day. No turning back. Ki-Hwa rose slowly and then remembered Kanegawa's midnight interruption. *Did it really happen just as planned? Or is he on his way here now to arrest us all?*

Just like the morning after she committed murder, she paced the room consumed by doubt; wondering, waiting for news, unwilling to leave for fear of missing something. She tried to find things to occupy herself, but all she could do was stare at the floor where the red stain had been and go over the plan piece by excruciating piece. It was the longest day of her life. By mid-afternoon there was still no sign of him.

As the magic hour approached when Kanewaga should arrive, she walked through the shared washroom to Asako's room. "Victoria just left," she said. "I'm going to walk a little. Would you like to...?" her voice trailed off.

"No thank you," she replied softly. "I'll wait here."

Asako sat in the center of her bed gently turning three posts on a long, stringed object decorated in opaque white and burnt yellow. Ki-Hwa had seen it before, but never up close. "I prefer *niagari* tuning for relaxation."

"Oh?"

"Tuning is half the talent of the *shamisen*. If you cannot tune it correctly, then there is no sense playing it." She frowned a little. Ki-Hwa's mind was again flooded with too many thoughts to get a word out. She had briefly seen the instrument with Saeko after she donned her geisha outfit for an evening of entertaining, but never dreamed an ordinary girl would know how to handle one. Unable to imagine how an object so fragile and valuable could have found its way to Rabaul, she assumed it was a prop used for effect.

"This is a *bachi*. It is used to pluck the strings." Asako held up a triangular piece of what looked like lacquered wood and began to play the most exquisite music, peaceful and wistful at the same time. As if soothed by the touch of a healing hand, Ki-Hwa became lost in the chords and didn't dare interrupt. But when the song was finished, she abandoned self-control.

"Wherever did you learn?"

"In the okiya. I was a geisha." She looked at Ki-Hwa. "I was not trying to hide it. But offering it would be foolish no matter how close our friendship."

"Why hide it at all? It can only make you more valuable." Ki-Hwa was stunned, taken back by the sudden confession. Asako had not been the same since the rape, but this day she seemed especially reflective.

"Because I wanted to forget that part of my life, though I do not think I will ever be able to." She looked away. "I was sold to an okiya when I was ten, not the best age to begin training. I hated it but I was determined not to bring dishonor to my family, so I trained hard and became geisha." She played the first few notes of a song and stopped, seeming reluctant to remember any more. Ki-Hwa thought she knew everything about this woman. Yet here was a secret that should have been plainly obvious.

"Why are you here?"

Asako paused long. "I was brought here for someone." She wrapped the *shamisen* carefully and placed it back in its protective case.

"Who?"

"I thought you were going for a walk."

She wanted to know more, but there were bigger things to worry about. Ki-Hwa stood and departed, leaving Asako in silence, not wanting to prepare for the evening, but knowing she had to. She fought off the nagging doubt and managed to keep up appearances, but nothing was the same. She could still see her assailant, feel him, and smell him. He permeated her thoughts and desecrated her soul, just as he had that night she'd never be able to forget. She hated this life.

"Is she going to the place?" A man's voice came from her doorway. Startled, she stood, covering herself. The shamisen case fell to the floor. "I'm sorry, I didn't mean to scare you," he said entering the room and rolling the door shut quietly.

"You are not allowed to be here, Takeo," Asako said.

"I don't follow instructions very well." He crossed to her sake cabinet and poured a cup, emptying it straight away. "By God, this is good. Is this *Junmai*?" He brought the bottle to his face to read the label. "It is." He held it like a trophy and looked over his shoulder at her, smiling. "This is very expensive." They gazed at each other, but her face was hollow. He dropped the sake. "You were thinking about it again."

She nodded. He crossed the room to her. "Healing takes time."

She nodded again, this time with a tiny smile. He opened his mouth, but nothing came out. He always had trouble finding the right words. He snuck out to the plantation night after night since learning of the rape, making it his personal crusade to undo the damage. He reached out to her during hushed conversations so the loathsome colonel in the next room wouldn't hear. They stayed up many nights when she couldn't sleep, her keeping him at arm's length and him respecting it. No physical contact was ever made. That was the rule. So they spoke. And spoke more.

"There is so much you want to hear me say," she told him. "Just know this; when I find my trust again, I will give it to you. "

He hugged her until it nearly hurt. He rubbed her slender back, and buried his face in her neck. She gently ran fingers through his hair. She was touched by his desire to protect and love her; something no other man ever dared. She wanted to care for him, and yet could not. She was unwilling to commit, to believe, to be led astray again. She pulled back and stared at his boyish face.

"Tell me," he said looking into her dark brown eyes. "Tell me it's forever. Tell me it won't change, no matter what happens to us in this world."

"What do you mean?"

"Just tell me. Tell me the feeling we have right now will be ours forever. Tell me you'll never forget. That if something happens to me, you'll remember me as I am right now; unashamed to admit weakness, unafraid to feel."

"What is bothering you?"

He looked to the ground, his arms draped around her waist. "I'm just, I'm afraid something will happen to one of us and this...whatever this is will be lost."

"It will never be lost," she reassured him. "Our connection can never be trivial. It can never be taken no matter how strong the tides."

He couldn't take his eyes off of her. "Losing you would be unthinkable. After I worked so hard to be someone."

"You know, I was-- " She stopped, looking around the room for the right words. "I lost someone close once before. I do not want to do it again." She put her head on his shoulder as he held her tight again. "And though I do not want to, I care for you."

"And because of that, no harm will ever come to me. No man with something to fight for can be defeated."

# 23

## Men shut their doors against the setting sun
*-William Shakespeare*

"How?" Kanegawa asked the walls repeatedly, pacing his cell four steps from end to end and back a thousand times. How did this happen? "How did Bishamonten get into that American's hands and how does he know so much about me? What happened to the body?"

He had to focus. "I gave Victoria the letter opener. Somehow it vanished from her room. So how did it get from Victoria's room to Ki-Hwa's just when she needed it? Assuming she's telling the truth, it is hard to believe it's a coincidence. She must have stolen it; there's just no other explanation. It's not possible someone could have foreseen her needing it that night and planted it there. Did Asako have access to Victoria's chambers? Yes. Could she have foreseen the Sergeant attacking Ki-Hwa? Unlikely, although this man had attacked her before, so she has a motive for revenge and he clearly set a pattern by traveling to the plantation during raids. Maybe she felt they needed protection and stole the opener as a defense weapon. It doesn't really matter how it got there. It did. Let's assume Ki-Hwa stole it and go from there. But then how did the American get it? No one knew I buried the Sergeant up there. No one. The American is not a scout; he's a pilot, which is so obvious to everyone but that idiot Sato. Unless he's an assassin acting the part of an aviator, in which case he's very talented. But how would he know so much about me and what is his motivation for framing me? And how did Sato know I was going to be there last night when I did not know myself? There has to be a connection between Sato, the American, the dead Sergeant, and Bishamonten. Could they be colluding in this operation together or are they the puppets and another master is pulling the strings? The question we must answer is who has the means to know I buried the Sergeant on the mountain, make a deal with the Allies, AND devise a plan with them to frame me? Ki-Hwa is the common thread but the frailest of spirit. What would the Allies want in return? The general? The Port? The new Zero…"

Stopping in the middle of the cell, he looked up, amazed that he hadn't figured it out before. He knew exactly who the lynchpin was.

"Deceiver!"

\* \* \* \* \*

By the time the wind told Victoria of Kanegawa's incarceration it was well past midday and she wasted no time summoning Abongo to take her to the Rabaul city jail just as the orange sky of dusk erupted in brilliance over the island.

"I'm here to see Colonel Kanegawa," she stated to a deputy as she walked past him.

"I cannot let you go in there madam," he said jumping in her way.

"What do you mean? Do you know who I am?"

"Step aside, Haruki." Sato's commanding voice came from behind the young deputy as he stepped from his office. "I'm surprised it took you this long to show up." Without saying a word, he held out a hand to lead her down the darkened hallway along the row of sixteen cells. She followed the oversized chief, but down the hall Sato turned on her. He grabbed her by the shoulders and pushed her up against the wall as though she were a common criminal. "Any weapons?" he asked as his hands found their way around her body.

"Get your hands off of me." She stared at the Chief, maintaining eye contact while his hands made their way around her. When he was done, she straightened herself.

"Do anything I don't like and you'll be in the cell next to him."

"And I suppose you'll be popping into Chang's room immediately after?" she said in a huff, straightening her blouse. He led her to Kanegawa's cell where he sat motionless in a chair against the bars. Sato said nothing as he turned to leave the two alone, but left a long stare behind him. Victoria was prepared for the worst, but she was still shocked to see the legendary colonel incarcerated. He sat quietly, waiting for her to speak first, when she finally put her hands inside the bars to grasp his.

"How did this happen?"

"Contrived charges born of conjecture and cunning."

"Well I see you haven't lost your talent for words."

"And I see you have not lost your warm, caring persona. I am surprised to see you here after our little spat."

"Our 'relationship' transcends superficial tiffs, Nibori. At least I'd like to think so. Now are we going to insult each other until Sato runs me through or are you going to tell me what happened?"

"What happened is I was deceived by a deceiver; a hustler who brilliantly planned this charade and quite possibly my execution."

"They wouldn't execute you."

"My dear, the Emperor himself would rather cut off his nose than let a mole grow on it. Perception is reality in the Imperial Army. I was very fortunate the last time."

"What's the charge?"

"Treason, but of that I am innocent I assure you. It is the conspiracy I am guilty of."

Victoria looked puzzled. "Chinatown? Nanking? Do you think this is about that?"

"Not those conspiracies, a more personal one involving a Sergeant and my ianfu."

Victoria leaned back a little. This was about helping *her* commit a crime? She didn't need to ask.

"She killed a Sergeant who tried to rape her," Kanegawa said.

"What? Another rape at my plantation?" her voice rose.

Kanegawa lowered his. "Yes. The rapist seems to be the same individual who attacked Asako. Ki-Hwa stabbed him with Bishamonten. The very Bishamonten we argued over last night. When I agreed to hide the body for her, I failed to retrieve the weapon and was not even aware she had used it until last evening." Kanegawa paused to look down the hall before continuing.

"That's why you brought hell with me? That letter opener was the murder weapon?"

"I went to reclaim it and the Chief caught me, only now there is suddenly no dead Sergeant."

"That's a fair tall tale," she said.

"Yes. What's more, now an American claims I am in cahoots with him to commit treason."

"An American?"

"An officer. Sato says he caught him in the jungle and that he knows me. He produced a Bishamonten-- your Bishamonten. The same one Ki-Hwa used."

Victoria's face contorted. "Bear with me, please. You went to dig up a body of a Sergeant that Ki-Hwa killed at my plantation but he wasn't there. Now an American suddenly has my letter opener, which is the murder weapon, and claims you're working together?" She took her arms back from the bars and outstretched them to the heavens.

"I am sure Lieutenant Hashimoto is responsible for removing the body, replacing it with a radio and tipping off Sato. He somehow discovered I buried the body up there and has struck a deal with the Anglos. I believe he offered his airplane for my head."

"Lieutenant Hashimoto?" Victoria paused, looking at Kanegawa the way a child looks at a lunatic. "I know you like to big-note yourself, but you're suggesting that a twenty-something lieutenant has masterminded a plot to frame you for treason by somehow discovering a dead digger you buried, replacing it with an American radio and giving the murder weapon to a Yankee so when he's captured he can call you a spy? And for this he gets what?"

"He gets life."

"And why is that?"

"Because I was about to expose him for who he really is, for which he would be executed."

"And he is?"

"An imposter. He is not who he seems."

"Then who is he?" she grew weary of his game.

"I do not know that. But I do know the real Takeo Hashimoto was found dead in a Hiroshima alleyway almost two years ago."

"You've known about this how long?"

"I only recently was informed. News takes time to travel from a local police precinct in Hiroshima to the outskirts of the Empire in a time of war. "

"So why haven't you placed him in irons?" He did not answer. She cocked her head to one side, knowing why. "You wanted to toy with him. Scare him a little, you brute." He looked away and shifted in his chair. "But instead you pushed him to the other side." She smiled, but quickly dropped it. "But getting you arrested doesn't stop you from exposing him. He should want to silence you for good."

"Or run away."

"Run away?"

"He has an airplane. In fact, he flies the type 52 Zero. The Allies would be willing to sacrifice one of their own to get their hands on it."

"The Yank bloke that was caught?'

"Yes."

Victoria stopped. "Then he would have to escape tonight, before you could talk."

"Precisely. They pitted Sato against me so we would both be preoccupied. Find him and you'll free me, as well as do a great service to the Emperor for which I am sure you would be generously rewarded."

"And where would I find him exactly?"

Kanegawa sighed. He grew just as weary of her, but needed her too. "Wherever his airplane is. You know where my men are. Have them detain and question him and that friend of his. Tell them to do what they have to. You go and question your girls, but only the ones who may know something, like Asako. I caught him outside her door once. You have a gun, do you not?"

She nodded. "It still seems a grand conspiracy that you should be telling a barrister."

Her doubt crossed his line of patience. "Let me remind you that without me you would have few, if any, allies in the Imperial hierarchy who would honor our current arrangement."

"My dear Nibori," she squinted her eyes and leaned forward the way a woman does when scorn overrules judgment, "You could have gotten a lot farther with talk of how I should do it for us, rather than threaten me with your waning power. Even if it was a lie, hearing you proclaim your faith in me..." She put a hand underneath her blouse and plucked out an object, dropping it into his hands through the bars. Kanegawa looked down at a ring with sixteen keys on it as she turned to leave. "Sato shouldn't get so close when he frisks someone." Kanegawa smiled for the first time in days. "He'll notice soon. You haven't much time."

* * * * *

Ki-Hwa returned to her room as night engulfed the island, bringing more swells of apprehension and determination. "We're so close," she muttered as her feet mounted the verandah and walked toward her room.

"To what?" A man's voice replied suddenly from the darkness just in front of her.

Startled, she let out a little yelp and put a hand to her heart. "Oh, my God, you scared me! Chief of Police Sato? What can I assist you with this evening?"

"I apologize," he said bowing without a smile. "You're so close to what?" He ignored her question and pressed his own.

"I was so close to making it back by dark. I wanted to get in my room before nightfall. I have entertaining to do." She found her composure and pushed past him to her room to find two policemen rummaging through her things.

"Where did you go?" the Chief asked.

"I went to the wharf and back."

"Why?"

"I wanted to get out, that's all."

"You wanted to get out?"

"Yes, Sato-san. Feigning interest in men night after night and forcing yourself to get worked up over uninteresting company is not easy. I have to get out once in a while." Sato smiled, which she returned. Ridiculing Kanewaga, his nemesis, had the desired effect. "The man you entertain is the cause of this search. Colonel Kanegawa has been arrested for a crime."

"A crime?"

"Let's just say he's in very serious trouble."

"Oh, my!" she exclaimed. "Is it serious? Will he be hurt?" Ki-Hwa changed tactics and began to cry only because a weeping girl is a nuisance to even the strongest man, as Seo-Sung had taught her. She covered her face, hoping to make him uncomfortable and grabbed the railing to keep from falling.

"Take it easy, miss. He's just being questioned right now. I know this is hard, but I need to ask you a few questions." He took an arm and led her inside, seating her in the colonel's favorite chair. "Did he ever speak English around you? When does he typically come and go? Is he always alone? Have you ever been to his quarters?"

She did her best to answer honestly while continuing to sob at the right moments. Sato was a fish on her hook. A few minutes later a deputy shrugged at him when they finished searching the room and he ordered them out.

"Be sure to let us know if you see or hear anything we talked about..." Sato said. But his words were interrupted by the distant sound of air raid sirens growing louder in the city. The three policemen froze, looking to the sky. "Let's go," he barked as they all ran down the verandah to their car. In an instant, girls scurried out of their rooms and made for the bunker with pillows and personal items. Ki-Hwa wiped her eyes and slid her door shut.

"I thought they'd never leave," Asako said as she entered her room with a roll of clothing tied over her shoulder. For the first time since Ki-Hwa met her, Asako was wearing pants.

"Kanegawa has been arrested," Ki-Hwa blurted out.

"I heard. Where is your pack?"

Ki-Hwa opened her window, moved a palm leaf, and grabbed a roll similar to Asako's that was hanging just outside the window. "No turning back," Ki-Hwa said for her own benefit.

"Right," Asako said. "No turning back, unless you want to wait for Sato to figure out that it was you who killed that Sergeant."

Ki-Hwa gasped. "You knew?"

The sound of Ki-Hwa's door sliding quickly open followed by the metallic *CLICK* of a gun's cocking hammer stopped the conversation.

"Knew what?" Victoria said.

# 24

## We have scotched the snake, not killed it
*-William Shakespeare*

"Those are surface ship rounds!" Rear Admiral Iseki growled at the senior staff and other personnel gathered in the island's command bunker. "They're using surface ships!"

"How can you be sure?" Major General Fukuda replied.

*WHUMP WHUMP*

An explosion close by made everyone in the room pause as dust filled the cave.

"...hear impacting are being fired from ships offshore that our spotters can see!"

"Is this the prelude to an invasion?" A colonel asked from the back corner of the room.

"Yes!" the Army Deputy Commander yelled over the noise of war in the cramped cave.

*WHUMP WHUMP*

"No!" Insisted the Admiral. "There are only destroyers and battleships, no troop carriers! But it's damn arrogant of them!"

Somewhere nearby, a bomb exploded with a violence that made the entire bunker shudder. Part of the interior ceiling suddenly cracked and fell to the floor. The Admiral grimaced in pain as a thin trail of blood ran down the back of his neck. "They're trying to make a point. They control the seas now!"

"This is *obviously* an artillery preparation for their invasion!" Fukuda insisted.

"Whether it is or not, we can't risk sending up the few planes we have in the dark. That was a tactic in vain the last time." The calm voice of Vice Admiral Jin-Ichi Kusaka entered the fray. He turned to his terrified driver. "Get word to the Kokutai to stand down."

All around the island, those outside the shelter of the bunkers and even those inside waited to hear the Empire's response. The roar of Zeros, Bettys, Kates, Irvings, and Vals rising skyward to meet the foes of the Empire was a comfort to those who desperately needed it. Planes streaking to the heavens meant they were taking the fight to the enemy. It meant hope that the terrible suffering on the ground would soon stop. But this night, that hope never came.

* * * * *

Colonel Kanegawa walked down the center of Malaguna drive toward his office, impervious to the explosions rattling the island, debris flying past his head, and frightened people running about. Escaping from jail was too easy once the sirens started and the police deployed to keep good order. Unfortunately, his Kempeitai would be out doing the same, so finding anything to stop his new enemy would be a challenge. A sword from his standing valet and a revolver from his desk was a good start.

Standing back in the street as shells impacted in the distance, he surveyed the city. "No planes," he mumbled. "Afraid of the dark...pitiful." Massive flashes from the muzzles of at least three battleships glared in the harbor. He searched the skyline and ridges. "Just a raid. An audacious one at that." Two explosions rocked the docks closest to him, followed by two more. But the sounds were different; not the loud WHUMP of large munitions, but a smaller signature. "Grenades?" Kanegawa looked toward the docks to see four of the Navy's fastest pursuit boats in flames as two shadowy figures jumped into a staff car and sped away, pier guards firing at them.

"Sir!" a young soldier yelled from a truck that stopped suddenly behind him. "You should take shelter, sir."

"Who do you have with you?" Kanegawa asked.

"Sergeant Matsushita and..." A shell landed close by, destroying part of the Malaguna marketplace.

"No matter," Kanegawa said jumping into the passenger seat and forcing Matsushita to move over. "They're bound for the North Coast road. Go!"

\* \* \* \* \*

"So it is true!" Victoria said, aiming her gun at Ki-Hwa's face. "By God, I didn't believe the old man when he told me, but here you shits are conspiring together!"

Ki-Hwa remembered the revolver as the one from Victoria's dresser that day she stole Bishamonten and now that it was pointed at her, she wished she'd taken it instead.

"I always knew you were trouble," Victoria said. "From the day I saw you, just knew you'd be a handful." She gritted her teeth and shouted as bombs rattled the room. "You killed a Sergeant. Right here in this room!"

"He tried to rape me. He raped Asako!"

"You could have told me!"

"And you would have done what?"

"I may not be your best mate, but my girls are my business. Your burden is mine as well. You should know that by now. Instead you ran to Nibori and put him in jeopardy."

Ki-Hwa flinched at the mention of his first name. "I didn't know what else to do."

"And you!" She swung the gun to Asako "I can believe her doing this, but you?" She stood swaying back and forth, shifting her weight from one foot to the other like a nervous boxer. "You've been the perfect girl. A model I tell the others to be like. How could you betray me like this?"

"This is only about our freedom," Asako said.

Victoria stared at Asako, not paying Ki-Hwa any attention. "Then why did you even come here; especially with your training? You don't need to be in this place, unless this was only a weigh station to keep moving on. Did you plan all along to escape from here? That lieutenant roped you into this didn't he? The one Nibori says is an imposter. He planned this to take you away from me."

"Imposter?" Ki-Hwa said without meaning to.

She swung the pistol back to Ki-Hwa. "This is not about you, Victoria. We don't want to..." Asako started.

"Do you have any idea what you've done?" Victoria snarled.

"Nothing worse than what you've done, Vikki," a male voice said slowly from the verandah. Victoria froze. Her jaw dropped and her eyes opened wide. Ki-Hwa knew the voice and the moment she saw the hair on Victoria's outstretched arm rise in goose bumps like raindrops falling on a still pond, she knew she knew him too. Without dropping her gun, Victoria turned, straining to see him standing expressionless, his own gun pointed at her. "You didn't check for a backup. I expected better from you, Jillaroo."

"You are David I presume," Asako said. "We were told to expect you about now."

"Yeah. Now off you go." He motioned with his gun toward the doorway.

"NO!" Victoria demanded as she sidestepped to block their exit, her gun still trained on the pair. Dave stepped forward and pressed his barrel through Victoria's finely combed hair and into her scalp. "You know I will, Vik."

Ki-Hwa believed him. He didn't seem like one to bluff. There was a long silence before Victoria finally accepted the inevitable. Her arm fell. The revolver hit the wooden floor with a loud *CLUNK*. The girls sprinted past the big Aussie and out the door. "I'll see you down there," Dave said as they left, not taking his eyes off Victoria. All that remained was a room filled with animosity and the occasional sound of shells hitting trees to the north, an uncommon direction. She refused to turn, choosing instead to stare at the ground. "Time for your atonement, love," he said. But Victoria remained unflinching and silent. "Why'd you do it? Why'd you turn traitor?"

"The word 'traitor' would imply that I had some loyalty to one side or the other at some point in this madness," she said. "I never had that. I never had anything but a nice pair of tits and the will to use them." She glanced around at the room and house and life she'd built after all else was taken. "I thought you were dead. Or at least gone."

"Never doubt the power of hate," he said.

"Well then, we both did what we had to. Unlike you, I've always known I was selfish and would never have anything to call mine unless I took it." She lifted her head and stared out the window, listening to the faint sound of bombs slamming into the island, but still kept her back to him. "These girls have nothing, but what's worse is they have no ambition, either. They care not to change anything. No spine, no drive, no strength. They wait for someone to give them something." She finally turned to him. "Well I don't! I saw an opportunity and I took it!"

"Committing treason in the process."

"Against whom?"

"Humankind."

"Oh, come down from the self-righteous glory horse, David! Do you really think you have the right to take the moral high ground here?"

"Yes."

"On what pretense?"

"Because our people don't believe in the wholesale slaughter of other people, combatants or not, in the name of religion or for a man playing the role of a deity. They're butchers with no remorse or common sense and you their accomplice." He was calm and spoke as if he'd rehearsed his words a million and another million times.

"I helped myself. You draw the battle lines and claim superiority in determining who's to be on which side, not caring that there are those who don't see things in black and white! You fight for the green and gold of mother Australia while they fight for the red of the rising sun. What's the difference?" She turned to him as a series of nearby impacts rattled the windows. "Well, Victoria Lynn Foster fights for the glory of no color but that of money, whomsoever provides for it." She took small but threatening steps toward Dave. He'd committed himself to killing her years ago, but suddenly found his trigger finger numb to the woman he once called a friend.

"Why exactly do you hate them so?" Victoria asked. "And don't give me that rubbish about your family being displaced. You know as well as I do the hardships of life on this island."

"Why do I hate them? They don't believe in freedom. This is freedom's frontier. Right here, this room. This is free man's land as long as I control it, while right over there, just out of that door, is oppression and denial of even the most basic human dignities. They deny people that which God bestowed. They murdered our friends. "

"They murdered *your* friends!"

"They were *our* friends, Vikki! The Diggers, the Jackaroos, the Sheilas, all of them. And they died with their arms held high! They died wearing Red Cross armbands, on stretchers as they lay helpless and bayonetted. They died on the boats crammed to the gills. They were proud Volunteer Rifles and they were slaughtered. I saw it all." He paused as a long series of bombs impacted the earth, making the ground heave and shake under their feet. The gas lamps swayed and flickered.

She lowered her head. He dropped his arm holding the gun and walked over to Ki-Hwa's cabinet, keeping his eyes on her. He looked at the sake bottles and let out a sigh. "After all this time living off rainwater, you'd think I'd have thirst for a drop." He paused again to allow her to reply, but Victoria stood in the middle of the room, arms crossed and sullen. "Do you remember when we used to take coconut juice and ferment it out by the drying racks?"

"Don't try to play on my memories, David. It wasn't exactly a joyous time."

"You seemed happy."

Tears appeared in her eyes as she looked around the ceiling to keep them from falling. "Until that vile brew took control and they tried to have their way." She turned to him. "Oh, you were never privy to that were you?" She took a big breath and pulled on the waistband of her pants. "I had to fight those drunks off so many times..."

Dave looked away. "So how'd you do it anyway? How'd you get to be owner of this place?"

"Simple. I wiggled my assets like a lure until the right fish came along to take a bite."

"Kanegawa?"

"He was the man in power at the time. We shared a common trait."

"Ambition?"

She nodded. "I just had to prove I could run the girls efficiently and it was mine for a paltry tithing."

"Until he got tired of you."

"I got what I wanted."

"Yes, you did. And I'm about to do the same."

\*   \*   \*   \*   \*

"We need shelter!" Sergeant Isogai shouted as Colonel Kanegawa's official staff car came to a halt at the gate of POW Camp 7. The soldier didn't even think of stopping him.

"Over there!" he yelled, pointing to a small cave dug into the hillside where the faint glow of a lantern flickered. Denbe drove quickly into the camp's large open courtyard, parked, yanked Frank out in handcuffs and headed to the cave.

Inside, three soldiers sat around a worn *kotatsu* table. Two stood as he entered. "I'm transporting this prisoner," Denbe said. "Need to wait out this bombing raid here."

"*Hai*," a soldier responded as all of them sat back down to continue their game of mahjong. Denbe peered at the soldier who refused to stand. A corporal, and one with a bad attitude by the looks of it. Denbe forced Frank to take a seat against the cave wall and looked back at the courtyard where a lone guard stood rigid, his rifle at the ready while bombs continued to fall some distance away. "Why is he out there?"

"Test of courage for the new guys," the corporal said. "We've all had to do it."

"He's not new," Denbe said. "He was sent over from Camp 151 because he couldn't be retrained. I remember him."

"All I know is he's the new guy so he goes through the same test that we did," the corporal said. "He'll stand guard out there and we'll play mahjong in here until the Yanks decide it's over. So what's his story?" The corporal asked, looking at Frank.

"Caught him today. Pilot. Shot down. Haven't had a chance to question him yet. Taking him to KT HQ."

"Did I see you come up the road from the city, though?"

"We were almost there when the bombing started. Decided to come back here."

"I didn't see you go by the first time."

"Guess you were winning," Denbe said looking at the mahjong tiles.

The corporal was indeed winning, but it was Denbe who was quickest on his toes.

"Sounds like this one," a soldier said, pointing at an Anglo major at the back of the cave, wrists and ankles bound. Denbe looked at his uniform. A New Zealander and from the blood around his nose and mouth one that had been captured recently. "Caught him in the jungle today as well. We watched him bail out of his plane days ago. Very sneaky to avoid us for so long," he kicked the major's feet.

"Go fuck yourself, mate" the major replied.

"What did he say, Chikaki?"

"He said he wants water," Chikaki the interpreter said. The soldiers laughed as Chikaki looked nervously at Denbe. "I came out to speak with him when the raid started, same as you. The colonel doesn't want either of them harmed."

Bombs rained down, loosening dust and debris from the cave ceiling with every impact. Air raids were usually concentrated on the city of Rabaul, but tonight the shells landed very close to prison camp NG 7, testing even the seasoned recruits. After several moments of silence pocked by intermittent explosions a soldier spoke. "They say sex before battle is a good omen, right?"

"I hear the older folks say that," the corporal replied as he shuffled the tiles for a new game. "But this isn't battle. It's just a bombing that we have to sit through."

"Says who?" a soldier interjected. "For all we know the entire Anglo Army is on the high seas."

Two bombs exploded not far away, drowning out the sound of his voice. The corporal eyed the two ianfu huddled against the far wall of the cave on an old *goza* mat. The soldiers weren't used to being around premium girls and it showed. "They just happened to be walking by when it started, right?" the corporal asked.

"They begged for shelter, but Nobuo wasn't going to let them in."

"I would have."

"You didn't want to until I said we had a cave."

"Enough," the corporal stopped them. He looked at the girls for a long moment as sweat built up on his forehead.

"I think it's exciting," Jin-Min finally said, looking at Nobuo. "I mean the danger of the situation."

"You see! She even wants to!" he exclaimed, not waiting for permission.

"Hey," the corporal started.

Nobuo scooped her up in his arms and made for one of the three goza mats in the far reaches of the cave as Jin-Min let out a giggle. The worried guard watched them run off and immediately looked at the corporal.

"Go ahead! Just save some for me!"

He grabbed the other girl, Sun-Cho, by the hand and ran for a mat.

The corporal pointed at Frank and spoke to Chikaki. "Tell them not to get any stupid ideas."

275

"I have to pee," Chikaki said.

"Again!?" The corporal refilled his sake cup. "I'm thankful you had sake to share, but you're not very good at holding it in." Chikaki stood from the table. "You're not going to puke are you?" the corporal laughed at the civilian who didn't look a day over eighteen.

"I don't think so." Chikaki walked quickly outside and peered toward the front gate of the camp. The guard in the center of the court stood perfectly still with his back to the cave. Chikaki checked the cave one more time to make sure no one could see him and pulled a small flashlight from his belt. He flashed it into the jungle across the street three quick times.

In the bush overlooking the camp, Asako and Ki-Hwa breathed heavy from running all the way from the plantation. Two shells slammed into the hillside, exploding not three hundred yards from their position, shattering trees and spraying mud. Chikaki's signal light was clear flashed three times.

"That's it," Asako said. Chang, the Chinese girl who so brilliantly manipulated Sato, handed Ki-Hwa a knife. She held it to her palm and paused as Asako looked away. With a slice that would make a surgeon proud, she cut hand across her palm. She winced and inhaled sharply, her eyes squeezed shut in pain, but she kept the arm steady. After stabbing a man to death she knew how to go deep enough to draw ample blood but shallow enough to avoid tendons. The blood pooled in her hand until there was enough to smear across her face, neck and left shoulder. Ki-Hwa stood and walked down to the road that led to the front gate of the camp until the moonlight discovered her and stumbled like a wounded animal toward it, moaning loud.

"Are you hurt?" the guard yelled as he ran to her. Ki-Hwa collapsed in arms, limp and heavy. He turned and dragged her across the open yard to the cave. Upon entering he exclaimed, "Corporal. She needs help."

But she didn't. And in fact the seemingly lifeless Ki-Hwa suddenly sprang to life, holding her knife, tucked into her blouse, to the soldier's throat. In a second, Chikaki ran into the cave with Chang following closely behind. He grabbed the guard's rifle and brought it to bear on the corporal. "Don't move!"

But the corporal would have none of it. He lunged for his weapon, grabbing it quickly from the inner wall.

"I said don't move!" Chikaki shouted. But his warning fell on deaf ears. The corporal stood and aimed at Chikaki.

"Shoot him!" Frank shouted.

*CLICK* The corporal's rifle misfired.

*CRACK* A shot rang out. Like a marionette whose strings are unexpectedly cut, the corporal went limp and fell to the floor, his legs collapsing under him. Blood splattered his chest in a scarlet stain that quickly soaked his shirt. Chikaki stood motionless, his mouth open. Slowly he turned to see Denbe, the proverbial smoking gun still aimed at the dead man.

Frank leapt to his feet as Chang slashed his wrist bindings. He grabbed the corporal's rifle from the dead man's hands and gave it to the New Zealander. "You know how to use one of these, Kiwi?"

"I can learn," he replied, studying the Arisaka. The New Zealander struggled with the bolt on the Arisaka, finally freeing it. "There's no bullet in the chamber...no wonder it didn't fire." He loaded a magazine from the dead corporal's gear.

"Are we escaping?"

"Yep...getting out of here."

"Jolly good. What about them?" But the major's question didn't need a reply. Jin-Min and Sun-Cho had the soldiers tied at the wrists and ankles in seconds.

"Let's go," Frank shouted as he ordered everyone out of the cave.

But Denbe was frozen, staring at the man he'd just killed. "Why didn't you just stay put?" Denbe said. Frank put a hand on his shoulder. "I knew him," Denbe mumbled. "Or at least I saw him in training."

"Yeah...we gotta go, Hoss," Frank said.

The party ran across the courtyard to two Army cargo trucks parked side by side and started them. The Kiwi major, who introduced himself as Lovasz, jumped into the passenger seat next to Chikaki, the pair looking at each other. "War makes strange bedfellows, eh?"

"So far so good, I think." He put the truck in gear and drove to the center of the courtyard, followed by Denbe moving the second one. The shelling continued all around the camp for three more minutes, never once hitting a single building inside of it. And then it stopped.

"Break," Denbe shouted. " Fourteen minutes and this place will be dust!"

"We're doing our best," Frank yelled, emerging from a hut, a group of sick and lame men walking and hobbling toward the trucks behind him. Five minutes passed. Then six. Then seven. Finally Frank stuck his head in Denbe's window. "They're all in. I'm shotgun in this truck right?"

"Shotgun?"

"Passenger."

Denbe didn't respond. He put the truck in gear and looked out the window, trying to drive  on a road illuminated only by the radiance of the moon. The trucks were moving. The plan was working. Escape suddenly seemed plausible. But Denbe was silent and Frank knew why.

"Don't be so hard on yourself," Frank said. "Killing isn't easy. We do what we have to for freedom."

"You Yanks," Denbe said shaking his head. "Always blaming everything on freedom."

In the back of his truck, Ki-Hwa and Asako sat across from each other at the end, the last to board. "When did you know?" Ki-Hwa shouted over the truck engine.

"It was not hard to decipher," Asako said. "When I heard Kanegawa was arrested, I put the pieces into place."

"We had an agreement to keep everything separate. Remember?"

Asako nodded, remembering the pact that everyone had a role in the escape but they would never learn of each other's involvement in case one was caught. But information brings peace and Ki-Hwa needed some right now. "The Anglos and I came up with a way to get him locked up, at least for this evening."

"And it involved killing the rapist who attacked me and pinning it somehow on the colonel?"

"You're not angry?"

Asako looked around the truck of sweaty, smelly POWs. "I wish you had told me when it happened, but no matter. You seem to have found a way to use it to our mutual benefit and you killed the man who raped me. How can I be angry? We all have secrets."

"Yes. Now tell me yours. You came here looking for someone. Who?"

Asako looked out the back of the truck at Chikaki driving the other truck very closely. His nose was practically inside the back of her truck. "Should we really do this now?

"Who?" Ki-Hwa repeated.

Asako looked at her. "Takeo."

"The pilot?"

"I came here to kill him."

Asako, a geisha and master of body control, suddenly had none. She breathed heavily and shouted. "My family name is Hashimoto. I changed it to Nagumo when I came here looking for the man who killed my brother. His name was Takeo."

"Takeo is your brother? But that's not..."

Asako shook her head. "The man who claims to be Lieutenant Takeo Hashimoto is not my brother. He is an imposter. He has been impersonating my brother since stealing his life a few years ago."

Ki-Hwa no longer heard the truck, felt the sting in her hands, or smelled the malodor of the POWs. The world stopped. "Finish," she said.

"My father made bad decisions. He lost all the money our family had, so he sold me into an okiya in Kyoto to be a geisha."

"Your father sold you? Just as mine did?" Ki-Hwa looked down at the dirt and coral of the passing road. *So many lies!*

"To regain our stature my father then called in some favors from his friends in the Navy and secured my brother an appointment to the Academy at Etajima. But on the night he graduated, he was murdered. At a moment that should have been his proudest and most honorable, he was cheated out of it by a dropout; a street thug who was unhappy with his own life. So he stole Takeo's." She looked at the passing jungle and stared as if watching the story unfold in front of her.

"I lived in a well respected okiya, entertaining powerful people. Those people aren't around the house much when there's a war on, so the geisha would get together and talk and form networks where vital information is easily obtained. It turned out that a geisha in Tokyo named Mae had been with Takeo the night he was killed. She told me of what transpired and I learned he had assumed Takeo's life, attending flight school in his place. But I was too late to catch him there. I had to follow him to Rabaul."

Ki-Hwa shook her head. " Who is he?"

"I do not know. Only an imposter with ambition for battle."

"So you came here to kill him, but then you fell in love with him instead?"

She shook her head and looked at the floor of the truck. "No. I found him easily and knew that killing him would be easy, too. Or maybe he would die in the air. But he always returned from every mission. But he was changed. He was less of a man each time. So I watched him suffer. He killed my brother and stole his life and deserved no less than to be tossed into his own hell. I wanted him to either go down in flames or live a life of pain as he watched his friends die one by one." She finally looked up and stared Ki-Hwa in the eye. "Once I even hoped he'd kill himself when he slipped so deep into alcoholism. He was so reckless, and so distraught over all the friends who died. Killing him would only have set him free from that. The war did much worse damage than I could have. So I kept close tabs on him."

"But you cared for him? Developed feelings?"

Asako looked back out into the jungle. "I couldn't help myself, much to my dishonor. At first it was just a shoulder to lean on while I looked for an opportunity to destroy him. But then he was so sincere. He hurt so deeply when his friends were lost. He was so outspoken against the Empire. I waited too long. Then things got worse."

"Worse?"

"Kanegawa somehow discovered his ruse. He knew he was an imposter."

Ki-Hwa frowned at the mention of his name. "What will happen to him?"

"He killed my brother. No amount of laughter can bring back what sorrow has driven away."

"But what will happen to him?" Ki-Hwa repeated the question, but Asako only looked away to the jungle.

Dave had chosen the route well and prepared the drivers with the utmost care to keep the probability of error to a minimum. They stuck to the seldom used but rougher back roads between the camp and the rendezvous beach near Nonga on the island's northwest side. The old Toyota truck engines were noisy, but the constant shelling covered them as Chikaki and Denbe forced them up and down the winding roads in the black night asking them nicely to be dependable just one more time. Just shy of Nonga, the impacts lost their ferocity and the bombing seemed like a harmless storm passing in the distance except for an occasional pair of rounds hitting the road behind them in case anyone was following. "They've shifted fire already," Frank said. "We need to dismount the men fast and be ready."

As they turned the last corner to the rendezvous beach an Imperial staff car sat in the loose sand where the road ended. "That should be our sabotage party," Frank said.

"Why are the tires spinning?" Denbe asked, stopping just behind the car as Frank dismounted and ran to the passenger side, its door wide open. "God dammit," he mumbled. Chang jumped out and followed him, gasping at the sight.

"Shin-Dae?" the normally effervescent Chinese girl whispered. In the passenger seat Shin-Dae bled profusely from her abdomen and gasped for air.

Shin-Dae gathered her strength. "We did it," she gasped. "We destroyed all of them." She smiled, proud. Her hands clenched tightly at her stomach where blood continued to seep through her stained fingers.

Chikaki ran to the driver's side where a dead corporal named Jiro slumped over the wheel. Denbe and Chikaki had no trouble recruiting their fellow Kempeitai; a disenfranchised young man who wanted none of the Imperial cause. He and Shin-Dae had only one task--steal grenades and sabotage the Navy's fastest pursuit boats

Shin-Dae took a deep breath and uttered a word. "Kanegawa."

"What?" Frank said.

"She said, Kanegawa," a male voice said from behind him. Frank spun to see the head of the Kempeitai mere feet away. He brought his rifle up, but the colonel's sword was quick and he found it poised at his throat, the razor-sharp tip breaking the skin ever so slightly. In a second, four Kempeitai soldiers leapt from the jungle surrounding the trucks screaming at everyone to get out and drop their weapons. Suddenly it made sense. Shin-Dae's wounds were from a blade-- the same blade that now threatened to run Frank through. Kanegawa and his men somehow found out the plan and got here first.

*We just lost the initiative,* Frank thought.

Ki-Hwa, Asako, Chitose, Jin-Min, and Sun-Cho were removed from the back of the trucks, led to the beach, and forced to their knees followed by Denbe, Chikaki, Lovasz, and twenty or so scraggly POWs. Finally Kanegawa himself led Chang and Frank to the gathering near the shore break. As they huddled in the sand, weaponless and surrounded by a squad of Kempeitai led by a man with a reputation for barbarity, hope faded.

"My own interpreter, my driver, and my consort," Kanegawa gloated as he glared at Chikaki, Denbe, and Ki-Hwa. "And I suspect you are responsible for bringing Jiro into this as well. The lot of you conspiring with this American to ensnare me." No one spoke.

He paced the lot, stopped behind an anonymous POW and with one swift strike, beheaded him. Everyone flinched, but no one panicked even as the head landed near the conspirators. Their relationship with death was familiar.

"What fantastic tales do you have to tell now, American? And my own men...what will I do with you?" He paced again and stopped behind Chikaki. "Tell them they will all die this night." Chikaki did not speak. "Tell them," Kanegawa demanded placing the blade of his sword against the back of his neck, warm blood still dripping from it.

"He says he is going to kill all of us tonight," Chikaki said in English.

"Go ahead asshole," a POW said. Frank gazed at the man and then the other men he risked his life for. Their eyes were blank and void of emotion. They cared not what happened to them this night so long as it was swift. "They would welcome a meeting with their savior at this point," Frank said. Chikaki translated.

"I can arrange that." Kanegawa strode to a prisoner and raised his sword when a gunshot broke the air, followed by several more from the sand dunes closest to the jungle. One of Kanegawa's men fell and did not move. All the POWs laid face-down in the sand, an instant reaction to danger while bullets flew overhead into the gathering, striking the Kempeitai guards and grazing Kanegawa himself. Only Jin-Min made the mistake of leaping to her feet to run and was instantly cut down by a Kempeitai in the confusion.

"No!" Ki-Hwa screamed.

Kanegawa's three remaining soldiers fled to take cover behind the trucks while returning fire in a general direction toward the dunes. Frank picked out the muzzle flashes of at least two weapons that pinned the Kempeitai behind the trucks with the water to their backs. The only thing that was clear was that no one was shooting at the POWs, saboteurs, or comfort women, so Frank took charge.

"Down the beach!" he yelled. "Away from the trucks!" But that was easier said than done with so many men who were barely mobile. The able bodied grabbed the sick and frantically tried to get away from the firefight, running in loose sand that might as well have been wet concrete.

In the fog of war, no one noticed Kanegawa, unwilling to retreat, moving along with the pack, swinging his katana, cutting down one, then two, then three POWs. He sliced Denbe's back, sending him face first into the sand, cut from one shoulder blade to the opposing ribs. "Traitor!" he screamed.

He raised the sword for the killing blow when a yell pierced the air and Kanegawa was forced down onto one knee in the sand by the weight of Ki-Hwa on his back. She slid a forearm under his bony neck and started choking him, forcing the old man to gasp for air and swing his blade wildly as he tried to stand.

Frank turned from the fleeing pack of prisoners and women to see Ki-Hwa locked in like a lioness on its prey and ran to them.

"Ungrateful woman!" Kanegawa yelled. He dropped his sword in the sand and reached up to grab her hands to pry them loose.

"Ahhhh" Ki-Ha yelled as he dug his fingers into the wound on her palm. Her grip was slipping. She saw the sword in the sand, let go of Kanegawa and lunged for it when a blade suddenly pierced Ki-Hwa as effortlessly as a fillet knife through raw fish, entering just below the left collarbone and exiting above the shoulder blade. Kanegawa's dagger, hidden in his belt, had found its mark. She cried out and fell to the sand as he pulled back.

"Oh dear," he said looking at her writhing in pain.

"Mother fucker!" Frank shouted as he finally got to the colonel and tackled him. But Kanegawa was more nimble than he looked.

285

He quickly got to his feet, grabbed his katana, and swung it at Frank, narrowly missing his chest, but creating an opportunity the American needed. As Kanegawa's arm was outstretched from the failed swipe, Frank lunged, getting inside his striking range and landing several punches on his head like a South Philly boxer. Some found their marks while others grazed him, but the assault was enough to disorient the old cavalryman and force him to bring his free hand up to protect himself. One of Kanegawa's soldiers ran from the cover of the trucks to assist, but was cut down by the shooters in the dunes.

As Frank bore down on him with swinging fists, Kanewaga backed up, planted his good leg and spun around on it, bringing the katana in an arc that found Frank's right forearm and sliced it off cleanly three inches below the elbow. The tip of the finely honed sword also caught him just above his eye, starting a trickle of crimson across his face. Frank grabbed his stump and backed away, blood running into his eye, just as Denbe closed in on the scuffle and found himself unarmed and face to face with a grisly scene. Kanegawa raised the katana into the air and stepped toward his driver, anger seething from every pore. "Impetuous boy!"

Denbe reacted as anyone would, by backing away from the charging threat. But he tripped in the loose sand and fell, the open wound on his back stinging as he landed. Kanegawa rushed forward to finish the job when a shot rang out, followed by another, felling him to his knees in front of Denbe. His sword arm dropped and his free hand felt the wounds in his back. His face gaped, but he was far from finished. With all the strength of the mighty Japanese Empire flowing through him, Kanegawa raised his sword, determined to eliminate the traitor before him.

But Denbe wasn't easy prey and raised a leg to kick Kanegawa squarely in the chest and knocking him backwards. Denbe grabbed for the katana, using his palms to squeeze the sides of the blade and wrest it from the colonel. In an instant, Denbe scrambled to his feet, flipped the sword and plunged it into Kanegawa's chest. The weary warrior groaned and grabbed wildly at the blade, trying to sit up and pull Denbe closer, blood pouring from his sliced hands before his life faded. The Imperial warrior, Colonel Nibori Kanegawa fell backward and then fell silent.

"That is for Seo-Sung," Denbe said. He then looked at Frank seated in the sand next to his severed arm. He wrapped the stump, muttering something about hoping it could be saved. The firefight between the dunes and trucks had silenced. Two men appeared from behind the dunes and walked up to them, rifles at the ready.

"Are you well Sergeant?" a voice asked.

"Chief Sato?"

From behind the trucks another man appeared. This one white and dragging a woman on a leash.

"Miss Victoria?" Denbe said. He hands were bound at the wrists. He shook his head, wanting to know, but not wanting to know. "He's a friend," Frank said to him. Denbe stared at Dave and then the four dead Kempeitai soldiers littered in the sand behind him. Finally he needed to know. "Explain," Denbe said.

"Compartmentalization, remember?" Frank said. "Everyone only knows the task they're responsible for. Only he and I knew the whole plan." He motioned at Dave.

"Yes, but...I am very confused."

Dave looked at the wounded sergeant, sweating and panting after emerging victorious from the life and death struggle. He deserved to know, at least the basics. "The good constable was always on our side. He is the Chief of Police. Not military. His mission is good order among the people, not fighting the war."

"Sato-san?" A woman's voice cried out.

"Chang?" Crumpled and bleeding on the beach, Chang whimpered. Sato rushed to her and ripped open her shirt to find a bullet hole just below her breast. Denbe fell to his knees and dropped Kanegawa's sword.

"Is he dead?" Ki-Hwa asked, walking over to help Denbe and seeing Kanegawa in the sand, his eyes fixed and his jaw open.

"Dead as a doornail," Dave said as he moved to Frank to inspect his wound. "Gonna be a bugger to make tea like that," he joked.

"Where are the boats?" Chikaki yelled looking toward the ocean, desperation in his voice. Frank grabbed his severed arm and looked at the watch on its wrist.

"Relax. They've got time." The last thing he needed was fear in the ranks, though confidence in his own Navy was certainly in doubt and the possibility of bleeding to death on this beach was true.

"Sergeant...can you get the men ready?" Frank said to Denbe. The gash on Denbe's back was bad, but not mortal. He would survive. Denbe nodded and moved to the group, finding Asako with them, trembling.

Ki-Hwa pressed on the hole in her shoulder and struggled not to cry out. She surveyed the wreckage of humanity. In the stolen staff car, Jiro and Shin-Dae were dead. The bodies of three dead Kempeitai lay strewn about the trucks, another one on the open beach just feet away from the lifeless Jin-Min as her dear friend, Sun-Cho, held her hand and cried. Only feet away was the head of the executed prisoner. Like rice falling from a bag, the bodies of three POWs killed by Kanegawa littered the sand in a neat row and then the colonel himself, whom she so underestimated, stared blankly at the stars, his soul riding among them with the horsemen of the apocalypse. The sand absorbed his lifeblood like a dry sponge sucking what was left of him away so that New Britain would be eternally stained by his wickedness. Twelve bodies...twelve! And Frank's arm. And Chang...the energetic and fearless one who never swayed in her desire to be free, was badly wounded. And it was all her fault.

*I'm responsible for this,* she thought. She vomited, but made sure to turn toward Kanegawa's body first to wretch on him. A final fitting farewell. Her brothers would be proud. *My family,* she thought. *They'll never know. About this. About me. About anything.*

Denbe led the prisoners to the best spot on the beach where a boat could get close. They were a motley crew of beaten, gun-shy souls, barely resembling men at all. Yet they smiled wide and thanked him through missing teeth, the newfound hope of liberty gripping their minds. They looked at him as a savior, a look that the young sergeant did not take for granted. Their beaming faces buoyant with dreams of home, made all his doubt and pain disappear. His waning confidence was rejuvenated in the realization that he was about to give the greatest gift of all: freedom. "Yanks always blame everything on freedom," he mumbled.

"Engines!" Chikaki yelled. "Boats!" A deep rumbling sound made its way up the shoreline from the southeast.

"Yeah, but whose?" Frank asked.

"We'll be in the crapper if they're not yours, mate," Dave said. The escape and firefight had taken so much out of the party that they let their guard down and now sat in the open on a moonlit beach, exposed to whoever was approaching.

"Come on boys," Frank mumbled, clutching his stump. "Let me see those lights." "Mind you, they'll probably expect a signal in return," Dave said.

Frank looked around in a panic. "Shit. My signal light."

"Where is it?" Dave said.

"In the truck!" Ki-Hwa had never run faster in her life, not even when a monsoon caught her in the paddy farthest from the Kim household. She found Frank's bag in the cab of the lead truck and sprinted back, dropping it in his lap as she clutched her wound. In no time Frank signaled four small American boats that made their way to shore while three more stayed farther out beyond the breakwater providing security.

The POWs loaded into the first two boats followed by Dave and Sato, who loaded the fallen ones as Frank argued with the Navy lieutenant in charge. Ki-Hwa watched intently, studying the body language of the hostile American who clearly did not want to take anyone that wasn't white. Crew members stared at her and Asako, and at the other women, and images of the wharf at Pusan flooded her mind. She watched Dave hand Victoria over to the lieutenant, still in bindings, all the while smiles creasing sailor's faces at the sight of the blonde, curvy madam. Dave and Sato handed the last dead POW to the crew and bowed. Then they bowed to each other as Dave boarded the boat and Sato backed away.

*There is respect among these men,* Ki-Hwa thought. *But will there be any for me?*

Finally, the lieutenant shook his head and pointed at the third boat. Denbe and Chikaki, under careful watch, boarded first, a crewman taking Kanegawa's sword from him. Chitose and Sun-Cho then stepped on. Sato helped Chang on board, giving her one last kiss. "You have your freedom. Use it wisely," he said before turning from her weeping eyes and going back to the beach. Frank held out his one good hand to help Asako on board and then turned to the last person.

But Ki-Hwa's feet would not move. Sato was a friend. Victoria was captured. Kanegawa was dead. All loose ends were tied up. No one on the island knew about her involvement this night. She could get on the boat and word of her treason would never make it back to the plantation or Rabaul or Japan or Korea. She stood on the precipice of a new life and only had to take one step to claim it.

But still she stood, clutching a wounded shoulder as waves licked her toes. Waves drawn higher by the moon each time. And somewhere under the same moon her family cried out to know what happened to her while their trusted patriarch wept and lied, "I wish I knew," he would probably say. He would raise her brothers to be like him, but only she knew how men betrayed everyone but themselves and how he would teach them to be the same. To climb over everyone else in order to save yourself. To push down the drowning man so you could float.

She looked at Frank and then Dave, the only men she respected because they were the stalwarts who refused to run away no matter what hardships they faced. She stood alone in the low surf, not knowing what her destiny in life was, but knowing it was not in running.

"I cannot," she said.

"Ki-Hwa?"

"I cannot. I have to make amends."

"You will perish here!" Asako yelled. "Please get on the boat. I cannot do this without you."

"Yes you can." She threw her bag onto the boat at Asako's feet. "So I know something of me will survive if I'm wrong."

Ki-Hwa backed away until she stood next to Sato, her gaze fixed on Asako as she continued to hold out her hand and plead with her to join them. Frank took a long look at her, understanding, but not agreeing. He signaled to the lieutenant that it was time to leave. The bombardment had long since ceased; the cargo was secure, the mission accomplished. Four American PT boats backed away from the beach, turned in the deeper waters, and roared out to sea to link up with Destroyer Group 12 as two rebels stood and watched. Just as she had on the night she was taken from Kyeongju in handcuffs, Ki-Hwa was alone, but unable to give up hope.

# 25

**Home they brought her warrior dead.**
**She nor swooned nor uttered cry.**
**All her maidens watching said,**
**'She must weep or she will die'**
*-Alfred, Lord Tennyson*

As an imposter, Takeo was used to a life in the shadows. Lying was easy. Acting was easy. Hiding behind a wall of misdirection and dishonesty was easy. But hiding in a South Pacific jungle in full flight gear was maddening. Every ten minutes he peeked from his hide sight at the Kempeitai waiting patiently near the command tent. They may have known everything about him or they may have known nothing. If all had gone according to plan, Kanegawa was still locked up and hadn't figured out his secrets, but he couldn't bank on that. He wasn't taking any chances and waited patiently for the inevitable. Around mid-day it came. Air raid sirens came to life and pilots and mechanics sprinted to start powerful engines up and down the airstrip.

Takeo jumped to his feet, spotted the Kempeitai and waited until their view was blocked by the crew chiefs, always the first to the flight line, running from their tents to make a move. He ran from tree to tree and paused behind storage sheds and fuel tanks until he was only twenty feet from his plane. But they were the last, open twenty feet. "Almost there," he mumbled as his crew chief started the Zero's engine. Takeo's plan relied on the lackadaisical pace of young pilots who dropped gloves, goggles and self-confidence like children trying to hold a thousand marbles close to their chest and he was right. As they passed him, he sprang, getting lost in the crowd, and ran.

"Don't be amateurs!" he barked at the younger pilots, jogging to his Zero. He hid behind the wing for a brief second and stared at the Kempeitai who scanned the flight line. So far so good.

"All ready, sir!" A voice startled Takeo. His crew chief had the Zero up and running in record time. "For the glory of the Empire, sir!" he shouted over the grumbling engine that seemed to be protesting this mission in exchange for sleep. Takeo returned the salute, but kept his eyes on the Kempeitai. "You take care, comrade," he said running up the wing and jumping into the cockpit that wrapped around his frame like a welcoming bathrobe. Looking back over his shoulder, he watched Hideki do the same and then looked back at the Kempeitai who stood stoically watching the planes take off, emotionless, not making any attempt to stop him. They looked him in the eye as Takeo let off the brake and the plane moved. But still they stood, one even smiling at him.

*Whatever you're up to...* Takeo thought, *I don't like it.*

The Zero strained to gain altitude. Turning southeast, the wing commander gave a last-minute pep talk about God, the Emperor, and blah blah blah over the radio. Below him dust rose from the islands' five airfields as planes of all types rose to the sky. The Allied formation descended, back dropped against the clear tropical sky like a biblical swarm of locusts ruining a perfect day. They flew in the normal pattern: Corsairs up front, bombers behind, Hellcats spread out and Lightning's up high searching for a target to dive on like pelicans hunting fish.

"Sergeant, the Gods smile upon your skillful hands," Takeo commented as he felt the Zero respond like his own limbs, nerves, bone and muscle. He jammed the throttle forward and pointed straight for the lead Corsair with the same brash audacity as always.

"Banzai!"

Three planes followed as he flew headlong into the formation, forcing them to break and scatter in pairs and threes. He looked quickly for a loner to get behind while the other Zeroes turned toward the bombers, only to meet the mighty guns of the Hellcats.

*Where are you?* He thought before answering his own question. *There.*

Below him at two o'clock, heading inland over the island was a single Corsair with the familiar skull and crossbones of the Pacific's well-known 'Jolly Rogers.' The markings were distinct...exactly what he wanted. He dived hard right, pushing the stick forward to its maximum. Straightening out and throttling back, he was in perfect position to pursue the deep blue Corsair. Through the incomprehensible clutter of panicked radio traffic, a voice uttered a clear exclamation.

"I've got your wing, sir."

Straining to look over his shoulder, Takeo was surprised by a familiar white and black shadow situated perfectly to the rear right of his plane. *Hideki. Just as I taught him.* "No need, I can handle this lost sheep. Go after the bombers!"

"No, sir. We shall make quick work of this one and return to hunt with the pack."

Takeo moved closer to the Corsair, who spotted him and made a run for the cover of a nearby cloudbank.

"I said I could handle this! Get back to the others!" But there was no response. Takeo's engine roared as he throttled up to cut off the Corsair before it could reach the safety of the clouds.

"He's in range, sir! Shoot now!" Hideki shouted.

"Jammed! My guns are jammed!"

There was a long pause. Hideki throttled to full speed to get within range, but it was too late. Like a squirrel reaching the safety of his tree, the Corsair gracefully disappeared into the cloud, taunting the Imperial pilots as he escaped.

"The clouds are too thick. He's gone. Our brothers need us," Hideki shouted as his Zero peeled off high left. But Takeo continued on, disappearing into the blanket of obscurity. Surrounded by the dull gray mist of a cloud nearly bursting with rainwater, he listened in silence as his comrades shouted in excitement, fear, joy, life, and death. He surveyed his instruments. He sat still, on the verge of a life-changing moment as the Zero flew onward. The aerial battle raged, but Takeo took no notice of it, numb to the world.

"I'm burning!" a pilot cried out. But his thoughts were no longer of the others. There was only he...and her. He closed his eyes and continued on; the plane gliding straight and level through the endless white-gray oblivion, not changing altitude or azimuth even slightly. It was blissful solitude.

And then he emerged, with nothing but blinding sun, clear sky and open ocean surrounding his miniscule, lonely airplane. The view was more magnificent than ever. He scanned the heavens and the earth below that he had rarely noticed, cleansed of his sins and hopeful he would not commit them again.

Like clockwork, the Corsair, camouflaged by the ocean below, revealed itself from just underneath him. He slid behind it and followed in silence, each unaware of the other's frequency. His hopes confirmed, Takeo relaxed. For the first time he was able to put the hell of war behind him.

"What are you doing, sir?"

*Hideki?* The transmission startled him, but not as much as the ominous sight of his Zero at the seven o'clock high position;

perfectly situated to open fire on him at will. The ingenious warrant officer had flown through the cloud to stay with his leader and Takeo had no one to blame but himself for training him that way.

"I found that lost sheep." Takeo's excuse lacked conviction.

"Are your guns still jammed?"

"They are, but I couldn't let him go. I'm hoping they'll come back up so I can get a shot at him."

"I will shoot. He doesn't see us," Hideki said.

"He's mine as soon as my guns come back up."

"But you're needed back over the island. They're bombing Rabaul!"

"They're always bombing Rabaul!" Takeo shouted, the sound of his voice echoing off the canopy. Whatever peace he'd felt before was completely shattered now. Silence fell over the radio and he sensed an impending disaster.

"So it is true," Hideki finally said; his voice ripe with disbelief. "They said you would run, but I didn't believe them. I told them they were wrong. I said you would not do this!"

The jig was up and out of respect for his friend, Takeo refused to lie anymore. "Yes, it is true. I'm looking out for me now and no one else! I refuse to bow in blind faith to a system...a concept...a flawed ideal that has no place in the modern world. We die while they enamor themselves with medals and swords. They sip cognac and smoke cigars, telling stories of how great they were in battle while you and I fight and die. Well no more!"

"What about your family? What about their honor?"

"My family and their honor are no concern of yours. I have taken their best interests to heart. Now you should too. Get out of this madness!"

Hideki did not hesitate. "I cannot and you know it."

"You can, but you won't. You're just the Emperor's loyal dog!"

"I gave my allegiance, as did you!"

"Yes, but I didn't mean it."

With incredible agility, Takeo's plane suddenly executed his signature barrel roll / split-S to the left instead of its usual right, cutting off Hideki's angle for pursuit. The move was timed brilliantly. Hideki managed his throttle to increase speed without being noticed. He was almost ready to fire, but instead found himself cut off and out of position. The Zero lost altitude at an unbelievable pace, leaving Hideki befuddled. Taking a page out of the Corsair's playbook, Takeo dove toward a large, low cloud.

"You have committed treason against the Empire, sir," Hideki said. "There will be no quarter, no shelter...no mercy!" He shrieked as his plane nosed over in an almost vertical dive to pursue his new adversary.

Takeo's body went weightless as the plane fell. Within seconds the Zero reached the sanctuary of the cloud where everything again turned gray and water blanketed the canopy. . He was forced to trust his instruments as he flew blindly. But pilots rely on feel just as much as manmade devices, and he pulled the Zero gently out of its dive, leveling off inside the cloud. Despite being the hunted, Takeo was in control of this fight. It was his prerogative to decide when and where to engage, and Hideki's task not to let the tables turn. He chuckled at the thought of the young pilot chastising himself for letting him get away, knowing that he was now at a disadvantage. He held his course steady through the cloud, feathering the throttle masterfully to slow down without stalling.

"Now!"

He pulled up suddenly and popped out into a blinding sun. Hideki was exactly where he'd expected: one o'clock high. He aimed and pressed on the throttle and gun triggers simultaneously, feeling the entire Zero shake as the cannons let loose. Bullets crashed through Hideki's fuselage, resonating a loud *THUMP THUMP THUMP* as they smacked against its outer steel skin.

"You maintained speed and altitude over the cloud enabling me to get behind and underneath you. Did you learn nothing?" He taunted his silent friend.

Hideki veered off to the right and pulled the nose upward, but almost immediately stopped and turned back.

"Don't do that," Takeo said, "Or this will be disappointingly quick." Hideki jerked the Zero back left and dived sharply down, cutting off Takeo's angle and negating his advantage. "So I did teach you something." Small puffs of white smoke escaped from Hideki's Zero, making the first encounter of this duel a victory for Takeo. The damage was light, but he scored first nonetheless as the two flew off in opposite directions at nearly 300 miles per hour.

"You can't go back to Rabaul, sir!" Hideki shouted.

"I don't intend to." *If I can wear him out...make him burn up his fuel...* Takeo searched the sky, straining to find the white Zero against the pale blue backdrop that merged seamlessly into the darker blue of the ocean below.

*There!* As if he merely had to think and the plane reacted, he nosed over from the climb to pursue again. But Hideki had managed to turn more quickly and was now rising rapidly to meet him head on. Just as his brashness forced him to attack, his equipment dictated otherwise. Hideki's plane sputtered and lost power, unable to sustain the severe climb he demanded of it.

*He's in trouble*, Takeo thought. Hideki's plane slowed, leveled out, and then dived underneath Takeo to rebuild speed. *I must've hit something.* He followed the youngster as his body ached from the intense G forces. He didn't want to take his eyes off Hideki for a second, but had to.

*Quick check...gauges good; no damage. Heading southeast again. Where is he? There...*

He was in good alignment and pressed on his guns again, sending more 20mm bullets ripping through the fuselage and tearing away a chunk of his right aileron.

Hideki pulled straight up out of his dive and raced the engine's throttle, taking Takeo by surprise. In mere seconds, Takeo had gone from delivering a deathblow to wondering out loud how the hell he'd been tricked. Hideki vanished upward into the sun, leaving Takeo to his own bewilderment. He was so surprised by the ploy, he failed to notice that he was continuing straight down as he strained to find his foe.

Takeo tried to pull up, but the shot was there and Hideki took it. Bullets ripped through his aircraft. A rain of steel hit the right wing and tail fin breaking away two chunks of metal and tearing across his left thigh. His flesh burned, but the older pilot was nowhere close to being finished and once again slowed his plane to near-stall speed. Hideki suddenly found himself vulnerable, having strafed without setting up a follow-on shot. Both planes dived toward the ocean, nearly parallel as Takeo tried to forget about his mangled thigh and get into position. It was a game of chicken; each one waiting for the other to make a move, expose a weakness, create an opportunity.

Banking hard right and pulling up steeply, Hideki broke off and tried to get back up to altitude and away. It was what Takeo wanted, but he would not follow. He lacked the strength to wrestle the plane upward and continue trying to kill his friend. He just wanted out and decided on the option no Imperial pilot ever chose.

*Retreat now.*

He stayed low to the water, dropping down to a mere five hundred feet above sea level and banked southwest, looking for the Corsair that was his guide. He knew it would take Hideki several minutes to realize he wasn't being followed, and then another couple to search for him. Or at least he hoped.

*I can't turn nearly as hard as I need to,* Takeo thought, rubbing his thigh. The bullet hadn't grazed him, but it hadn't penetrated either. It removed a chunk of muscle the same way it had done to another pilot in the 251st who had survived by wrapping his scarf around it. *I just need to do the same and get out of here.* He opened the throttle to full power and flew straight and level, checking the skies all around him every few seconds. The radio fell silent. He removed his scarf and started to tie it around the wound when two bright red 20mm rounds suddenly buzzed from the upper left in front of his cockpit, seemingly inches from his face. Three more rounds slammed into the plane, cutting a hydraulic line that sprayed fluid into the cockpit and onto the canopy. Hideki's plane roared by from above and banked hard right to swing around on his tail.

"It doesn't have to end this way, sir!" Hideki called out.

"And I suppose we'll just head back to Lakunai and all is forgiven?" Takeo prodded him. But his defiance masked his concern. The strafing hurt. His left wing flaps were suddenly stiff and nearly unresponsive. Coupled with his injured leg, the plane was difficult to control. He'd made a serious misjudgment and would have to run for his life. He jammed a throttle that was already fully open. More red and orange tracer bullets flew by him. Hideki was fully on him, but his shots were inaccurate. He banked, pitched and rolled hard in each direction, diving and then pulling back up, but all to no avail. All he could do was take enough evasive action to avoid his guns. Hideki had been trained too well. Outflying him was draining every bit of energy he could find. It was as if his every move was anticipated and countered. Every thrust blocked, every slash parried. There was only one trick left. He pulled straight up and banked hard right, trying to bring Hideki into a tight turn that he wouldn't be able to recover from.

"Aaaaahhhhhh...," he groaned as the G forces pulled and stretched his body to new proportions, introducing him to a higher level of misery. But Hideki followed. Tighter and tighter they turned, mustering every ounce of strength each man had to pull the Zeroes through the climb. Still Hideki followed. He prayed the angle was too tight. Their altitude increased rapidly...eleven thousand feet, twelve, thirteen. And still Hideki followed.

But then the unthinkable happened. The mighty Zero that he'd ridden to victory countless times coughed and sputtered. *Oh no,* Takeo thought, checking the gauges. *Oil pressure...he must have hit the pump.*

*THUMP THUMP* A pair of bullets crashed into his plane, but caused no real damage. Instinctively, Takeo nosed the Zero over and dived downward, straight into Hideki as he ascended. This was it. Face to face. One or both would not survive. Both pressed on their guns, too close for the 20mm cannons and opting for the twin 7.7mm machine guns instead. Takeo's nose was out of alignment and he could see all his rounds miss Hideki and sail harmlessly by. He was convinced this was the end, so when Hideki's plane suddenly burst into flames, he was dumbfounded.

"Oh my God!"

As Takeo dived past Hideki he could see the cockpit engulfed in flame. A pair of silver flashes crossed across his canopy from left to right.

*American Lightning's!* Takeo thought. *We got too high.*

He leveled off and looked back to see Hideki's plane gently reach its apex and nose over slowly to begin its final dive. His heart sank. He'd won, but lost at the same time. Miles from Rabaul and any of his compatriots, the Zero plunged toward the ocean, alone.

Takeo did not want to watch the last moments of his only friend's life. He banked away from New Britain and stared at the ocean he'd flown over so many times as it grew to encompass his field of view. There was nothing he could do but reflect. He thought of his home and his life up to this point. He thought of his family and how proud they'd be if they ever knew how brave he was in the air, or what a fine officer he'd become.

*But how disappointed they would be too.* He thought of his treason and recalled his mortal atrocities, feeling nothing but shame for his life and all the pain he'd caused others. He was damaged by war and the misplaced ambition to be a part of it, but he would no longer be a slave to it. He would finally be free to live and love as he saw fit and refused to weep for such good fortune. But he could not help weeping for Hideki and let the tears flow until a deep blue Corsair slowly came up to meet him, the skull and crossbones emblazoned on its fuselage.

*Is she worth it?*

# 26

## The easiest way to be cheated is to believe yourself to be more cunning than others
*-Pierre Charron*

"Welcome back, Frank!" A twangy voice bellowed, nearly indecipherable through its strong southern drawl. Frank stepped off a transport ship on Bougainville a year after being shot down over New Britain and shook hands with his old boss. "Guess we'll have to call ya stumpy now."

"Wild Bill, I assume?" Dave asked over Frank's shoulder.

"The one and only. Guessing yer the Coastwatcher this guy told us about."

"Dave Ladd. Pleasure."

"Been a long time since Port Moresby," Frank said. "How's the fight here?" They all turned to walk off the dock toward an immense logistical base whose size and activity Dave struggled to comprehend.

"Third Marines took Bougainville in November and the American and 37th Army Divisions took over from them in December. We got ourselves a nice base and airstrip on Cape Torokina over yonder but Japs don't like it too much. They's still in the highlands refusing to give in. Banzai chargin' our boys on occasion, but it's only a matter o' time before they get the quit in 'em." Frank looked toward the jungles just outside the port, but the hard slap of the colonel's hand on his back prevented him from appreciating it. "Damn, I was tickled bigger 'n shit when I heard you's coming back. All that target data you fed us was dead on the money. Now what else you bring back? Some women?"

"Yes sir. Thanks to you for getting that on the up and up from the brass."

The colonel threw one hand in the air as if to shoo away a pesky fly. "I'd do it for any o my flyboys. Besides, you earned it. You gave us some good shit that'll paralyze them Japs in Rabaul." Rodgers disproportionate ratio of balls to brains was surely the secret to his continued promotions.

"So this is Bougainville," Frank said. "I remember when we called you and said the Injuns were on the way to reinforce it." Frank turned to look at Dave, who openly gaped at the myriad of American ships anchored in the harbor unloading vast amounts of equipment. His astonishment left him several steps behind the Americans.

"Yer coastwatcher there trustworthy?" Rodgers asked.

"Yes sir. A real trooper. Wish we had a few more like him."

"Say, you ain't sweet on him are ya? You didn't go homo on me in the jungle, didja?"

"Hell no, sir! I managed to bring you back some women, didn't I?" They laughed as Colonel Rodgers led them to the medical tent while Frank proudly told tales about Dave's worth to the Allied cause. They were bound to tell stories both true and far-fetched around a grog of some foul-smelling homebrew of the most toxic sort while Frank healed, but that would have to wait a few days.

"You know the deal, son. You gotta do some de-briefing and those spooks gotta do some interrogatin' on y'all," Rodgers said.

"Yes sir. With pleasure."

\* \* \* \* \*

There was no room in Asako's heart for rest. All the planning, all the speculation, the fear, nerves, running, fighting, shooting, waiting, wondering, worrying and the questioning was over. She should relax, but couldn't. It wasn't the Army cots, canvas tents, strange food, or the constant drone of war that kept her on edge. It wasn't Chang's life-threatening wound, or Takeo's incarceration, or even Ki-Hwa's ridiculous decision to stay behind. She was trained to reason through those things that she could not control. Something just wasn't right.

Dawn broke early to the sound of bombs echoing in the distance. She emerged from the shared tent and caught sight of the massive Mount Balbi in the center of the island, venting steam and ash from its 9,000-foot-high peak. After living under Mount To for so long she would have thought this to be a welcome sight, but it only made her think of Ki-Hwa.

Asako, Chitose, Sun-Cho, and Chikaki walked as a group to the mess tent for breakfast, escorted by a freshly bathed and shaven Frank, Colonel Rodgers, and another young officer who Asako quickly surmised was a curious assistant who wanted to see the yellow defectors up close.

"You could just show us the way colonel," Chikaki said.

"I want the boys to see you with me so's they know to keep their mitts off."

"How is Chang?"

"She's still on sick call, but I get the impression from the docs she'll recover. Strong constitution on that one."

"And you, lieutenant?"

Frank held up his amputated arm. "I'd rather Ava Gardner broke my heart, but they stitched me up okay. No infections yet."

Torokina was nothing like Rabaul. It had been fought over and both the land and the soldiers who had done the fighting bore the unhealed scars. Cape Torokina was home to the American Army's XIV Corps; 62,000 strong and growing. The Allied base was a small city that had been won, built and stocked all within four and a half months, a task that would have taken the Imperial military at least twice as long. The immensity of the Allied operation was breathtaking. They walked among giant tents, stacks of supplies, hastily built structures, and enough equipment to make the Japanese effort look like a children's camp. Ships arrived, unloaded supplies, loaded wounded, and were gone in mere hours. There was no shortage of anything and no one went hungry, though they seemed to complain about it a lot. It was like moving up from the compound to the plantation overnight.

The land was scorched a deep black and everywhere Asako looked, trees were charred and the undergrowth around them was burned away. Craters littered the landscape and she imagined the battle here had been immense and thousands of men had died on the very ground where she now walked as a free woman. The same would surely happen to Rabaul, which saddened her, not for the Imperial garrison, but Ki-Hwa, the only flower on a soon to be barren landscape. Until this day Asako thought the earth could no more be tamed by man than a snake could be a household pet. Now she saw that an island was no different from a woman in the eyes of the greedy. If men wanted it they would take it and if they couldn't take it they would disfigure it so no one else could possess it.

In the mess tent Frank told them of the two Divisions manning the perimeter against the remnants of the Imperial Army, who lived in the jungle and were cross at their defeat, vowing to win their island back like a prize fighter who loses his title. She avoided the eyes of the leathernecks and dogface soldiers that stared through her. They had the same menacing, hungry-eyed look like the one she'd seen in the rapist Sergeant that fateful night that frightened her. She gave shallow bows and said 'hello,' since it was pretty much the only English word in her vocabulary. But they rarely said anything in reply, unless it was amongst themselves after she'd passed by. She knew how to manipulate Japanese men, but these combat hardened Anglos were wayward souls that seemed to have no anchor. In a land where she was supposed to be welcome for her bravery, she instead felt like the young girl in the okiya; afraid and excluded.

After breakfast each of the group found care packages in their tent-four sets of olive drab overalls to fit in better and a welcome sight. "Denbe!" Chikaki gushed. He sat on a new cot in Army overalls, released by the military police to the care of Colonel Rodgers with a small bag of ointments and bandages for his wounded back. One by one the girls thanked the colonel and gave him a hug and a kiss on the cheek, making him blush a deep pink.

"Damn! I'm gonna have to sleep with boxin' gloves on tonight," he muttered, turning to Frank. "Ladies and gentlemen," Rodgers said aloud as Chikaki interpreted. "You shouldn't be thankin' me at all. It's us who should be thanking you. And I have someone here who would like to thank you themselves."

Rodgers opened the flap of the tent to let in two men: the New Zealand Major Lovasz rescued from Rabaul and another officer they recognized as one of the former POWs, gaunt, and sickly, but clean and smiling. He thanked them all one by one and recounted stories of atrocities inflicted on him and his men during their imprisonment. No matter what their personal reasons for escape were, they were subservient to the good they had done for this man and the others like him who now had what the Americans always treasured above all else; freedom.

It was all very well and good and everyone shared a caring tear, but Asako was still unsettled. Alone in the tent that afternoon while the others wandered about, she reached into Ki-Hwa's bag and pulled out her journal in the hopes of discovering something about the cricket who did not fit into a jar. Maybe the one item so valuable that she went back for it during an air raid would hold a clue. What was it about these words that they were so important to someone who had half the formal education as her?

She thumbed through the poems and random entries finding nothing but anger at Ki-Hwa for leaving her alone so selfishly. She might as well be reading a suicide note. There were thoughts, but nothing coherent. Poems...bad poems...borrowed poems...a confession that she'd named three volcanoes after her brothers. Another confession that she named three POWs after her brothers as well. One silent and domineering like Ki-Chul, one clever and resourceful like Tae-Hyun, and another you but caring for his fellow man like Jung-Hwan.

"Maybe that's it," she mumbled. "A father sold her, a colonel owned her...even Frank used her. But only her brothers ever loved her." She looked out the tent flap as a breeze blew in from the ocean and remembered the day her father came to the okiya to ask her to avenge her own brother. "Like mine."

# 27

## Long is the way...and hard, that out of hell leads up to light
### -Milton

"Well, I guess you gotta be a colonel to get your own tent around here?" Frank said, entering without a knock or announcement.

"Yessir. So just put in a few more years an you'll git chers." Rodgers held out two bottles of beer.

"Oh, blimey!" Dave exclaimed taking one. "And it's even cold!" He sat in a portable canvas chair that was not made for comfort, but was anyway, while Frank did the same. Both took a long tug and smiled broadly. "By the grace of God, that's good. Never thought I'd find that so refreshing."

"Home of the brave!" Frank held his bottle up and clanked it against the other two. The three sat quietly, appreciating the rare pleasure they'd done without for so long, savoring all the long moments until this one.

"So, Dave...you gonna go back?" Rodgers asked. "We can sure use ya here."

Dave thought for a long moment, looking at the center post that held the tent up as if trying to remember something. "Well sir, I've certainly had a good feed at your cook's expense, but I'm a mite attached to that island."

"It's gonna get worse, ya know...we're gonna pound it to hell. I don't want none o my boys to hit ya."

"Yessir..." He replied, not trying to mock the colonel, but doing so anyway. "But me daddy used to say the one thing that didn't require a decision was going to hell."

"Ha!" Rodgers let out a laugh, looking at Frank. "Guess ya knew him pretty well, after all." He plucked a dollar bill from his pocket and slapped it into Frank's good hand. "How's the arm, stubby?"

"Why does everyone keep asking me that?" Frank laughed, "Like it's unusual to see a man with half an arm?"

"And a big old scar above his eye," Rodgers added.

"I'm already teaching myself to fly one-handed, see?" He mocked the motions of a pilot with his three good limbs. Rodgers smiled, knowing Frank was serious and their future held an unavoidable confrontation about that very subject. He would most likely present a convincing argument that he could fly as good as ever with limited range of motion and the colonel would champion him, but Army Air Corps policy wouldn't allow it. It would be an uncomfortable conversation, but that was for another day.

When his limited beer supply was exhausted, Rodgers retrieved two canteens and three tin cups from behind his chair. A cup appeared suddenly in Frank's good hand as Rodgers grinned broadly, revealing the wide gap between his front teeth. The 'USA' normally printed on the side of his canteen carrier was drawn over with a marker to read, 'GSA.'

"I can only imagine what that stands for," Frank said, smelling his cup and quickly retreating from it.

"Good Shit of America!" Rodgers held his hand in the air for a toast. "To you boys. Damn good work you done!" Rodgers knocked his back, but Frank and Dave were reluctant. "Relax, boys...it's just coconut juice I been fermentin' for a while. Now don't be a Nancy there Francis...down the hatch, son or I'll pee in yer cup."

Frank took a tug and winced. "I can feel my hand growing back."

"You know we ain't gonna go into New Britain, right?" Rodgers aimed his comment at Dave.

"Aye. I figured it out a while back. Can't say as I blame ya."

Frank's eyes widened and his smile vanished. "Wait! Sir, we're not going to invade New Britain? Why?"

"Strategic Isolation." Rodgers said it succinctly, taking great care to pronounce the words. "Why invade it if we can go around it?"

"Go around it? And then what? We have to deal with it eventually."

"But not now. The powers that be decided we can do just as much damage if we leave 'em to wither on the vine as we can by takin' the isle by storm."

"But they'll still be able to influence the area with all their aircraft," Frank insisted. "They have over a hundred capable planes, fifty thousand troops and a blue water Navy in harbor, including destroyers and submarines. It's their largest hub in the region, strategically, logistically. We'd be fools as fools get to just drive around and wish it away!" He looked to Dave for help.

"Well, some smart folks thought o' that. Seems we're gonna take the western half of the isle and leave the eastern half to the Japs. Then we bomb the livin' tar out of 'em with the Fifth Air Force. From what I heard from Lieutenant Hashimoto, most o' their planes went to Truk yesterday, any-hoo." Rodgers took a long pull from his cup.

"You'll have to translate for me later, mate," Dave said to lighten the mood, but Frank was inconsolable. "Take half the island and then what? Wait for them to surrender? They won't, by God."

"I know...so does MacArthur and he's wearin' the stars, son. The Philippines is more important." Rodgers was indifferent to Frank's protests, but he ranted anyway, knowing none of them had the power to influence national strategy. So many nights he dreamed of getting back into the cockpit, flying over Mount To and declaring, "Here's one for you, Rita!" He wanted to be there when General Imamura surrendered and watch the Rising Sun being torn down from the house on Namulan Hill by American G.I.'s. Now that dream was dead...or at least postponed indefinitely. He was adamant that Rabaul had to be destroyed but in the end conceded his inability to change anything with a metaphorical epitaph. "That's just crazy eights."

"Well, you can debate it all you like. In fact, debate is healthy as long as it don't get violent. When the talking stops that's when the decline starts." He raised his cup to his lips. "That's the way of our good friend, the Jap."

*That's one smart redneck,* Dave thought.

Rodgers opened a case of C Rations. "Sir, what about all the folks we brought back?" Frank asked. "What's going to happen to them?"

"They did good and it won't go unrewarded. They don't have a lot of value to be honest. Not a deep set o skills there, but I talked with Bull Williams this morning and I think we got an idea on how to use 'em. Except for that lieutenant with the Zero. The spooks think Hashimoto is hidin' something and ain't too keen on givin' him the run o' the roost until he comes clean."

"They gonna keep 'em all here?" Frank asked.

"Well, like I said Bull Higgins thinks he can use 'em in his intelligence outfit. Prob'ly teach 'em all English and get 'em working with the spooks or put 'em out there with some generals who need translators in the islands. One thing we ain't gonna do is get 'em workin' in the clinics. Can you imagine a wounded troop lookin' up and seein' a Jap working on his guts? He'd shit 'em all out!" He laughed and took another sip. "I dunno, but we'll use 'em, one way or the other. They's gonna have to live in their own area though. Fence it off and keep the boys out. For their own good. Never know what Joe's gonna do when he gets worked up sometimes. Gotta keep 'em separate.

"And in the long run?" Frank pressed him.

"Well, if they earn their salt then when the war's over and we're sittin' like this in Tokyo around a bottle of proper libation we'll leave 'em there with some money or take 'em back to the States, whichever. We just won't tell 'em that just yet. So's they work a little harder, you know." Rodgers took a drink and stared at Frank's stump. "So I gotta present for ya." He reached behind his chair and pulled out Kanegawa's sword and handed it to Frank.

"Blimey," Dave said.

"Is that?" Frank started.

"Yep. The Navy boys wanted to keep it, but that's the good thing about wearing eagles on yer collar. I figure you earned it." Frank looked it up and down, pulled the katana from its sheath and admired it for several moments. "So I gotta ask..." Rodgers said. "how'd you git that colonel framed and locked up anyway?"

"Well, it's a long story, but the short version is he brought a body up the mountain one night and buried it very close to our favorite OP. We learned from Ki-Hwa that she actually killed the man in self-defense during an attempted rape and Kanegawa agreed to hide the body for her. So we got an idea, right? Let's frame the colonel, get him arrested, and that way he's out of our hair during the escape."

Dave nodded and looked at Rodgers through glassy eyes. "He's a hard bugger. Needed to put him somewhere for safekeeping."

Frank continued. "So we dug up the body, got rid of the smelly thing, loaded the same hole with a radio to make it look like he was aiding the Allies. Then we got Chang to lead the Chief of

Police, Shitoke Sato, up to the spot where he miraculously found the incriminating supplies and set a trap for Kanegawa. He was in on the plan, but we still had to make it look like an accidental discovery, so they went through the movements.

"And this colonel fell for it?" Rodgers asked.

"Hook, line and sinker. Everyone said he was obsessed with his letter opener trinkets and since one was with the body, he was easy pickings. Ki-Hwa was sure he'd come back for it, which he did. Then Bingo! The coppers nabbed him red-handed. Took us several nights of watching that hole, but we got him in the nick of time."

"And then you arranged to be captured so you could get close to the POWs?"

Frank nodded.

"And then they took you to the POW camp?"

Frank smiled. "Well, after some beatings, yes. I think Sato took the whole 'let's rough him up to make it look real' thing a little far, but them's the breaks. I've had worse. So Denbe took command of me and took me to NG 7. That's where I prepared the men for escape."

Rodgers turned to Dave. "And you, son? How'd...or I guess why'd you bring that little filly back here?"

"Vikki?" She committed treason against the people of Australia. I want her prosecuted."

"Well, that might be a tough cookie to sell, but we'll see what the Aussie liaison officer says. Either way, cheers to you both." Rodgers held up his cup. "Good t'hear you boys boil up a cockamamie plan and make it work. Now if we can git that pesky lieutenant to talk, the world'll be right as rain."

# 28

## When your house burns down,
## you have a clearer view of the moon
*-Japanese Proverb*

"I think I'm going to get along with these people," Denbe said.

"Why do you say that?" Asako asked.

He looked at the curious woman with a sincerity she'd never seen in him while frigate birds squawked in the trees overhead. A platoon of soldiers ran along the beach in front of them in nothing more than shorts and boots, an American flag proudly flying at the forefront. "These people...they are very casual. What is the English word? Easy going?"

"To you, yes," Asako replied.

"They care what I think."

"They won't when they have what they want."

"Why do you mistrust so?"

"Because I've worn the mask of the geisha and have heard what men say when they think no one is listening."

"You're paranoid. They just like being themselves. Theirs is not a class obsessed, devote-yourself-to-the-Emperor-or-die society like ours. There are no delusions of grandeur or pressure to contribute to the cause. They're just people." Denbe was drunk on hope.

"Are you not worried of what will happen to your family?"

"Well if all goes right and they do what they say they will then you and I will just go down in the books as another dead soldier and comfort woman whose body was never found." He looked out over the beach. "I trust them."

316

Asako rolled her eyes. "You've only been here five days."

"Yes, but it's been remarkable. They even have ice cream."

Asako finally allowed herself a laugh, but then fell silent once again, staring at the waves.

"I want to thank you for including me in your plan," he said. "I doubted you. I shouldn't have."

"You know who was really responsible for that. For bringing you in."

He stared at Asako even when she looked out to sea as a submarine, not yet submerged, rounded the point from the main harbor. "She would be proud of us I think."

"Do you see it?" Frank suddenly bellowed as he ran up the beach to join them. "Do you see the sub?"

"That one?" Denbe asked, squinting and pointing out to the water. Silhouetted by the setting sun, the submarine glided gracefully through the calm waters of Empress Augusta Bay.

"Yeah, there he is," Frank said, breathing hard.

"David?" Asako asked.

"Yessir. He's heading back."

"Do you think he'll be all right? He's been away a while."

"That man is harder than woodpecker lips. He'll be fine."

"What is a woodpecker?" Denbe asked. They watched the sub for several long moments as the sea spray foamed around the conning tower.

"You're going to miss him aren't you?" Asako asked.

"What? Me? No. I don't get emotional. It only leads to confusion. Clouds judgment."

"So saving Chitose had nothing to do with emotion? It was just a calculated decision that you made to benefit your cause?" Asako asked.

Frank looked at the beach. "The rule doesn't apply when there's a damsel in distress. I'm a sucker for that. I get involved even when I shouldn't."

Denbe looked at his watch. "Dinner in thirty minutes. What will we feast on this evening I wonder?" he left, leaving Asako and Frank to watch as the sub slowly disappeared beneath the surface.

"Will he be able to tell us how Ki-Hwa is?" Asako asked. Frank nodded as a battery of artillery guns suddenly came to life in the distance, making Asako flinch. Frank pulled an object wrapped in cloth out of his fatigues and handed it to her.

"Well, she probably wanted you to have this." She didn't need to unwrap it. She knew what it was without looking and gazed out to sea, taking it in her hand and stuffing it into a cargo pocket of her overalls. A gust kicked up and the butch look of a woman in overalls with her hair blowing in the wind on a beach was strangely arousing for Frank. He felt himself look at her the way the other troops had. "I would have thought you would be happier to get that."

"Yes, maybe."

"Well, then what's eating you, doll?"

"I do not know," she said, suddenly vulnerable and not wanting to hide behind her stoic exterior anymore. "Maybe it is the loss of so many. Maybe it is the uncertainty of what will happen to us. Maybe it is the thought of starting a new life with the scars of the old one so easy to spot. I was geisha. They were ianfu. In your country that is dishonorable."

"I think you're too concerned with appearances."

"Is that so? We are tainted, damaged. We can never be cleansed of the filth that has touched us, violated us no matter how much we wash; at least not in a man's eyes. We are the scraps thrown from the table for the dog after the master has eaten the choice cut. We are unworthy to keep, but too young to kill out of mercy or even spite. We are no longer what gentlemen want."

"What gentlemen are we talking about here? What am I, fish livers?" He held his arms out, but she failed to understand. "Look, I think you need to get a little perspective."

"A what?"

"Perspective. Answer me this: is anyone shooting at you?"

"Well, sort of."

"No, I mean right now. Is anyone aiming a weapon at you and pulling the trigger?"

"No, but..."

"Are you sleeping under the stars tonight? Are you scrounging for your next meal? Are you walking around naked?"

"No."

"Half the people in the world cannot answer these four simple questions with a 'no' like you can. You lost a friend. It's terrible. But this is a war and people die. We fight it so more people won't die. I feel for you, but let's put things into perspective. "

She felt small where she should not. She wanted to lash out. She wanted to break down and cry. She wanted to do something, anything except sit there and let the world tell her who she was. She was always the one in control or holding the reins of it. She was always the one telling men what to do and how because she knew what they wanted more than they did themselves. She knew a man within moments of him stepping in her door better than he knew himself over the course of a lifetime and yet here everyone was different. Even Frank. He was not like any man she'd ever known and she was faced with the reality that all Americans were this unpredictable. In one minute they were polite and mannered and the other looked through her to eat her heart. She couldn't control them anymore than she could control

Ki-Hwa to make her get on the boat and leave that life behind. Still, it was a far cry from the stagnant life of the plantation and she knew Frank deserved gratitude for that.

"I am happy you were shot down," she said at last.

"Well...thank you. I think." He looked away and then back again quickly. "That was a compliment, right?"

She smiled faintly. "I was born under the sign of the Monkey. We are erratic geniuses if the soothsayers are to be believed."

"And Takeo?"

"What of him?"

"He lives day to day in a tiny tent surrounded by barbed wire at the opposite end of the airfield. He's next to a makeshift brig for deserters with its own firing squad execution line, but he's still mum. He's uncooperative and only asks about you."

"Then he only has himself to blame."

"I thought you cared about him." Asako stayed silent and looked back at the sea. Frank continued. "Look, his stubbornness isn't going to get him killed, but he is getting one thing...a boat load of scrutiny from the brass not just for him, but the accomplice he keeps asking about. You."

"I have proven my loyalty to you Americans."

"Yeah, but see, here it is. People are wondering if it's really possible that he defected and gave his plane to the enemy for the love of a woman who he's never even been, you know, intimate with, according to her? And if true, what powers of persuasion does this woman possess and is she using them to throw us off her own true plans? His silence is brining heat on you."

"He knows nothing. Nothing you would find useful anyway. He was only told to fly his plane here and turn it over. What else do you want from him?"

"It's not that we want something else so much as it's apparent he's hiding something. Something about himself. His story is full of wild goose chases. Inconsistent shit. It's hard to trust him even if he skeedaddled and turned traitor to the empire."

"So what happens if he chooses to stay mum as you put it?"

"It's a difference of comfort, see. If the intelligence guys think he's good to go then he gets freedom, or at least a baker's slice of it. But he'll get to be with you and your friends in your own little area. If they think he's not safe to let go then he stays in chains there in the brig and gets dumped on the Emperor's doorstep when this whole shebang is over."

She looked at the ground and then back to Frank and nodded. "Did you tell him I am here and safe?"

"Yes."

"You are right." She looked at him and then back out to sea. In her pocket her hand felt the blade of Bishamonten. "There is something he is not saying. I can tell you. But first I need something."

*     *     *     *     *

Takeo stood outside the door flap of his incarceration tent on a rainy afternoon with nothing better to do than stare at the ocean hundreds of meters away. A plot of land fourteen by eighteen paces encapsulated by barbed wire eight feet high with steel pickets every six feet surrounded his tent. Ten identical holding tents made a neat row, stretching a hundred yards south with a guard area directly to its front with an identical one to the rear. Almost no prisoners occupied the tents, since the Japanese would rather die than surrender and the ones that did, Takeo had no desire to speak with. They were the enemy now, or so he hoped.

Intended as a holding area for POWs with intelligence value, the area worked just fine for Japanese defectors who suddenly landed with an intact Zero. The solitude was suffocating and with no end in sight, Takeo was forced to relive his actions indefinitely, his memories spanning a range wider than the ocean itself from denial to acceptance and back again.

One morning he saw her. She did nothing but stand in his line of sight, hundreds of meters away where the last trees met the beach, staring at him in the same dress as the last time he saw her. The night they embraced for the last time. He rubbed his eyes to be sure. She was alive and well and on the island. His heart leapt.

That same day Army intelligence decided he was no longer a threat and released him to Frank who put Takeo on a boat and took him from Bougainville to Puruata Island a half-mile offshore. Colonel Rodgers had a simple, yet brilliant plan to keep the defectors away from the troops and put them to work-"give 'em a corner o that little island out yonder."

In only a few short hours a platoon of Marines erected a barbed wire fence that cordoned off the northern tip of Puruata and two general purpose medium tents occupied the last grove of trees that remained. Puruata was only 500 meters wide by 700 meters long and was mostly scorched from the battle to overwhelm its thirty Japanese defenders. The defectors' corner was little more than a quarter of that size spit and lay directly under the glide path of Torokina airfield and a stone's throw from a large stockpile of oil barrels. But it was private and it was secure and the Allies wasted no time reeducating the group to be translators so they wouldn't be bored. It was perfect.

"May I come in?" Asako asked feebly, peeking her head in Takeo's new quarters that he shared with Denbe and Chikaki after

322

Frank dropped him off. As she entered he zipped a worn flight suit he'd acquired from a G.I. in exchange for his Japanese aviator goggles. A great deal in the mind of the G.I. and something Takeo no longer wanted anyway. The sight of her, even in her American coveralls, was overpowering. He held her like an addiction, squeezing almost too tightly, smelling her wonderful hair.

"Let's take a walk," she said. "I can't stand being in these tents anymore."

His internal demons refused to rest during his incarceration, continuously eroding his faith in Asako and her grand scheme. Pessimism became a bedfellow that waged a battle with faith. Her smile quieted his fears, but he wasn't without burning questions that needed answers. They walked along the beach at dusk, barely aware of the sky's beauty as the South Pacific sun set around them.

"So how have you been faring?" she asked.

He shrugged. "Same questions every day."

"Have you answered them?"

"I told them everything I know. I think they must have become tired of it. How is it that they did not keep you locked up longer?"

"I don't fly warplanes."

"But you are a comfort woman. Did you trade your body for your freedom?"

"Takeo!"

He stared at her, looking for a crack in her armor but didn't see one. "I'm sorry. My mind wandered a lot in there."

"It matters not."

He gazed over the water watching a flight of four Corsairs preparing to land. They stood on the beach in silence until Asako walked to a fallen palm tree and sat. Takeo watched like a fascinated child as planes he'd only dreamed of seeing flew over, landing with grace on the airstrip across the bay. Asako kept her hands in the pockets of her baggy and unflattering coveralls. Behind them the thick, creeping kunai grass had begun to regenerate, forming a dark green contrast to the blackened earth of Bougainville. From this tranquil spot, it was easy to forget that a world war was being fiercely contested in every direction.

"You know...I was never concerned about the bullet with my name on it," Takeo confessed, "It was the one labeled 'to whom it may concern' that scared me." Asako smiled, but offered no comment. "Do you ever regret it? That we can never go back to Japan?" Takeo asked as two Warhawks growled overhead, momentarily drowning out the conversation.

"No. When they said they were escaping, all I could think of was how badly I wanted a new life. No more okiya, no more madams, no more plantation, no more fathers to be ashamed of, no more men treating me like a plaything or having to serve. It was an opportunity to be someone else."

"Why do you want to be someone else so badly that you would risk so much?" He walked to her and sat on the tree.

"Why did you?"

"I am who I am."

"Are you? Are you really Lieutenant Takeo Hashimoto?"

He stared, the cold shock of truth sending tremors through his body as his face went numb. His ears and neck grew hot. "What do you mean?"

"Do not lie to me anymore. You are not Takeo Hashimoto. Why do you think they suddenly had a change of heart and released you today? It is because I revealed to them that you are not who you say you are. That you are an imposter who stole someone's identity to reinvent your life. To become a glorious combat aviator and return home to praise and triumph. Only it did not work out that way did it?"

He was a naked man on a stage in front of millions of judgmental eyes, exposed, and caught in his greatest lie by the one person he never wanted to know the truth. He looked to the sky to escape her gaze. He closed his eyes and thought of his Zero and the way it felt to command such a remarkable work of art and how he never would again. Just like he would never hold her again.

"Where did you get this information?"

"From you. It is my duty to read people. To gracefully balance desire and expectation and to know what people want and who they are before they even do. You never carried yourself like a true graduate of Etajima or Tsuchiura." She stared at him, unflinching. "Despite all this," she continued. "I told them that they have nothing to fear from you. That if you are holding back information it is only of your own tortured past, not some grand Japanese strategy. You are not valuable enough to know anything that would hurt them."

"Why do you do this to me?"

"Because the man you killed has a powerful family-- now at least. And they want to know who you really are. So tell me...who are you really?"

He bowed his head. "Shigeki," he said without pause, his voice low. The name he thought he'd worked so hard to forget came back with remarkable ease like a canoe turning down river against a strong current. "Rin Shigeki." That is my name. My real name."

In a second her hand leapt from her pocket and buried a blade deep into his chest in almost the exact same spot where the real Takeo, her little brother, had stabbed him that dark night in Etajima.

But Takeo, or Rin, was never an easy target, on the ground or in the air, and had a long and comfortable relationship with death. The wound was severe, but not mortal and the sting of metal only unleashed the pain of a broken heart and betrayal. He grabbed Asako's outstretched arm and tossed her past him and into the sand. She tumbled as he jumped to his feet to look at the wound. He knew better than to remove the blade, at least not here. That would only make the cut bleed more. But he had to finish the job whether he loved her only moments ago or not. She knew who he was and tried to kill him. Now it was her turn to die— just like her brother.

He grabbed her and pulled her up off the beach to look her in the eye one last time. "Ianfu!" he growled. He reached back and slapped a backhand across her face. She pulled backwards toward the fallen tree, trying to escape his clutches but couldn't. He struck her again, this time with a fist. Her head swam as it did the night she was raped. Still she pulled away from him and toward the fallen tree just behind her. He cocked his fist again to strike, but Asako was a quick learner. With one hand free of her, she lunged for the blade still in his chest and pushed on it. He screamed and fell to his knees while she jumped over the fallen tree. In seconds he pursued her but as Rin came over the tree, a katana ran him through. The same katana she had placed next to it hours before. The katana she convinced Frank to let her borrow. The katana the sailors took from Denbe. The katana belonging to Colonel Kanegawa. The katana that had ended countless lives and now would end one more. She held the blade in his midsection while Ki-Hwa's words echoed in her head: *Men cannot be trusted. Only manipulated into doing something predictable.* If there was one thing Asako knew how to do, it was manipulate men.

He fell to his knees and then backwards into the sand, his eyes wide on the brilliant orange sky above him. She straddled him like she'd done so many times before with so many men and grabbed Bishamonten with both hands, pulling it out and then pushing it back into the center of his chest with all her might. What her brother had started, she was sure to finish this evening. She collapsed on top of him, face to face, gripping Kanegawa's Bishamonten in one hand and his katana in the other as the sun's brilliant red radiance faded to the west.

"Ironic," she said looking at the weapons. "It appears the colonel will get his bidding on you after all."

He gasped and spit up blood into her face while trying to bring his hands up to her throat, but could not find the strength. "Why?" he sputtered.

"Look into my eyes. See the ones you saw in him. See what you saw when you took my brother's life. I am not him. But I will leave you the same way you left him. Alone." She stood, wiped her face, and stared at him for a long moment. "You killed a man to escape a life of mediocrity. I am killing you to escape a life of slavery. We are really no different. And that is what I fear most."

Asako turned and walked down the beach leaving him to his own suffering with only one regret: that she'd asked his name. That made the murder too familiar. He was no longer an imposter or even a target, but a person. Rin Shigeki. But learning his true identity was necessary for the ones who sent her here. They wanted to know. They demanded it. It was the last task she needed to repay her debt and say farewell once and for all to a life dedicated to someone else. She walked away from one life and into another, free.

*Other books by Kelly Crigger:*
*Title Shot, Into the Shark Tank of Mixed Martial Arts*
*Curmudgeonism, A Surly Mans Guide to Midlife*
*Dark World, Into the Shadows with the Ghost Adventures Crew*
*I Am Haunted, Living Life through the Dead*

*Coming soon: Reverse Polarity*